PLACES AND TERMS

CADROOT — leaf with sedative properties; dried, ground, and smoked with rolled paper

CELDIA — small denomination of currency

CONCLAVE WARDENS SUN — judicial arm of the Senate

CONIFOR — northern city; Anji's initial destination

DORODAD — desert expanse in the far west

DREDGER — result of prolonged Rail usage

KALAFRAN OCEAN — giant body of water separating Kardisa from the continent

KARDISA — island chain off the eastern coast of Yem

KASKATIAN MOUNTAIN RANGE — range of mountains bisecting the northern territory

KIVA — largest settlement between Kaskatians and Tideron; known for flour exports, textiles, and medicine

LINURA — capital city of Yem; home to Anji, Kit, and Rolandrian; seat of House Demuratia, Senate, and Sun Wardens; port city

MAKONA — continent

OLANGAR — small village in the northern territory

ORDER OF INHERITANCE — centuries-old religion emphasizing
gratitude for the Nine Gods and
the world they left to mortals

PEAK — leader of a Spur

RAIL — powder made from refined coal coral; amplifies strength,
increases awareness and reaction time; causes sickness
of the lungs and transmogrification after prolonged use

RHODA — large denomination of currency; paper bills;
100 Celdia = 1 Rhoda

SHEERTOP CATHEDRAL — ruined cathedral and small
town; deserted; prior seat of
the Order of Inheritance

SILVERTON — last town before Kaskatian mountain
range; known for its silver mines

SPUR — name for any drug gang operating in Makona

THE ONE PATH — new state religion

TIDERON — port city north of Linura; destination
for Kit and Anji; major port

TUMBLEDOWN PASS — mountain pass known for
frequent avalanches

YEM — largest country on the continent of Makona; borders the
entire coast and much of the north of the continent

ANJI KILLS A KING

ANJI KILLS A KING

EVAN LEIKAM

The Rising Tide – Book 1

TITAN BOOKS

Anji Kills a King
Paperback edition ISBN: 9781835414613
Broken Binding edition ISBN: 9781835415559
E-book edition ISBN: 9781835414620

Published by Titan Books
A division of Titan Publishing Group Ltd
144 Southwark Street, London SE1 0UP
www.titanbooks.com

First edition: May 2025
10 9 8 7 6 5 4 3 2 1

A CIP catalogue record for this title is
available from the British Library.

EU RP
eucomply OÜ Pärnu mnt 139b-14 11317 Tallinn, Estonia
hello@eucompliancepartner.com +3375690241

Typeset in ITC Usherwood Std 10/14pt.

Printed and bound by CPI Group (UK) Ltd, Croydon, CR0 4YY.

For my mother, Angela

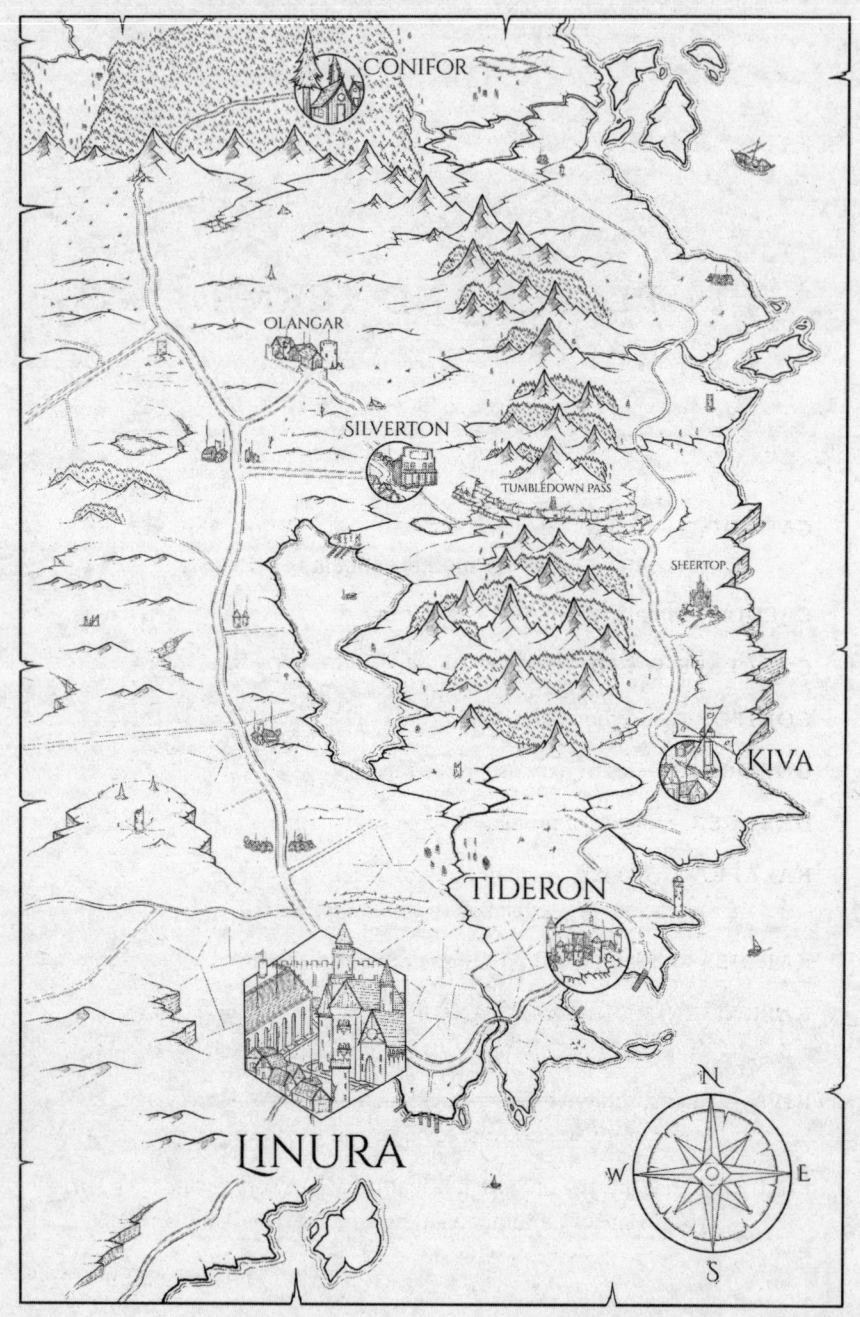

THE MENAGERIE

THE HAWK — Sword Master. Wears a mask of black metal.

THE GOAT — Navigator, Maxia. Wears a mask of blue stone.

THE OX — Muscle, Second In Command. Wears
a mask of sanded wood.

THE LYNX — Scout, Sharpshooter. Wears a mask of jade.

THE BEAR — Leader. Wears a mask of white ceramic.

THE MENAGERIE TENETS:

1. Let no charge learn your face

2. Let no charge learn your name

3. Let no crime be announced before trial

4. Let no lie befoul your lips

5. Let no other take your charge

Before you embark on a journey of revenge,
dig two graves.

Confucius

✦ PROLOGUE ✦

Hot noble blood pumped over Anji's hand. She clapped the other to his mouth and held it tight as he convulsed like a fish pulled from the sea, his bare feet squeaking against the marble floor. A fresh surge of crimson caked her fingers as she dug the knife deeper into the hot ruin of his neck and forced him to lie flat. He gurgled and groaned, his thrashing tongue soaking her palm with spit.

His gray eyes met hers, wide and confused.

"Shut up, please, shut *up,*" she hissed, stepping aside at an awkward angle to avoid the still-gushing blood. There was so *much* of it.

His chest finally stilled. His eyes grew distant. Fingers trembling, Anji wrenched the blade free and stuffed it under the mattress. She snatched a silken sheet from the ocean of bedding and bundled it around her blood-smeared arm. Then she took a final look at his lifeless form under the open window and allowed herself a silent, satisfied breath. Up so high, the air was clear, free from the reek of the city streets below.

The guards outside paid her an indifferent glance as the doors clicked shut at her back. She scurried on her way, hoping her eyes weren't too wide, grateful for the baggy trousers hiding her shaking knees. A terrified squeak bubbled in her throat, but she swallowed it down and took the carpeted stairs one at a time, her unbloodied hand clutching at the polished railing. Her vision tunneled as she descended.

She was sure she would faint, that she'd tumble down the steps and wake the entire castle.

The landing was empty, the corridors dead to either side. She ignored the pulse pounding in her ears and stole through the entrance hall, past the ballroom's double doors, and into a narrow servants' passage. Not a soul passed as she ducked behind a tapestry hiding the stairs to the basement where laundresses were kept.

Kaia and Libby and all the others were asleep. Angry snores issued from Matron's quarters.

Anji stepped lightly between the cots, past her own, then down a short hall and into the washroom. A latticed window cast half-moon light onto the toilets, the sinks, the beaten-copper basin. She dumped the length of silk into the tub and dunked her stained hand into a pail of clean water.

She scrubbed in silence. Her mouth felt stuffed with cotton. Fingers clumsy and cold. Her breaths were clipped and rapid chokes. The low light made it difficult to tell if she'd removed all the blood. She held up her hand in the moon's pale glow. Blood was still caked under her nails, but she'd rubbed her hand raw. It would have to do.

She snuck back into the sleeping chamber to her cot. Underneath was a box she'd never opened in front of Kaia and Libby—certainly not Matron. She eased it across the stone floor, lifted it, and set it on the thin sheets above. Inside were a thick bronze coin, a dagger in a leather sheath, and a clutch of silver

Celdia pieces she'd managed to stow away, the hollow iron rings looped to a length of frayed rope.

The Celdia jingled as she pocketed it. She clutched it tight, staring around the darkened room, but the other laundresses didn't stir. Matron's snores droned on. A steady thread of air escaped Anji's lips and she turned, grabbed her father's coat from its peg, and said a silent goodbye to her friends as she slipped out the door.

The catacombs were an ancient maze, lit by sconces throwing flickering orange light to the dirt floor. Her breaths echoed off the rock walls, each scuff of her shoes like a hammer blow she swore the whole castle could hear.

Pale, barred light appeared down the passage, and a tension released in her throat. She hurried forward, clutching her coat tight. The grate opened on oiled hinges onto an empty cobbled path. The sky had eased into the cloud-dusted pink of early morning.

Linura's city streets began their new-day bustle as she walked. It didn't take long to find a wagon, even less so to convince its owner to let her on. She dropped a few Celdia into the old man's callused hand and climbed in between bulging canvas bags. The cart rattled through the main gate, past a pair of constables leaning on their halberds. Anji watched the road lengthen as the wagon took her up the Roseway, blinking at the sun climbing higher over the city's receding rooftops, shining red on the sea beyond the docks. Linura Castle's thin spires dwindled as the bells began to ring.

Anji clutched her dagger's hilt with cold fingers, felt her coin buzzing against her thigh. She settled against one of the canvas bags and a turnip tumbled into her lap. It was filthy, but she took a bite, smiling as she chewed.

⊹ 1 ⊹

Anji was shitfaced, and likely about to get stabbed.

She'd made it two days on foot in the pounding wind and snow with an empty stomach and piss frozen to her shins by the time she'd found the town—whatever it was called. The old farmer had kicked her out of his cart after a day of travel, all for eating a few turnips. Bitter old fuck. Walking through the barren tundra had reduced her feet to stubby blocks of ice, numb and cumbersome and swollen in her ragged shoes. She'd thrown up the moss she'd eaten.

The town had sat in darkness as she'd approached—dead apart from a scattering of lit windows and a fat column of smoke rising from the thatched roof of a two-story building just off the main road. There'd been a sign swinging on rusted hinges over the building's front door. A faded relief of a burly blacksmith, hammer raised high in one hand, beer stein in the other.

THE HAMMERED SMITH.

Four days past—before she'd become a murderer—she'd have heeded her father's wisdom and avoided bars altogether. They were haunts for thieves and drug fiends, mercenaries for hire. The low places for downtrodden upstarts.

Hell, she'd thought, *I'll fit right in.*

Regardless, by the time she'd stumbled up the main thorough-fare of this ramshackle village, lips flaking, fingers frozen to brittle twigs, she'd been too exhausted to care. She'd clattered into the cavernous space, ignoring a poster depicting a hazy likeness to the girl she'd once been tacked to the door. She hadn't even stopped to check the bounty.

Now she sat sweating and drunk and hating the inside of this bar more than the road she'd crawled down to get inside. She hated the shriveled bartender and the sickly way he rubbed his hands together as he puttered around the tables. She hated the ceaseless wind outside, clapping the tavern's shutters against the brick. She hated the rotten, pestilent stench of mushrooms pervading every crack and pore of this town. She hated the huge framed poster hanging over the mantel depicting a dark, gangly creature she'd never seen. The shape seemed to shift slightly, its bony shoulders rising and falling, its ugly face contorted in a snarl. Above the moving image, bold letters proclaimed:

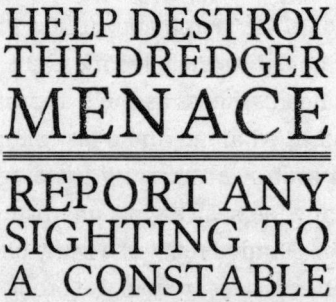

HELP DESTROY
THE DREDGER
MENACE

REPORT ANY
SIGHTING TO
A CONSTABLE

Most of all, she hated the incessant gurgling grunts issuing from the man opposite her as he shuffled and shuffled and threw Celdia onto the table's center. Made her want to pop his fucking eyeballs out.

Four, five.

Anji pressed her fingers tighter to the cards. An old deck with chipped, greasy edges. Smoke hung rank in the stuffy air, stinging at her eyes, creeping through the rafters, into the long-silent kitchen behind the bar. She scratched at her cheek, adding a layer of filth to the blood still caked underneath her nails.

I could afford a bath after this hand, she thought, blinking at the blurry duo opposite with cards held before them, at the grungy sod staring her down. *Should probably buy one for him too.*

Best not count your fish before pulling in the net, sprout.

More fatherly wisdom. She pictured him hunched over their little table, varnished deck in hand, in the quiet hours after her mother had gone to bed. His mischievous grin as he taught her how to count cards—strictly academic, of course. Her mother would never have approved. Anji pulled her coat tighter despite the sweltering fire. The sharp scent of boiled leather racked her nose and her breath came a bit easier.

"Final draw," the grungy sod said. "Come on, boy, you in or out?"

Anji narrowed her eyes, feigning confusion—mostly feigning. Her hand twitched to her rough-shorn hair, but she stilled it. Somewhere along her mad dash north she'd gotten the bright idea to shave her head to look more like a stableboy and less like the girl who'd shoved a letter opener through a king's throat, though without a mirror she couldn't be sure if the change would be enough to fool anyone searching for her. She seemed to have gotten lucky with the Hammered Smith's few patrons, all of whom appeared well past even Anji's state of drunkenness, but she'd nearly corrected the man calling her a boy. The word floated to her lips, but she caught it like an eel in her fingers.

Keep it together, Anji.

She set a hand to the rim of her mug, to the handle, brought its lip to her mouth. The beer tasted flat and bitter, nothing like

7

the clear spirits she'd grown accustomed to in the laundry. She pictured Kaia passing her a bottle, an ever-present lock of blond hair dangling over her eye. Libby giggling on her cot, the three of them nursing sore heads and sharp words from Matron in the early hours before their shifts. Anji doubted she'd see them ever again. Her bottom lip twitched at the thought, the loss like a weight settling deep in her chest.

Here in the tavern, her drinking had started in seclusion. She'd polished off three mugs of cloudy beer like they'd save her from the Senate's headsman, then had the audacity to look into her coat pocket. Empty save for a stray button and eleven measly Celdia—enough for a few more drinks, perhaps, but Conifor was still days away on foot. She needed more money. Gulping down beer on an empty stomach, wondering what she would do, she'd been on the edge of tears when the man in the seat across from her now had begun shuffling cards. She couldn't help herself. She'd had to do *something*.

Seven, eight . . . no, nine . . .

"Piss drunk," the man said, dragging on a greasy cigar. He stabbed a pudgy, dirt-stained finger at her mug. "How can someone with so much booze in them win this often, eh?" He exhaled a blue plume of smoke and barked out a sticky cough.

"Ale's got nothing to do with it, Jom," said the wispy, middle-aged woman to Anji's right. "Hot streaks come and go."

Jom wrinkled his bulbous nose. "Hot streaks," he murmured.

Anji darted a glance at the deck, counting as best she could despite the fuzzy cloud nestled where her brain had been. She did a quick mental dance, keeping her face still, and tossed two Celdia into the pile. She rubbed a thumb at the heavy circle of bronze pulsing in her pocket. The tension in her shoulders eased.

The chair groaned as she sat back and sipped at her mug. The thought that she really should stop drinking made an appearance, but was quickly dismissed. The buzz felt nice, and though this man Jom had a murderous look in his eye, there was no chance he suspected her.

Eleven, twelve . . . right, and the next one . . . Suns?

Jom flipped a card off the deck: Suns. The woman cursed and threw her cards facedown onto the scarred wood. Her scuffed brass earrings shook as she slumped back in her seat, arms crossed. She clicked her tongue and snapped bony fingers at the barkeep. "I think it'll be a nightcap for me and I'll be getting home," she said, still glowering at her hand.

"Not alone you won't," Jom grunted, glassy eyes still on his cards.

"I hardly need an escort." The woman sniffed as the barkeep ambled over and lowered a foamy mug to the table. He'd feigned disinterest for the duration of their play, seeing to other customers and checking in on the trio now and then. Now, with the denizens of this poor excuse for a town turned in for the night, he seemed more inclined to watch.

"You might listen to him, Tela," said the barkeep, his wattled chin bobbing up and down. "Dark times to be wandering the streets by yourself." He stuffed the tray under one arm and glanced at the latticed window. "Quite literally dark."

Jom exhaled another plume of smoke. "Roff still hasn't turned up?"

The barkeep shook his head.

The woman, Tela, furrowed her brow. "The lamplighter?"

"Not seen in days," said the barkeep. "And Alma Woodward came in yesterday raving about a Dredger prowling about, keeping to the shadows."

Tela gaped. "You don't think Roff . . ."

"The change comes on fast," said the barkeep, picking at his chin. "Man has no wife, no family to speak of. Lonely sort of life.

Nine know folk are struggling enough these days with what little they have, and he didn't have much."

"But even so, resorting to snorting that awful stuff," the woman'seyes widened, "knowing what becomes of you. I'll never understand it. Then again, lamp lighting isn't much work, is it? He should have found himself more to keep his hands busy." She sighed. "That's the trouble with young people these days. Laziness. This will happen when you don't have a proper job."

"And no telling the damage a Dredger will do," said the bartender, frowning. "I hear they'll dig right through cobblestone looking for Rail. More places for my taxes to go."

Anji flicked her eyes briefly from her cards to the pair as Jom screwed up his face in concentration. He dragged at his cigar, the exhaled smoke sailing straight into Anji's nose. She breathed in the fume and wished she had the stomach to ask for one of her own. Somehow looking at Jom she didn't think he'd offer.

Jom dropped two of his own coins into the pile, metal clinking. He slid another card off the deck (Ravens) and slipped it into his hand, glowering at Anji as she glanced once more to the pair.

Tela wrinkled her nose. "Vermin," she said. "The whole lot should be rounded up."

"Shut it, you two," grumbled Jom. "Trying to think here."

A shutter outside slapped against the window and the woman jumped in her seat, one hand to her chest. She raked her fingers through graying wisps of hair. "Darkness and drugs and everything in between," she said, eyes fixed on the window and the black streets beyond. "Plague in Kardisa. And now King Rolandrian murdered in his bed."

Anji bit her lip and made a show of rearranging her cards as the two spoke.

"I say the old ruin had it coming," said the barkeep, and Anji's earlier distaste for the man ebbed a little. "Rolandrian's legacy will be letting Governors fatten like pigs off our hard work. This tavern has been in my family for six generations, left to me by my father, who would rise out of his grave just to die again if he heard the rates I'm paying—for a place owned outright, mind you."

Jom huffed a heavy sigh through his nose, but the barkeep rambled on.

"I've had next to no custom now everyone is working triple shifts out in the fields. All that strain on the crops—it'll bleed the ground dry. Anyone of an age to drink is too exhausted to do anything but go straight to bed after work. On top of that, they're terrified of the new constables—Sun Warden tax collectors in all but name if you ask me. Trussed up in yellow, tacking up their *decrees* and handing out pamphlets, accusing *us* of impiety with one hand while they drain our pockets with the other. Last night two of them came in and told me to hang that up." He dipped his head to the poster over the mantel. "Wouldn't leave until they were satisfied it couldn't be ripped down. Then the pictures and words started moving and about scared the whole bar out into the street. Hardly anyone's been back since." He glanced out the window again. "All this muster and bluster and maxia, and for what? So they can carve up a little more for themselves when they've already got the world." He snorted. "I've got half a mind to pack up and join the Tide."

"All talk," said Tela, waving a hand. "That's as much a revolution as this bar is a brewery."

"Rumor is it's growing in strength," said the barkeep, but his voice trailed off into a mutter.

Tela rolled her eyes. "I'll join when I've got more than mushrooms and potatoes on my plate."

"King's dead, isn't he?" said the barkeep. "It's a start is all I'm saying."

"Would've gutted the bastard myself if I'd had the chance," said Jom. "Nine, if the girl were here I'd buy her a drink."

Anji allowed herself the tiniest smirk and took a sip of her ale.

Tela scoffed, "Of all the taverns in the world, I doubt she'd choose this one. Most the realm couldn't find us on a—"

Jom pounded his fist on the table, nearly toppling Anji out of her chair. The pile of Celdia rattled and a few discarded cards flipped over to show their stained faces.

"Dammit, boy, you going to bet or not?"

Tela put a soothing hand on Jom's shoulder. "Jom, dear, really."

The tavern rang with silence. Anji's stomach churned, her hand twitching toward her dagger, but Jom relaxed into his seat, waving Tela's hand away. "Streak like this, he might've figured out the rules by now." Then he guffawed and pointed a swollen finger at Anji. "You scare pretty easy, don't you? Gap-toothed little shit."

Anji took a steadying breath and hunched once again over her cards. "Waiting for a card, *dealer*."

Jom stared across the table, his beady eyes bright, but flung a card across to Anji and leaned forward, cigar dangling from his bulbous lips. "Speaking of traveling alone," he said, "where was it you came from, boy?"

Anji's heart fluttered.

"Silverton," she said, fitting the new card into her hand. "And it's your call." She gripped the table's edge to keep the world from spinning. Tela gulped her drink, a dribble of amber liquid beading onto her rough-spun shirt. She wiped it off and gave Jom a sidelong glance. Was that tension in her shoulders? Or was Anji just eight mugs deep? Anji blinked and directed her hazy gaze to Jom's watery blue eyes.

The man tugged at his ear (the tell he'd been showing all night), then fanned out the three sets of pairs Anji knew he had: two Steeds, two Suns, and two Ravens. She kept her face straight.

Jom grinned, his cigar tipped up as he bit down into the paper and leaf. "Beat that, scrawny fuckarse."

Anji lay her cards down, glossy faces flickering in the candle-light. Jom's face screwed up first in confusion, then realization, and finally—rage. His hand inched closer to his belt.

"Issa packed house," Anji said, arms raised, her words more slurred than she wanted them to sound.

A dead quiet settled over the table, through the empty tavern. Anji reached for her mug. "Sorry, old man," she said, relief flooding through her, "looks like tonight isn't your—"

Jom slammed his hands flat on the table, and in one motion got to his feet and kicked the chair behind him. He slid a thick dirk from its belted sheath, teeth bared.

Anji rolled her eyes and began gathering her winnings.

"You cost me more tonight than I've made in a month, boy," he said, face purple. "*Nobody* wins like this without cheating."

"Jom, dear," Tela said again, voice even. She patted the man's forearm, sparing Anji a glance. If she'd been more sober and less desperate, Anji might have taken the look as a warning, a plea to run out of the bar, to forget the winnings and spare herself a gutting.

But Anji couldn't run. Not yet. She eyed the money amassed in the table's center.

She tensed, ready for Jom to bound across, for his weight to carry him past her so she could spin around and—

The tavern door crashed open with a screaming gust of wind.

"We're closed for—" the barkeep faltered. His tray clattered to the floor, empty clay mugs shattering on the planks.

Heavy bootsteps rang in the empty tavern as a specter in all black strode across the room. The figure wore a black mask fash-ioned into the face of a bird of prey, smooth angles forming into a beak curved to a sharp point.

Anji jumped to her feet, then stumbled into the table's edge. Her head felt soaked in tar. A wave of confusion and fear washed over her. Wasn't it enough that she'd gone this far? She'd just wanted to celebrate, to rest. She cast a longing look at the money piled on the table, *her* money.

"Nine Gods," said Jom at Anji's back. "It's the Hawk . . ."

The Hawk stopped an arm span from Anji, the open door framing her slight form. Anji dug her nails into her palm, cold panic roiling in her gut.

Nine, not now. Not when I was so close.

"Excuse me," said the bartender, his voice shaking, "are you here for someone?" He gulped. "Because I can assure you I do not harbor—"

The Hawk pointed a gloved finger at Anji. "I'm here for the girl."

Anji ignored the confused glance Jom and Tela shared. She palmed her dagger's handle, kicking the chair aside. "C'mon then," she said, her words jumbled. She spared a glance at the others, now shrinking in unison toward the back wall. Cowards.

The Hawk stepped closer—too close. Anji nearly had the blade singing out of its sheath—

Then the blinding pain came, darkness hurrying after.

✦2✦

Her feet were *freezing*.

Anji shifted, eyes shut tight, trying to twitch the covers over her toes. The Matron had left the window open again—resigning her to curl under her sheet like a mouse in its den. She groaned and flipped to her other side. Still cold. Another piercing gust of wind tore through the window and she put out a hand. Her other hand followed with a metallic clink.

She opened her eyes.

No bare stone above her head or candle left burning to push back the darkness. No murmur of the other girls waking for their shift. No sheet, no cot, no open window.

Only tundra, and wide, empty sky.

The expanse of Yem's northern territory stretched out in wafting tufts of heather and sedge and tall, stringy grass. Pitted, moss-covered rocks littered the ground, which lay under a deep purple sky, pink on the jagged horizon.

Anji tried to sit up and found her wrists locked together with iron manacles, her legs tied together with a length of thick rope. Another short span of rope connected her chains and the binds around her ankles. She twitched her head from side to side so quickly the headache from the night before came calling between her eyes like a knife wedged into her brow.

A camp. This was a camp. A thin mare was tied to a stake beside a flapping gray canvas tent. A neat stack of pots and pans near a crackling fire, and behind the flames, writing in a leather-bound notebook—

"You."

Only the word sounded more like *ooo*. Anji gagged. A bolt of rough fabric had been wrapped around the base of her skull and jammed between her teeth. Icy panic lanced through her stomach.

"Good morning," came the voice behind the mask, that sonorous rasp. "I'll thank you to keep silent while we're exposed. There are others hunting you."

"Mmmph phukooo viish!" Anji said, squirming in her bonds. She tried to scramble to her knees, but only slammed into the dirt.

The Hawk sighed and tucked the notebook and pencil away. She filled one of the pots with water from a metal canteen and settled it on a rock near the fire. "You're only tightening those knots. Lie back and be quiet. You'll have water and something to eat in a moment."

Anji worked the gag, sawing at the cloth with her teeth. The dense fabric held, digging into her neck, cutting against her ears. She strained until her tongue ached, until saliva dripped down her chin, catching in the chill wind like ice forming on her skin. She let out a muffled scream, eyes shut tight.

"Enough of that," the voice sounded again, and now the woman was on her feet, stepping around the fire. She squatted down next to Anji, gloved hands out as though calming a wild animal.

Anji recoiled, spitting through the gag, arms and legs flailing. She could feel the grip of the bindings digging into her ankles

16

more with every turn, but she didn't care. Her heart slammed against her ribs. She needed air. She had to get up and unbound and away—*far* away. She twisted and thrashed in the cold dirt, her throat raw from screeching through the cloth. Dust caked the side of her face, her nostrils, the corner of her eye. She had a hazy view of the Hawk kneeling down, then felt the iron-tight grip of a hand around her arm. The pain made Anji freeze.

"I'll remove the gag, so long as you're quiet," the Hawk said, her voice calm, "but you stay tied. Fair?"

Of course it wasn't fair, and if Anji had the use of her arms she'd skewer this bitch right here on the spot, let her blood cake through the permafrost. Then she'd steal the horse and the tent and head north until she reached Conifor—where she'd never be found again. She cursed herself and the throbbing pain behind her eyes, her aching face. *Why* had she stopped running? How could she have been so stupid?

Anji whimpered, tears leaking out onto her cheeks to join the dribble of spit lining her jaw. The tears etched frozen lines on her skin as the wind began to rise with the sun.

"Idiot girl," the Hawk muttered, and Anji heard the scratch of steel on leather. The bird mask loomed overhead. "I'm going to cut you loose, but if you scream or try hopping off I swear to the Nine I'll slit your moronic throat myself."

Anji stared, chest heaving, and blinked at the mask. *The Hawk, and if she's here, that means . . .* She glanced about the darkened hills, searching for signs of movement before the Hawk gave her a rough shake, maneuvering Anji so the mask filled her whole vision. The black metal gleamed in its contours, covering the woman's entire face save for the ridge of her wrinkled jaw. The dagger's burnished steel reflected the fire's light.

"Deal?"

Anji nodded. Felt a tug at the base of her skull, then a release of tension in her arms and shoulders as the shorter rope was cut.

The gag fell away and Anji worked her mouth, spitting fibers. The Hawk reared back on her heels and sheathed the dagger once more.

"There," she said. "Never liked gags much anyway. Cruel things." She surveyed Anji, then stood and padded to her previous spot near the fire.

Anji heaved herself up. The manacles were connected by three fat links, heavy and coal-black. They clinked together as she inched toward the rim of firelight. A blast of wind scratched at the tattered remnants of her hair, at the scabby cuts where her dagger had slipped. With the icy gale scraping at the sides of her face, she wished she'd kept it long.

The Hawk resumed her seat behind the fire and stirred at the pot, her mask reflecting the flickering flames. Anji shuffled a bit closer to the light. The warmth spread out like welcoming arms, and she edged nearer, sniffing up a trail of cold snot. She'd never felt more pathetic.

A long silence settled on them, and Anji watched through the remnants of her drunken haze as the woman stirred in slow circles, the spoon's metal tip never scraping against the bottom.

"How did you find me?"

Her voice sounded empty on the air, devoured by all this open space.

The Hawk didn't respond. She merely kept stirring, her mask giving nothing away.

"I can't believe they sent the Menagerie after me."

"You murdered a king."

"A shit king," said Anji, but the Hawk said nothing. The fire crackled, the woman stirred at the pot.

"Where are the others?"

"Out there somewhere," said the Hawk.

Anji stared across the yawning tundra. The hills and boulders stared back, still and silent. Here she sat, hands bound, without a sword, opposite one of the Menagerie: the most hardened warriors in the world. A cadre of bounty hunters in service to Rolandrian, and by extension the Senate, the judicial arm of the ruling monarchy Anji had just squashed. Her hands began to shake at the thought of masked figures stalking her through the wilderness like a pack of hungry wolves.

The Hawk divided the pot's lumpy contents into two metal cups and offered one to Anji. "Should help with the pain and swelling."

Anji glanced at the cup.

"Poison is not my trade, girl," the Hawk said, her arm still outstretched. "Though you had your fill in that tavern."

Anji reached her bound hands awkwardly to the lump on her brow, still tender, still throbbing. Her fingers came away dry. That was something at least. She twisted in her bonds, looking to her belt for her father's dagger.

"It's in my tent," the Hawk said, "along with your other possessions. You've no use for them anymore." She gestured with the cup. "Eat," she said, voice firm. "You'll need the strength."

"Those things are mine," said Anji. "Give them back to me right now or I'll—"

The Hawk scoffed. "Or you'll what? Thump me to death?"

"You don't know anything. I have training. I could have handled myself back there, I just needed another—"

"What you needed was to stay sober when you knew someone would eventually find you. You're the most wanted criminal in Yem, and you decided to stop for a few drinks and a card game?" The Hawk sniffed. "Stupidest thing I've ever seen. How you managed to kill Rolandrian and escape is beyond me. I expected some fight out of you."

19

Anji ground her teeth and raised the manacles. "Take these off and give my knife back then. You could die impressed."

The Hawk exhaled a long breath. "Eat."

The cup's warmth was ebbing, so Anji took a sip. Hot broth, salty and coarse, filled her mouth. Complex flavor hit her in waves —sage, cumin, and purple carrots swam in the salty broth along with brined chunks of white meat. She tried remembering the last time she'd tasted something so satisfying and came up short. They'd been given mostly brown bread and oats in the castle laundry, the occasional piece of fruit on a holiday. She gulped the rest down fast enough to singe the back of her mouth and ran her finger along the inside of the cup.

"This is fucking delicious," she said, sucking the last of the broth off her finger. "You eat this good on the road?"

The Hawk's mask revealed nothing, but the woman behind it said, "I see no point degrading my meals for a degrading task."

Something in that smelled of an insult, but Anji didn't care right then. The Hawk was right: new energy sparked at the edge of her dulled senses. The aches in her limbs seemed a far-off thing now, the spot where the Hawk had struck her still throbbing, but less so. She was about to ask for more when the woman sat straight and flipped her mask off.

Anji blinked. The Hawk was *ancient*. Not a day younger than sixty. Specks of gold flecked her leaf-green eyes, the skin around them wrinkled. A thin, shiny scar ran in a curving line from her bushy left brow to the center of a sallow cheek. Anji wouldn't have called her beautiful, but there was something about the face —something alluring, as if time couldn't quite fully harden what edges had once been soft. Her long, liver-spotted face shone in the firelight, gray wisps of hair whipping in the wind.

Anji frowned, self-conscious of staring. She picked up a pebble and rolled it between her fingers. "I thought the Menagerie never removed their masks?" And then, though she felt childish for asking, "Are they really maxial? What does yours do?"

The Hawk sipped at her cup. "Mostly it itches," she said. "Besides, no use standing on ceremony."

Anji's eyes narrowed. "And why is that?"

Something whistled through the air to Anji's left, and before she had a chance to register what it really was, the woman across the fire held up a long, glass-tipped arrow. Anji flinched back, mouth open, as the Hawk rose soundlessly to her feet. She pointed the arrow's tip toward its origin.

"Lynx!"

A scuffling sound came from behind a massive boulder lying on a rise toward the horizon. Anji strained her eyes and watched a figure slide out from behind the rock, a small, curved bow held in one gloved hand. The figure wore a mask much like the Hawk's, but made of worked green stone. It covered his entire face, but where the Hawk's mask was all curves, this one was boxy and angular. The face of a snarling cat, with squat points for ears.

The figure traipsed across the rock-strewn ground, stowing the black bow on a clip at his waist. He wore black leathers like the Hawk's, though his seemed to be in better repair.

The Lynx. The Menagerie's sharpshooter and scout. Anji recalled a sweltering day with her mother at the Linura docks, waiting for her father to arrive and moor their little boat for the night. As they sat amid the bustling harbor, her mother reading a thick book and nursing a thin cigar, a ship adorned in Rolandrian's house colors had sidled up to the dock, attracting a murmuring crowd. The Lynx had strode down the ship's gangplank with a tattered prisoner in tow, tall and lean, wide shouldered, and masked like he was now. The crowd had parted like wind-blown branches as he walked silently away from the ship, whispering and jostling for a closer look—some had even given the odd cheer.

Anji had been as swept up as everyone else, waiting to see if any other Menagerie members would appear, but her mother had only glared at the man's back as he'd met with gathered Senate officials and guards at the top of the ramp leading into the city. Before Anji could see anything more, her mother had led her to the dock's far end, away from the noise and excitement.

The man before her now was certainly tall, but much larger around the waist than Anji remembered. He walked closer to the fire, the campfire and lightening sky revealing gray tufts of thinning hair around the top of the mask.

"Hawk?" The Lynx chortled. "Look at you! Back at it. Bear will be tickled to hear it. She's been moping about you for months. I kept telling her you just needed some time. Heals everything, I always say—"

"Lynx—"

"What are you doing all the way up here? Why aren't you masked?" He took another step, his mask tilted toward Anji. "Who's that you've got?"

The Hawk flicked her green eyes to Anji and back to the Lynx. "Nobody. Where are the others?"

The Lynx stopped within twenty strides of their camp, towering head and shoulders above the Hawk. He waved a hand southward. "Still on their way, I expect. I was headed to Olangar for a separate job when I got the notice to change assignment. Didn't Bear fill you in?" He began walking toward the Hawk, but she held up a hand. The Lynx stopped, but his posture stiffened.

"Why are you—"

"You haven't seen us, Lynx," said the Hawk. "Go back to your horse, back to the others, and report the northern territory clear."

A muffled chuckle issued from behind the Lynx's mask. "Come on, Hawk, what is this?" He shifted toward Anji, then pointed at her. "Hang on. Is that her? The one who killed—"

The Lynx sputtered, the arrow perched in the Hawk's slender fingers moments before now jutting from his neck. Even in the dim light, Anji could see blood pooling where his leathers met at the collarbone. The Lynx fell to one knee, desperate gulps issuing from behind his grotesque mask. He jerked a hand to his neck, feeling at the mess of flesh and bone, of smooth wood, the glistening point of the arrow sticking out under the base of his skull, and fell to the ground, spasming once before lying still.

The Hawk marched to where the man lay like a crumpled sheet and squatted for a moment. She tore away the Lynx's mask and shoved it under one arm. Then she untied his boots, wrenched them off, and carried them back to the circle of firelight before tossing them on the ground at Anji's feet.

"Try those on," she said, settling back to her place at the fire. She picked up her cup, frowning at the leftover contents.

Anji gaped at the woman, her tongue going cold in the rising wind. She closed her mouth, opened it to say something, then closed it again.

"You look like a fish, working your maw like that," the Hawk said, flipping her thin gray hair out of her face. She took a final gulp out of her cup and flicked the remnants over the fire.

"What—why did you do that? You *threw* that arrow?" Anji said, finding her voice once more. "You just—you—Nine, you didn't even have a bow!"

The Hawk narrowed her eyes, her head tilted just to the side. "How observant of you. They should have written that on the sheets: 'Miracle girl, understands what people don't have in their hands.' " Then she shoved the Lynx's mask into a satchel Anji hadn't yet seen. It was silk of such a deep blue it seemed out of place among the Hawk's other things. The fabric shimmered like liquid, and Anji felt the sudden urge to reach out and touch it. It might have been a trick of the light, but Anji couldn't quite see where it opened, and by the time the Hawk had twisted the sack and tucked its strap under the bulging contents, she couldn't be sure she'd seen it open at all.

A gust of wind tore at the flames, and as though it were a cue, the Hawk stood and began kicking the fire out with one boot. Anji gaped at her.

"Why was he so surprised to see you?"

"None of your concern."

"I thought the Menagerie all worked together?" said Anji. "You're—you're friends, aren't you? Why did you kill him? It sounded like he—"

"*Leave* it, girl," said the Hawk. "I'm not here to answer questions or fulfill your childhood fantasies."

"But you let him see your face," Anji stammered. "I thought—"

"I'll not hide my face from the dead."

A weight dropped into Anji's stomach, like a rock plunging into an icy river. She scratched at the back of her hand with one jagged nail. "The dead . . ." she trailed off, her voice quivering.

The Hawk shot her a scathing look and cleared her throat. "You're to be tortured and executed. Publicly, I imagine. And I'm on my way to the biggest payday of my life." She spared a glance for the man lying dead on the moss-covered ground not twenty feet from the fire. "I'll not let you or anyone else stand in my way."

A lump welled up at the back of Anji's throat. She'd come all this way, braved the elements wearing nothing but laundress homespun and her father's old coat, only to be dragged back in chains? Rolandrian had been a terrible king; everyone knew it— everyone talked about it, in the castle, on the streets. As a girl, she'd stayed up many nights listening to her parents talking about him when they'd thought she was asleep. The image of the two of them hunched together over stacks of paper at the oak table under their only window still burned in her mind.

The king of Yem had been responsible for every horrid thing happening in the world, so Anji had snuffed him out like a candle. She'd done the country and its people a favor, and in return she'd receive only torture and death.

But that couldn't be. Yem wasn't some backwater country like Dorodad, with no governance or order. Her parents, her aunt Belle, they'd taught her that much at least. Even the worst criminals were given their fair trial, just like everyone else.

"There'll be a trial though, right?" Anji said, holding on to the hope like a drowning girl to a piece of driftwood.

The Hawk's mask wagged. "No trial."

"But the Senate—they have to—"

"Linura is your home," said the Hawk. "You worked in the castle. Did you not notice the Senate were no longer in charge?"

"I wasn't exactly invited to their assemblies," said Anji. "Besides, servants aren't allowed outside the castle."

The Hawk's mouth twisted. "Well, if you had ventured out, you would know the Sun Wardens hold near-total control of the Senate, and, by extension, Yem. With Rolandrian gone they've likely firmed up their grip."

"Those psychos in the yellow robes?"

"All who worked in any sector of government will be under their influence," said the Hawk. "Whether they know it or not."

The news hit Anji like a rogue wave. When she'd been living on Linura's streets, the Sun Wardens had been nothing more than old men shouting on street corners about their new religion. How had they gained so much power in only six years? Anji thought about the last time she'd seen one of them, standing on a crate with a thick book in hand, brandishing it like a sword to a jeering group of onlookers in a muddy alley where she would beg for food. They would be the ones administering her punishment—and all without a word of defense from her.

25

The Sun Wardens in their yellow cloaks cutting into me like a pig.

"I'll just run," she said, "I—I'll run the first chance I get. You're old. You're old and you're horrible and you can't keep me here like this. It isn't right. You don't understand. He *needed* to die, or else—"

"Run if it makes you feel better," said the Hawk. She pointed at the cup still in Anji's limp hands. "I poisoned you. A week with no antidote and you'll be in more agony than any torture the Sun Wardens can drum up."

Anji stared. "You said poison wasn't your trade!"

The Hawk lifted one bony shoulder. "I lied," she said, giving the fire one more kick. "I'll administer the antidote as we travel."

"You—" Anji sputtered, "you're not supposed to lie! It's in your rules." Then another thought occurred to her, one that presented Anji the tiniest, faintest glimmer of hope. "I'm also not allowed to see your face. How do I know you're even really the Hawk? You could have killed her and taken her mask. Why should I believe a single word you've said?"

"Believe what you wish," said the Hawk. "It won't make you any less poisoned." She jerked her head to the limp form of the Lynx lying in the dirt. "And you can ask him who I really am."

Anji bit her lip, trying to ignore the cold chill running up her back. Hawk or no, the woman had killed the Lynx like he was a fly on the wall, and he'd at least had a sword. Anji was manacled, hungover, unarmed, and though she'd rather eat horse shit than admit it to herself, likely poisoned. The thought made her skin crawl. Some black toxin seeping into her stomach, her veins, like a parasite she couldn't shake off. Pictures flashed through her mind—Rolandrian dead on the floor, her escape from Linura Castle, the old man's cart, her frantic race toward Conifor.

She'd been so *close*.

It really is all over then.

The Hawk coughed hard into her fist once, twice. She gathered her mask from the ground, set the pots in a neat stack, and laid the spoon inside. Without looking at Anji, she opened the entrance to her tent and said, "There's a blanket on the horse. Use it if you like, but you sleep outside."

✦ 3 ✦

Anji stared at the tent flap.

Granted, she knew next to nothing about bounty hunting, but leaving your captive to their own devices while you slept seemed ten kinds of stupid. Something chirped overhead, drawing Anji's gaze to a brown and white bird beating its wings on a northerly tack. Anji flexed her freezing fingers. If the Hawk wanted to make the mistake of underestimating her, that was her business. Anji wouldn't just sit and wait to be taken to her own execution.

She counted a hundred seconds, then bent to untangle the rope digging into her ankles. Her fingers ached as she fought with the unyielding knot. A frustrated hiss burst through her clenched teeth and she gave it up. If her father had known this knot he'd never shown it to her. She cast about for something, anything she could use to cut through rope. Hope had nearly fled when her eyes landed on the pot near the smoldering fire. She shuffled around the pit and snatched up the Hawk's spoon, careful not to let it clank against the other metal. The spoon was old and cheap, its edges rough.

Anji set to work.

The sun had cleared the distant mountain peaks to the east by the time she'd sawed herself free. She massaged blood back into her tingling ankles, then began working at the manacles. Twice she checked the tent flap for an angry, masked woman brandishing a knife, more than willing to deliver Anji to Linura with her throat slashed, but if the Hawk heard her, she didn't stir. A trickle of blood ran down her right wrist as she tried forcing her numb hands out of the iron loops. Holding back a scream, she slammed the cuffs against her thighs. She'd have to find a way to get them off eventually—for now she needed to get as far from the Hawk as she could.

She sprinted away from the camp, flitting amongst the heather like a rabbit fresh out of its hole. A cramp tightened in her thigh, but she pushed on. She'd run for the day, find a spot to hide out somewhere in the far-off hills. There wasn't much to eat out here, but she could manage a few days of eating moss and move on to a city farther north than—

Something tugged at her right ankle and the world blurred. The hard-packed earth rushed up and white pain shot through her skull like a thousand arrows. Hot blood bubbled out of her nose, spilling over her lips and into her mouth. Her palms stung where they'd slammed into the ground. She lay there in a daze, chest heaving, speckled light lancing across her vision, before she rolled to one side. Legs shaking, she got back to her feet, hunched over, gasping and spitting bits of dirt. She looked around, sure she'd tripped over something, but there was nothing there. No tree branches, no large rocks poking through the mossy earth—just empty, howling air as far as she could see. She took one step, then another, but at her second step something tightened at her ankle.

Anji kicked out her right foot, and the tug increased. She tried to step forward, away from the camp still visible not two hundred feet away, and something pulled on her ankle like a rope lashed to stone. She tottered for balance and nearly fell over again before righting herself. Her nose was throbbing now, her vision still clouded with pain.

Shit.

She gathered her shirt into a bundle at the hem and pressed it gingerly to her bleeding nose, cold air clawing at her stomach. She needed to get back to the fire, back to the horse. Perhaps she could break this tether, whatever it was, at a full gallop? Would it simply rip her leg off? She'd chance a leg if it meant getting the hell out of here.

Anji palmed the left pocket of her trousers, missing the familiar lump of coin she'd kept there for nine years, so close at hand. The last remnant of her mother, and she'd left it behind. Guilt swam in her gut at the thought of her father's dagger—also forgotten.

Had she been in such a rush to leave that she'd forgotten her only remaining links to her parents? What would she have done when she'd realized, some miles distant from the Hawk, that she'd left the dagger and coin behind? Not so many nights ago she'd been curled in her little cot, her father's coat bundled like a pillow, breathing in the boiled leather, tears pouring silently down her cheeks. She'd been so desperate, so foolish and pigheaded, that she'd nearly resigned herself to that true loneliness, the kind she'd cried herself to sleep fearing for close to a decade. She set her jaw as she trudged back.

The camp lay undisturbed, the only evidence of her presence the empty cup she'd used to dose herself with poison. A thin trickle of silver smoke wafted from the smothered coals, spiraling into the relentless wind. The mare gave her a bored, one-eyed glance and nickered.

"Oh, shut up," Anji hissed. She snatched up the rusted spoon, hoping its rough edge would cut a neck easier than it had the ropes. She edged toward the tent flap.

Surprise her, she thought, *cut her throat and grab your things. Quick. Quick. Quick.* She slipped inside and stole on silent feet over the canvas floor, eyes adjusting to the dark.

For an old woman, the Hawk didn't keep many luxuries. She slept on a cot in the far corner—no blanket, not even a pillow. In the near dark, her face was serene, its harsher lines smoothed, her chest rising and falling in the rhythm of deep sleep. She'd bundled the blue-dyed silken satchel between her legs, one thin hand clutched around the strap. A pair of swords, one long and one short, lay nestled alongside her body in their black sheaths. Anji pictured herself slipping one of the blades into the Hawk's chest, but dismissed the idea. She'd wake up before the sword was even free.

Beside the cot, a diminutive oil lamp sat extinguished next to a long burlap bag lined on each side with bulging pockets, and next to the lamp—her mother's coin.

All thought fled from her, and she padded across the space, holding a shaky breath. Right there for the taking. Her world, the life stolen from her, was contained in that glint of bronze. Anji hunched over and had barely gathered the burnished metal into her palm when the Hawk's gloved hand shot out, grip iron-tight on Anji's wrist. Pain flared through the bones in her arm as the rest of the woman's wiry body slid off the cot and to her still-booted feet, eyes hard. The Hawk brought the point of a small dirk to the hollow of Anji's throat.

"You're bleeding."

Anji tried wrenching out of that grip, but it remained firm, the knife's wicked tip sticking at her exposed skin. She didn't acknowledge the blood caked to her face, but took another shaky look around the tent, a last desperate hunt for her father's knife. Her skin throbbed where the coin's edge dug into the meat of her palm.

"I'd have thought it was obvious," said the Hawk, hauling Anji toward the tent's open flap, "but I've taken steps to ensure you can't escape. You're poisoned, and I have the only antidote. I'm better trained than you—much better trained." Her mouth was a thin line, her eyes bored. "And, as you've now noticed, you are tethered to my person by a maxial link. Is this all clear to you now?"

The Hawk pushed her out of the tent, knife point digging into the back of Anji's neck. Anji growled and wrenched away, and to her surprise the Hawk let her go. They stared at each other for a heartbeat, and in that gaze Anji realized how truly cornered she was. The Hawk had done this—all of this—a thousand times. She'd likely tied dozens of criminals to the tether around her ankle. She'd marched scores of thieves and rapists and degenerates to the gallows. Why should Anji be any different?

She looked away from those searing green eyes. The Hawk stepped into the clearing, slipping the knife back into its sheath. She set her hands on her narrow hips and peered around the camp, as though surveying for any other trouble Anji had gotten into while she was asleep.

Was she even sleeping though? Anji thought. *What if she was awake this whole time? Did she know I would run away?*

"We're making for the coast," said the Hawk. She blinked at the sun, raising a palm toward the horizon with one eye closed. "Now that you've gotten escape out of your head you should get some rest before we—"

Anji shrieked and swung the spoon for the tender spot where the Hawk's neck met her shoulder. She didn't need a knife or a sword or a bow. She was sober now, and more than a match for this old woman. The Hawk had gotten the slip on her, gotten lucky finding Anji drunk and underfed in some no-name town. Everyone had a lucky break, and it was this old woman's turn, simple as that. The Hawk would take the blow and crumple at Anji's feet.

Only the blow didn't land. The woman snaked away like molten metal, sidestepping and spinning in a graceful motion that made her look as if she were dancing underwater. Anji barely had time to register her footwork before she felt a searing pain, heard the hollow jolt of her skull being rattled. She held a hand to her already-broken nose as her ass smashed into the hard earth. The spoon clattered against a smattering of chipped rocks. Her only weapon—her only hope.

Someone was hammering a nail into her nose. Through the tears flooding her eyes she could make out the shape of the Hawk bending down, the light from the risen sun flaring at her back. Anji felt a hand on her shoulder and jerked away.

"You're slow," the Hawk said, "and sloppy." She backed up a step, arms crossed. "A spoon? You wanted to kill me with a spoon?"

Anji growled and scrambled to her feet, blinking tears from her eyes. She could still fight with her hands, manacled or not, could still smash that maddeningly stoic face to bits if she could just—

She swiped at empty air. Once. Twice. Heard a boot crunching gravel. A black shape shifting, then nothing, only light, and a sharp rap to the side of her head. Then another to the small of her back, making Anji stand straight up as though she'd sat on hot coals.

"You're embarrassing yourself, girl, just—"

Anji screamed and threw her full weight at the Hawk, or at least the spot the Hawk had just been. She sailed through the air and gasped as she collided with the earth and inhaled a nose full of dirt. Coughing and sputtering, she tensed for the blow, the blinding strike to her head, or maybe she'd be flipped over and stabbed right through the heart.

Just end it, she thought. *Make it stop.*

But the final strike never came. Anji lay there, chest heaving, spitting rocks and slivers of grass from her teeth, blood coursing from her pulsing nose. She blinked tears away, trying and failing to hide a whimper as the Hawk squatted down in front of her.

Anji spotted it too late, the glint of her coin in the tufted grass. She swiped for it but the Hawk plucked it from the ground. She held it to the light, one eye closed.

"Fair bit of maxia in this," the Hawk said, voice even.

"Give it back."

The Hawk pocketed the coin. "A little more insurance, then."

"Fuck your insurance," Anji said, lip quivering. Fresh tears brimmed at the corners of her eyes and she bit her tongue, shutting them away. "You've already got my knife, isn't that enough?"

"It's a nice knife."

Anji jerked her head, snarling. "It'll be in your heart before long!"

The Hawk rose from her squat. "I know you're a bit dim," she said, "so I'll make myself clear. You're my prisoner. Worldly possessions are no longer yours to claim. What was yours once is now in a satchel only I can open. You must accept this if we're to continue."

Anji bit back a retort, a swirling mix of loss and defeat settling in her stomach. She spat a glob of blood into the grass, grateful she didn't see any teeth.

"If you're finished trying to kill me," said the Hawk, pointing at the mare, "I'd suggest you fetch that blanket and get some sleep. I'll wake you before midday. Steel yourself for a hard road. We're likely to meet more unfriendly faces before we arrive at the coast."

"You're an unfriendly face," Anji said, sitting up in the dirt, holding her nose shut.

The Hawk cleared her throat.

"Sleep," was all she said. Then she disappeared back into her tent.

4

"Why don't you just kill me?"

Anji walked ahead of the mare, wrists chafing, pain radiating from her skull. She'd hardly found sleep before the Hawk had roused her, commanding Anji to march forward despite her protests for more rest. The small of her back ached, she was dizzy with hunger, her nose was a ruin. The Hawk had given her a rag soaked in what Anji'd hoped was clean water, but dabbing at the wound only made it throb all the harder.

She'd lost count of her attempts at conversation, the Hawk silent from her perch atop the horse, ignoring her every word. So Anji was surprised when the woman finally answered.

"Thought about it," she said, that monotone voice reverberating off the metal mask she'd donned once more. "Still thinking about it, but unfortunately you're worth double with a heartbeat. I expect there's not much fun in flaying a dead regicide. Though I'm sure you'll chatter the Wardens into putting you out of your misery within an hour."

Anji's gut clenched. They wouldn't actually *flay* her, would they? She dug her fingernails into her palm. Focusing on the pain brought her to the here and now. She wanted to keep this woman talking. At some point the Hawk would let something slip, some weakness Anji could exploit, something she could use to get the hell out of this mess. She kicked at a tiny chip of lava rock and watched it skitter through the grit. The Lynx's boots had fit, at least. Anji had decided to relish the comfort they gave compared to her laundress flats, rather than picture their previous owner.

"If you're so annoyed with me, why not cast a charm to shut me up?" she said, looking over her shoulder. "You're a Maxia."

The Hawk barked a laugh, twitching the reins, her voice like a bell inside the metal mask. "If you think that tether is a spot of impressive maxia, you haven't seen much of the wider world."

"I never said it was impressive." Anji tugged at the ever-tingling knot around her ankle. "How much did this set you back? You've got it active at all times. I bet it's costing you a month per day."

"It costs what it costs."

"I wouldn't pay anything if I were as old as you," said Anji. "You can't have much time left as it is."

"I'd gladly give a year of my life to shut you up. Eyes front, girl."

Anji narrowed her eyes. "I have a name," she said, turning back to the rutted road. "It's Anji."

The Hawk said nothing.

They trekked in silence down the narrow easterly road, tundra stretching to either side. The sky spread wide and azure above, empty of clouds, the sun a useless yellow disk. And always the ceaseless, droning wind.

Anji had been this far north only once, when her family had been selected for passage on a caravan to sell pottery in Conifor. Her father had still been an apprentice fisherman, still struggling to bring money home, when he'd burst through the door to tell Anji and her mother. He'd called it the Pottery Lottery, seeing as well-paid work came infrequently to low-born citizens. Anji remembered her mother's stern face folding into a frown at the news, but she'd simply nodded and started packing their things without a word.

The journey had been cold and dull, bumping along in a caravan led by a group of Repulo from the Southwest Shelf. The Repulo rode giant, flightless birds with cruel, curved beaks and chewed strips of stained wood as they chorused the long, sorrowful laments brought from their homeland. She could still see her parents bundled up against the latticed sides of the cart, heads jostling, one sleeping while the other watched over her. They'd done their business on arrival, but that night Anji had also accompanied her parents to a dismal warehouse on Conifor's outskirts. Scores of people had gathered there, their conversations hushed, their faces drawn and tired. Anji's parents had left her in a filthy office, given her a book, and told her to mind herself while a heated debate had commenced in the adjacent room. Anji had only caught a few words of the exchange, but her parents had come out looking frustrated and hadn't spoken to each other till they'd returned to Linura.

This trip was proving much more exciting.

"How much farther do you think?" she asked, her voice light, airy as the plains sweeping out to either side. "I don't have a compass to hand, but I'd say we're headed east, not south."

"Again, your observational prowess knows no bounds," the Hawk said. She cleared her throat and Anji heard what might have been a wheeze, or the wind. The woman had certainly come down with something on her way north. Anji hoped it wasn't catching.

"So . . ." said Anji, "we're not headed for Linura?"

"We're headed where I point us."

Heat rose in Anji's cheeks. She pictured the map of Yem tacked to the wall in her aunt's tiny apartment. The barren trail the Hawk was forcing her down now would eventually connect to the

Queen's Road, which ran east from Yem's border with Dorodad across the entire country until it ended in Tideron, Yem's largest city apart from Linura. There had to be other villages and even towns dotted along that route. Towns meant more people. People she could bribe for information or protection or both.

Besides, even the Hawk would have to sleep again sometime. Opportunities would present themselves, just as one had in Rolandrian's bed chamber. Anji had escaped Linura Castle's many constables—she could escape one old woman who, from the look of it, had severed ties with the Menagerie.

"Well, we haven't run into any more of your friends," she said. "Why aren't you working together anymore?"

"Not my friends," said the Hawk, "and certainly not yours. If they catch us up they'll try cutting my throat and take you for themselves, as was plain this morning. I can't have that. So we're avoiding the passage south, taking the long way through Tideron and the Kalafran Ocean."

Then down the coast, right into the Port of Linura, Anji thought.

"How are we going to navigate through towns, through Tideron, with everyone looking for me?" Anji asked, genuinely curious. "My face must be up on every bare wall by now."

"True enough," said the Hawk, "but you've only a slight resemblance to the girl in the drawings. A spot of luck, that. The artist had a clumsy hand. Also, your hair is shorn, and now your nose is an altogether different shape."

"Right," said Anji slowly, "but I'm traveling with *you* now. Won't that make people suspicious? What better prisoner for a Menagerie member than a king killer?"

The Hawk cleared her throat. "Most folk see the mask and they're smart enough not to prod me with questions."

"Kill me then," Anji said, glancing over her shoulder, "if I'm so annoying."

"Don't mistake me, girl. You're worth more alive, but my patience has its limits. Even so, I'll keep my head now and collect on yours later."

"What do you even need all that money—"

Anji yelped and tumbled into the dust, her toe throbbing despite the boot's thick leather. The Hawk cursed and yanked at the rope until Anji scrambled back to her feet, teeth clenched. Stupid road filled with stupid rocks. *Cold and wind and rain and lava rock.* Anji forced a breath through the stabbing pain in her nose. Every hero in the stories she'd read had braved forests and swamps and endless beaches. They'd fought ogres and trolls and sand shrikes, commanded armies, and rescued children from cruel witches. Nothing about this barren tundra seemed worthy of a book.

"The bounty on my head must be huge," she said, "if the whole Menagerie is up here chasing after me."

"Enough to fund an army," the Hawk said. "Eyes on the road."

Anji walked on. The knowledge that the Hawk had reason to keep her alive was like a weight off her chest, but the woman at her back was no ordinary captor. Anji shuddered, picturing what an experienced member of the Menagerie could do with a blade in hand and murder in mind. The cool, casual way she'd beaten Anji, so unlike the street brawls of her youth, so—refined.

"So, the Menagerie," she said, more a statement than a question. "I've heard stories about you since I was a girl. *Legendary* bounty hunters. Is it true the Senate hired you into service after you captured the Ghost of Linura? I heard you were all barely into your twenties."

The Hawk coughed, but said nothing.

"Must pay a lot, that sort of job. Why did you leave?"

The Hawk said nothing.

"We used to play 'Menagerie' when I was little. Five of us as each animal, and the others got to be our bounties." She looked over her shoulder. "Have you heard the song?"

The Hawk said nothing.

Anji cleared her throat and began to sing:

How many animals does it take,
To catch the wicked and make us safe,

"Stop it, girl, I'm not in the—"

Anji spun around despite the lead and danced along backward. She continued,

Ox is strongest, loyal and true,
Goat is cleverest, valor anew,

"Quiet! There's—"

"Come on, I'm not even to your line yet!"

The Hawk sprang off the horse and strode toward Anji.

"Nine, I'm sorry, okay?" said Anji, staggering back as the Hawk advanced. "I said I'm—"

"Shut up," the Hawk hissed. Anji swallowed a curse as the woman grasped her shoulder and spun her back to the trail.

Over the rise ahead, a covered wagon jostled toward them, wheels squeaking on the washboard terrain. Two horses pulled it along, one a dappled gray, the other a roan stallion. Burnished gold tack and harness glittered in the sunlight as the wagon came closer. The cart's canvas covering fluttered on the breeze, spotless white with gold embroidery stitched in a deft hand at its edges. Two figures sat atop the horses with a third hulking in the cart at their armored backs. All three wore longswords, grave faces, and colors matching the purple and gold of the Linura City Constabulary.

Anji knew those colors. She'd seen them every day of her life while working in Linura Castle.

Rolandrian's colors.

No, no, no, no. Her heart skipped. She cast around for some place to hide. *Not now, not so soon, it can't be over now, it can't—*

The Hawk leaned close to Anji, one hand still tight to her shoulder, and whispered, "Keep your mouth shut."

The cart creaked to a stop a few yards away, close enough for Anji to make out the haggard faces of the two constables atop the horses. The third sat in the shadows of the covered wagon, armor glistening where it stuck out into the hazy day. Whoever it was, they sported a golden cape likely worth more Rhoda than Anji had ever seen.

"Ho there," said the man on the horse to Anji's right, a lean, middle-aged brute with salt-and-pepper streaks at his temples. A band of woven white rope circled his upper arm. He peered down his hooked nose at the Hawk, and as his gaze slid over Anji she took a meek step back.

The Hawk inclined her head, then clicked her tongue at her own horse, who ambled to her side. She grabbed at the reigns.

"Corporal," she said.

The man leaned in close to the woman at his side and muttered something in her ear, still looking at Anji.

"We've no wish to delay you on what business you're about," said the Hawk, ushering Anji along. "Safe travels to you all."

"Wait," came a voice from the shrouded figure in the wagon, another man. Anji thought she heard the Hawk sigh as the man stood, the cart creaking as he stepped into the sunlight. Whatever hair had once occupied his scalp looked to have fled for the bushy pair of eyebrows protruding over ice-blue eyes. His jowls quivered as he surveyed the Hawk.

"Captain," she said. "Really, I would not—"

"This is the girl," said the captain. "The one who killed King Rolandrian." The constables on horseback swiveled to stare at Anji, their faces hard.

So much for my disguise, Anji thought.

"You've come far enough, hunter," the captain went on. "Tell your Wardens you've given her over to us and you'll be paid your due when you return to Linura."

"Are you sure, sir?" said the Corporal, smirking. "The girl on the poster was a lot prettier than her. She looks like a stableboy. Worth a pig or two, but not a million Rhoda."

The Hawk gripped the reins so hard Anji could hear them squeak in her gloves. Anji pushed down the urge to gape at her. *A million Rhoda?* she thought. *No wonder she wants me all to herself.*

"She cut her hair," said the woman opposite. "With a rake, by the look of it."

Anji ground her teeth, but kept silent at the pressure of the Hawk's fingers digging into her shoulder.

Why hasn't she turned me over yet?

"I mean no disrespect, Captain," said the Hawk, inclining her head once more, "but I have tenets I keep to. I'm sure you understand. Once in my possession, I cannot give up my charge. I'll see the girl is taken safely and without spoil to Linura, on my honor."

The woman on the horse guffawed. "The honor of a Sun Warden hound," she said, spitting into the road. "Speaking of animals, where are the rest of you, eh?" She glanced at the empty expanse about them.

With a deep frown, the captain raised his eyes to the landscape as well, then back to Anji and the Hawk. A spiral of fine dust wafted between them on the frigid wind. The Hawk stood still, her legs like tree roots dug deep into the earth.

"I'm afraid I cannot acquiesce."

The captain barked a laugh and waved this last away. "Enough of this," he said, drawing a long, polished sword. "Kill her if you must. Take the girl."

The two on horseback dismounted, armor rattling. Tiny puffs

of gray dirt clouded around their polished boots as they slammed into the ground. The corporal gripped the hilt of his longsword.

The Hawk darted forward, sword in hand as though it had always been there. She shot like an arrow around the roan stallion's head, her sword slipping neatly between the man's jaw and chest piece. Blood spurted and dribbled down his white tunic. Anji stared, the food she'd eaten earlier threatening to come back up.

"What the fuck—"

The corporal gurgled and fell to one knee, eyes wide, his hand twitching toward his neck, but the Hawk's blade was already out and ready to catch the sergeant's steel with a clang that rang out across the plains.

The sergeant grunted and whipped her sword around in a wide, scraping arc, separating her blade from the Hawk's. The Hawk sidestepped, feinted, and swung at waist level, ostensibly going for a side cut. The woman raised her blade to block it, but the Hawk swung up, dodging the incoming slice, and drove the point of her sword into the woman's unarmored armpit. Blood-drenched steel burst out her shoulder's other side, through leather and cloth, scraping against metal. The sergeant screamed, her eyes wide, and dropped her sword to the dirt. The Hawk twisted and wrenched her blade free, letting the woman crumple into the dirt.

Sucking in a breath, the Hawk pointed her sword at the Captain as he leapt off the wagon, his broadsword raised, the hilt poised at the side of his head in two gauntleted hands. He advanced on the Hawk with quick feet and sliced the giant blade through the air.

"You'll pay for that, you cu—"

The Hawk twirled, the broadsword's edge passing within a hair's breadth of her leathers. She bent, poised her steel against the Captain's hamstring, in the space between plated armor, and slid it up with a jerk. The Captain bellowed as the Hawk dodged a blow that would have broken bone.

With the Hawk occupied, Anji grabbed up the short sword the sergeant had dropped and gripped the hilt close to her chest, her manacles clinking. It felt marvelous, having a real weapon again, something with a point and an edge. She sprinted at the Hawk as she took the Captain's head from his shoulders with one clean blow. But the Hawk stepped aside, letting her fly past to collide with one of the now-riderless horses. The horse nickered and danced away in its reigns, startling the other so they dragged the wagon forward a few paces. Anji spun away, the leather hilt soaked in sweat already. She gritted her teeth and sidestepped as the Hawk raised her blade, point poised straight at Anji's chest.

"Don't even think—"

Anji screeched and bound forward, lifting the sword's edge high, aiming for the neck. The Hawk brought up her blade without taking a step, the clanging steel reverberating up Anji's arms. Remembering her footwork, Anji cross-stepped and twirled the sword once in her fingers. The Hawk circled with her, one arm extended, her sword steady and shining.

"You can't win," she said, that insufferable mask and the voice behind it setting Anji's blood to boiling.

With another yell, Anji leapt, striking once, twice, a third time. The Hawk was so *fast*. The calm, indifferent way she deflected each of Anji's blows carried a silent insult, each parry a new flavor of shame. Anji spun, the sword raised, and brought it down with a strangled cry. The Hawk batted the steel from Anji's hand and it tumbled end over end in the dirt. Anji scrambled after it and gripped the hilt, her breath like a bellows in her chest. She couldn't see for the hate and embarrassment and filthy desire to *end* this woman and her maddening poise. With a final burst of rage, she rounded on the Hawk once more, tears blurring her vision.

Strong fingers gripped Anji's wrist. With no thought, she lurched forward and sank her teeth into the meat of the Hawk's gloved hand. The Hawk cursed as the acrid taste of boiled leather and sweat filled Anji's mouth.

A blinding pain rang in her temple like a bell and she reeled back as her wrist was released, sword still clutched in one hand. She raised her manacles to cradle the agony blossoming in her head.

Anji stood still, chest heaving, and watched the Hawk step toward her, flexing her bitten hand.

"Drop it," said the Hawk, her sword still leveled at Anji. "Now."

Anji glanced at the carnage underfoot, the gory remnants of the three officers that had sat full of life just moments before. Well-trained soldiers, and the Hawk had cut through them like shears through linen. She hadn't even made a sound. The only blood the woman had spilled was either leaking into the dirt or dripping off her blade. Not a drop on her leathers.

Anji, however, was starving, exhausted, and chained. All the training she'd had, the days spent learning poses and nurturing purple bruises. Useless.

She threw the sword into the dirt.

The Hawk lowered her steel but kept it out of its sheath. "We need to move," she said, adjusting her mask. "First, climb into the wagon and destroy a few things. Take what food you can find. They'll have water as well."

Anji stared at the blood still streaming from the captain's severed head.

The Hawk snapped gloved fingers and pointed to the wagon. "Food. Water. Silverton is still half a day's walk from here and we're running low on both."

Fists clenched, Anji stepped around the headless captain and into the wagon.

"Make a mess. We want it to look as though they've been robbed."

"I get it," said Anji, letting her eyes adjust to the dark.

Inside was an assortment of chests, crates, and bundles of cloth. Anji opened what chests weren't locked and dumped the contents onto the floor—mostly papers, but some fine silver utensils and picture frames she might have stolen if she'd still been alone. She cast around and found a burlap sack filled with packaged, cured meat and a hefty block of white cheese. Glass clinked as she picked up the bag, and she shuffled the contents around to find two small bottles of wine.

"There's wine!" she called, kicking another chest clattering to the floor. She tossed a few bundles of clothing across the small space for good measure.

"Water, I said," came the Hawk's voice from outside the wagon. Anji looked up to see the woman unlatching the horses and slapping them away. She scrambled out of the cart, the bag slapping against her leg.

"What are you doing?" she said. "I could have ridden one of those! My feet are killing—"

"You walk," said the Hawk, snatching the bag from Anji's hand. She crossed to her horse and began tying it to the saddle.

Anji scoffed but resumed her place in front of the mare as the Hawk climbed back into the saddle and commanded her to walk. The trail yawned endless ahead, rock-strewn and overgrown with sedge and heather. She glanced over her shoulder as she began to pace forward, the sun starting its slope toward the horizon.

"Why didn't you let them take me?"

The Hawk said nothing.

✦5✦

Anji's father had been a fisherman before he was murdered. In company with his knowledge of sailing and storms was an endless supply of sea-related sayings, which he would pester Anji with to no end. One of his favorites was "You can bait the hook however you like, sprout, but the fish still has to bite." As a child, Anji had always thought it was her father's way of telling her to be patient, but a full day in the Hawk's shadow had given the phrase a whole new meaning. Anji tried shouting, crying, and pleading for the Hawk to let her go, but her every word was met with either silence or the occasional command to shut her mouth. As the day faded, Anji traded frustration for curiosity and began plying the Hawk with more questions about the Menagerie and the Hawk's blatant disregard for their well-known rules. But the Hawk remained stubborn as a rockfish with a full belly no matter what she asked or how she asked it.

If she even is *the Hawk,* Anji had thought. *The real Hawk would never have killed those soldiers. She should have given me up the moment they asked.*

After a day of fighting, shivering, and what seemed like endless walking (on Anji's part at least), they'd finally stopped atop a ridge overlooking a cluster of shabby buildings bisected by a wide, potholed street. A thin stream trickled over a rocky trail at their backs, winding down the ridge where it joined a larger tributary that lined the town's north edge like a silver ribbon. No sound issued from the houses or empty alleys. If not for a scattering of candlelit windows and wisps of smoke rising from a few chimneys, Anji would have thought the place deserted.

"Do all the towns up here have to look so sad?"

"Try living off this land yourself," said the Hawk.

Anji's teeth chattered as the moon broke free of a bank of clouds in an otherwise empty sky. A black shape darted through the air above their heads and dipped toward the stream, making barely a ripple as it beat its wings silently upward again.

"Just saying," she said, "town with a name like Silverton—thought it might be a bit livelier." She recalled a sign somewhere on the road days past, indicating the town lay some way off her frantic course. She'd put it to memory in case anyone had asked where she'd come from.

And a load of good that did for me, she thought, and for the first time in days, she laughed to herself.

The Hawk stiffened. "What's so funny?"

Anji sniffed and shook her head, peering down at Silverton again. On the road, she'd imagined a sprawling, affluent mining village—not this poor, broken thing sheltered between two prominent hills, dwarfed by the towering mountains to the east. "Barely any light down there. Do people just sit in the dark when the sun goes down?"

"Likely can't afford the fuel," said the Hawk. "They've few exports now their mines are dry." She hunched over the saddle horn, her nose grazing the pages of the tiny notebook she'd been scrawling in that morning. She sniffed and dragged a finger down one page, then squinted through the darkness at the expanse to either side. "The land here is infertile, and what they do manage to grow is taxed." She cleared her throat. "Or stolen, depending on who you ask."

"What's the notebook for?"

The Hawk clapped the book shut and stuffed it back into her leathers. She dug into the heavy brown sack attached to the saddle, dismounted, and thrust a piece of dried meat at Anji without a word before gathering the reins and pulling the horse away from the ridge's lip. More dark shapes joined the first in the air, flitting over the stream and chirping in a strange chorus as they darted in and out of the water.

"What the hell are these things?"

"Bats," said the Hawk. "Likely from the abandoned mines nearby." She tugged at the horse's reins. The mare bobbed her head and huffed, took a single step forward, then reared at the swift approach of one of the bats.

"She's scared," said Anji. "You have to—"

"I know how to handle a horse." The Hawk untied the large sack attached to the saddle and tossed it jangling to the ground.

"It isn't the weight, it's the—"

"Eat and keep quiet, girl. I don't need your help."

Anji pressed her lips into a thin line and watched the woman struggle. She gnawed at the meat, wondered vaguely what animal it had come from, but suspected she wouldn't get an answer even if she asked. As with everything the Hawk had given her to eat so far, it was bursting with flavor. Spicy yet sweet, it melted in her mouth like butter and burned going down. The woman couldn't match Kaia or Libby for company, but Anji hadn't eaten so well in years.

Not that I'm living in luxury, she thought, frowning at her manacles. She'd cartwheel down this hill naked for a cigar and a cup of clear spirit, but the bounty hunter seemed determined to drink only water. Earlier, the Hawk had upended a few drops of some clear liquid into the dregs of their canteen and instructed Anji to drink. The antidote for the poison coursing through Anji's veins.

As the hours had passed, Anji's anxiety had heightened. She'd been alert to every sensation, every pain or tingling in any extremity, unsure of whether the poison was having an effect yet. The thought of poison running through her veins made her feel unclean, corrupted. Despite the cold, her palms were slick with sweat. She wiped them on her pants as the Hawk finally coerced the horse to the stream's edge despite the bats' flurried dance above. The mare stared down at the stream, then whickered and danced back.

"Come on," said the Hawk, "drink up, that's it."

"She isn't used to a stream," said Anji. "Try a different container. A bucket or a trough—"

"We don't exactly have any of those to hand."

Anji sighed and stepped forward. She bent and unclasped the large brown sack and fished inside.

"What in the hell do you think you're—"

Bootsteps thudded in the dirt as the Hawk advanced. Anji's heart thundered as she stood and raised the pot like a shield.

"Try this," she said, trying to keep her voice even. *Nine, she's so damn fast.*

The Hawk stood like a statue for a moment, fists clenched, before snatching the pot out of Anji's hands. She stomped to the stream, filled the container, and lifted it to the mare, who began drinking at once.

One of the bats flapped close to Anji's head and she let out a tiny shriek, waving it off, but it was already well toward the stream once more to join its fellows. For the first time since she'd escaped Linura, she was glad she'd cut her hair so short. The mare's tail whipped once at the frenzy of movement above, but it kept drinking after such a long day's ride.

The Hawk guided the pot and the mare's head to the ground and shot a glance at Anji. "Thought you were a laundress."

Anji lifted a shoulder. "They had me working in the stables for almost a year when I was first brought to the castle."

"Why did your work change?"

A gust of wind blew across the stream, wafting through the horse's mane. This close, just the smell of horse brought back memories of Anji's short time in the Linura Castle stables. There she'd learned how to muck out stalls, which saddle and lead repairs would last, and the proper cleaning of hooves. As the weeks had passed, she'd found a sort of gratitude for the work —for the horses especially—but also the fresh air, the endless number of things to learn . . . the sense of purpose that had kindled a warmth in her she hadn't known she could feel again. Even so, her parents' deaths were still a raw wound across her heart, and a loneliness without end still plagued her sleepless nights.

But anything was better than sleeping on the street.

Working in the stables might have kept her from her current course, if not for Gnab, the red-haired son of the stablemaster. Gnab had shoved horse shit down her pants, tripped her as she walked with arms full of harnesses, and berated her with insults about her dead parents, her thin arms and legs, the gap in her teeth—until the day she decided she'd had enough and sank a bony fist into his cheek.

Linura Castle's stablemaster—a gruff, impatient man at the best of times—had been the one to break up the fight. Unwilling to hear a word against his son, he'd allowed Anji a minute to pack her paltry belongings, then marched her by the elbow to the laundresses' quarters beneath the castle, away from the horses and her musty pallet in the tack room's far corner. There he'd left her with Emelda, the castle steward and servant master, who preferred the title of Matron. And there she'd stayed, until she stabbed Rolandrian.

"I got in a fight."

"Of course you did," said the Hawk. She shook out the pot, patted the horse's neck, and stuffed it back into the bag before tying it to the saddle once more.

"We'll make for the center of town," she said, donning her mask.

Anji looked over the ridge at the bulbous building hogging all the town's scant light. "Looks like the perfect spot to rest up," she said. "Separate rooms, then? We could share a bed, but I don't think our relationship has—"

"We're not sleeping here."

Anji picked a sliver of cartilage from her teeth. "Right," she said, "you've got a tent and a cozy cot for yourself. I don't suppose you care, but I've had my fill of sleeping on the ground." She spat the sliver out, watching it catch on a particularly strong gust of icy wind. "A nice goose-feather bed and a drink would be—"

"Stop your prattling. We're getting supplied and making our way. No interruptions, or I'll—"

"Slit my moronic throat," Anji finished, scratching at the skin under her manacles. "I'm well aware."

"I'll auction your things to the lowest bidder, girl. That dagger of yours is Sevenfold steel, and the coin is so full of maxia I could sell it to the Dean of Exorcia himself."

Anji froze. "You wouldn't."

"I hardly think it benefits you to assume what I would or wouldn't do. We're here for food, and I need to ask about Tumbledown. Then we're off." The Hawk hoisted herself back into the saddle, sawing at the reins as the horse sidestepped away from the bats above.

Anji frowned. "Tumbledown? You didn't mention . . . I didn't know we were going that way."

"Forgive me for not drawing my plan out on a map for you."

Anji shifted her gaze to the mountains standing sentinel over the village, so much larger now after a day of travel. Their sawtooth tops cut a black line through the swath of stars overhead.

"You're sure we need to take that route?" Anji said, hating the quiver in her voice.

A bat screeched and dove straight for the horse, startling her into a rear that almost knocked the Hawk out of the saddle. After shifting back into place, the Hawk leaned forward and rubbed a gloved hand against the mare's neck.

"Did you hear me?" said Anji. "I asked if we—"

"Yes, we're taking the pass," said the Hawk in one breath, the mask shifting to watch the bats flying past. She levered herself straight in the saddle, then craned the mask down toward Anji. Sitting so high on the horse, the woman made Anji feel tiny as an insect as she went on in a cold voice, "I've no wish to come across more of Rolandrian's patrols, and they and everyone else looking for you will think twice before taking such a route."

Anji scoffed. "They're right to. You might be willing to risk your skin, but I want to keep mine as long as I still can."

"And what would a stable girl turned laundress know about a mountain pass four days' travel from Linura? Have you even seen these mountains before today?"

Anji bit back a retort. Working in a castle full of people, she'd heard her share of stories of the wider world. Soldiers and couriers liked to talk. There was no way for Anji to have verified their tales even if she'd had a mind to. But as far as she knew, Tumbledown pass was home to myriad horrors. Vengeful storms,

53

snowfalls, landslides that had buried entire caravans. Insects, poisonous snakes that hid in icy fissures, bears twice the size of a house that could rip your limbs off. She crossed her arms. "Go fuck yourself."

She couldn't be sure, but something in the Hawk's bearing told Anji the woman was grinning behind that mask. Leaning over the saddle, she said, "If you're afraid, just say so. No need to be so crass. That may have fooled a couple drunks in the Hammered Smith, but it won't work on me."

"I'm not afraid," said Anji, forcing herself to keep her foot still lest she stomp it like a child. "Besides, how will you get paid if I disappear down a crevasse?"

"You'll not die before you're supposed to," said the Hawk.

The horse reared again at the approach of more bats.

Silver flashed. The Hawk drew her right-hand sword and sliced into the air. A pair of squeaks broke over the wind, followed by soft thumps to the swirling heather underfoot. Two bats, cut cleanly in half, lay in pools of dark blood at Anji's feet. The Hawk sheathed her sword and steadied the horse. The mask's metal contours shifted under the half-moon, reflecting Silverton's scattered lights and the unveiled stars overhead.

"Move."

Anji gulped down the last bite of the meat, and at a gesture from the Hawk, preceded the woman and her horse down the ridge.

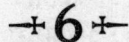

If Silverton looked a drab settlement from above, it was down-right depressing up close. Trash and soiled clothing lay strewn across the branching dirt lanes and piled against the cratered brick facades of shabby houses, their roofs sagging on their frames. Warped wood planks covered many of the windows, likely salvaged from neighboring structures. Tiny wells of firelight flickered behind ill-fitting doors.

Someone had vandalized one of the walls, which read:

THE TIDE WILL RISE

Though this slogan had been drawn over with a giant white cross, and beside it in the same white paint, a symbol Anji had never seen:

"What's that?" said Anji, jerking her chin toward the symbol.

"Keep walking," said the Hawk.

Little of the populace was present, but a scant few darted like malnourished phantoms between narrow alleys. A persistent coughing issued from a squalid dwelling up the road; from another the high-pitched whine of a child, though whether they were laughing or crying Anji couldn't say. The air reeked of coal smoke and boiled linen and spoiled meat. As they approached the tavern, the sharp smell of human excrement wafted through Anji's nose, and she felt the urge to retch. Anji would never forget her year living on Linura's streets, but the state of Silverton made Mudtown look luxurious by comparison.

"Why don't they leave?"

"Why don't you ask them?"

Anji crossed her arms against the cold and squalor, as though it would keep the stink and dread off her skin. Something cold splashed against her shins, and she realized she'd stepped into a puddle of black mud, which now caked her new boots.

Piss and shit and Nine know what else in there too, she thought, shaking off what she could. She scanned the grubby town as the Hawk barked at her to keep walking for the hundredth time. *All this thanks to Rolandrian, no doubt. I should have killed him sooner.*

One of the gaps between the buildings caught Anji's eye. A sliver of pale moonlight illuminated a row of molded planks leaning against the brick wall in a makeshift shelter.

The planks shifted, clunking against one another, then . . . something emerged from the shadows.

"Hawk," said Anji, eyes still fixed on the alley. "Hawk, what—"

A tug at her manacles jerked Anji around to face the building ahead—the only one emitting significant light through filthy windows. The Hawk stopped them at a vacant hitching post. The tavern's veranda harbored a few drunkards pulling on cigars, sparing occasional glances at the masked woman and her chained cargo. A wind-scarred sign hung past the awning above, but whatever it had said was faded beyond relief.

The tavern's front doors crashed open with a burst of noise and shifting light. A middle-aged man in overalls and a patched straw hat was being forced outside by two constables in gleaming silver armor, yellow cloaks clasped to their shoulders.

"They'll work you all to death!" the man cried, his voice strangled with grief. "It's a gods-forsaken cult! The Tide will rise! The Tide will—"

One of the constables snarled and sank a gauntleted fist into the man's stomach, forcing him to double over with a wheezing gasp. They hauled him back up and handled him down the steps and into the street, sparing barely a glance for Anji and the Hawk as they marched away from the tavern. The man seemed to gain his voice back as they walked, and he started to yell something else before the armored woman at his side kicked at the back of his knee and sent him sprawling to the dirt.

The men and women on the front porch all watched, eyes wide, their mouths shut tight. The man was now pinned down in the middle of the street by one constable while the other clapped him into manacles and gagged his mouth. He was still struggling and crying out, but his words had become an indiscernible garble. The constables yanked the man to his feet once more and shoved him along, his muffled shouts fading to silence as they turned a corner and disappeared. One by one, the bar's patrons averted their eyes and looked back back into their drinks.

Anji wanted to shout, to tell them all they were drunks and cowards and worse. How could they just stand there and watch a man be corralled like that, with no argument, not a single one of them asking why he was being taken away? She looked around at the Hawk, who was still staring at the empty street.

"Aren't you going to kill those ones too?" Anji said, jerking her head.

"Murder doesn't solve every problem, much as it may surprise you."

"So you agree they shouldn't be hauling someone off just for—"

"Those are Sun Warden constables," the Hawk cut in, sliding out of the saddle. "They'll not stand in my way, unlike Rolandrian's." She shook her head and tugged at Anji's lead. "No more questions. Stand over here."

The Hawk maneuvered Anji and the horse to a hitching post on the tavern's far side, away from the front door and the figures on the porch. She looped the reins around the post once and adjusted the mask. Anji noticed the woman's hands were shaking, but she couldn't bring herself to judge. Her whole body was quivering despite her oversized coat. The cold down here seemed to dig deeper than it had on the ridge with the bats. The Hawk spun on Anji, a slender finger pointed at the ground.

"You stay put, and keep your mouth shut."

"What was that he said about the Tide?"

"I said no more questions," said the Hawk, turning toward the tavern's steps. "I'll only be a moment."

"I want a cigar," Anji said.

The Hawk raised her hands. "I want you to stop talking," she said, her voice muffled against the mask. She tugged at her gloves and marched toward the tavern.

"I'm just going to steal the horse," Anji called, hating how petulant she sounded.

A gust of wind swirled between them, and the Hawk turned with it to face Anji. Anji shivered despite herself, though she kept her chin raised.

"Do as you will," said the Hawk. "You did so this morning and left your nose a wreck. If I were you, I'd conserve that energy for the pass and cherish what remains of my face."

Anji ground her teeth and watched the Hawk mount the steps and stride past the silent stares of the porch patrons. She pushed into the tavern, the chorus of voices lifting and dying as the door closed behind her.

As soon as the Hawk was out of sight, Anji snatched at the blue pack on the horse's flank and felt for a fastening. She flipped the bag over, turned it side to side, and dug her ragged nails into the silken fabric.

Nothing. No buttons, no buckle—no discernable way to get inside.

She cursed and slammed the satchel against the horse's stomach, eliciting an annoyed whinny from the mare.

"Sorry," she said, wiping at her face with her bound hands. Anji tried the bag again to no avail. Sealed like a bladder. Likely maxial. *Not a Maxia*, she thought, frowning. *Right, and I'm not tied up to a horse like a common thief.*

But no. She *wasn't* a common thief. She was an assassin now. A king killer. A regicide. And indeed, she *was* bound to a horse, and to the Hawk herself—but not for long. In a few days she'd be back in Linura, carved and flayed while still breathing, at the mercy of a hundred old men in silken robes, their faces passive and sweating, watching as she pleaded and cried and begged for mercy.

She considered calling out to the people on the porch; explaining who she was, that she'd been kidnapped, that she was innocent and this was all a giant misunderstanding. Any decent person could see she was no more than a skinny young girl. Hardly a threat.

But these folk had shown their colors already. They'd watched one of their own dragged away shouting about the Tide, something about a cult, and they'd done nothing to intervene. None had even said a word. Why would they help her? Likely they would just call on any other constables that happened to be inside, or worse, gang up on her and the Hawk and take the bounty for themselves. Judging by the dozen posters tacked on the bar's wall, they likely knew how much she was worth. Anji ducked her head down and scratched at her chin, staring at the mare. She had to escape. Now.

Maybe I wasn't going fast enough before, she thought, lifting her foot to finger the ever-tickling loop of maxia bound around her ankle. The tether was invisible, about the width of her thumb. At its touch, her fingers tingled, but it wasn't unpleasant. She tried working her jagged nails under it to no avail. It was stuck tight like a second skin. *But with the right force anything can be broken.*

Anji untied the reins and hefted herself into the saddle, a rebellious thrill taking hold as she glanced at the tavern doors. The men on the porch disregarded her. She was alone in the street with only the muted clamor of the tavern's interior and the gusting wind at her back. The mare knickered under her but moved not an inch.

Anji slipped her boots into the stirrups and kicked.

The mare didn't budge.

"Come on," Anji whispered, kicking once more. She gathered up the reins and pulled, and finally, reluctantly, the horse wheeled away from the tavern and the Hawk.

Darkness shrouded the street ahead, but Anji nudged the horse into a trot, then a canter, hooves clopping through the mud and rock. Cold air streamed past her ears, into the gap of her widening grin. Her spine twinged as the saddle bucked against her backside, thigh muscles tight and poised. She urged the mare faster with a flap of the reins and they picked up speed. Houses and broken storefronts and tiny fires blurred past as the mare gained more ground—nearly out of the stretch of buildings now, speeding away from torture and death and—

A yank at her ankle. Something in Anji's knee popped and she was flying back, stars and rooftops wheeling overhead. She landed like a cord of wood in the middle of the street, cold mud splattering into her face. All the air in her lungs blew out at once and she gasped, blinking grit from her eyes.

The horse skidded to a stop some distance away, whipping her head up and down before turning back to where Anji lay in a shivering heap. The mare snorted and stood over her, one eye gazing down as Anji lifted herself to one elbow and slapped a hand to the frigid earth.

"*Fuck,*" she said through gritted teeth. Tears stung her eyes. She was twelve again, humiliated and bruised after trying to jump the small gap between the chandler's shop and the butcher's across the alley. All the other kids had managed it, but she'd smacked her chest against the lip of the opposite building and tumbled to the cobbles below, snapping a bone in her wrist that had needed six weeks to mend. The same hot flush of embarrassment seared through her now. She whipped around in the dirt, sure someone was watching, ready for the Hawk's rebukes or a blow to the head. But the street was silent and dark and still. She groaned and got to herfeet . Putting weight on her knee made it sting with a sharp pain, but it didn't feel broken. She tested a step and released a shaky breath. She could still walk.

The mare nuzzled her shoulder. Anji patted the matted hair of her flank, took the reins in one hand, and began the short trudge back to the tavern.

"Why'd you fall off your horse?"

Anji whipped around, reaching for a dagger that wasn't there.

A little boy stood behind her, keeping a wary distance from the mare. A spattering of filth etched his thin face, his hollow cheeks, watery blue eyes blinking up at her. One of his feet was shod in what she could only describe as a bundle of rags. The other was bare, caked in dirt, and lined with a nasty black wound gone far past infection.

He held a knot of fabric close to his chest, and in the dim light Anji could make out a sort of face on the shock of white cotton that may have constituted a head. A doll. The ugliest doll she'd ever seen.

Anji had never been any good with kids—even when she'd been one. She clicked her tongue at the horse and walked a bit faster, hoping the boy would take the hint, but he matched their pace, favoring his bad foot and glancing sidelong at her. He trailed along in silence until they came back into the tavern's sickly yellow light.

"I was tied up," Anji said. "I thought I could get away, but . . ." She stopped the mare once more in front of the vacant hitching post.

"Why were you tied up?"

A shout issued from inside the tavern, but the doors remained still. Anji scratched at the tether, then eyed the boy standing solemn and shivering at her side.

"She's prolly a prisoner!" he said, shaking the doll in both hands, talking out of the corner of his mouth.

The boy's eyes widened.

"Why, Mr. Poop," he said, a hand to his chest, "what an awful thing to say!"

"Well, she's tied up, ain't she?" the doll, Mr. Poop, said. The boy twitched his eyes to Anji, then back to the doll, giving it another shake.

"If you'd been *listening,*" he said, "you would have heard that I already asked." The boy rolled his eyes to Anji and held the doll at arm's length. "He never, *ever* listens. Sometimes I wonder why we're friends."

"Some folk don't much like hearing what others have to say," said Anji.

The boy furrowed his brow, as though this were a nugget of information he'd keep to himself for later. "Why *are* you tied up?"

A dry clatter of wood issued out of the darkness up the road. Anji squeezed her fingers into a fist, hoping she and the boy weren't about to be set upon. What was keeping the Hawk in the tavern so long?

"I was . . . running," Anji said, "and I got caught."

"Like in a game?" The boy's eyes lit up.

Anji's mouth twisted. "I guess so."

The boy tilted his head to one side, taking another step toward her, the doll limp in his hand—forgotten. "So you lost, then," he said, his voice low, solemn. "That's okay. I lose at games all the time. Ma used to tell me, she said, 'You just have to keep playing, keep trying no matter what.' " He shrugged one shoulder. "And eventually you win."

Anji sighed. "I won before I lost, I think."

The boy narrowed his eyes, as if unsure whether Anji was pulling some kind of trick on him, using the esoteric words adults wield when they'd prefer a child stop talking to them.

"Where are you and the horse going?"

"Linura," said Anji, then, thinking he might not know where or what that was, she added, "A city far south of here."

"I know where it is," said the boy, affronted. "That's where the yellow men come from. They took my friend Sarella and her parents in one of their big wagons." He held his hands out as far as they would reach, his eyes wide. "We used to play together . . ."

The boy toddled closer, blinking. Purple bruises clustered about his neck, around his right arm above the elbow. Anji stepped back, as though whatever horror he'd been through would seep into her, and felt a rush of shame.

"Do you have any food?" the boy asked, blinking up at her.

Words fled Anji, like water trickling from her cupped hands.

The boy ventured closer, and Anji could see he was shivering. *Of course he is,* she thought, *My teeth are chattering and I have a coat. He doesn't even have* shoes.

"Where are your parents?"

She knew the answer to this question might further break her heart, but she had to hear it. The boy cast around with wide eyes, as though his parents would turn up around the corner if he looked hard enough. He muttered something about his mother. Anji caught the word "gone."

Anji opened her mouth to speak when the noise from the tavern rose once more. She twisted to see the Hawk bounding down the steps, a rough burlap sack and a metal canteen sloshing with water in one hand, tucking something into the folds of her black leathers with the other. Anji turned back to the boy, but he was gone, doll and all.

"Well, look at you," the Hawk said, fastening the burlap sack to the mare's saddle. "Following directions for once." Anji whipped around the horse, trailing the slack line behind her, looking everywhere for the kid.

"What's got you spooked?"

"Nothing," Anji said, still casting around. "There was a boy out here . . ." She swallowed, her spit brackish. Nine, she needed a drink now more than ever. "He asked me for some food."

The Hawk grunted and finished fastening the sack to the mare. "Didn't expect anyone would come right up and talk to you."

"He said his parents were . . ." She couldn't finish the sentence.

The Hawk grunted as she mounted the horse. "Well," she said, "let's be off. Couple of louts on the porch followed me in. More curious than the usual sort. They asked after you and I told them you'd murdered two children in Conifor."

The words took a moment to sink in, but Anji sputtered when she understood. "You *what*? Why would you tell them that?"

The Hawk kicked at the mare's sides and they were off again, walking down the wide road separating the dilapidated houses, gray smoke trickling from the thatched roofs. They passed out of the village in silence but for the horse's hooves, Anji still keeping a close eye out for the little boy and his doll.

"If I'd told them you'd killed Rolandrian," said the Hawk once they were out of the village, "they would have cut my throat and made you their new queen."

✦ 7 ✦

Anji collapsed to the dirt, fine grit wafting into her nose. She coughed, more powder coating her blistered lips. Every muscle trembled with fatigue and bone-deep cold; her knees and ankles ached like they'd been hammered into shape by an angry blacksmith.

Unmoved by Anji's attempts at conversation, the Hawk had set them on a southeasterly course out of Silverton with all haste. Once beyond the town's sight, she'd jerked Anji away from the Rose Road and onto a smaller track that pointed like a dusty dagger toward the sawtooth peaks eating up the lightening sky.

They'd traveled in stony silence as the stars disappeared, the growing day revealing signs of strife that had plagued Yem and its people: a broken wagon left to weather on the road's edge, a distant cluster of blackened huts in the lee of a craggy hilltop. They passed an abandoned farmstead, its windows broken out, the once-tilled land gone over to weeds and spiraling dust. Remnants of a windmill lay in a heap on the house's south side, the sails torn and fluttering on the breeze.

The Hawk had bothered to speak only once, when Anji had

stopped to gape at the remains of a man long dead, sitting tied to a fence post. A sign had been looped around his head, the word "debtor" spelled in bold letters. Under the letters was the same strange symbol Anji had seen on the wall in Silverton, the hollow orb over an downturned semicircle. Anji's insides squirmed at the sight of a black bird pecking at the poor man's intestines, which hung like blue-gray rags in the dirt. Mouth dry, Anji had asked what happened, but the Hawk had only muttered something about the Sun Wardens and ordered her to get a move on.

Now Anji lay shivering on the ground, curled on her side and listening to the lap of water on rock.

They'd stopped on the shore of a lake so perfectly circular it seemed drawn by a child. Its water reflected the cloud-speckled sky, not a ripple stirring its glassy surface. A copse of stunted trees pocked the lake's far side, bisected by a rocky stream that weaved into the larger body of water. The road, still visible from their camp, wound like a brown snake into the mountains ahead, so large now Anji felt she could reach out and touch them.

The Hawk slid off her horse, removed the tent and bags and set them in a neat pile, then trudged to the mare and began unbuckling the saddle, seemingly unaffected by the hours they'd been traveling. Anji pulled her coat tighter, the thin leather doing little to warm her trembling limbs.

Must have been out of my mind, she thought, *fleeing into the north.*

On top of being captured, she was being dragged through the coldest part of the country. Through ceaseless, frigid wind that cut at her cheeks and clutched at her fingers. Here, the sun hung in the sky like an ornament rather than the warm orb it was in the south, soaking the back alley above her childhood home. She longed for afternoons spent on the basement steps, basking with her mother in the warm golden glow with books and cups of tea. Now, however, returning to the city's warmth would herald only her torture and death. At least she wouldn't be shivering when she was set into with the knives. Probably. She closed her eyes against the thought.

"You're not laying there all night," the Hawk said from above —Anji hadn't heard the approaching boots over her chattering teeth—"Brush the horse down."

"I'm your prisoner," Anji said to the ground, "not a valet. See to your own damn horse."

Anji gasped as pain erupted in her side. The Hawk drew her foot back again and Anji held her hands out to catch it, but the woman only sidestepped and gave another swift kick to her leg. Anji curled in on herself, waiting for another blow, but it didn't land. Raspy breaths rattled through the Hawk's old lungs.

"Brush it down or you don't eat," she said, tossing a horse brush to the ground by her head. "I don't mind getting you back to the city scrawnier than you already are." She turned and stomped toward the bundled tent.

Anji narrowed her eyes at the brush, but clambered to her knees and snatched it up. She shook her manacles at the Hawk. "It'd be a lot easier if I—"

Fabric cracked like a whip as the Hawk flapped out the length of gray canvas. "Your hands stay bound."

"Why?" Anji said, standing. "Afraid of what I'll do with them?"

"Terrified."

Anji scowled. "I need to wash them."

Without a word, the Hawk fished inside the large brown sack at her feet and tossed over a sloshing canteen.

Anji splashed some water onto her hands, wincing at the cold. She rubbed most of the day's dirt away and dried her skin on her soiled pants. Not exactly refreshing, but it would have to do.

"Thank you," she said, setting the canteen against a rock. "See? You can be civil after all."

"Stop pestering me and get on with—" The Hawk sputtered and twisted away, hacking and coughing so hard she had to screw her eyes shut.

"Hey, what—"

The woman held up a gloved hand, as though warding Anji away. Anji was too transfixed to think of doing anything other than staring.

"You keep coughing like that. Are you sick?"

The Hawk's head wagged, nose red, tears running down her wrinkled cheeks. "Just brush the damned horse." She coughed once more, spat something into the dirt, and set to pitching the tent as though nothing had happened.

Eyebrows raised, Anji crossed the camp. The horse's tail twitched as she approached, and she made sure to stay within its line of sight.

Last thing I need right now is a hoof to the chest.

"You're a pretty thing," she said, touching her palm to the mare's glistening coat. "Been a rough time for you? Same here, but we'll get you brushed down and well-fed. How's that sound?" The horse lowered her head toward the tufts of heather underfoot. Anji looked around at the Hawk, who tore her gaze back to the half-finished tent.

"What's her name?"

"Didn't bother giving her one."

"Every horse should have a name."

"Call her what you like," said the Hawk. She snatched up a fist-sized rock and began hammering a stake into the tent's corner flap.

Anji studied the mare's brown coat, noting the flattened hairs where the Hawk had cinched the saddle too tight. Her overgrown mane shone inky black where it wasn't matted with road dust. She whickered and bobbed her head, one eye rolling toward the level plains opposite the mountains.

Kaia and Libby, Anji's only friends in the laundry, loved a good scandal. They'd all hardly been introduced before the pair had begun gossiping about the girl Anji had replaced. Raven-haired and sulky, the girl had a habit of staring out of windows at the city beyond the castle walls, at the streets the servants were forbidden to walk. A diligent but quiet worker, she'd kept to herself, hardly interested in making friends or causing a fuss. One night, however, she'd slipped into the laundresses' sleeping quarters well after Matron had ordered them all to douse their lamps. She'd thought, apparently, that she'd gotten away with being out past curfew, but Matron had been awake and waiting for her. The girl had been locked in the castle dungeons for a week, then demoted to cleaning garderobes and toilets. They later found out, through the endless chain of castle gossip, that the girl had been out with a guard she'd met, carousing in upper Happerdam.

The escapade had caused quite the stir at first, but apart from Kaia and Libby, the other laundresses had developed a habit of falling silent whenever the subject had come up. Before long, even Kaia and Libby had let the gossip die. But Anji had spent many restless nights thinking about the girl. All she'd wanted was a night to herself, away from the castle's confines. The servants were an embarrassment, something to be hidden away from local gentry and visiting nobles, but the girl had simply not wanted to be a thing ill-used and ill-kept, even for one night. She'd been a trapped, tamed thing, at the behest of those who thought her less than deserving of freedom.

"Molli," she said, patting at the mare's back. "How about Molli? You like that one, girl?"

Molli only inched forward to get at a fresh bundle of yellow grass.

"Poor girl," Anji said, "stuck out in the middle of nowhere with a mean old woman."

The Hawk snorted at her back, but said nothing.

Anji raked the brush against Molli's flank, and after some time she felt the tension leak out from her neck and shoulders. The work was soothing in a way, like folding linens. Just a series of monotonous motions that eventually left her with a job done. She'd found a sort of comfort in that, locked away for hours in the stuffy confines of the castle basements, brick walls sweating, the reek of soiled sheets and mildewy wash basins thick in the air. She'd been kept there so long she could bring the image up like a stage play in her mind: fourteen servants in matching homespun lined up along rickety tables, scalding water slopping in giant tubs at their backs while they repeated the same motions over and over. Gossip and chatter weaving in and out of their work, Kaia the chief instigator. Anji would participate as she liked, but the hours passed without a word were like traces of gold in black rock. The crinkle of fresh sheets, the smell of lavender and rose petals, cotton and silk chafing at her fingertips.

Molli's left flank finished, Anji started on the right. She leveled a look over the horse's back, at the Hawk now marching back from the shoreline, her pot sloshing with water. Anji hadn't even noticed the woman had left.

The Hawk settled on crossed legs in front of the finished tent, dug a bundle out of the burlap sack, and began pulling apart strips of dried meat. Her hands trembled despite the black gloves she always wore.

"Can't we start a fire?"

"No."

"It's freezing, I can't keep—"

"No fires. Anyone searching would spot us too easily."

"I don't understand you," said Anji, shaking her head. "You killed your own friend—"

"He wasn't my—"

"And *then* you killed three royal guardsmen." Anji threw up her hands, her manacles clinking.

"They were trying to take you."

"But the constables in Silverton—you weren't worried about them. Why?"

"Because they—" A muscle twitched in the Hawk's jaw. Without looking at Anji, she said, "I don't have to explain myself to you."

Anji shrugged a shoulder and kept brushing.

"You could put up a barrier," she said, pulling a knot of horse hair out of the brush. "Something maxial? If you can keep me tied like this I don't see why you wouldn't be able to—"

"If I could do that don't you think I would have by now?" said the Hawk, wrapping a portion of meat into a wad of brown paper. She scratched at the leather covering her neck and cleared her throat.

"You've been coughing," said Anji. "I'm only saying, a fire would—"

"I'm fine," snapped the Hawk. "Get to my age and we'll see if you don't let out the occasional cough."

"I think you're afraid."

"Fear keeps a body breathing."

The words caught Anji off guard. A memory flitted through her mind like a bird, of her and her mother nestled together in the rocking chair on their front stoop, her mother's nail gliding under a line of text while she read out loud, as Anji had nodded off to sleep in her embrace.

"That's Gale Summering," said Anji, "from the *Fireheart Chronicles*. Book three, right?"

For an instant, their eyes met, deep brown and ancient green. Then the Hawk snatched up the blue satchel and, to Anji's surprise, opened it like any ordinary sack. She fished out a paper-wrapped bundle, tied the sack up with a deft motion, and set it back down.

"What happens if they catch up to us?"

The Hawk slipped a knife from her belt and sliced the package open, held it up to her nose, frowning. "Who?"

"The Menagerie," said Anji, laying a hand on Molli's neck as she shied away.

Something rustled behind Anji and she whipped around, eyes wide, but it was only a snow-white raven lifting off from a boulder and away toward the mountain peaks. She felt a hollow ache in her stomach as she watched it disappear into the lightening sky.

The Hawk folded the package back together and stowed it once more in the blue satchel, sealing it tight with a flick of her wrist. "We fight over you, I expect."

"And you'll kill them all? People you've known and worked with for years? Your own friends?"

"Three against one is foolish."

"You took on three of the king's own yesterday," said Anji, still not quite believing the words as she said them.

The Hawk lifted a bony shoulder. "They weren't the Menagerie."

"So you *are* afraid," said Anji. "You don't think you can win."

"I didn't say that either."

"I hope they kill you."

The Hawk cleared her throat and pulled out a hand-sized hunk of brown bread. She broke off a piece and shoved it in her mouth.

Anji watched the Hawk eat, ignoring the empty rumble in her gut. "Why aren't you with them anymore? The Menagerie?"

"Not your concern."

"Sounds like my concern," said Anji. "For all I know they're coming to save me from you."

The Hawk leveled a look at her, chewing in a quick rhythm.

"Think you'd be better off with them?" she said, tearing off another piece. "They'd start torturing you long before Linura."

Anji shook her head. "The Menagerie aren't torturers. They're warriors, bound by a strict code of honor."

Still chewing, the Hawk rolled her eyes, but Anji went on, "I saw you all together once, walking a pair of prisoners through the Water Gate. You had them chained on top of a cart so everyone could see. And the Bear . . . I've never seen a woman so tall, so . . . regal. Like she was cut right out of a story." Anji glanced at the Hawk. "One of Gale Summering's, maybe. Anyway, I'd never seen even one of you before, apart from the dolls some of the other kids had, and there you all were, right in the middle of Mudtown."

"Dolls," said the Hawk under her breath.

Anji continued, brushing a difficult knot from Molli's mane. "The crowd was so thick I could hardly see, all cheering and shoving. The Bear called the Ox over and they stopped and waved and tossed out a handfuls of Celdia. Then the Goat and the Lynx and . . . and you. You all waved and even though you were wearing masks I swore I could see you smiling."

"Likely Goat was," said the Hawk, leaning back on her palms. "He loves bringing prisoners in. Like a parade, every time we came home."

"You were out catching murderers," said Anji, as though she were explaining the concept to a child. "And rapists and corrupt politicians. Why wouldn't you be happy to bring them to justice?"

"Do you even know what that word means, girl?"

That caught Anji short. She narrowed her eyes and said, "It means someone gets what was coming to them."

The Hawk rubbed at the bridge of her nose.

"You're a fool if you believe they're in it for anything but the cruelty they're allowed. We followed our tenets, for a time . . . but they've been twisted as the Wardens have gained power." The Hawk measured out another sliver of meat, portioned a hunk of bread, and set them on a bare rock at her side, gesturing for Anji to eat. "Does your song mention Lynx's affinity for skinning children? What about the Bear? Any lyrics about her boiling debtors alive?"

As grisly as the words were, Anji chose not to believe them. What did this woman know? She'd likely been thrown out for being a crochety old bitch. "And what do you do it for?"

"I *did* it . . . for the money, of course. Assuming the price was right."

Anji gave Molli a final glance over before stowing the brush on the saddle. She strode around to sit opposite the Hawk, wincing at the pain in her back. "A million Rhoda," she said, and snatched up the meat and bread. She crammed the lot into her mouth, ignored the cramp in her jaw as she chewed and continued, "Never understood how little slips of paper could pass as money. Silver I understand—it's valuable by itself. But paper? Doesn't feel as real, somehow. I escaped with twenty-four Celdia. Took me three years to stash it all away. Even as I left, I knew it wasn't enough to get to Conifor." She picked up a stone and tossed it into the dirt. "Should have waited till I had a full Rhoda at least."

The Hawk sniffed.

"Suppose it'd have been easier to hide from you. Could've folded it up and hidden it in my shoe or something. What are you going to use all that money for?"

"We're not here to get to know each other."

"It's a long trip. Might as well talk to pass the time."

"I don't make friends with assassins."

Anji guffawed, and a sliver of gristle shot onto her knee. She flipped it off. "If I'm an assassin after killing one man—one who deserved it, I might add—what does that make you?" She pointed to the pair of swords sheathed at the Hawk's belt. "How many throats have you cut with those?"

"You know nothing about me, girl," said the Hawk. "I'm through with all that nonsense."

Anji rattled her manacles. "Could have fooled me."

"I think that's enough out of you."

There's the crack, Anji thought.

"Shame we don't have any arrows to hand. You'll have to skewer them the old-fashioned way." She widened her eyes. "But no, I forgot—you quit. You're through with such *violence,* aren't you?"

"I'm warning you, girl."

"Of *course,*" Anji said, clapping her hands together, "you're a walking storybook. A wise old warrior, so tired after a life of gutting peasants and chasing after criminals . . . but you've hung it all up, right? Now you're sailing straight. You're better than all that *now.*"

"That's none of your—"

"Oh, this is perfect," Anji went on, cackling. Pain lanced through her nose when she laughed, but she ignored it. "A washed-up bounty hunter coming out of her well-deserved retirement just for me. It must be so *difficult* for you, after swearing off torture and murder for good, to kill four people just to bring me all the way back to—"

"I said shut your mouth!"

The Hawk rose to her knees, chest heaving, knife drawn at her side as the shout echoed across the lake.

"Ah, ah," said Anji, manacles clinking as she patted her chest. "Worth more alive, remember?"

"I could cut your stinking tongue out."

How is she so fast? Anji thought. *Aunt Belle couldn't draw a knife like that even in her prime.* Anji felt that rush of familiar panic, like a rising wave. Perhaps she'd pushed a bit too far. "I'd prefer the gag, myself," she said lightly, though her pulse still pounded in her ears.

The Hawk settled back, her lips a hard line.

They sat in silence but for the howling wind, the flapping canvas at the Hawk's back. Anji wiped her greasy hands on her soiled pants. It wasn't much to eat, but it gave her something to focus on apart from the slow dread creeping into her every moment, rising like a high tide with her chained to the beach.

"If it makes you feel any better, I can't kill you either."

"I wasn't much worried about that."

"I mean the tether," Anji said, fingering the invisible binding. "It's a maxial charm, right? It'll never break if you die without the disarming incantation." She chuckled. "I'd have to haul your corpse around, still on the run. Not exactly a nice thought."

A terse silence passed, then the Hawk said, "How would a laundress know that?"

"You hear all sorts of things in a castle," said Anji airily. She jerked her head toward the blue satchel. "That bag is maxial too, isn't it?"

The Hawk said nothing, but Anji pressed on.

"The coin in there, the one you said felt full of maxia? Well, it is. My mother—" Anji bit her lip, then said, "She found it. She gave it to me before she died."

The Hawk's mouth twisted, but she looked away, clearly uninterested in Anji's sad story.

"Can I have it back?" Anji said. "It doesn't do anything else, and it's the only thing I have left to remember—"

"The coin stays in the bag."

Anji got to her knees. "Please, I can't sleep without it," said Anji. "It's mine, and I—"

The Hawk locked Anji's gaze. "Nothing is yours," she said. "Not anymore."

"I'm not going to do anything with it," Anji said, hating herself for the desperation coating the words. "I just want to hold it." She inched closer, licking her lips despite the cold. "Please."

"You need to get back—"

"Just for a moment, I just want—"

"I said get back!"

The Hawk rose to her knees once more, hand clamped to a sword hilt. Her shoulders rose and fell in a rapid pace, like she'd just run a full sprint. Anji found herself kneeling before her, stopped short by the ugly twist of the woman's mouth, the hatred filling her green eyes.

"Fine," said Anji, settling back with a sigh. She wiped at the corner of one stinging eye. "I just thought—"

"Shut up."

"Would you stop interrupting me for one fucking—"

"I said quiet!" the Hawk hissed, gathering up her mask. She slipped it on and rose to her feet, her hand still squeezed around her sword's hilt. "Someone's coming."

Anji narrowed her eyes. She heard nothing save for the clap of water on the shore and the ever-present wind.

But no, the bump and thud of wagon wheels became barely discernable over the breeze, bringing with it the sound of low voices.

Without thought, Anji bounded across the camp, putting herself between Molli's flank and the Hawk's back. "Who is it?"

"Quiet," said the Hawk.

A heartbeat later, the wagon crested over the slight rise ahead. It gleamed brilliant white, its gigantic golden wheels flashing in the sun. Anji's mouth fell open at the sight of what drove the wagon toward her.

A pair of monstrous black birds pulled against their tack, their hooked, pale yellow beaks the length of Anji's arm. Their heads bobbed with every step, white irises with pits of black holding Anji in their gaze, studying her with an eerie intelligence. Taller than any horse, they strode on slender, scaled legs, three-toed feet digging grooves in the earth. A squawk issued from one of them, echoing over the low-lying hills.

On the wagon's flatbed sat a cage made of iron and dark wood.

Though Anji couldn't quite tell what lay inside the cage, she could make out the figure sitting on the wagon's box. A bent old woman in plush robes of purest yellow.

A Sun Warden.

8

The wagon trundled down the slope, rocking side to side. Whatever lay in the cage shookwith the motion, piled like a mound of filthy rags. Something hairy and gangly draped through the gap between two of the bars.

"Not a word," murmured the Hawk. But for the first time in days, Anji didn't feel much like talking.

Her only true brush with religion had been born out of necessity. In exchange for a bit of food, she'd attended sermons given by the poor priests of the Order of Inheritance in their dusty cathedral. The Order's weekly allowance of potato bread had kept her from starving as a street urchin more than once. But where those priests had kind, jovial faces, the woman approaching now could have melted a candle without flame just by looking at it.

The Sun Warden hunched forward, her face pallid and fixed in a heavy frown, cheeks and lips sagging with wrinkles. Dark sacks welled under each heavy-lidded eye, contrasted with thinning snow-white hair she'd pulled back in a tight bun. She hunched forward, neck outstretched, elbows perched on her knees, the oversized robe swallowing the subtler angles of her body. Her gray eyes narrowed as the wagon drew within twenty strides, darting from Molli to the tent to the half-open bags at the Hawk's feet, then finally snapping to Anji.

At the Warden's side sat a reedy man in a waist-length white coat and black breeches that flapped in the wind. His silver hair was combed over a balding pate. Anji thought she'd never seen a man with a face so set in a grimace, like everything he saw was the color and smell of shit. His eyes were a purple so dark and brilliant they seemed to dim the light of day. A Maxia, so infused with time's mysterious essence it was impossible to guess his true age. He looked into Anji's eyes, and she felt the wind that had been buffeting them settle for an instant before picking back up again.

The Warden leaned over and whispered something in his ear, still glaring at Anji and the masked woman as the wagon came to a stop.

The Hawk stepped forward with a palm raised high, but she kept her other hand close to her belt. She dipped her mask and ran a slender finger down the middle of its face.

"Warmth to you, Illuminess," she said, her mask muffling her voice. "My heart lifts to see a Warden of Sun so far—"

"You travel without your companions, Hawk," said the Warden, her voice cutting the air like a knife. "Explain. And know you speak before Illuminess Hectate, Fifth Column Cleric of the Sun Wardens, under the One's ever-watching eye."

Anji chanced a glance at the Hawk, who inclined her head and went on with even more deference.

"My superior was ordered by High Cleric Escadora to dispatch the Menagerie, Illuminess. As to my traveling alone, it serves only to bolster the Menagerie's precision and efficiency. To better spread Their Warmth."

"Indeed," said Hectate. "You have proof of this order?"

The Hawk produced a thick piece of folded vellum, atop which she placed a wad of Rhoda fastened into a shining silver clip.

Both figures atop the cart might have been statues for all they moved. After an interminable period of stillness and silence that made Anji want to scream, however, the Warden held out a hand.

The Maxia muttered a strange, complex series of words. The slip of paper and the Rhoda floated out of the Hawk's fingers, across the space between them, and into Hectate's waiting palm.

Without acknowledgment of the sheer amount of money the Hawk had just handed over, the Warden slipped the Rhoda into her robes and unfolded the paper, her eyes darting across the surface. After a moment of windy silence, she creased the vellum and tossed it spinning back to the Hawk, who snatched it out of the air.

"Your prisoner," said the Warden, "of what is he accused?"

"I cannot say, Illuminess," said the Hawk, her mask twitching toward Anji, who took an involuntary step back.

The Warden's eyes widened. She drew herself up straighter and said, "You *dare* withhold information from me?"

"I keep to strict tenets, Illuminess," said the Hawk, her posture not folding one bit. Anji's brows rose. If anything, the woman was standing even straighter. "I am forbidden from announcing my charge's crimes."

The urge to admit she'd been the one to kill Rolandrian flashed through Anji like a bolt of lightning. The Hawk was obviously terrified of the Sun Warden and her Maxia companion. How satisfying it would have been to defy the woman in front of her betters. To feel the waves of disbelief rolling off her captor, to finally have the upper hand, to do *something* of her own accord. But that tiny victory would die in an instant. There was no telling what twisted tortures the Maxia could summon while keeping Anji alive for the real show in Linura. Anji almost laughed: the only thing keeping her safe at present was the Menagerie's stupid tenets.

But why was she willing to break them before? Why not now?

The Maxia leaned to whisper in Hectate's ear.

With an impatient wave of her hand, Hectate leaned against the bars of the cage at their backs. "Have it your way then, hunter. I care not what the vermin did."

"Of course, Illuminess."

The Warden reached into her robes and drew out a bulging, fist-sized sack of silken gray cloth, tied at the top by a white string. With twitching fingers, she unclasped the string, then withdrew a bright blue marble of rock sugar. She slipped it in her mouth, sucked loudly, and said, "Do you have a scrying sheet?"

"I do not, Illuminess," said the Hawk. "I'm afraid that privilege rests only with my cadre's commander."

The Warden tutted around her candy. "Unwise," she said, more to herself than to the Hawk. "So you've not heard . . . One of your companions was found dead near Olangar. The Lynx."

The Hawk's mask twitched side to side as she said, "I had not, Illuminess. A tragic loss to my cadre."

"Tragic, yes. The report suggests the nature of his wounds was . . . unnatural. Butchered by his own arrow."

"Many dark forces plague the land of late, Illuminess," said the Hawk.

"'Dark forces.'" The Warden bit into the candy, the hollow crunch sending a cringe up Anji's spine. "*Vagrancy* is the plague, hunter," she said, swirling the pieces around her ancient mouth. "Neither spirit nor demon walk the earth without the One's design. Your friend was likely robbed, raped, left to bleed out on the rocks." She swallowed and waved a hand. "The price paid for arrogance."

"Of the Design are we so made to serve."

Anji had given up trying to figure out the deeper meaning of this conversation. Her gaze drifted past the Maxia to the cage at his back, the thing inside now shifting, its matted fur tangled with bits of straw and slivered wood.

"You," said the Warden, pointing a gnarled finger at Anji. Anji blinked and looked around. She hadn't realized she'd been stepping toward the cage. She had to find out what was inside.

The Warden popped another rock sugar between her lips. It clacked against her teeth as she asked, "Have you seen a Dredger, boy?"

Biting her lip, Anji shot her gaze to the cage once more.

The Hawk gripped her arm above the elbow, her fingers digging into Anji's skin. Anji hissed a breath, white pain shooting through her sore muscle.

"Answer when the Illuminess speaks to you."

Anji leveled a look at the Illuminess, now stowing the bag of sweets back into her robes. The woman swept a blue-veined hand toward the cage, her lip curling. "Quickly, Alphoronse, the criminal would like to see. A demonstration before we depart?" She jabbed her finger at Anji once more. "You wish to see the fruits of idleness, child? The sequelae born of the earthly disease of delight?"

Still in the Hawk's grip, Anji staggered toward the cage, into which she was now afforded a clearer view.

The bottom of the enclosure was filled with soiled straw, black and brown and soaking wet. A fresh gust of wind pushed the stench of stale urine into Anji's face, making her nose crinkle, her eyes water. White-winged snap flies buzzed in lazy circles around the inside of the cage, flitting from the bars to the snout of the creature inside, its eyes yellow and piercing and staring a thousand miles away. Its mouth hung in a rictus snarl, bile and pus and shining saliva coating its thin gray lips, its pale gums where mangled teeth stuck out at awkward angles like broken fence posts.

"Miserable thing," said Hectate, following Anji's gaze.

"Where are you taking them?" asked Anji.

"Them? There's only one, you stupid boy."

Anji gestured at the cage. "I don't know what gender they are."

Hectate sputtered laughter, sugary saliva splatting against the wagon bed's boards. "As though you looked upon a baker in his shop! You'd so soon grant personhood to such vileness? Better to befriend a Scorphice in its den. And you can thank the One there's iron between you and the wretch too, else it might have your face for a meal. Wicked, gluttonous, despicable creatures, the lot of them. We're taking it from town to town, to show the populace the scum slinking under their feet. Folk must see with eyes as yet unknowing the consequence of indulgence, of meddling with the One's own flora, plumbing the depths where Their Warmth does not shine." She rapped a knuckle on the cage's top, and the Dredger flinched, letting out a pitiful snarl.

"Observe," she said, waving a hand at Alphoronse.

The Maxia murmured again, eyes flashing, and a swirl of dust lifted from the ground, collected in a disc, and hovered to the grated top of the Dredger's cage. With a soft *thwump,* the disc fell inside, sprinkling dust over the Dredger's back and the splintered cage bottom.

The Dredger unfolded like a spider, its gangly limbs snapping and cracking, the matted fur and hard bits of scale that ran down its arms and legs glistening in the light. With a snarl, the creature was on all fours, running its snout along the wooden planks of the cage, snorting up the dust and grit, mewling and panting and spraying dirt up past the bars. The noise startled the giant birds in their harnesses, tack jingling as they flapped their miniscule wings.

"Desperate for the stuff," said Hectate. She let out a throaty cackle, watching the creature, her eyes wide with fascination and hatred. "They'll snuff up anything resembling a powder. Not too bright once the transformation has taken place. Like I said"—she grinned, her teeth shiny with sugary spit—"gone to animal madness."

Anji had to look away—her stomach churned at the sight of the poor thing, still snuffling about and now letting out a frustrated sob, its emaciated shoulders racking back and forth as it combed every last inch of the cage floor, leaving wet streaks against the wood. A dull pain radiated from her elbow. She'd nearly forgotten the Hawk's hand still clenched around her arm, fingers digging like worms into her flesh. The Hawk stared silently at the Dredger, rigid and unmoving.

"Would you let *go*?" Anji said, jerking away, and to her surprise, the Hawk released her grip. Anji nearly tripped over her feet, massaging the sore spot on her arm.

Hectate inclined her head at the Hawk. "Everything you hate, isn't it, Hawk? Perhaps when you're through with this one you could help us round them up."

"What does it want?" said Anji, her curiosity battling the unease building in her chest.

"Quiet," snapped the Hawk, but Hectate waved the question away.

"Peace, Hawk," she said. "We are on a mission to spread knowledge, after all. Alphoronse?"

The Maxia cleared his throat. "It is addicted to a stimulating powder," he said. His voice was much higher-pitched than Anji had anticipated. "A drug which has gained in popularity these past years and recently been outlawed. Apart from general euphoria, it bolsters mental acuity, provides endless energy, and enhances eyesight, hearing, and taste. With it you can work and fight for days without sleep, though the eventual physical toll it takes on the body is substantial, as you can see. It has an incredibly short half-life, resulting in a withdrawal which makes the user lethargic, yet strangely affable and loquacious. Amazing concoction, really —the refining process consists of—"

"That will do," Hectate cut in, slicing at the air with a wrinkled hand. "Don't teach the lout how to make the stuff. Fascinating as the effects are," she sneered at the cage and the Dredger now curled back into a ball at its corner, "one need only observe the end result. Monsters, all. I say we eradicate the lot, save what we use for demonstration. Hopeless, pathetic curs racing to the grave. And all for some ground-up coral." She slapped a hand against the cage, her voice rising. "Was it worth throwing your life away?"

"Coral?" said Anji, ignoring the tension emanating off the Hawk still hovering at her side.

The Maxia's mouth twisted. "Coal coral, to be exact. Native to the Kalafran coast. The polyps themselves have no effect, but the black exoskeletons are harvested, dried, then ground to powder. The Spurs call it Rail."

Anji had no idea what a Spur was, but before she could ask, Hectate continued.

"Ingenious, I'll admit," she said, "what these addicts do for a high. They dive for it, risking reef sharks and sting jellies. Coal coral only grows on certain types of rock, volcanic stuff . . ." She snapped her fingers at Alphoronse.

"Basalt, Illuminess."

"Basalt, yes," said Hectate, "horrid black stone—unnatural. Those mangy Inheritance priests used to build those awful cathedrals out of it." She sniffed. "Gaudy structures."

Anji thought that was rich, coming from a woman in a robe of such a bright yellow she'd have had to shade her eyes if not for the bank of dark clouds rolling in from the west, eating up the sun and its light. Hectate hobbled back to her bench, sat, and slipped the sack of candy out again.

"Listen to us," she said, squinting at the lowering sun, "prattling

87

on." She slid another piece of rock sugar between her lips. "We'd best hasten to Silverton while the weather agrees with the road."

The Hawk inclined her head and shoved Anji out of the way as Alphoronse got to his seat and gathered up the reins. He twirled the leather around one slender hand and looked around the camp as though seeing it for the first time, his violet eyes finally landing on the Hawk.

"Forgive me if I'm mistaken," he said slowly, "but I was under the impression that of your cadre, only the Goat was trained in maxia." He gestured toward the invisible tether around Anji's ankle. "You've managed quite an impressive pair of charms—strong, both of them. And efficient for one unattended."

The Hawk didn't flinch. "An undeserved boon from our esteemed leader, Maxia Alphoronse. The High Cleric saw fit to teach me charms of Seizure and Sealing. You know how he rewards those who please him."

"Indeed," said Alphoronse. "I do, however, detect a third pooling on your person? Perennial, but weak . . ."

"A trinket," said the Hawk, "of mere sentimental value, I assure you."

This seemed to be enough answer for the Maxia, though he didn't look like he quite believed the Hawk. Anji wondered how the Menagerie compared to the Wardens. Where did the Maxia fit in? And had the Hawk left her old companions or not? If she hadn't, why had she killed the Lynx? She felt like a tiny boat in a roiling storm, though for now at least it seemed she was undetected by the forces blowing about.

"You are full of surprises, Hawk," Hectate said as Alphoronse flicked the reins. The wagon rolled forward. "Fare well with your charge." The Maxia turned to cast a final glower at Anji, then snapped the birds into a full trot, up to the road above and on to Silverton.

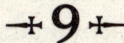

As soon as the wagon slipped out of sight, the Hawk lurched away from Anji with a curse. She crossed the camp in one bound and began stuffing things back into the bags, muttering to herself in rasping breaths.

The meek laundress in Anji harbored an instinctive desire to let the woman rage, to allow whatever fire had been kindled by their meeting with the Sun Warden to burn itself out. Though she hated to admit it to herself, her exhaustion paired with her situation's crushing weight weren't making it easy to push back against the Hawk's formidable, seemingly indomitable spirit. In fact, the more time she spent in the hunter's proximity, the more the Hawk's reputed skill became hard, sharp reality rather than the fanciful legend of her youth. That quiet castle servant urged caution; to fade back, to recede into the shadows until her presence was forgotten.

But Anji was her mother's daughter, dammit; her father's sprout. What would they say if they could see her now? Going along with the Hawk's every flip from Menagerie to rogue, the few remaining days of her life depending on a woman who lied as easily as she breathed. Anji chewed at her lip as she watched the Hawk scuttle around the camp. The woman was an enigma, a walking contradiction whose mystery made Anji feel unsafe and unsure. Well, she was sick of unanswered questions, of being interrupted, of this old woman and the hurtful words she wielded like the swords at her hip.

Above all, she was sick of being forced across this cold, desolate place. Of being beaten and bruised and castigated with no information, conversation, or humanity. She eyed Molli, who at least had the freedom to roam a little distance away to graze should she choose to. Anji tugged at the invisible tether wrapped around her foot, feeling that wire-tight tension against her ankle. She glowered at the Hawk as the woman finished cinching up one of the saddle bags.

"Are you going to explain what the hell just happened or . . ."

The Hawk ignored her—again.

"Hawk, I think you—"

"Don't call me that," the woman snapped. She ripped her mask off as though she'd just remembered she was wearing it and clipped it back to her belt.

Anji lifted a brow. *So she doesn't like her old name.* She'd pack that away for later. For now she balled her hands into fists, and said, "Fine, but why are you—"

"We're leaving. Get your things."

"Ah, of course, my things," said Anji, scanning the ground. "Oh that's right, you stole everything I own."

The Hawk ignored her gibe and twisted the canvas sack closed.

"Hey," said Anji, pushing down an anxious flutter in her chest. She'd never seen the woman so flummoxed. "Can you relax? We haven't even—"

"She might have bought the note, but the Wardens have a protocol. They'll send word to the others as soon as they reach

Silverton. Bear hasn't disclosed my absence, but that doesn't mean—"

"Wait, the others—"

"I said get your things! We've precious little time. The Bear knows Lynx is dead, which means they're on our trail now. They've likely split up to cover more ground. We have to make the pass before—"

"Wait a moment—"

"I am speaking, girl, not you! Shut your mouth and do as you're told," said the Hawk, bounding toward Molli, who jerked away at the woman's approach. "We'll have to ride together," she said, her breath rasping. In one fluid motion she bent and grabbed up the saddle and heaved it jangling over Molli's back, forgetting the half pad lying in the dirt, which should have gone on first. Molli whickered and stepped farther away. The Hawk stomped after her, grasping for the dangling girth strap.

"Stop!"

Anji's voice echoed across the tundra. Her throat ached with the force of her yell. The Hawk actually spun around, her face showing the first hint of surprise Anji had ever seen it hold.

The bounty hunter cleared her throat, her eyes flicking to the wall of clouds now closing over the distant sun. Black smudges marred their light-brushed-edges.

"We have to leave," said the Hawk, enunciating every word like a school teacher, locking eyes with Anji. "Right now."

But Anji was through taking orders from this old bitch, not without *some* sleep at least.

"I walked all fucking night," she said, clenching her hands into fists. "I haven't slept more than a couple hours since Linura—"

"And whose fault is that—"

"I'm likely to drop at any moment," Anji said, raising her voice. "Our horse is—"

"*My* horse—"

Anji groaned and yanked at her remaining tufts of hair. "*Your* horse is dead on her feet." She gestured to Molli, whose head was now drooping far too low for Anji's comfort. "Is it Menagerie policy to ride your horses into the ground? Just look at her!"

The Hawk crossed her arms, scowling like she'd rather do anything else in the world. Finally, she twisted and scanned the horse's face.

"What am I looking at, exactly?"

"Her eyelids are too heavy," said Anji. She jerked her head at the pot of water at Molli's feet. "She's hardly touched her water and her coat was covered in sweat when I brushed her down."

"She rode without issue these last few days," said the Hawk, her eyes flicking along Molli's flank. "Looks fine to me."

"Well, she's not. Horses will run until they drop. But if you're so set on killing her, go ahead, force her up a fucking mountain."

"I'm growing tired of your language," said the Hawk, but her eyes were still fixed on Molli.

"Well, I'm *growing tired* of walking," said Anji. Then she sank to the ground like a sack of potatoes. She threw one leg over the other and leaned onto one elbow, looking up at the Hawk. "Kick me all you want. I'm not going anywhere."

The Hawk pointed at the invisible tether around Anji's ankle and stepped forward, looming overhead. "You don't get a say in where you go." Her voice was like iron, cold and rigid. Anji wondered fleetingly if she'd finally crossed a line into a beating she wouldn't recover from. She decided to bet against it.

"Drag me then," she said. "As long as I'm lying down I can sleep through it."

The Hawk's lips pressed into a thin line, as though she were seriously considering it. She sucked in a breath to speak, then covered her mouth against a chalky cough born somewhere in the bottom of her throat. Anji watched, frowning, as the Hawk spat into the dirt, her eyes red, tears running in shining streaks down her dusty cheeks.

"What the hell is the matter with you?" said Anji.

"I'm fine," said the Hawk, wiping at her face. She hitched both hands on her hips, staring out across the darkening landscape, chest still heaving a little.

With a wary glance at the woman, Anji said, "The pass isn't going anywhere. You're coming down with . . . whatever you've got. My legs feel like broken glass, and it would be stupid to risk the horse. We have to rest. All of us."

The Hawk tapped her fingers against her belt, looking as though she were fighting for the right words, the argument that would make it possible to spirit Anji and the horse across the pass in the next few minutes.

"Fine," the Hawk said, wiping at her nose. "Two hours. You sleep out here. Then we go, regardless of your dainty little legs." She sniffed and tossed the saddle back to the ground, followed by the thin blanket Anji had used the day before, then spun on her heel and trudged back toward the tent. Before crawling inside, she bent and grabbed up the blue sack Anji had forgotten about, slinging it over her shoulder.

"Could I please—"

"Shut up about your gods-damned coin."

And with that the woman disappeared into the tent, leaving Anji alone in the darkening expanse.

Anji bit at the inside of her cheek. She'd won a small victory, she thought, as she settled to a soft spot on the ground, drawing her knees to her chest. But still, sleeping without her mother's coin was like losing her all over again every night. She swallowed past the lump in her throat. Tears blurred her vision as she wrapped her coat tight and lay on her side atop the blanket, adjusting around a rock lodged into the hard-packed earth. She wedged her fingers between her thighs and curled against the howling gale.

The pass would afford its own opportunities for her to escape. With every breath she drew, every second she still had her wits and some use of her limbs, constrained as they were, she could fight. She could run.

She lay on the rigid earth, silent tears freezing on her cheeks, and watched the swirling clouds crawl over the sun until darkness took her.

✦ 10 ✦

She dreamed in flashes.

The demolished basement door.

Her parents' bodies lying in a bloody pile, torn newspaper stuffed into their mouths.

Running through a rain-slicked alley, constables yelling, their boots clapping on the cobbles. The reek of coal smoke and molten iron. Heavy, stinking bodies pressed together to watch a hanging. A man in a yellow robe shouting and pointing, his face a snarling mask of rage.

On her knees in a stone-walled chamber, hair lank over her battered face. Sweat and muck and piss sticking her soiled clothes to her skin.

"Not much fuss, really," a man's voice said behind her. "Skinny as a pole. Another day on the streets might have done her in."

"Start her in the stables."

Sconces flickering, whirring past. A tugging at her arm.

"Come on, girl," the man said, "I said—"

"Come on, girl." The guard whirled around. "Up," came a voice behind a gleaming metal mask.

95

Anji squeezed her eyes tighter. Where were her parents? Why was the door open? Didn't they know she'd freeze to death all alone in here?

She reached out.

Moss.

Rocks.

Mossy rocks.

"Wha—"

"I said get *up*!" Something shook her shoulder.

Her eyes flew open. The Hawk was crouched at her side, gray wisps of hair spinning in the rising gale. Cold mist swirled like pipe smoke among the scattered boulders. The wind swelled into a roar so loud Anji had a hard time hearing the Hawk's words until the woman bent forward and shouted:

"Funnel cloud! Get in the blasting tent!"

Anji pushed up, blinking the sleep from her eyes. She surveyed the far horizon, or at least the horizon that had been there when she'd fallen asleep. Now there was only a wall of black cloud surging toward them like a landslide. And under the blanket of roiling storm—a funnel of twisting white vapor throwing up dark dust and rocks at its base.

"How did—" she sputtered, gasping as the Hawk jerked her up, eyes still fixed on the vortex speeding toward their camp. A pulse of bright light illuminated the wind-churned tundra.

"Go!" bellowed the Hawk, her voice drowned out by an ear-splitting crash of thunder overhead. She spun for the tent, one arm still clamped to Anji's elbow in a vise grip. Anji stumbled forward as a second thunderclap rent the air. They scrambled across the clearing, the Hawk's breath a haggard wheeze in Anji's ear.

"Why are you—"

A crackling sound issued from the ground. To Anji it sounded like the earth was dissolving in acid at her feet. She looked down, frowning, at what appeared to be thousands of fist-sized holes opening in the dirt. Her stomach lurched.

Spiders.

Silvery, bulbous bodies lifted themselves on jointed legs from the holes like a rising tide. Scores of red shining eyes stood out amongst the sleek hairs on their spindly limbs. They rose in unison on their hind legs, mandibles pointed at the sky as another thundercrack boomed overhead, then began scuttling in a frenzy around the camp.

The wind rose to a shriek as the Hawk shoved Anji inside the tent.

"What about Molli?" Anji said as the Hawk climbed in after. She took a final glance at the mare, hooves stamping on the ground as the swarm of spiders chittered forward in a single mass, legs clacking against the rocks. She yelped as the Hawk yanked her aside and slammed the tent flaps closed against the canvas floor, looping strands of string through riveted holes.

Above, the pattering against the tent's roof rose to a roar. Tiny indentations bloomed across the fabric.

The Hawk shoved Anji away from the entrance and began fastening the tent flaps closed. Molli squealed outside and Anji heard a loud, fleshy thump. A flash illuminated the tent's walls, white and stuttering, before another clap of thunder sounded outside like an ocean upending onto the plain.

"She's dying out there! Those things are eating her alive, we have to—"

"There's nothing we can do!" The Hawk darted to the support pole at the tent's center. Anji heard a heaving rasp as the woman bent down and grasped the bottom of the only thing holding the tent upright.

"What are you—"

The Hawk yanked at the bottom of the pole. The tent roof collapsed, flapping as it settled dark and musty over Anji.

"Keep still," came the Hawk's voice, right beside her now. Anji groaned as the woman pushed her prone against the ground.

"Are you fucking crazy? This is our only shelter!"

The Hawk grunted, her scratchy breath blowing warm against Anji's neck. Currents of air pounded like a god's hammer at the flattened tent.

Nine, let me outlast this.

Nine knew she'd outlasted everything else.

Then the ice started falling.

"Cover your head," the Hawk said. She raised her manacled hands to her scalp, the chain scraping against skin. Every muscle and tendon strained and shook against her bones. Cold snot seeped from her crusted nostrils and she sniffed it back, whimpering and miniscule and drenched in frozen fear.

The deluge outside was like a rockslide: thousands of icy boulders tumbling from the heavens. Hailstones crashed against the rocks outside, pounded into their matted, makeshift shelter. Anji curled tight against the Hawk, wishing she could dig under the hard permafrost below.

They laid huddled together, the sky tearing open above, Anji's vision marred by the darkness of the canvas and the intermittent spikes of light on all sides.

She listened to Molli's dying squeals. Her stomach churned at the scurrying, teakettle screams of the spiders as they set to the mare like a hungry fire. Anji wondered which breath would be her last, picturing that churning flume of wind and rock lifting the tent into the sky, sucking air from her lungs as she dangled above the earth. Her heart slammed against her ribs, pulse pounding in her ears as chunks of ice punched into her arm, her torso, her legs. She could only whimper under the onslaught, could only lie in dark confusion and fear curled up against the Hawk and the storm.

Finally, the mare's nauseating cries gurgled to a stop, and Anji heard the scuffing crawl of thousands of legs before the innumerable tiny pinpricks scuttled over her body with only a thin layer of cloth to protect her. The Hawk cursed and shifted, her limbs flailing. She swatted Anji on the head, kicked out and rolled away before a crunch followed by a tiny scream issued from somewhere in the tent.

Anji panted through the chaos, the reaping storm heralding her end, eyes clenched so tight her temples ached. Shuddering with fear and cold, she retreated into memory, like she had all those lonely nights on Linura's streets, in the hollow hiding places she'd found to tuck herself inside. The images stung like open sores, but she let them fester, allowed them to blanket her mind, better by far than facing the truth. Better to think of better things, to take herself away.

To an afternoon on the low brick wall behind Mudtown's best bakery, her parents to either side, her father still in his knee-high fishing boots, the bells over Laurelside Square clanging as factories loosed their tired crowds. Tearing into brown seedbread still warm from the ovens. Her mother shoving a piece in her father's ear and both of them laughing like idiots. The glow of sunlight in her father's green eyes, the gap in his teeth she'd inherited from him, which he'd stuck his tongue between when he'd been thinking hard or annoyed with her mother. The conversation they'd had, faded to unintelligible words like music playing in another room. That feeling of warmth, of belonging and love and exactitude that she would kill to get back.

Then it was over.

The crawling sensation ceased. The wind died to a whisper. Stray hailstones clattered among those already fallen, then stopped altogether. Thunder cracked, far off and sullen. The tent flapped around them as Anji exhaled a ragged breath and got to her knees.

The Hawk rose with her, chunks of ice clinking overhead as they pushed the fabric up. Anji sidled through the maze of damp canvas, wafting her aching arms toward the tent's opening.

"Wait," came the Hawk's voice from within the folds. Anji spun around, disoriented, panic at being so confined building in her chest. A wave of dizziness and nausea hit her. She pushed down the acrid taste of bile. The Hawk's lithe form crawled forward and pushed the fabric away from the tent's clasped opening. "Do you hear anything?"

"I need to get out of—"

"Shut up. Listen."

Anji wanted to scream and vomit and cry all at once. She wanted to slap the Hawk and tear through the tent with her filthy nails. Her lungs pleaded for fresh air. She noticed a damp warmth between her thighs and realized she'd pissed herself. But she listened for the sound of chittering legs.

Nothing.

"I think they're gone."

The Hawk loosed the tent's opening with a deft flick of her fingers. Anji scrambled through into the light, stumbling to all fours, and sucked in a lungful of cold, clean air. Inhaling stung at her nostrils, at her raw throat, but she didn't care. She leaned back on her calves, eyes closed, soaking in the feeling of empty space.

"Gods take it," came a husky voice at her side.

"Just give me a moment," said Anji, eyes still closed.

"Shit!"

Anji opened her eyes at the word, wincing at the bright light already peeking out among the blanket of gray clouds. The Hawk stood at her side, hands on hips, jaw locked tight. Anji followed her gaze.

Molli's body lay in a bloody tangle across the ruined camp. White bone stood out amongst a mangled pile of brown hair and fibrous lumps of muscle and sinew. Anji's stomach lurched. She held a hand to her mouth, manacles clinking, then bent double and retched onto the mossy rocks. Tears stung her eyes as she spat out a string of bile, then she pictured the swarm of spiders burrowing from the ground once more and vomited again as the Hawk kicked at a tuft of grass.

"*Shit!*"

✠ 11 ✠

Anji had a cat years ago.

It wasn't *her* cat, exactly, but she named him Oliver and claimed him just the same—nobody else ever came calling for him.

Oliver was entirely black, save for a spot of white on his chest. Anji had no clear memory of finding him—he had simply appeared one day atop the basement steps, mewling and slinking back and forth across the stone. Her parents forbade her from bringing him inside and refused him food, grumbling about the added expense. But her father never kicked at him or scolded Anji for cradling him in her arms, though many of Mudtown's stray animals were infested with fleas. She'd even spotted her mother bending to scratch his head once as she'd left for work.

Oliver began to learn Anji's routine, following her to school (before Rolandrian had the schools closed down), trailing behind her and her father on their way to the docks so she could see him off for the day. Mudtown's streets were chaotic with traffic, but Anji could always spot the cat's tail bobbing through the tangle of legs and carts.

This went on for some time, until winter settled on Linura—one of the harshest in living memory. A garrison of Mudtown's denizens had been formed to scrape mounded snow off the roofs of houses and shops. Even the factories came to a standstill as the remaining population worked to rid the streets of ice. Anji and her parents had huddled together in front of their tiny hearth as the heat was sucked into the cold brick walls rather than their bodies. The poorest died where they slept, crammed into alleys, some lucky ones sleeping in crates, while others battled with the exposure.

Anji hadn't seen Oliver in days, cooped up in the basement as they were. After what felt like an eternity the snow and ice had receded, and with reluctant permission from her parents she'd ventured outside to find him. She'd opened the door, creaking and crackling with melting ice still clinging to the wood, and stepped out to find the cat stiff against the brick wall of the shop across the alley. She'd just been reaching toward his ice-coated fur when her mother appeared and snatched her wrist away. But at the sight of Anji's stricken face, she'd pulled her into a hug and let Anji cry into her shirt.

Anji had tossed and turned on her pallet in the loft at home, waiting for the release of sleep, but hardly finding it. Oliver's lonely, frozen form stained her memory from then on. She could see it still, even trudging up the sheer incline of the mountain underfoot, and wondered whether Oliver had been as cold as she was now, at the end.

It had been her fault, of course, not bringing him in, letting him die alone and scared with her so close. She'd begged her parents to let her out to look for him, but they'd refused. She should have ignored them and done the right thing, but she hadn't. And now Molli was dead because of her. If they'd just gone up the pass when the Hawk had told them to, if they'd just left before the storm and the spiders and the vortex had hit, if she'd just been a little bit less concerned for her own comfort, the horse may have lived. They could have made progress away from the storm and still let her rest, in the lee of one of the large rocks they'd already passed, in the shadow of what looked to be ruins looming ahead. The only consolation to Molli's death was the fact that the poor horse didn't have to freeze her ass off alongside Anji any longer.

The Hawk had directed them up the slope, past rocky outcroppings growing heavier with snow until they'd found a long, crooked trail that ran the length of a deep chasm yawning to Anji's right. Another mountain towered across the gap, its crenellations glowing orange as the sun sank toward the western horizon.

Anji pushed through the torrent of white, manacles jingling, searing with cold where they touched her skin, her legs trembling in her scavenged boots. The mountain air cut like twin knives through her crusted nose, but by some miracle the wind seemed to have died as they'd gained elevation, more a patient sigh than the roar of the storm in the foothills. She'd slipped and tumbled into the snow three times, unable to balance on the unforgiving terrain with her hands bound. Now she concentrated on putting one foot down, then another, powder crunching and squeaking under her weight. A blister stung at her right ankle, rubbing against her sweat-soaked sock with each plodding step.

Silent and steady, the Hawk loomed behind like a shadow. Snow clung to her leathers, in the contours of her mask, along the folds of the silken blue bag jostling over one shoulder. Every resolute step the woman took rang like a bell in Anji's head—a reminder of her unyielding determination to shepherd Anji to Linura and onto the torture rack.

Anji stopped for a breath at a particularly level section of trail, raising her hands to cradle the back of her head as she turned fully around to face the Hawk.

"How much farther?" she called, panting. The volume of her

voice surprised her, reverberating off the rocky tors above and out across the chasm. She spat out a flake of snow from her top lip, glancing again at the woman tramping up the path like it owed her a stack of Rhoda.

"Don't shout, idiot," the Hawk breathed, coming even with Anji, her chest heaving. "Why do you think it's called Tumbledown?" She shoved at Anji's shoulder to turn her back around, then pointed a thin finger at the squat, snow-caked structure perched on a rise above the path, still some distance ahead. "Those ruins mark the halfway point. We'll stop there and catch our breath for a moment, eat something . . ."

"Eat what?" said Anji, her stomach grumbling as though listening to their conversation. The earlier bombardment of hail and wind had destroyed the Hawk's cooking supplies and scattered most of her ingredients across the plain. Anji had resigned herself to a full day of hunger pangs, at least until they got to the other side of the pass and into the next town.

The Hawk tapped gloved fingers on the blue bag's strap. "I stored some extra food in here," she said, then slapped at Anji's shoulder. "Along with your antidote. Get a move on if you want your next dose. It's mostly flat or downhill from here, so you can quit whining."

"I wasn't whining," said Anji.

"You were about to."

The Hawk stomped past Anji toward the structure, hitching the bag higher on her shoulder. Anji just stood there, her jaw clenched so tight she thought her teeth might break. She was being forced through the mountains on foot, with an empty stomach, a pounding headache, and the worst company she'd ever kept. So what if she complained a little? She put her hands on her hips and gathered more breath, peering across the chasm. The wind roared between the peaks, but Anji thought she heard something else—a distant rumbling from far below. The tether tugged at her ankle. Anji wiped her nose and started forward.

As she walked, the mountainside to her left came into clearer view. Its face ran in stony rivulets, deep basins of snowpack where narrow valleys formed. She craned her neck, following the veins of rock to the summit, and her eyes widened.

A hulking tower of tiered black stone had been constructed in the saddle between the peaks. Its western edge soaked in the day's fading glow, an icy sheen glittering off the molded brick. It stood against the pale white slope like a giant charcoal stick left standing in the snow, its arched windows dark and silent. Black steps wound by the score in a switchback lane from the tower's base to the smaller structure overhanging their path. As she came closer, Anji saw it was made of the same black stone as the tower, albeit much shorter in stature—the skeleton of a not-quite-finished structure. No roof that she could see, only black brick walls and empty spaces for windows.

Anji huffed through the Hawk's tracks, eager for the small shelter the ruin would provide. She tried to resist licking her lips, which only dried further as soon as she slid her tongue over the flaking skin.

She'd nearly come level with the Hawk when the woman stumbled to one knee.

Anji's heart leapt as the Hawk doubled over, shoulders shaking with deep, hacking coughs. The Hawk reached a hand out, grasping for some unseen support, then sank to her other knee. Anji stumbled through the snow to her side.

"Hawk!" she said, her voice hoarse. "Hawk! How do you open the bag? You're not going to—"

"Stop—"

Anji tightened her grip. "How do you open the bag? Tell me the disarming charm!"

Though the Hawk's mask was still on, Anji could just make out the labored, scratchy breathing behind it. Was she going to die right here? Anji relished the thought, but she had to find out how to get into that damned satchel. She shouted in her face again, but the woman only flailed a thin arm. Dodging the weak blow with a curse, she ripped off the Hawk's mask, then nearly tumbled back into the snow.

The Hawk's face was choked red—blotches of purple blooming at her cheeks. A dribble of ink-black spit trickled down the side of her mouth and onto her wrinkled chin. It began to freeze. Anji sank to one knee.

"The words, Hawk!" she yelled, shoving the mask into the woman's lap—it felt much heavier in her hand than she'd imagined. She squared up, glared into those sea-green eyes. "If you're going to die out here you can at least let me have my things back."

The Hawk gave her head a quick shake, pawing at her chest.

"And take this fucking tether off me!"

The wind gave a hard push at Anji's back, harder than any she'd felt since taking the pass, and she stumbled forward. Sharp pain blossomed in her cheek as the Hawk backhanded her. She fell on her ass into the snow, eyes wide.

"Keep," the Hawk gasped, "quiet." She sputtered and spit into the snow. Then she sat up straighter and began digging around in the folds of her clothes, chest heaving like a punctured bellows. Anji felt fresh tears burning at her eyes and wiped them away as the Hawk took out a green glass vial and shifted so the wind blew at her back. She tipped the opening against one slender, shaking finger, then held the contents to her nose and snorted hard before tilting her head back, blinking at the sky.

Anji felt her jaw drop as the Hawk stood, knuckled her nostril, then slipped the gleaming, snow-crusted mask back over her face.

"Come on," she said, turning south once more.

Anji gaped at her. "Where—" she stammered, climbing to her feet. "What the fuck was that?" she yelled. Her feet seemed to be moving of their own accord again, following after the old woman. "What did you just—"

Like a snarling beast, the Hawk spun on her heel and marched the few strides to Anji, grabbing up her shirt in both fists. The mask was close enough to kiss the tip of Anji's nose.

"This is the last time I tell you before you get the gag," said the Hawk through gritted teeth. "Shut. Up."

"Thought you didn't like gags?"

"I could—"

"Cut my stinking tongue out, yeah." Anji mimed buttoning her lips, then whispered, "Quiet as a mouse."

"I'm getting awfully sick of your cheek, girl."

Anji cocked her head and grinned. "What was that you were snorting? Was it that Rail stuff?"

The Hawk only grunted and released her, but Anji hissed a curse. How had she not guessed?

"It is!" she said, barking a laugh. "Oh, this all makes so much sense. *That's* why you were able to beat me earlier. Not because you're any better. I mean, I'll grant you must have been amazing in your prime—but now, you're old as shit! You just have a massive amount of strength because of the Rail. Like that Maxia said, you're . . . enhanced!"

"I'd have beaten you without it," the Hawk said, her gait much easier now as they clambered up the trail.

Anji sniggered. "Still," she said, "the Hawk, using drugs. Nine save us all. When did you start up? How much longer do you think you have until you turn into . . ." Her smile faltered. "One of those things?"

As though Anji hadn't said anything at all, the Hawk shoved

her forward and barked a command for her to move. They plodded on for half a minute.

"Can I get a hit?"

"Not a chance."

"Come on, you're taking me to be tortured," Anji said. She stopped and turned to face the Hawk. "It's not like I've got enough time to transform. You could at least give me—"

"I'm giving you nothing, now walk."

Anji shuffled forward. "Just a little hit, we both know it would help—"

The Hawk's hand shot to her belt and the sword attached to it. "What do you think you're doing?"

"I just want a taste," Anji said. "I saw how much you had in there. It's more than enough to get us both over this mountain."

The Hawk flipped up her mask. "Stop. Rail is not a toy. We are not at a party and I am not your bed friend to be experimenting with. I use it as medicine, and I won't be doling out doses which cost more Rhoda than most make in a year. The withdrawal would make you talk even more than you already do, which would kill me faster than any mountain could."

Anji darted a hand toward the Hawk's pocket. The Hawk dodged away, slapping at Anji's wrist.

"You really want to do this here?" she said, hand hovering above her sword's hilt. "In the snow, a sheer drop to one side?"

Anji spat through chapped lips and made for the pocket of the Hawk's leathers once more. "Just a tiny bit," was all she said. The woman cuffed her on the ear like she was disciplining a dog.

"No more of that—"

"I don't see why you can't—"

"Fool girl, you'll get us both—*killed*!"

Anji felt a hard shove, then the snowy ground at her back.

"You old fucking *hag*—"

109

"Stop!"

The Hawk's voice rang across the pass, the word echoing as she marched toward Anji. "I've had enough of your pathetic—"

Anji shrieked and scrambled up, throwing her weight into the woman and pinning her thin form to the ground. She beat at the Hawk's shoulder, manacles clinking with every blow.

"See how you like it!" she screeched.

"Stop it, you idiot!" the Hawk said, twirling out of her grip. She got easily to her feet, eyes darting to the blue bag now lying in the snow some feet away. Anji moved for the bag, but the Hawk closed the distance, snatched at her arm, and spun her so they were face-to-face. She held up a finger between them and opened her mouth to say some other rude thing to Anji before a sound drew their attention to the ridge.

A crack.

Anji heard another, then another, then a slight hissing trickle followed by a heaving, heavy rumble, like thunder on glass. The Hawk drew in a gasp and shuttled Anji from the ridge as the patch of snow they'd been standing on rolled away with a roar, bringing the blue satchel down with it.

"No!" the Hawk screamed. Anji struggled in the Hawk's grip, but the woman held firm.

The snow gathered and flowed down the slope like water, spilling across exposed rocks, tumbling through the air, sending chunks of ice careening far below. Eventually the sound dissipated, leaving the pair standing at the chasm's edge in a hollow silence.

Pain lanced through Anji's arm.

"What the fuck!" Anji sidestepped as the Hawk advanced on her, fist raised to strike again.

"How could you be so—so—" said the Hawk through gritted teeth. She stopped and pointed down the slope. "That was all our food! The rest of my—" She sputtered, closed her mouth, then, "That could have been us down there!"

"You started it!"

The Hawk's eyes widened. "I can't believe how stupid you are."

"Well, start believing it!" Anji said.

Then the Hawk gave her a look of such confusion and disgust Anji would have laughed if she'd been anywhere else, with anyone else.

Just push her down the fucking mountain, Anji thought, getting to her feet. Pulling her jacket tighter, she walked warily toward the Hawk's side, brushing off crusted snow.

The Hawk gazed down at the mess of powder and ice piled a hundred feet below.

"Sun's almost down," said Anji, narrowing her eyes at the mountain peaks. She swung her gaze to the now snow-packed chasm's bottom. "Can't be that far under, can it?"

The Hawk glared at her. "How should I know?" she growled. "I've never buried the last of my possessions under an avalanche before."

"First time for everything, I suppose," Anji said, "though I imagine you'll make me do all the—"

A shriek issued from below. It took Anji a moment to register the noise. Not like a bird's cry or the scream of another person, but the high-pitched hiss of an insect, loud enough that Anji flinched as it rang out a second time. Anji scanned the chasm, her trickle of uncertainty thickening to a stream of fear as a large patch of the slope near the chasm's floor bulged out, then bowed back in.

"What is it?" said Anji, glancing at the Hawk. "Hawk?"

The Hawk only took a step back, then another.

Then she drew her swords.

⊹ 12 ⊹

"What the—"

Anji tottered forward, her eyes glued to the mound rising under the snow. Whatever it was, it was massive. The Hawk cursed and snatched at Anji's arm. "Get back."

But Anji couldn't take her gaze away. What could possibly move that much snow?

A titanic shape exploded from the slope—blue of so light a hue it was almost white. Chitinous claws raked against the ground, sending sprays of fresh powder careening into the gully. Another high-pitched keening sound rent the air, this time loud enough to echo off the peaks. Anji winced and crouched low, eyes on the shape still emerging from the hole. A body layered in milky, segmented armor scuttled out, carried on a dozen spindly legs, the two at its front raised high: a pair of gigantic, crablike claws. Anji felt the urge to retch, revulsion tightening her throat.

"Scorphice," the Hawk hissed. "Behind me, girl."

Anji sputtered, but no words would come. The thing before her *couldn't* exist. It was too grotesque, like it had been plucked from a story and thrown at her feet by a mad god. But it grappled up the slope, chunks of ice and snow crackling under its churning legs. Anji scrambled back into the snow, her sweating, shaking hands rattling the manacles. Perhaps the thing hadn't seen them? Could it smell? She glanced once at the Hawk, then at the monstrosity screaming up the slope. It faced them fully now, its face a churning nest of serrated fangs under a cluster of black dots shining in the dying light.

Nine, are those its eyes?

It unleashed another howling cry, louder this time—so loud it set Anji's ears ringing. The Scorphice was halfway up the slope now, body undulating like a snake, its legs chewing through the frozen earth.

"Give me one of those," Anji said, pointing at the swords in the Hawk's hands.

"Like hell." The Hawk shoved her away from the chasm's edge.

"Do it!" Anji said, stumbling along, rattling her chains. "I can help! I can distract it!"

"I can fight it on my own," the Hawk said, her eyes darting back to the ridge. "Head for the storehouse." She shoved Anji away with a grunt, sending her tumbling into the snow. Anji spun and climbed to her knees.

"You won't even let me defend myself—"

"I said—"

The Scorphice cried out again. It was nearly level with the ridge.

"Come on!" Anji yelled. "What use is money if you're dead?"

The Hawk glanced at the ridge, then flipped her short sword hilt first and slapped it into Anji's waiting palm. Its balance was incredible, the hilt just long enough for both of Anji's still-manacled hands.

Instinct told Anji to shove the blade through the woman's gut right there. But killing the Hawk would only serve to chain Anji to her person forever, and by the look of it, forever would only be until she was alone with the Scorphice. She pictured herself freezing and screaming while her insides were sucked out, or whatever these vile things did. No. Fighting alongside the Hawk was her only chance. She squeezed her stinging fingers against the hilt's worn leather and stood at the Hawk's side, sword bared as the sun dipped behind a distant mountain, its last warm rays glancing off the rocks around them.

The Scorphice took the ledge just as the light died. It reared, two pairs of legs ascending along with its gleaming claws, each the size of a pony, eyes black and glittering like obsidian. Anji gripped the sword's hilt, bile building at the back of her throat. The cold was gone. Her aching limbs and freezing skin gave her no pause. The frigid, dry air welcomed her movements. The monster jumped.

It cleared ten feet of ground, then crashed in front of them, claws swiping. Anji dodged away from the left claw, running to the side where the disgusting confusion of clacking legs skittered over loose rocks, punching holes in the packed snow below. Anji swiped at one of the legs, the sword glancing off the rigid, glassy carapace. She had time for a silent curse before she was knocked to her back by a crushing weight in her gut. White flashed in her vision and she scrambled up, spitting snow and bits of rock. She tasted blood and spat that out too, a red trickle staining the snow.

The Hawk shouted, and Anji caught the glint of her mask behind the Scorphice's tangle of legs. Anji stumbled away, and though she knew she should be helping, knew she should start hacking at any part of the beast she could, she had to watch. The woman moved like liquid, dodging in and out of the monster's heavy swipes. She jabbed at the eyes, puncturing one with a sickening crunch, loud enough for Anji to hear over the rattling legs and howling wind. The Scorphice shuddered, a guttural growl radiating from its entire body. The Hawk wrenched her sword back and made another greedy swipe at the nest of gleaming eyes, but the right mandible caught her in the chest. Anji gasped as she watched the woman fly through the air and land on her back, sliding through the snowpack like a stone. She lay still save for one hand groping desperately for the sword just out of reach.

The creature whipped its dripping face, splattering black blood on the snow in a dribbling arc, a short, gasping shriek echoing off the mountain faces as it bounded toward the Hawk.

Without thinking, Anji yelled. She was surprised to hear her own voice fighting for purchase in the clatter of the carapace, the susurrus of clacking legs on ice and rock. She threw her arms up. "Hey, ugly!"

The Scorphice skidded, legs clicking in unison. Anji stared wide-eyed at the bloodied mess of eyes over a gaping maw, snapping open and closed. Rows of tiny teeth, like hundreds of filed glass chunks.

Anji sidestepped as the Scorphice careened toward her, flailing claws thundering down into the snow, spraying powder and rock chips into the air. She hauled herself up an outcropping of rock, fingers digging into the pitted stone, sword slipping on the frost. At the top she waited for the monster to line up. There.

She jumped. Cold air streaked past her cheeks, her scalp. Time seemed to freeze; her thoughts centered on the writhing form below, the Hawk clambering to her knees, sword in hand, watching. Anji squeezed the hilt of her stubby sword. She was going to miss—the thing was moving too fast.

She landed on the armored back, wind bursting from her lungs, nearly slipping on the slick carapace. Balancing as best she could with it flailing, she scrabbled toward the Scorphice's head. She drew herself up and locked her knees, clenching the muscles in her thighs, willing her body to stay upright. The Hawk gave another strangled cry as one of the claws smashed down again, but Anji ignored it. She raised her sword in both hands and brought it down with all her strength directly into the mass of eyes.

The Scorphice shuddered under her, loosing not a roar, but a whimper. Anji heard a hiss from where she'd stabbed it, like steam issuing from a cooling kettle. She gripped the sword's hilt, pushing it farther, deeper—the cold steel digging into her palms until she couldn't press anymore—until her arms shook. The hilt trembled and Anji squeezed at the leather grip as the thing descended to the ground, its many legs clacking out of sync. Warmth spread around her knees as blue-black blood gurgled from the wound, glossy eyes twitching, taking a last accusing look at Anji. It clicked one claw in a spasm, the other dragging through the snow. Anji wrenched the sword out and made to stab into the soft meat again, more if she had to, but as soon as she raised the sword her leg slipped and she fell to the ground, her shoulder exploding in pain as the world upended.

The Hawk was there, a shadow blotting out the newly risen moon. She bent and tugged at Anji's jacket collar. Anji kicked her legs, trying to stand, to gain purchase on the slick ground, now an exposed layer of ice under swept-away snow. She finally got to her feet, chest heaving, shoulder throbbing, and let the Hawk hustle her away from the dying thing. They collapsed as the Scorphice crumbled in on itself, claws and spiked legs scraping huge gouges into the ice.

Anji knelt in the snow, watching the result of what her hands had done. She blinked at the Scorphice, beautiful even in its death throes, leaking steaming black blood over the trail. It scrabbled toward the ledge, toward its home far below, but collapsed in a heap of bloody limbs. She felt sick watching it die. Wished it would just get on with it, but much like Molli, much like Rolandrian even, death came slow, and traumatic, and gasping to the last. The Scorphice's legs clattered against the bare rock of the trail, sending bits of stone flying. It hissed and cried and whimpered, let out a horrid convulsion, and finally lay still.

Something crunched in the snow at Anji's side, and she spun, sword raised. But it was only the Hawk, back on her feet with one gloved hand out.

Anji gripped the leather hilt and jerked away.

"Don't—" the Hawk panted, her sword's tip at Anji's throat like it had been forged there. "You know better. Save your strength."

Every muscle, every frayed fiber of Anji's being wanted to strike, to fight to the last. But the Hawk was right. She was outmatched, manacled, and utterly exhausted. She just wanted to throw up and lie down and shut herself away in a dark hole somewhere.

Avoiding eye contact, she handed the sword over.

The Hawk sheathed it, her spare still poised at Anji's neck. She dipped her head toward the structure down the trail.

"Let's get out of the cold."

✢ 13 ✢

"What if there's more of them?"

Night had finally settled outside, stray flakes of snow drifting past the storeroom's narrow windows. A sliver of the crescent moon peaked through a break in the clouds above, shining weak silver light on the rocky bluffs, the mountain range trailing in the distance.

"We fight them off, I suppose," the Hawk said, lying back against the wall. "You aren't much for fighting hand to hand, but you can handle a blade, girl, I'll give you that."

"Thanks," said Anji flatly, pulling her knees to her chest. She cast around, eyes wide, as though another monster would crash through an undiscovered hole at any moment. Just outside, the Scorphice's corpse was still visible, lying in a tangled heap of blood and bone and carapace. Were there more waiting somewhere in the chasm below? She and the Hawk had obviously disturbed some kind of den or nest. Anji imagined the skeletal remnants of whatever the Scorphice ate—goats, foxes, people —scattered about the cave's floor. Or perhaps it had lain coiled in wait until it sensed its prey and sprang out of its hole to do its feeding on the slope, leaving the bones (if it left any) for the snow. Anji shuddered and curled tighter against her bit of icy wall. She wondered if the Scorphice had had a mate, or whether it was cooped in its den all alone. *Bit of a boring life,* Anji mused, *but better than being led to slaughter*. Then she remembered she'd just slaughtered it moments ago and shut her eyes, willing her mind to stop the million intruding thoughts clamoring for attention. Her heart hadn't quit hammering since she'd seen the thing. Fingers trembling, she ran a hand over the fringe of her scalp and sniffed a thin trickle of snot. She closed her eyes and let out as steady a breath as she could manage. Sleep might come easy enough tonight, considering her exhaustion, but she wasn't excited for the dreams that would follow, the Scorphice shuddering beneath her knees and screaming for its life an addition to the show that already played in her head every night while she tossed and—

"Where did you learn to fight?"

Anji opened her eyes and stared at the Hawk's unmasked face.

"Thought we weren't trying to get to know each other?" Anji said, licking at her lips.

"Stop doing that," the Hawk said, pointing at her mouth. "You keep licking those things and they're going to freeze off."

"You've got your own lips, you do what you want with them," Anji said.

The Hawk opened her mouth to speak but only choked out a cough, her eyelids heavy. Dark circles, much like the Sun Warden's near the lake, had formed below her eyes. Mucus dribbled in a continuous stream from her nose, now spiderwebbed with burst capillaries.

A cry echoed outside and Anji felt her stomach drop, but it was only a solitary bird circling the dark tower at the mountain's peak.

"What is this place?" Anji said. She didn't much care about it, but she wanted to shift the subject from her education, and by extension her parents. From the life soon to be cut short.

The Hawk's bloodshot eyes flicked to the tower. "The towers were precursors to the Inheritance cathedrals, all abandoned before the One Path even started gaining power. You said you'd lived on the streets . . ."

Anji nodded.

"So you likely got food from the Order," the Hawk went on. "Did you attend service?"

The services and the food they provided were the only things Anji had looked forward to for nearly a year on the street. She'd counted the days until the morning the cathedral doors would swing open to a crowd of waiting urchins. The Order of Inheritance was favored among all the poorest denizens across the continent of Makona. Theirs was a religion of generosity, of kindness and service. Above all, the acolytes of the Inheritance counseled gratitude to the Nine Gods who, according to the thin volumes they'd handed out freely on street corners, had birthed all creation out of a dance that had lasted a million years. After the dance, the Gods had apparently departed creation and left the creatures of the world to their own devices, never to intervene again.

"They wouldn't let us eat without staying for the sermon. I was cold and lonely and—" she stopped herself. She didn't need to explain herself to this woman. But the Hawk nodded as though what she'd said had made perfect sense.

"My father used to take me," the Hawk said, her voice slurring, stopping and starting a little at a time. Her eyes seemed to lose focus, but the corner of her mouth twitched up before she rolled her gaze back to Anji. "Did you notice where in the city the cathedral was built?"

Anji thought back to her days scrounging in Mudtown's reeking streets, the crowded buildings, the milling, stinking press of bodies, and the giant black spire of rock that towered above it all. Higher even than the belltower in Laurelside Square, which she used to climb with her mother to watch carrier pigeons roost.

"It was built on a hill . . . ?" she said, more a question than a statement, but the Hawk nodded.

"They build on the highest points they can," said the Hawk, pointing vaguely at the tower above, "to shorten the distance their gratitude travels, 'so it may permeate the skies.' " She scoffed. "Load of nonsense."

"You don't believe in the Inheritance?"

The Hawk shrugged. "Wouldn't matter if I did, would it? That's the whole point. Seems a strange thing to make a religion from, but everyone is entitled to their beliefs, I suppose."

"Even the Sun Wardens?"

The Hawk glared at Anji, started to speak, but was interrupted once more by another hacking cough. She bent with the force of it, her narrow chest convulsing.

"Hawk?"

The woman wiped at her mouth, gasped a little. "I told you . . . not to call me that."

Anji inched forward, knees still clutched to her chest.

"Are you alright?"

Groaning a little, the Hawk shifted against the wall, her legs straight, the tips of her snow-covered boots touching together. "Coming down," she murmured, and let her heavy-lidded eyes close.

Of course. The Rail. How long had it been since the Hawk had last used? An hour? Two? That also explained her chattiness. What had the Maxia said on the lakeshore? Something about the drug's half-life, whatever that meant.

Anji hadn't done many drugs in the castle, more out of short supply than any inclination to abstain. But whatever she had managed to drink or snort had worked wonders at keeping the

121

stray thoughts away, those of the life she'd led and lost what felt like three lifetimes ago. She couldn't remember ever saying no to something put in front of her, but she did have some less-than-fond memories of early mornings retching over a toilet in the laundresses' washroom, of shaking through the night after smoking too much Faze. Those weren't happy times, but she'd take a night of sleepless, senseless sweating over the insistent nightmares of her parents. She moved around to the Hawk's side.

"Do you need anything? Water?"

The Hawk shook her head, eyes shut tight, mouth a thin line, then she stuffed her hands between her thighs, the rise and fall of her chest like a tiny animal's shallow breaths.

"Do you need another dose?" Anji said, looking the woman up and down. "I can—"

"No," the Hawk said, her voice hard. Her eyes flew open, staring directly into Anji's. "Don't touch it. Need to save it. I'm—I have to start weaning off. I can still avoid the—" She gagged, her throat bobbing. "Gah," she spat. "Gods."

Anji unclipped the canteen from the Hawk's belt and took an icy pull, wincing at the cold biting her teeth. Water wouldn't satiate her much longer. Her stomach had become a tight knot of hunger like she hadn't known in years. She needed to get outside, to find that stupid blue bag. Apart from the scant food they still had, it also held her dagger, her coin, and of course, the antidote she needed. But going outside alone meant the possibility of coming across another Scorphice, or more constables . . . or another Sun Warden. She glanced at the scabbards still tied to the Hawk's belt.

"You'll die," said the Hawk, following her gaze. Anji nearly laughed at the woman's unflappable vigilance. The Hawk took her laugh for confidence and lifted herself up with a glare so hard Anji's heart fluttered. Comedown or no, the woman still scared her. "You've got another few hours," she said, her eyes like augers, "before that poison goes to work, and with no clue how to get the bag open. I'm—" She hacked a cough, so loud it reverberated off the structure's walls. "I'm all you've got," she rasped, then settled back to the floor. "I'm all you've got." But her eyes closed again, wrinkles standing out stark on her soaking skin. Then she yelled, a throaty cry of frustration and pain, of pure torment.

"Wouldn't dream of it," said Anji, and to her surprise, the words weren't entirely a lie. True, she'd yearned for the Hawk's death dozens of times since she'd met her out on the plains, pictured it as she'd slept, woke with the desire in the morning. But something had nestled next to that desire, something she couldn't name. Whatever her faults, the Hawk had saved her life more than once already. Anji wouldn't kill the woman in her sleep. She owed her that much.

Though she still harbored a gnawing hatred for her captor, Anji felt a pang of sympathy for the old woman, now shivering with withdrawal. She remembered a night in the laundresses' washroom, holding Kaia's hair back after a particularly bad Faze binge. Kaia had screamed and cried and pushed Anji away, screeching about chained specters floating out of the walls, moaning and covered in blood. She'd called Anji a whore and a liar, though all Anji had done was try to help. As Kaia lay sobbing near an overturned chamber pot, Anji had gotten up to leave, only for her friend to call her back. Anji sat with her till dawn, rubbing her back and whispering about her parents, her favorite books, the friends she'd had and lost. Kaia had eventually fallen asleep on Anji's thigh, golden hair spilling onto the floor. The next morning, Kaia had thanked Anji with a rose she'd cut from the castle gardens. Anji had left it in the box under her cot the night she'd escaped.

Anji flexed her fingers, willing blood to flow back into their tips. One of her nails was cracked down the center, another welling with a dark spot near the quick. She bit at the notched edge of her thumbnail, gnawing off a filthy sliver and spitting it away.

The Hawk convulsed once, then again, one leg kicking. She whimpered and rolled to one side, then the other, a crackling gurgle exploding from her throat. Anji sighed and sat straighter. She had no desire for closeness with this woman. The Hawk had taken her prisoner, had beaten and scorned and humiliated her. Her ultimate goal was Anji's torture and execution.

The Hawk yelped in pain or fear or both. Anji laid a hand to the woman's twitching shoulder.

What the hell am I doing?

"It's okay," she said, "I'm here."

The Hawk shuddered, her eyes shut tight.

Anji did what she could.

How many animals does it take,
To catch the wicked and make us safe,
Ox is strongest, loyal and true,
Goat is cleverest, valor anew,
Hawk is quickest, watch and fly,
Lynx is quietest, in darkness high,
Bear leads the pack with truest soul,
Sing for them in every role

Anji sang the song three times. Not in the lilting, childish way she had as a girl, jumping rope and giggling with the other children. She sang low and sweet, drawing out the notes like a tossed angler's line, reeling them back in with each new verse. The Hawk's shivering slowed, then finally stilled. They sat together, an old, sick warrior and a terrified laundress, in a cave surrounded by snow and death and unforgiving cold, and Anji felt a tension in her heart ease.

"I trained with my aunt," she said softly, "in secret. She came to live with us when I was ten. Just appeared one day with her bags, but my parents were happy to have her. Mom said she was in the army for years—high-ranked after so long, but discharged after the Dorodad Border Wars. She got work as a teacher right away, educated as she was. I happened to be old enough to be in her class." Anji's lip twitched. "Her name was Belle, and she seemed to know everything. My parents taught me some about Yem's history, but Belle filled in the gaps for the whole class; and she never read from Senate-approved books. She slept in our house, on the floor . . . her pay wasn't much, but she made enough to get us by while my parents—" Anji caught herself. It wouldn't have mattered anymore to say what they'd done, but something made her pause. The years of keeping secret her mother's maxial abilities. The silent oaths she'd kept to hold their late-night conspiracies close. She'd been so used to never bringing them up even when they were alive. She took a breath and went on, "Soon enough my aunt had saved enough to afford an apartment over the classroom. She had a pallet set aside for me. I slept there sometimes . . . and trained with her, eventually—after hours, of course."

While my parents plotted their revolt.

The memories returned with such fierce clarity Anji had to pause. She could see the classroom, the rickety desks, the lone molding bookcase. Her heart ached to return, to run into her aunt's wiry arms. She wiped at a tear and rubbed it against her filthy pants.

"Home was with my parents. A basement apartment—in Mudtown. We lived below a chandler who liked to experiment. Lots of different smells, of course, and sometimes they'd mix in terrible ways. Funny how a combination of sweet scents can make for something so foul."

The Hawk said nothing, but her eyes were open now, glassy and unfocused. She pushed her mask away and tucked her knees tight against her slender chest.

"As often as the bad smells came though, good ones always won out," Anji continued. "The owner would let me help when custom was slow, which it nearly always was. His name was Dannet." Anji pictured the brusque little man with his silver goatee fussing over his invoices, his wax stores and ingredients. "I'd spend hours there, sifting through the drawers. He put out a stool for me to watch him work, and after a while I started helping with customers. My parents never complained, though I imagine they worried I was a nuisance. If I was, Dannet never said so.

"We couldn't keep the smells out of our house—one of the reasons the rent was so cheap, I expect. Dad said cinnamon was a plague on the neighborhood. The smell still reminds me of them."

"Your parents."

Anji picked at the filth under her nails. "Dad was a fisherman, same as his own father. Not much money in it, but he loved the sea more than dry land—more than my mother, if you asked her. Taught me how to sail, and I took to it well, but I didn't have the makings of an angler like him. Never got used to gutting fish. I still hate the taste."

The Hawk murmured something, but Anji couldn't make it out. She went on.

"He loved to write at night—stories he'd make up for me and then read to put me to sleep. He gave me this"—she picked at her coat—"and that knife in your bag." She didn't mention the coin.

"My mother was . . . she worked for a newspaper." And then, since she'd already come this far and the damage was six years done: "An artist and writer. They both certainly preferred I read rather than practice with swords," Anji said. "My aunt was a harsh teacher, always knocking my legs apart, forcing me to hold a stave for hours. My arms were always too scrawny, my head up in the clouds when she lectured on proper poses and movements."

Anji pulled in a breath.

"Then Rolandrian outlawed schooling for all of Mudtown. Belle was let go, given textile detail. She packed her things that night. Said she was headed for Conifor to find someone. A woman I never met, but she must have loved her . . ." She picked at a hanging bit of skin at her nail. "I hope she found her."

Wind tore at the cave mouth, gusting and dying at Anji's feet. She perched her chin on one knee, watching the stars flicker above the glowing peaks.

"She was all I had left," said Anji, cradling her head in her folded arms, "I don't even know if she's really there—in Conifor, I mean. It was the only place in the world I thought I might have . . ." She swallowed, lifted one shoulder. "Someone."

Silence settled between them. Eventually Anji summoned the courage to look across the darkened space, to suffer whatever insults the Hawk had ready for her. But the Hawk's eyes were closed, her breathing deeper. Anji sighed. She wondered when the woman had stopped listening and finally drifted off. Probably for the best. If Anji hadn't stopped herself she might have told the woman all about her parents and the dreams they'd died for. She breathed a silent curse, knowing she'd overshared already. It had just been so nice to talk to *someone,* even an old woman who so obviously hated the air Anji breathed.

The Hawk twitched, muttered something Anji couldn't make out, then began hacking again, like something sticky and stubborn was caught in her throat. Each cough sent her frail form curling tighter in on itself, until finally the Hawk dribbled a wet black glob out of her mouth and onto the stone.

Anji grimaced. *How much has she been using? And for how long?*

Though her fingers itched to claw at the woman's face, a small piece of Anji couldn't help the concern she felt, regardless of whether the Hawk said it was hers to feel or not. They'd faced death together, hadn't they? That had to count for something. Up against a Scorphice the Hawk had lived up to her reputation as a merciless killer, but here in this cave, curled in on herself and shaking like a leaf, she looked anything but formidable.

Anji crept forward. Prodded the Hawk's shoulder.

Nothing. The woman was out cold, her mouth slightly open.

Anji's heart leapt. She'd finally been left to herself for the first time in days. But she was still a prisoner as long as this *thing* was tied around her ankle—as long as she was poisoned. She scanned the Hawk's seamless array of leather armor, trying to remember whether the Hawk had stashed Anji's antidote on her person by mistake. The inky-black material covered every bit of the woman's skin apart from her face. Anji leaned over the Hawk's still form, checking as many spots as she could without touching the woman's body.

No sign of the antidote. She'd have to go outside. She'd have to hope the tether was long enough for her to find the bag out in the snow. Hope it had ripped open on its way down.

Anji licked her lips, and with a final glance at the Hawk, ducked out of the open doorway.

⊹ 14 ⊹

Stars crowned the mountain peaks standing sentinel above the snow-filled gully, blinking in a milky swath across the void. The wind had died to a whisper, whistling through the boulders and crags and outcroppings like an icy chorus with neither beginning nor end.

Anji couldn't care less.

Cold crawled through to her bones as she clambered down the slope. It scratched at her crusted lips, fingered the holes in her shirt, the bare skin exposed by pants Matron would have forced her to throw out weeks ago. Her feet had fled from aching, past numb, and into pulsing pain in the few minutes since she'd left the cave.

And the *wind.* That incessant, wailing wind. It slapped the sword she'd stolen against her thigh. It stung her ears like a thousand pinpricks, found its way up her nose and down her throat.

She closed one nostril and blew hard.

Shame nipped at her heels as she scuttled over the incline, eyes peeled for any sign of color—a strip of black against the pale, moon-drenched white. She had left the Hawk asleep and alone, at the mercy of whatever else might wander into the ruin. Even out here nursing stiff fingers, sniffing icy snot up her nose, it seemed the essence of cruelty leaving the Hawk alone in the cold and dark.

Anji crossed her arms against the wind and glanced back at the ruins, still visible at the crest of the hill. *Maybe I could have started a fire.*

But no. The Hawk was better off in the dark. Better to be freezing and unseen than for one of the Menagerie to spot a flicker of flame and come investigating while Anji wasn't there to stand guard. It felt strange, taking precautions to protect a woman hell-bent on seeing her publicly tortured—but she needed to get into that bag. She had a plan.

I'll take the bag back, she thought, *wake her somehow and make her open it, and swallow the antidote whole.*

Then she'd simply take back her things, and be off north; poison-free and unburdened from the brooding bounty hunter. The woman had looked so weak, Anji thought she would have no trouble making her escape. She'd be surprised to find the Hawk still conscious when she returned to the ruin, which was now barely distinguishable in the distance.

Anji couldn't be sure, but it seemed to her she'd gone farther than the tether had allowed for back in Silverton. A wild thought crossed her mind then, which set her heart racing.

What if the charm has worn off?

If it had, she could run. Take her chances with the poison, find an herbalist to mix an antidote within the week. She had no loyalty to an old drug addict set on seeing her flayed. That Scorphice had attacked them both, hadn't it? Anji had saved the woman's life, and the way she looked at it, they were square, regardless of whatever miserable, lonely withdrawal the Hawk was enduring up above. It simply wasn't Anji's problem.

But Anji only stomped forward, her fists clenched with cold and bone-beating annoyance at the pitiful, panicky creature she'd become. So eager to flee. When she'd lived on the street, she'd fought other beggars. She'd stolen food and clothes, slept on rooftops, outrun constables. Then she'd been forced into the castle, where she'd grown soft and scared. Where was that urchin now?

She couldn't run. Not yet. Conifor was even farther away now, and she refused to make the journey without the dagger and coin. She'd carried them through the confused aftermath of her parents' deaths. They'd been on her as she mucked out the castle stables. She'd found a box to store them in under her cot in the laundresses' quarters. Those bits of metal were her only shreds of a life torn from her hands, and she'd die before continuing on with those hands empty. What was safety or warmth without the only pieces of herself she still cared for? How could she carry on?

The moon's silvery crescent had sunk past the mountain's edge by the time she actually saw the bag. A patch of black, stark against the dim white. Her heart leapt in her chest and she trudged faster, sending up puffs of powder in her wake.

Just a few more steps and she'd be out of this mess. She'd never step foot in the mountains again. She'd never even *think* about mountains if she could only—

Something tickled and tugged at her ankle and she plunged face first into the snow.

Her scream was muffled as she floundered and jerked like a jackal caught in a trap. She scrambled in the powder and scratched at the invisible tether.

"Fucking thing!"

The shout echoed off the crags overhead. Anji jerked around, staring wide-eyed at the ridge, at the silent ruins, at the Scorphice's dead carapace still lodged at an awkward angle at its edge. The world remained still.

Anji slapped at the snow, teeth clenched in a silent snarl, and twisted on the spot. As though mocking her, the tether tingled around her ankle.

The bag was only a body length away. Anji stretched herself over the snow, the strap inches from her clawing fingers. The tether pulled at her aching joints, a sharp pain shooting up her calf and knee socket and into her hip.

Her bare hands throbbed as she scooped uselessly at the snow. She cursed herself for not stealing the Hawk's gloves and kept digging, shards of ice cutting into her palms. She grazed the silken fabric with the tip of her middle finger and heaved an icy breath, stinging but clear and rejuvenating.

The tension pulling at her ankle released, and Anji flew forward into the snow once more. She spat flakes from her mouth and froze at the sound of heavy steps at her back.

"Well, well. What's got you out here in all this mess?"

⇥ 15 ⇤

Anji spun, her stomach plummeting. She ripped the stolen sword from her belt and faced the source of the voice.

The man striding toward her was over seven feet tall. *Half-starved,* she thought, *like he hasn't eaten in weeks.* He waded through the snow as though it were ankle-deep water, his tattered gray-and-black leathers snug against long, knobby limbs. He wore a stone mask of deep polished blue, its features long and sloped, the black meshed eyeholes wide-set over a prominent muzzle. Stubby horns curled from the top and over tufts of red hair spotted with gray.

The Goat.

Freckles spattered the bits of pale skin between mask and leather. His belt held a slender dagger in a faded leather sheath. A bandolier of glass tubes hung at an angle over the belt, glowing with a weak purple light. A wicker-woven quiver hung from a taut strap around one bony shoulder. And cradled in wiry gloved fingers: a crossbow, the gleaming tip of a bolt pointed at Anji's chest.

"Toss the sword. Nice and easy, girl," the Goat said, his voice muffled by the mask.

If one more person calls me "girl," she thought. She clenched her jaw, squeezing the sword's hilt so hard it hurt her fingers, then threw the sword into the snow at the Goat's feet.

"Hands up."

Anji raised her hands, then lifted herself to one knee.

"Ah, ah," the Goat said, mirth dripping off his words. "Slow. Nothing clever now." He gestured with the bow, and Anji got to her feet, her muscles tightening in protest.

Crossbow still trained on her chest, the Goat scooped up the sword and slipped it into a loop at his hip.

A bead of freezing sweat trickled down Anji's neck. She inched toward the bag lying in the snow near her feet.

"None of that," said the Goat, twitching the crossbow. "Let's go for a walk. Just the two of us." He tapped at the bolt. "Try to run and this goes in your back."

Anji's brow furrowed, hands still raised. Why did the Goat have a crossbow? He'd always been depicted as the Maxia, the navigator. In fact, in all the tales she'd heard of the Menagerie, he'd never even drawn a blade. The Hawk and the Ox were the warriors, the blade masters. *None of this makes sense.* She chanced a glance at the length of steel at his belt and pushed down the lurch in her stomach—the acid taste of vulnerability.

He must have cut the tether, she thought, *but not with that sword.*

"I'm worth twice as much alive," she said, embarrassed at the quaver in her voice.

The Goat chortled. "A bolt in the gut won't kill you for a day or two. A week with the charms I know. Oh, it'll hurt like hellfire." He lifted a shoulder. "But I'll still get paid. Now come along quietly, unless you want a new rib when we get to Linura." He pointed her in the direction of the ridge and the ruins at its top, to where the Hawk lay passed out.

"Up you get," he said. "Let's not wait for the grass to grow."

"Why—"

"Think I don't know where that tether leads? *Walk*."

Anji watched the Goat snatch up the blue bag. He studied it for a heartbeat, then tied it to his belt and made a shooing motion with one hand. She set her jaw and trudged up the slope.

Keeping her arms up made the trek more treacherous than the journey down. She stumbled a few times—much to the Goat's delight. They ascended in silence but for Anji's panting breaths and the man's boots stomping in a steady rhythm at her back. She wondered whether the Goat would shoot the Hawk while she slept or cut her throat.

Her knees buckled as they came level with the ruins. She gasped in air as the Goat aimed his crossbow into the darkness.

"Hawk!" he cried, voice echoing through the pass despite the mask. When no reply came, he motioned with the crossbow.

"You first," he said.

But no trace of the Hawk remained among the ruins, save for a spot of bare rock where she had lain. Keeping the bow pointed at Anji, the Goat slipped one of the glass tubes from his belt and shook it in one gloved hand. The walls illuminated in brilliant purple light, revealing nothing but snow and stone.

"Where is she?" said the Goat, rounding on Anji. Her hands shot into the air again without instruction as he shoved her back out onto the trail.

"How should I know?" she said, and though she would have lied just to spite the man and his hideous mask, she was being honest. "We're not exactly bosom friends." She scanned the ridge, vacant save for the Scorphice's corpse, in which the Goat showed little interest. Her stomach turned at the sight of it lying in a crumpled mess atop the slope, its eerie white carapace coming into vivid relief with the day's growing light. The sky was now empty of stars, lightening to deep purple.

The Goat clicked his tongue. "Blast it," he said, craning his neck from one side of the gully to the other. "Hawk! Show yourself! I've got your prize here. Shame if I were to walk right off without—"

"Will you shut up?" Anji hissed, slapping at the Goat's arm. "You'll start an avalanche, you idiot—"

Light flashed. Pain exploded in her jaw. She crumpled to the ground, a sharp rock digging into her thigh. Warm blood filled her mouth, wine red against the snow as she spit it out, crying out a curse or a plea. She couldn't tell through the haze of anger and confusion. The Goat bent over her, blotting out the stars above.

"You're not giving orders here, you little brat," he said, though he lowered his voice. He glanced about the white expanse once more, then gripped the crossbow so hard Anji could hear the leather gloves squeak on the wood. "*Hells,*" he muttered.

Still panting on the ground, cradling her pulsing jaw, Anji allowed herself a morsel of hope. Wherever the Hawk was, she'd turn up eventually, hopefully to cut this bastard's stinking cock off. With the tether broken, Anji would be able to escape in the confusion of a fight. *I can still get out of this,* she thought, though her confidence drained like filthy wash water as she watched the Goat adjust his mask and step forward, kicking a stone away with one of his giant booted feet.

"Get up," he said. "Time we got off this rock."

⊹ 16 ⊹

Anji slogged down the trail, hands raised, feet scuffing on loose stone. Sweat and melted snow dampened her soiled clothes. Every part of her ached and starved and smarted, every tendon and muscle wound tight as a drum. Her mouth pounded with each weary step, the metallic taste of blood ever present at the back of her throat.

Patches of snow littered the mountain's base, giving way to mounds of lava rock, windblown moss clinging in orange and green tufts. The sun had finally crept over the mountain's dome, scattering wisps of gray cloud as the masked man herded her down.

"Caused quite the stir in Linura, you did," said the Goat at her back. "Hear what they've got planned for you?"

"I'm to be tortured, apparently."

"Torture's a decent enough word, but vague. They always omit the details, those posters. Way I heard it, you're facing the Scavenger's Maid. You know what that is?"

If Anji had had any food in her stomach, it would have threatened to come back up. She'd often listened to her parents' whispered late-night talks, pretending to sleep in her loft bed. One night, her father had come home late and nearly fallen weeping into her mother's arms, describing an execution he'd seen. Anji's mother had fixed him some tea and sat up as their candles burned low, letting him vent out the horror of what he'd witnessed in graphic detail. The tremor in her father's voice as he recounted the scene had kept Anji awake long after her parents had finally gone to bed. Once more, the image of blood and sharpened iron filled her tired thoughts, and though it caused her knees to go weak, she wouldn't give the man at her back the satisfaction of seeing her squirm.

"Sounds alright," she said lightly. "I hope she's a redhead."

"They take this metal contraption, see, and you're folded into it. Then they'll tighten the metal, a little at a time. First you bleed from your nose and ears. Your spine separates, ribs and all that, then it's the vitals gone. Takes hours for you to die. But you'll be on your knees, limbs compressed, organs spilling out your mouth."

"If you're there," said Anji, "be sure to stand downwind, would you? Your stink is torture enough." She glanced to either side as they rounded the next bend.

"Think she's coming for you, eh?" said the man. "Hawk? She's a runner. Likely gave you up for good once she saw—"

"Fun little name, that," Anji said, ignoring the question. "The Hawk. Do you have one too? Or do I just call you 'Asshole'?"

Something slammed hard into the small of Anji's back. She flew forward, her shoulder smashing into the snow and rock. The Goat set his crossbow on the ground and rammed the tip of his boot into her side. Anji felt all her breath leave at once. She gasped, eyes wide as the man unsheathed his slender dagger.

Anji froze.

He squatted and sucked at his teeth, letting the blade catch in the sunlight.

"Let's get something straight, you and me," he said, touching the dagger's tip to her nose. "Far as I'm concerned, you're dead already. And dead girls don't jest. Dead girls walk when they're told, they eat when they're told, and they die when they're told. And they keep their jokes to themselves, don't they?"

Anji wheezed a reply, but the man's hand shot out like a snake and wrapped around her throat. His fingers were like iron barbs, tips digging at her neck. She yelped and kicked her legs against the hard ground, sending up a cloud of gray dust and clattering rocks skittering down the trail. She beat at his arm but it was like smacking a tree branch. Then a slice of thin fire streaked against Anji's cheek and he brought the blade back, dark blood shining on its edge.

"Answer me, girl, or I'll take out your fucking eye!"

Blood thundered in her skull. She needed air, the pressure on her throat a vise squeezing tighter—

She choked on a breath, tears spilling down her cheeks.

The Goat laughed and pressed the dagger's tip into Anji's shoulder. "Words, girl! Words!" The blade worked into her flesh like a hot iron. A streak of blood dribbled down Anji's arm. Her bladder released. She gulped a lungful of air.

"Th-they do!"

"They what?" said the Goat, digging the dagger deeper into her skin. She shrieked and kicked and sucked in another breath.

"They keep th-their jokes to themselves!"

The Goat shoved her away, standing straight once more.

"Looks like you've got a brain in that potato-shaped head of yours. You might put it to good use if you want to keep it on your neck for the next couple days." He sheathed his dagger and gestured down the trail. "Name's Goat," he said. "Now get up and keep your mouth shut."

✛ 17 ✛

Anji never thought she could hate someone as much as she'd hated Rolandrian, or the Hawk, or her parents' killers, but the Goat had climbed his way to the top of that list in an astonishingly short time. In just a few moments, with even fewer words, he'd made her feel small and useless in a way the Hawk or even Matron never had. The way he'd brandished the knife, the rise of his jawline under the mask, like he enjoyed torturing her. The careless way he'd cut at her face and wheezed and cackled. Like this was all one big joke.

They trekked in silence toward the tundra plains below, the Goat's bootsteps sure and solid, Anji's breath shuddering. She scanned the jagged slopes, searching for a sign of movement, the glint of black metal.

Anji chewed at the inside of her lip, annoyed with herself, with her seemingly inexhaustible ability to get herself further into trouble. The Hawk had *told* her how horrible the Goat was, and she simply hadn't given a shit. Some childish part of her must have hoped the Hawk had been wrong about her old friends, that she was just a bitter old woman who'd been kicked out of a club, tossed aside, abandoned. The idea of the Menagerie being anything but the heroes Anji had grown up pretending to be had seemed ridiculous.

Now, as she trudged in front of the Goat, shirt and face stained with blood, panic flooding through her in thick waves, she knew she'd been wrong about the Menagerie all along. How stupid she'd been, how taken in by fantasy, by childhood songs and Senate lies. Why had she not heard of the Goat's cruelty before? And where were the Ox and the Bear?

As if in answer to her question, a figure appeared down the snaking trail. The Goat whistled, and Anji knew he meant for her to stop. She halted, hands still raised, manacles jingling on her chafed wrists.

"You can lower your hands," said the Goat, crossbow still aimed true.

Anji's arms cramped as she eased them down, the manacle's cuffs sliding back into place. She wanted to sit, to rest her aching legs, but for all she knew the Goat would shoot her for it.

"Who is that?" she asked, nodding down the trail.

"Shut up," the Goat said, shifting his weight. He kicked a rock out from underfoot and Anji watched it clatter down the trail. She thought of the avalanche, wishing he'd been under the falling snow too. The Goat had tied the blue satchel to his belt, near the loop holding the Hawk's sword. Anji ground her teeth—her knife was so *close* and yet so far away. She felt ten years old again, jumping to grab at her shoe being tossed between two bullies, sprinting down a muddy sidewalk while bigger kids chased and jeered. She imagined sticking something sharp in this bully's gut and watching *him* piss himself.

A woman approached, stocky and thick-thighed and wearing a mask.

The Bear, Anji thought, her throat going dry. But no, the Bear's mask was white, or at least, the one Anji had seen that day in Mudtown had been. It was always painted white on the dolls as well. As the woman came closer the features of the mask came into better focus. Deep brown and carved of wood polished so smooth it gleamed in the low light. The only wooden mask in the Menagerie.

The Ox.

The Goat snapped a finger at Anji. "Sit."

Anji settled on a somewhat flat chunk of stone near the road's edge. She massaged blood back into her thighs as the woman came level with the Goat.

"Hawk?"

"Gone."

Alive, Anji thought. But the hillside was silent and still.

"Ha!" the Ox boomed, slapping the Goat's shoulder. "I knew it. Pay up." She held out a thick-fingered hand as the Goat grunted and reached into the folds of his leathers. Her voice reminded Anji of her aunt's—rich and raspy, ever on the edge of a laugh. Belle had taken to smoking cadroot in her later years, and before she'd left for Conifor the effects had started to show not only in her speech, but in the brownish tint of her nails and her efforts climbing the steps to her apartment. Judging by the Ox's hale movements, however, she'd never touched the stuff.

"Bet was that I'd kill her," said the Goat, but he still dropped two Celdia clinking into the woman's hand. "Not that she'd go missing."

The Ox pocketed the money and gestured at the empty trail. "Don't see a dead Hawk anywhere." She planted her hands on her ample hips and scanned the folded foothills. "And I doubt she's missing."

Anji followed her gaze, easing farther onto the stone seat. Her hand grazed a loose sliver of rock, sharp to the touch. She kept her head still.

"We'll sort her out," said the Goat, more to himself than the woman at his side, who hooked a thumb at Anji.

"Why is she bleeding?"

"Fell down."

The Ox sucked her teeth and stepped toward Anji. "I'm Ox," she said, patting her chest. "You must be Anji."

Anji raised a brow. This was much more like the Menagerie she'd heard of, the congenial and unshakable sort she and her friends had pretended to be. The heroes she'd sung about.

"Not too talkative just now," said the Goat, "but it's her."

The Ox jerked her head around. "Did you give her the Insights?"

"Figured you'd want to do it."

Heart hammering, Anji shifted her hand to cover the sliver of sharp stone just as the Ox rounded on her once more.

"Did Hawk recite anything to you when you were captured?"

Anji shook her head. "She didn't tell me anything. Mostly she wanted me to be quiet."

"Can't imagine why," said the Goat.

"Right," said the Ox, straightening. She set one hand on the hilt of a short, stubby sword scabbarded at her belt, and said, "You are hereby held in acquisition under the noble jurisdiction of the Conclave Wardens Sun and the Eighty-Seventh Senate of House Demuratia, long may they reign."

"Long may they reign," said the Goat.

"Oversight of said acquisition," continued the Ox, "conducted henceforth by First Constabulary Cadre Menagerie, Initiates of the One Path and eternal servants to the Conclave Wardens of Sun and the One All High."

Great, Anji thought, *more religious yapping.*

"By virtue of your worldly birth," the Ox went on, "you are afforded the following rights: the right of guarded passage, the right of neutral escort, the right of salt and sea, and the right of insight. All rights shall be enforced forthwith until judicial processing and termination of exchange. Do you understand and accept these tenets?"

Anji furrowed her brow. "I-I think so?"

"Basically, we have to feed you and see you don't die until your trial," said the Ox. "You're also allowed to ask any questions you like, though we can choose whether or not to answer."

"Don't much like answering them, myself," said the Goat.

"I, on the other hand," said the Ox, "see it as the least we can do. We are children all under the One's accordance, after all."

The Goat scratched at his neck, but remained silent. The tension held like a bowstring in Anji's shoulders released a little. He was obviously lower ranking than the Ox.

"If you've no questions at present," said the Ox, "we've got a camp below, about half a day's walk. We'll get some food in you and signal Bear."

The Ox reached out her hand and grasped Anji's wounded shoulder. At first Anji thought she was being helped to her feet, but the force of the Ox's grip only increased. Anji flinched away, but the fingers around her arm held firm. The Ox's other hand snaked around Anji's head and yanked her forward, her brow slamming against the wooden mask.

"With ruination comes the dawn," said the Ox in a voice dripping with glee, her mouth's rancid stench seeping under her mask and into Anji's nose. Blind fear and confusion raced through Anji's mind. The words made no sense. Was she supposed to say something? She would say anything if the woman would only—

The Ox released her and stepped back. Her posture, which had appeared so cordial moments before, now seemed crazed and precipitous to Anji. Without a word to the Goat, the Ox turned on her heel and began marching down the trail.

Trembling, Anji crept her hand another inch, palming the

jagged piece of loose rock into her sleeve. She raised her hands again as the Goat nudged her off the boulder and onto her feet, and felt the needle of rock slide down her arm to the notch of her elbow, past her shoulder, then against her side to where her belt met her tucked shirt.

+ 18 +

They reached camp as the sun scraped the far horizon's jagged edge, its dying rays birthing long shadows from the moss-covered boulders and wavering, knee-high clumps of sedge. Wind curled through the brush at Anji's feet, whistled and clawed at her ears. Along the trail and into the flatland, Anji had thought over what questions she would ask the pair, if any. But now as they approached their destination, she wanted only to drop to the ground and sleep.

A patched gray tent much like the Hawk's sat near a long, flat boulder at the bottom of a shallow bowl in the hills. Beside the tent, tied by their reins to anchored stakes, stood a pair of horses—one nut brown, the other speckled white. Two buckets sat on the bank of a tiny stream trickling near the boulder. The stream foamed over smooth stone and moss, the fading sun's light flickering as it flowed. Two slender poles of wood stuck out of the ground, a line between them festooned with the carcasses of small animals hanging upside down. They swayed like drying socks in the brittle breeze.

"Wait," said the Goat, and Anji stopped, her limbs begging for rest with a camp so close. She'd have laid down in the stream if it meant she could ease the pain in her thighs.

The Goat held out his hand and walked until the air around his palm rippled like a sheet of yellow-gold light. The light expanded, revealing a shimmering dome that covered the camp's perimeter.

"*Allantetea loranateanorathania,*" said the Goat, his voice low and precise, and the dome disintegrated.

"I'll fetch water," said the Ox lightly, ignoring Anji's gaping mouth. She patted the Goat's back and strode into the camp toward the buckets near the stream's edge.

The Goat tilted his mask toward Anji. "Well, look at you all astonished. Never seen real maxia, have you?" He gripped the bandolier of glowing vials around his waist, as though hopeful she would ask him about it. True, she was indeed curious, but Anji didn't want to give the man more satisfaction than was necessary. She had seen "real" maxia, her mother being who she was, but Anji was practiced in looking shocked when she saw it performed. Admittance to Exorcia, and by extension the use of maxia, was reserved for the upper classes, the well-connected, and outlawed for everyone else. Anji shook her head, hoping her widening eyes portrayed a girl beset by wonders unceasing.

"Trapped a fish!" came the Ox's voice from the stream. Anji and the Goat turned together to see the woman standing with one foot in the water, the other perched on the bank. She held a flapping silver fish by the tail.

The Goat corralled Anji into the camp, letting her collapse near the burned-out remnants of a cookfire at its center. She groaned with the release of tension in her limbs and watched the Goat ease himself onto the boulder near the tent, crossbow still trained on her chest.

"Alright, here's the plan," he said. "Ox and I are going to signal the Bear, and you're going to sit quiet and keep to yourself. Try to run, and"—he patted the bow—"well, let's assume you're not a total moron." He set the bow on the rock, its bolt still pointed at Anji, then folded over his boots and began untying the laces as the Ox ambled back into camp, water bucket sloshing in one massive hand, the fish already limp and gutted in the other. The Goat snorted a laugh. "Imagine, Rolandrian murdered by a simpleton. Wouldn't that just be—"

"Stop your chiding, Goat," the Ox said, setting the bucket down. She crouched and began tearing strips from the moss she'd also gathered, piling it into the cookfire's ashes.

"Apologies," the Goat said. With a grunt he yanked one of his boots off and tossed it aside. "Still, can't believe *she's* the one that did it." He unlaced his other boot, which he pulled off and threw next to its twin. With a relieved sigh, he snatched up the crossbow again, long legs splayed before him. A gust of wind pushed the stench of his unshod feet into Anji's nose, and she nearly gagged.

Tittering, the Goat gestured at Anji with the bow. "So. A laundress turned regicide. Won't that make for a song. Who helped you with it then, eh? You couldn't have done it on your own."

"Tenets, Goat," said the Ox with a tired sigh.

"Not used to fighting your own battles, I take it?" Anji said without thinking.

The Goat coughed a laugh, then shot to his feet with a snarl, one hand clapped to the hilt of the long dagger at his hip. He'd taken one step toward Anji when the Ox held up a hand, which stopped him in his tracks. "Peace, Goat," she said, her voice even. "Our charge is tired. Remember yourself." She gestured to the pair of dead rabbits dangling on the line near the horses. "Those coneys need stripping."

Anji cursed herself for the outburst, her throat tight, eyes flitting between the two. The Goat's impenetrable stare stuck on Anji for a heartbeat, hand tightening on his dagger's hilt. Then with a grunt he tore his gaze away and trudged toward the line. He ripped both rabbits off and strode back, the animals swinging in one huge hand, then snatched his crossbow from the rock and folded himself in front of the fire opposite Anji. "Just saying," he muttered, laying the rabbits on the ground in front of his crossed legs. "Choosing to run up this way, lass . . . one might forgive me calling you simple. Myself, I'd have run south. My dad always said, 'Son, if you're running, run someplace warm. That way, if you're caught, you won't die with your teeth chattering.' "

The Ox blew on the moss fire, heavy smoke billowing up from it. "Well, nobody is dying here. She's wanted alive and she'll arrive as such."

The Goat sniffed, unsheathing his dagger. "Hear that?" He jerked his head to the Ox, now lifting a copper pan out of a canvas bag the size of a pillowcase. "You're lucky you were picked up by such professionals as we."

"Luck has no place on this earthly realm," said the Ox. She fished out a square package of white butter and cut a square into the pan. "We move as the One wills us."

"As the One wills us," said the Goat. He slit into the first rabbit's fur, separating pelt from muscle with easy, practiced strokes. His long fingers worked like spiders along the creature's body, unwrapping it like a parcel until only gleaming muscle showed. He set it aside and started on the second without a word.

The One should get off their ass and will me out of here, Anji wanted to say, but she kept it down, her side still smarting where the Goat had kicked her, the wound in her shoulder a constant reminder of the pain he could inflict in a heartbeat. She watched the Ox lay the fish sizzling into the pan, and leaned back despite her aching stomach. The Ox had mentioned she was allowed to ask questions, so she thought for a moment as the woman added another pat of butter to the pan.

"Why don't you take off the masks?"

The Ox chuckled. "Everyone wants to know about the masks. We do take them off, in private."

"You know what I mean."

"Ask the right question." The Ox simpered. "And I'll answer it."

Anji ran a finger along the chaffed skin under her manacles. "Why don't you take them off in front of your prisoners?"

The small amount of jaw showing under the Ox's mask lifted. "Credit goes to Bear's grandfather, actually" she said. "He put up the funds for Bear to start the cadre, introduced her to the proper Senate rank and file, with certain conditions . . ." She held up a finger. "One of which being we stay masked while we're on a job, before and after we catch our quarry. Most instances, yours for example," she dipped her head at Anji, "we're escorting prisoners to an execution. There's typically a trial beforehand, of course, but you can bet if the Menagerie is called to task, the charge is a damn sight more guilty than their neck can afford."

The Goat muttered something about "vagrants" as he worked, but the Ox continued, swatting at a snapfly buzzing around the smoking fish.

"So," she said, "seeing as the days with us are usually their last, we afford them the anonymity of their captors. We're escorting a prisoner, yes, but still a person. It's a respect granted to you not to see our faces. Not to have to compare yourself to the living, which you will no longer be once—well, you know."

The Goat mimed drawing his bloody knife across his neck. A lump formed in Anji's throat, but she shifted closer. "Are they really maxial?"

"They are," said the Ox, "but not so much as all those songs make out."

Anji blanched and the Ox guffawed, lifting the pan off the heat and flipping the fish with a flick of her wrist. "They help us see in the dark, mostly. Another gift from Bear's grandfather. He was a Maxia."

"Damned powerful one too," said the Goat. The Ox ignored him.

"He enchanted the masks with his final breath," she continued, "so they're effective forever without draining us." She looked up from the pan. "Didn't Hawk explain any of this?"

Anji's mouth twisted. "She only told me how horrible the rest of you are. And that I was going to be tortured and executed. She was very clear about that."

"But you asked questions, yes?" said the Ox.

Anji nodded.

"And she refused to answer?"

"Nearly every time," said Anji.

"She's not keeping the tenets," said the Goat. "Ungrateful bitch."

"Goat," said the Ox, twitching her mask around, but she didn't admonish him further. Turning back to Anji, she slammed the pan against the rocks. "It doesn't matter—pointless to expect . . ." She cleared her throat. "I didn't think she had another job in her."

"You weren't expecting her to go after me?" said Anji.

The Ox picked off a flake of fish and lifted her mask to taste, revealing much smoother skin than the Hawk's. The fish must have been thoroughly cooked by now, but the Ox kept frying it as she talked. "None of us have heard from her in months. She hasn't been answering messages. Hasn't taken an assignment in over a year. I've no idea what's got her back at it."

"I can think of about a million reasons," said the Goat with a scoff. He leveled a finger at Anji. "Finally found a bounty worth her precious time, and she wants it all to herself."

Anji frowned. "Is that why she stopped working with you? You weren't paying enough?"

"Our needs are met," said the Ox. "The Wardens see to that."

A gust of wind barreled through the camp. Anji wrinkled her nose against the smell of the Goat's feet mixed with cooking fish. The Ox jerked her chin to the Goat, who set the skinned rabbits aside, rose, and dusted the seat of his pants, pointing the crossbow at Anji once more.

"Oh, put the piece away," said the Ox, waving a hand. "She's half-starved and sleep-deprived. You're just showing off now."

"She assassinated the damned king of Yem!"

"She's in our custody," said the Ox slowly, "and will be treated with the respect the damned deserve."

A moment of tense silence passed. The Goat's fist clenched so tight his leather gloves squeaked.

"Go," the Ox said with a shooing motion, "I'll watch over the big scary killer." She ignored the Goat's muttered curse as he dipped into the tent, then shifted back to curl her own gloved fingers around the pan's handle, shaking the burning fish loose from the bottom. Anji studied the fish's blackened scales, its single vacant eye staring at her. She tore her gaze away and scanned the rocky hills past the camp. Where was the Hawk? She was starting to fear the woman had *actually* died somewhere on the mountain.

Should have stayed put, Anji thought. *We could have dug the bag up in the morning. Fought the Goat off and avoided the Ox altogether. Stupid.*

The Ox slipped a black-bladed dagger from her boot and cut into the fish, divvying a portion onto one of the flatter stones near Anji's foot. Glancing sunward with squinted eyes, she bowed her head over the clump of flesh still crackling as she held the pan.

Beneath your blazing eye, we shine,
on your divine intent, we dine,
with your decree, in light of thee,
this feast we take, by your design.

Anji stared at her portion of burnt fish. Even in her starved state, she could hardly call it a feast.

Her new captor didn't seem to mind. She sheathed the dagger without wiping it, lifted her portion under the edge of her mask, and stuffed the whole charred mess into her mouth, grease dripping onto her tattered leathers. Anji cringed at the audible crunch behind the wood. The woman wiped at her lips, reached a finger between her teeth, and tossed a particularly large bone into the fire.

Something clattered inside the tent, and the Goat's head appeared through the flap. "Where's the map?" he said.

"How should I know?" said the Ox, not looking back at him. The Goat grunted and slipped back inside, barking a curse before something else crashed behind the canvas.

A full day had passed since Anji had last eaten, but the stink of fish and the Ox's smacking lips made her stomach turn. The Ox reached behind her and drew out a sloshing canvas canteen. She sucked at the bladder's spout, head tilted back, the tendons in her bulbous neck standing out, then swished the water around in her mouth and spat it into the sedge at her side. "You should eat," she said, gesturing at the burnt meat in front of Anji. She lifted the still-sizzling pan and shifted it farther from the fire. "We've got a long couple of days ahead of us, and that's assuming we don't run into—*hells*!"

The Ox dropped the pan clattering to the rocks, oil spilling over the ring of burnt grass circling the fire. Shoulders heaving, she clenched one hand around the other and doubled over, her breath hissing between her teeth. With a snarl she snatched up the pan, raised it high, and smashed it down into the fire, sending sparks and flaming grease in all directions. Anji scrambled away as the Ox shrieked and beat at the flames, the pan clanging off the gathered stones. After multiple strikes, she tossed the battered pan aside, and cradled her hand. Tiny beads of grease crackled on her thin leather glove as she finally ripped it off. She flexed her hand, an angry red spot welling just beneath the first knuckle where oil had burned through the leather and onto her skin. Anji blinked. The first finger of the Ox's hand was missing. Where the finger would have been was now only a lump of pink scar tissue.

The Goat burst out of the tent, crossbow raised in one hand, his other arm holding a bundle of cloth.

"What the—" he started, then his mask twitched toward the pan lying in the dirt. He lowered the crossbow. "Grand, Ox. You're not the only one that needs to eat, you know."

"Just signal her," said the Ox, stomping out a smoldering bit of grass. "And do it in the tent."

"Can't see in the tent," said the Goat, kneeling to the ground. He unrolled the piece of cloth, revealing a hand-sized silver hammer. After patting himself down, he produced a palm-sized, flame-orange stone and set it on the canvas. "Let her watch. She'll be dead in two days, anyhow." His words came out in a rush. Anji wondered what the man's eyes must have looked like behind the mask as he scanned the cloth. Were they purple, like Alphoronse's? Like her mother's without her glasses?

The Ox turned her mask to Anji.

"I told you to eat."

Anji glanced at the half fish, still untouched on the rock at her knee.

"I'm not hungry."

"Don't be ridiculous," said the Ox.

Heat rose in Anji's cheeks. "I'd rather have the crossbow bolt."

The Goat wheezed a laugh. "Haven't you been listening? You're wanted alive. The bounty for your corpse isn't worth the minimal amount of poison it would take to kill you. Now do as Ox says and eat before you pass out and become more of an inconvenience than you already are."

A jolt ran through Anji. The Goat's words reminded her that

indeed, she had already been poisoned. "The Hawk poisoned me," she said. "I forgot, the antidote is in that bag." She pointed at the horse.

The Goat let out a wheezy laugh . "Told you that, did she?" He adjusted his mask.

"More lies," said the Ox. The Goat nodded.

"We never poison, girl," he said. "Hawk least of all. She may have left the cadre—"

"We don't know she *left*—" the Ox started, but the Goat talked over her.

"But she'll still hold to her own principles. Reckon we wouldn't have half the rules we do if it hadn't been for her."

"So . . . she didn't poison me?"

"Are you feeling sick?" asked the Ox.

Anji opened her mouth, closed it again. She *had* felt sick, but only periodically. Whatever nausea she'd felt had been brought on by the Goat's kick to her stomach, and before that it had been a short-lived, negligible unease—more like anxiety than what she imagined it would feel like if her body were failing her. Now she thought about it, she hadn't noticed any serious symptoms of being poisoned since the Hawk had told her she'd been dosed. And any fatigue or fever she'd developed could be explained by the harsh trip she'd suffered over the past week.

"She said it would take a week to feel the effects," she said, more to herself than to the pair across from her.

The Goat slapped his knee. "A week! What kind of poison would take a week to gestate?" He gasped another laugh. "See? Dumb as a rock."

Anji bit her lip, humiliation boiling up in her gut. How could she have been so stupid? The Hawk wouldn't have taken the risk of poisoning Anji. She could have run out of antidote, or lost it on the journey, or Anji could have succumbed to the draught as soon as she drank it. Anji should have known one of the Menagerie wouldn't take such reckless measures, not out in the middle of nowhere.

She picked up the greasy bit of fish. The skin had gone cold, but she wedged it open and took a bite from the white meat under the scales. It mushed against her teeth, salty and scalding as it passed down her throat. No matter how much fish her father had tried to get her to eat, Anji had always hated it. But her hunger won out. She peeled another piece from the skin and slipped it into her mouth, chewing mechanically, working her tongue around the bones, a stray scale lodging in her molars.

"Hawk did all the cooking," said the Goat. "Only reason to miss her. Enjoy it anyway. Not many more meals for you, I imagine."

"Enough with your taunts, Goat," said the Ox. "Agreements, verse eleven."

" 'Over the wicked' and all that, yes," muttered the Goat.

Mollified, the Ox stalked to the Goat, her words oddly soft as she stood over him, her hand held out.

"Could you?"

The Goat looked up, then grabbed the Ox's wrist, said a string of unintelligible words. A blue-green glow erupted from the Ox's wound. She shook it as though she'd touched something sharp, but backed away with an audible sigh, saying a quick thanks that the Goat ignored, now engrossed in the cloth in front of him. He picked up the hammer and held it loose in his curled fingers. Anji inched forward for a better look.

Chief among her aunt's numerous interests had been her love for maps. Anji remembered nights after sword practice, lying in the cot Belle had set up in her little apartment over the classroom. It had been a drafty, sparse room, but better than her parents' musty basement in the dead of winter. Belle had tacked up many maps of Makona, her own pen marks denoting various places she'd been on this and that campaign, far-off cities she'd dreamed of visiting. Over the few years they'd had together, Anji had learned more about the outlying areas around Yem than she ever had under other teachers, underfunded and overworked as they were in Linura's poorer districts. Belle's maps were a thing of art, to be sure, but Anji had never seen anything like the canvas unrolled at the Goat's feet.

The map depicted not just the continent of Makona, but other land masses across the Kalafran ocean, swaths of earth Anji had never seen. They'd been painted in staggering detail. Lakes and rivers and inclines were marked in different colors. Makona's borders were clearly drawn in bloodred ink, the countries inside their bounds shaded in various hues: Dorodad far to the south-west, its coastline jagged and smattered with tiny islands. Above it Repulan, the narrow strip of thick forest and tangled rivers that stretched to meet Yem, which expanded far into the north and east and devoured most of Makona's central region—the largest country by far. Under Yem marshy Eltavan, cut nearly in two by the vast Blackwater Gulf. And past Yem's crooked coast the island chain of Kardisa, a collection of volcanoes and coral reefs in the middle of the Kalafran Ocean.

Anji leaned in closer, and could just make out what appeared to be scorch marks up and down the cloth, some bisecting lines representing roads, others circling smudges depicting cities and towns—more in the blank spots between.

The Goat picked up the hammer and held it loose in his curled fingers. He checked the mountains towering in the distance, the span between the base of the nearest peak and their camp in the foothills, then set the stone down on the map. Anji had to admit it looked to be exactly where they were. She watched, chewing on a nail now as he aimed the hammer, and—

"*Gilochtertetrona ammn meean.*"

—struck it down onto the stone. The steel met rock with a hollow smack. A flash emitted from the bottom in a perfect circle, burning a brownish-orange ring the exact size of the stone into the map where they were. The ring smoldered for a moment, tiny fissures of smoke curling from its edge, then darkened to black.

The Ox kept her visage trained on Anji, but Anji was too captivated to care. The stone had burned their location into the fabric, and Anji imagined the circle appearing on another piece of cloth somewhere out there in the mossy hills, past the net of streams veined across the tundra's southern reach.

Another circle appeared on the map. This one far off, but not so distant Anji felt at ease. The Bear could be along in a day on a good horse, which Anji didn't doubt she had.

"Sheertop," the Ox muttered. "We can be there before nightfall tomorrow if we hurry." She rounded on Anji. "You'll have to sleep in the saddle."

The words barely registered to Anji. She stared at the map once more, something clicking into place in her mind.

"That's how you knew where to follow the Hawk," she said, pointing at the map.

The Ox shook her head. "I told you, we didn't know her intentions. We were informed about your relation in Conifor and ordered to disperse. Bear sent the Lynx ahead, directly north, while I searched out farther west with Goat here, and Bear herself stayed south to cut off your retreat. We had no idea the Hawk had gone after you until the Lynx's body had been found."

"Got a nice tip from Illuminess Hectate," said the Goat, and though Anji couldn't see his face, she could have sworn he was grinning from ear to ear. An image of the shriveled old woman sucking on her candies sprang to Anji's mind. She'd likely been intending to contact the Menagerie from the very start, just like

158

the Hawk had said. What had she asked the Hawk about? A scrying sheet?

Hawk wanted to move right away, Anji thought, remembering her tantrum before the funnel cloud hit. Before Molli had been eaten alive. *She was telling me the truth the entire time, and I was foolish enough not to believe a word of it. I couldn't deal with a few more hours of discomfort, and now I'm stuck with these two psychopaths.*

But something else still caught in Anji's mind, like a fish fighting on a line. She wiped her grimy hands on her pants, sweat beading in her palms despite the dropping temperature.

"How did you know about Conifor?" said Anji, though a rumbling in her chest told her she didn't want to hear the answer.

The two bounty hunters shared a glance, having some sort of silent conversation despite their blank masks. The Goat began rolling up the map. "Tenets, Ox," he said.

The Ox scratched at the back of her neck, the dark meshed pits of her mask not quite level with Anji's eyes. "The first hours were chaos," she said. "You managed to escape so fast, nobody knew where to begin the search or who to search for, for that matter. The Wardens set us to work at the castle, starting with the men guarding Rolandrian's private chambers."

The king's rooms materialized in Anji's mind. Marble floors, gilded furniture, curtains billowing on the breeze, the letter opener on Rolandrian's desk. Warm blood, thick and sticky, coating her hands. The bored expressions on the pair of guards who'd let her pass without a word. She'd shared a shaky glance with one of those men.

"Then we moved on to your fellow laborers."

Something vile churned in Anji's gut. A buzzing filled her ears at the thought of the Sun Wardens, led by these two, pouring into the laundresses' quarters while the castle bells rang overhead, the confusion and terror her friends must have woken to. The minutes she'd had between murder and escape had swirled like a dream, led purely by an immediate need to flee, with no thought spared of what consequences Kaia and Libby and the others might face. Innocent all. She glanced up at the Goat, who leaned forward.

"Didn't consider them when you ran, did you?" he said, sniggering. "That blond friend of yours, Kira, was it?"

The world veered on its axis. Anji gripped at the grass. Pictured Kaia tied to a chair, screaming in a dark room while the Goat loomed over her with that long knife of his, his wretched stench the last thing Kaia would smell.

"Kaia," she said, pushing the name out like molten iron.

"That's enough," said the Ox.

But the Goat was obviously enjoying this, basking in Anji's mounting rage. "Names," he said, shrugging. "I only remember the sounds of their screams."

"I don't believe you," Anji said, her eyes brimming with tears. The Ox's arms uncrossed.

The Goat snickered. "They didn't last long, if it makes you feel better. Their bodies will be hanging from the castle walls by now." He clicked his tongue, his mask wagging side to side. "Aiding and abetting regicide. Such a shame."

The pale sunlight seemed too bright then, the world too wide, pressing down on Anji's shoulders. She wanted to scream, to cry and run and die right there on the spot. She swallowed back a mouthful of bile, unwilling to show weakness in front of these two monsters, but the tears flowed anyway, first a trickle, then pouring from her like blood from a gaping wound.

All thought for her own skin left her then, and she sprang forward with a snarl, nearly blind with anger and tears and the heavy terror of knowing it was all her fault, that she'd never see her friends again. She'd barely gotten to one foot, however, when a hand wrapped around her wrist and yanked her back to the ground spitting and screaming.

"Stop!" shouted the Ox, but whether she'd meant it for the Goat or Anji was unclear. Anji twisted in the dirt, flinging dust and grit into the flames. The Goat chuckled, which sent a fresh wave of white-hot, strangled rage coursing through her.

"You old fuck!" she bellowed, her throat aching with the force. "You didn't have to—"

"Little bitch has some fight in her," said the Goat around another laugh.

Anji twisted in the Ox's grip and made to rise again but the huge woman just grunted and rolled with her, pinning her to the ground with another thick-fingered hand around Anji's throat. The grip was just enough to hold her down without cutting off her air. Anji kicked her legs and screeched and choked out another sob, tears falling down her temples, her nose flooded with snot.

"Peace, Goat," said the Ox, then turned that wooden mask to Anji. It peered down at her in silence as she struggled and cursed until finally Anji's struggles relented, her chest heaving.

"I wouldn't expect any less for the loss of a friend," said the Ox, her voice even, "especially two. But what's done is done. You cannot best us in combat. I warn you now, girl, do not try that again." The mask hovered over Anji's face for another heartbeat before the pressure at Anji's neck released and the woman moved away.

Anji lay panting on the ground, fingers digging into the earth, the weight of her friends' horrid fates slamming into her with every pounding beat of blood through her skull. She looked over the camp and the indifferent stream, across the tundra's lonely expanse. The desperate girl in her hoped to see a figure jutting up over one of those shallow rises, mask glinting in the late evening light, silver hair billowing on the relentless breeze. But no figure appeared on the empty plain.

⊰ 19 ⊱

They rode like phantoms under the speckled night sky, Anji wedged between the Goat's knobby knees, nose wrinkled from the sour stench of unwashed skin and clothes, his or hers, she couldn't tell. She'd managed a fitful nap, her body shutting itself down regardless of the jostling flight over the tundra's folded expanse.

At dawn, the Ox spotted a group on horseback cresting the easterly horizon. The party galloped over the vast stretch, kicking up dust and grit, flying no banners, the men and women atop the mounts clothed in rough-spun tunics and bits of leather plate.

The Goat reared up, one hand gripping the reins, the other wrapped around Anji's upper arm as they halted.

"I'll talk," said the Ox, bringing her horse to a stop.

The Goat scoffed . "What's the point?" he said, though he stayed in the saddle.

Now the bedraggled company sat a short distance away, the sun rising at their backs. They'd ventured close enough to reveal their bodies and sallow faces. Three men, two thickset and bearded and the other lanky and clean-shaven, all carrying rough-looking weapons. The two women on either side of the trio sported spears, splintered and worn with chipped blades tied with silver wire to the staffs.

They all sat heavy in their saddles, faces grave.

"Nice day for a ride," said the Ox.

The clean-shaven man at the party's center cantered forward, one hand to the hilt of his sheathed sword. His eyes flicked between the Ox and the Goat before settling on Anji.

"Is that the regicide? The one who killed Rolandrian?"

"Of course it's her," said one of the other riders, a red-haired woman to Anji's left.

"Looks like a boy," another panted, his eyes wide. "We should move on, Fernand, there's no—"

"Let me handle this," said the lead man, Fernand, over his shoulder. He squinted back at the Ox. "Is it her?"

"We do not speak our charges' crimes," said the Ox. Anji expected her to say more, but the only sound that followed was the chopping wind at their backs, flapping against the other riders' dreary dress.

Fernand nudged his horse a step closer.

"Rode all this way just to die," said the Goat under his breath.

The horse stopped.

"There's no need for this," Fernand said, voice quavering. He blinked and wiped at his sweat-drenched face. "I mean to say, we don't want to fight." Anji felt a stab of sympathy for him, but was also impressed as he went on. "There's five of us and two of you. Release the girl and"—he swallowed—"and we'll let you pass."

"She is ours by right of conquest and acquisition," said the Ox. "You've no claim without steel."

"We don't hold to your tenets, Warden," said the woman to Anji's right, spitting the last word like poison. Fernand jerked around.

"Quiet," he said, then turned back to the Ox. "As I said, we're not here to fight."

"Then you shouldn't have ridden up," said the Goat. "We're not Sun Wardens, by the by."

"Just their dogs," said one of the bearded men.

The Goat groaned and shifted in the saddle. "Must we go through all this every time?"

"Tenets," said the Ox, and Anji's brow furrowed.

"Fucking *tenets*," the Goat muttered as the Ox went on, raising her voice to the mounted men and women.

"If your force be superior," she said, "we shall bow to your blades. Accept or exhibit."

"We can take 'em, Fernand," said another of the bearded men.

"A *million* Rhoda," muttered the woman to Anji's left.

Fernand chewed at his lip. He bunched his horse's reins in one fist, and with a final glance at his fellows, inclined his head.

"We will exhibit."

"'Bout time," said the Goat. He slapped at Anji's arm. "Off you get."

Anji spun in the saddle, but the Goat was already shoving her off and onto the ground.

"What are you—"

He put a boot on her shoulder and kicked her across the small space between his horse and the Ox's. With one arm, the Ox hauled her up and maneuvered her into the space between her thighs.

"Meet at Sheertop," said the Ox, tugging on the reins. "May your exhibition—"

"Yeah, yeah, exhibition." The Goat waved at them with one gloved hand as he hopped out of the saddle. He strode away from his horse, arms wide, and began to sing.

How many animals does it take,
To catch the wicked and make us safe,
Ox is strongest, loyal and true,
Goat is cleverest, valor anew

The other riders began edging their mounts forward, baring their crude weapons, calling to each other to get into formation. The Ox kicked her horse into a trot, but Anji twisted in the saddle, eyes fixed on the display.

"Why are we—"

"Quiet," barked the Ox.

A call came from the mounted fighters as the Goat flipped his mask off and tossed it aside. Anji tried to make out the features of his face, but the angle at which the Ox was spiriting her away made any clear visage difficult. He slipped off his bandolier, removing one of the vials, the purple liquid inside pulsing and brightening. Then he smashed the vial against his chest in an explosion of glistening glass and vapor.

A single heartbeat passed before a roar exploded from the Goat. Anji blinked and he was doubled over. Blinked again and he staggered, back arching as he released another ear-splitting cry. His legs extended, his torso widened, and a pair of arm-length horns burst from his head. Black fur sprouted from his body, tearing apart the leathers that had clung to his skin moments before. Towering amidst the tall grass, shoulders heaving, a monster stood where a man had once been.

The gathered horses reared and screeched, hooves clawing at the air as their riders shouted confused commands to one another. Their leader, Fernand, tore away from the group as the Goat set upon them all with a snarl. He kicked his horse into a full gallop, headed straight for Anji and the Ox. The Ox sawed at the reins and brought her horse to a stop as Fernand closed in, the whites of his eyes wide, his teeth bared. Light glinted off his raised spear, and Anji felt the Ox shift behind her, then a glint of silver flew from the Ox's hand across the narrowing gap between horses. The blade sank into the man's face where his upper lip met his nose and wobbled there for an instant. Fernand's head snapped back so hard Anji thought it a wonder it didn't fly away, then he slid from his saddle and crumpled into the ground like a sack of bricks. Bone crunched, the sound joining the screams and shrieks of horses and riders as the Goat ripped and tore at them. Anji lifted her eyes from the mess that was Fernand to watch the Goat, just as the Ox maneuvered them around.

One of the women stabbed her spear at the Goat's leg, but he snatched it and backhanded the rider off her horse, a booming laugh issuing from his cruel muzzle as she tumbled through the air.

He laughed and tore at the horses, the men, the remaining women. Blood spurted from ripped limbs, panicked shrieks echoed through the open air, horses cried and wheeled. One horse sprinted away from the maw, a headless torso bobbing in the saddle until it flopped to the ground.

"What—" Anji sputtered. "How—"

"He's a berserker," said the Ox overhead. "As likely to kill us as them. He'll catch up when he shifts back."

The screams of the dying were out of earshot now, but Anji glanced behind once more at the creature, now on its knees, throwing bloody ribbons of gore behind him. The horses were scattered, ruined bodies littering the ground around its hulking form.

Anji thought about the numerous vials in the bandolier and shuddered as the Ox led them over a rise and across the plain.

⊰20⊱

Sheertop Cathedral towered on a lonely rock-strewn rise amid the vast, multihued plains. Its spire jabbed like a crooked finger into the deepening sky, the arcade underneath a black and tumbled ruin grasping at the hill's edge. Tiny wooden frames littered the mound from base to crown, the dusty remnants of a settlement; thriving once, perhaps, but now gone to ruin.

They'd ridden all day, Anji catching snatches of fitful sleep, plagued with disturbing dreams of her parents and friends that forced her awake in a panting, sweaty tangle between the Ox's bouncing legs. They'd been forced to slow the horse to a trot along the route, and once stopped to fill the Ox's canteen at one of the many rivulets that veined Yem's southern reaches like strands of hair. Anji had complained about her exhaustion, her sore limbs, and her hunger—but the Ox had offered neither response nor rebuke. She'd seemed interested only in answering Anji's questions, of which Anji had only one.

"Will you please just let me go?"

The Ox had shaken her head, lifting her mask just enough to drink deep from the canteen before handing it over to Anji.

"Doesn't work like that," she'd said, stuffing a wad of meat and white cheese into her mouth. "You and me? We're not friends. I've answered your questions, listened to you chatter. You've got spirit, for what that's worth. But you're a regicide. You've an execution to face, and the One will see you face it."

Anji had thought of running again—of throwing the canteen at the Ox and sprinting for the nearest town. But while the Hawk had been gruff, the Ox's near-fanatic adherence to her tenets and faith made Anji too nervous to ask again. Anji wasn't a person to the Ox—just a doomed bit of walking flesh, fixed on a track and barreling toward an end already designed by the god she worshipped. She'd swallowed whatever nonsense the Sun Wardens believed like a piece of charred fish, bones and all.

And even if Anji did somehow get away, what then? She had no food, no weapons, and no money. Manacled as they were, her hands served no function past lifting a canteen to drink and holding herself straight in a saddle. Her only possessions were a dead man's boots on her feet, the ragged clothes on her back, and the trinkets locked away in a bag still tied to the Goat's horse, wherever that was now.

This is the most thoroughly fucked I've ever been, she'd thought, and climbed back onto the saddle. She'd entertained the idea of throwing herself from the horse while they rode. *I could break my neck and end it all on my terms. No crowds, no torture, just a crack and then . . . hopefully, nothing at all.* The notion had scared her into silence and dread, the heavy, clawing hopelessness of it all galloping at her side like a ghost over the rolling terrain.

The Ox pushed them hard until Sheertop had crept into view over a shallow rise, the sun falling to the west as they approached the abandoned cathedral and its town. Even from this distance, Anji could tell the cathedral's construction matched the one she'd frequented as a girl.

"The holy houses of fools," said the Ox at Anji's back. "But beautiful in their own way, I'll admit. Such devotion to build so high, as though in the unknown depths of their hearts they were reaching for the One's grace."

Anji shared the awe she heard in the Ox's voice, though the way the woman spoke raised the hair on her skin. She craned her neck as the horse took the slope, the giant structure looming overhead like a raven over her eggs. The Ox led them through the detritus of a long-forgotten village, its empty lanes caked over with dust and weeds. Wooden houses drooped on their cracked brick footings, overgrown with mold and moss. A wind-beaten cluster of gravestones stood on a plateau overtaken by brush. Anji wondered what the ruins would have looked like in their prime, why they'd been abandoned at all, and why here in the cold and unforgiving north, where resources like wood and metal were likely prized, nobody had thought to scavenge the place.

The Ox led them up the switchback trail to the cathedral's base, through the press of dilapidated homes, past a long-dried well, its hatching splintered and scattered over the faded road underfoot. Anji scanned the vastness at their backs. From the high vantage, the untamed, uncaring wilderness looked so beautiful she felt a sudden urge to paint it, to lock its beauty forever on a canvas. Anji suppressed a laugh—she'd never painted in her life. She wished she'd tried to learn. How many things might she have found a passion for if she'd been allowed to live a normal life? If the abnormal one she had wasn't about to be cut short?

They passed beneath the flying buttresses, arched and carved with runes Anji couldn't make out, then rounded the front corner under the watchful spire standing quiet sentinel over its desolated hill. Finally, the Ox clicked her tongue and tugged at the reins, and they stopped in the cathedral courtyard—what remained of it, at least.

Broken cobbles lay buried under decades of grit and dust, sedge and moss grown thick out of cracks and gouges in the earth. Dead, stunted brush lined the outer rim of stone, once tended, Anji thought, but now a copse of reedy corpses convulsing in the icy breeze. A pair of winged, humanoid statues flanked shallow steps, their faces long blasted away by the elements. The building's facade harbored weathered double doors, twenty feet tall and banded with bolted iron. A wide, bronze disc sat where they met, dark green with age, but despite its patina Anji could just make out the nine-pointed star that had lifted her spirits on so many hungry days.

Anji rolled her eyes to the shattered rose window and beyond: the spire, so spindly from a distance, now stretched like a black road into the yawning sky. She averted her gaze from the massive presence the heap of rubble still commanded.

The Ox nudged Anji out of the saddle and dismounted, her boots sending up puffs of gray dirt. Without a word, she grasped Anji's forearm and ushered her toward the entrance.

"You've nowhere to go," the stout woman said, voice low behind the mask. "Try to run, and you'll find naught but miles of wilderness and tundra and no food. If you want to eat and sleep somewhere warm tonight, you'd best stay put, no matter what happens in there. Got it?"

Anji pressed a hand to the door. She felt she'd been lugged around the whole of Yem's northern reach and not moved an inch. The only thing she had to show for this journey was a collection of bruises, knife wounds, and an aching stitch in her side. Her only friends in the world had been murdered because of her. Running had become an ethereal, useless notion. As had the thought of speaking another word. She'd devise her elaborate, daring escape tomorrow, if only she could find a flat bit of rock in this old ruin and block out her guilt and shame and fear with the recess of sleep. She met the mask's bovine stare with a nod.

It must have been answer enough. The Ox gripped Anji's shoulder and pushed open the giant doors.

✦ 21 ✦

At first, Anji felt she'd walked into a lightless, musty cave. The air smelled earthy and thick, like a basement gone over to mold. Her footsteps reverberated off the black walls and crumbling pillars set in twin rows along a central aisle scattered with shredded paper and broken brick. Whatever grace or grandeur the cathedral once held had vanished with its flock—a once glorious structure, now a ruin lit by columns of yellow light shining at angles from its many missing rooftiles.

The vaulted ceiling stretched away overhead, arches protruding in thick bands like a giant's rib cage. Anji lifted her eyes to a sight so familiar it made her heart ache.

A symphony of color and shape, dazzling gold and yellow like summer wheat mixed with blues so deep pieces of the twilight sky might have been chipped off for paint. Figures in flowing dress spread across the curvature, the firmament of bodies and clouds and sunrays so meticulous in their detail, so lovingly brushed it clutched at her heart. She drank in the majesty, the movement frozen in a moment, faded and forgotten and rotting over the empty nave.

The Last Dance. The Nine Idols' sowing of the physical realm, their ultimate gift bestowed to the newborn races and peoples of the world in those tender millennia past. According to the Order of Inheritance's scripture (the little of it Anji had read), the Nine had given the world's dead lands and still waters life and light, with no price and no expectation. They'd handed the keys to their own kingdom to mortals and left this plane of existence to govern itself. The Order's philosophy being that though the Nine had created this world, they asked nothing in return from its inhabitants—no worship, no reverence, no wars in their name. Their scripture spoke only of gratitude, of community, of sacrifice for fellow peoples, and respect for all living things.

"You must be freezing."

Anji blinked, lowering her gaze to the cathedral's altar, to a giant, shattered art-glass window and the tiny fire flickering at its base. She clenched her stiff fingers and stepped over the rotted remains of a pew, carpet squelching beneath her boots.

A lithe figure stood near the firelight's rim, arms spread wide.

The Bear was one of the tallest women Anji had ever seen. She towered over the cluttered nave, her back to the fire, the flames casting her shadow toward Anji like a drawn blade, splitting the dying sun's stained glow. Despite herself, Anji felt her feet inching closer, as though commanded to do so. As she approached, Anji could make out the strong lines of the mask, bone white, cut as if by a saw from one solid hunk of granite. Where the Lynx's mask had been etched in a snarl, the Bear's was stoic—thoughtful, even.

"Have a seat," said the Bear, gesturing at the uncluttered floor around the altar. "I have prepared some food and a little to drink." She looked sidelong at the Ox. "One knows I've had plenty of time to prepare for you."

"We got held up—"

The Bear cut the air with her palm, silencing the Ox at once. She kept her mask fixed on Anji, who was now fully in the fire's light.

Around the fire lay an assortment of pots and pans, rope, a cutting board made of burnished wood, and a cloth sack bulging at the sides. A sleeping roll and woolen blanket lay outside the fire's ring, brown and homespun and thin, but it made Anji's back ache at the thought of lying down.

"Sit," the Bear said, her voice slapping against the inside of the mask. "I'll not have it said we were inhospitable."

Anji had no response to that—none she felt comfortable voicing—so with a final look at the Ox, whose mask betrayed no emotion, she sat.

The warmth spread to her torso and limbs like a salve the moment she crossed her legs over the dingy carpet. She held numb hands out to the popping flames, flexing and wincing at the pain in her fingers as blood began pumping into her veins once more.

"Better?" the Bear's voice sounded, followed like a wraith by her body, which settled across Anji on the fire's opposite side.

In the full light, Anji guessed the woman was of an age with the Hawk. Her jaw was wrinkled and liver-spotted, hair receding and streaked with wisps of gray mixed with jet black.

"You were admiring the fresco," said the Bear. She pointed a gloved finger toward the ceiling.

"Yes," Anji croaked.

The Bear clicked her tongue and gave her head a tiny shake before leaning to the fire's side and picking up a polished brass pot. "The cup next to you, dear, if you please."

Anji glanced about and spotted a matching brass cup near her foot, dented at the rim but otherwise in fine condition. She handed it over, careful not to let the fire's heat bite at her wrist. The Bear plucked it out of her hand and filled the cup, the lumpy contents of the pot dolloping in and splashing over the rim.

She offered it to Anji.

The Ox coughed behind her, and Anji whirled. She'd forgotten the woman was still at her back. It made her nervous that she hadn't bothered to sit down. Or hadn't been ordered to. The Bear cleared her throat, and Anji wheeled back to the proffered cup.

Though her father would have called her a fool, she took the cup and wolfed its contents down in two swallows, sparing a thought for how the Goat had laughed at her the day before. The spice caught at her tongue, the scalding liquid and lumps of meat and slimy vegetables tumbling like lava down her throat. She didn't care. The hunger writhing in her gut had become more than a nagging, passing thing. It had taken over her vision, her hearing, and even her exhaustion.

The Bear leaned back, hands settled into her lap, the leathers she and the rest of the Menagerie wore creaking like the bits of splintered wood in the fire.

"Good?"

Anji bobbed her head and set the cup down with a hollow *thunk* on the destroyed carpet. A gust of wind tore through the scattered holes in the cathedral walls. One of the horses bleated outside. The Bear passed Anji the cutting board, on it a pair of bread slices and a hunk of yellow cheese. Anji accepted it, balled a piece of bread in her trembling fingers, and pushed it into her mouth. The rough texture made her jaw cramp, but she chewed and swallowed and began balling the second piece as the Bear's mask twitched up.

"Goat?"

"We were interrupted," the Ox said. She shuffled into Anji's line of sight. "I can wait for him outsi—"

"Stay for this, Ox."

The Ox halted, setting her boots shoulder-length apart, hands behind her back. The Bear untangled her legs and rose to her knees. She stared across the flames at Anji, the light gleaming in those carved pockets of black.

" 'The Nine's Gift,' " the Bear said, gesturing toward the ridged ceiling. "Those filthy Order priests' *celebration* of their so-called stewardship."

Anji thumbed the second wad of bread into her mouth. Swallowing past the pain in her throat, she said, "There's still a cathedral in Linura." She gestured around the ruin. "They taught us all about—"

"Then you know also," said the Bear, "of the Latent Truth, the first of the One's Dialects, spoken in the Earthen Ash?"

Anji's brow furrowed. She had no clue what this woman was getting at. Orphaned, wandering the streets of Mudtown terrified and starving, she'd been grateful for any dry spot she could lie down, any person willing to give her something to eat—she didn't have the luxury of caring what robes they wore or what they'd said. She'd regurgitated the proper prayers to get bits of bread and clean water, but nowhere in any of the many hours of sermons she'd forced herself to sit through had she ever heard of a "latent truth."

"I'm sorry, I don't know," she said, part of her curious, the other part of her hesitant to stoke whatever fire burned in this woman. The Bear's mask and the visible strip of face beneath remained impassive. She clapped her hands together once, the sound echoing off the stone walls all around.

"My dear Ox! We may have the makings of an initiate with us here in this nave of the naive."

The Ox huffed. "Not much time for full rites."

The Bear's shoulders slumped.

"That's right," she said. "Not the path chosen for you, of course." She waved a hand, as though swatting at a fly. "No matter. We unworthy do not besmirch the One's course with suggestion. You'll face your fate with an honest heart." Her jaw muscles flexed, the tendons in her exposed throat rigid. She stood in one graceful movement, arms outstretched.

"Oh, what times we endure, child. A plight of dissenters and doubters has descended upon Yem! Linura chokes with indolence and dishonor and *debauchery*." Her body quivered with the words, voice rising in pitch. "Addiction! Thievery! Buggery! Beggars and tarts and fiends walking the streets. Murderous, villainous scum, the lot of them. Filth that stains the One's design."

What in the hells is this woman blathering about? Anji curled her knees to her chest, the fire a pleasant glow beside her. If the Bear wanted to yap about her religion until they all fell asleep, Anji would sit and listen, just like she had as a girl. There was no point trying to escape. Not yet.

The Bear backed away from the fire, yet not wholly out of its embrace. She lifted both hands to the ceiling, breathing in a lungful of air, then let it out in a rush before she went on.

"The Order issues false doctrine, my dear. There was no Last Dance, no inheritance, no accord between gods and mere mortals. If there exists *any* accord, it is between the One and your very soul! You walked into a cathedral much like this one, looking for succor, duped by grand paintings and pretty words—but you were deceived. The Order acolytes bake lies into their bread, their welfare, flavored with the callow wish that you spread the good word of *hope*." She spat this last out like poison, rounding on one heel, her finger still pointed at the ceiling. "To whore your soul for progress, for equality, for tolerance. They would have you starve yourself of the very thing, the *only* thing which will bring you that ever-elusive strength to carry on: acceptance."

She gestured around the cathedral, the broken pews, the shattered windows.

"The One's intent speeds us ever toward decay. You think the world revolves around peace? You think these dark times the endcaps between eons of good? No, Anji. We mortals occupy the interminable gulf between lit beacons. The fires of peace gutter before the hungry dark that looms over their fragile light, and our sole liberation from this morbidity, this reality of sin and death and disease and corruption is to *accept*. Accept and conform to the One's decree, Their divine architecture."

The rebellious animal in Anji perked up at this. She'd been taught by her parents, by her aunt, by Mudtown's filthy, freezing streets, *never* to accept, never to fold. Her parents' deaths had been the anvil to poverty's hammer and still, she had pushed on. And that drive hadn't been born out of faith or fear or even love, but a determination, a reckless *knowledge* that her life could improve. That she could see herself through and . . . to somewhere else. Somewhere better.

But sitting in this ruin, after all she'd seen, all she'd done . . . Hadn't she felt a glimmer of what the Bear was saying, even over the last few hours? After learning of her friends' torture, the persistent image of their bodies draped over the castle walls. She'd entertained a feeling so similar to what this insane woman preached, so frequently and so deeply it gave her chills, that the woman before her might have been reading her mind as Anji had walked into the cathedral.

"So you just . . . give up?" Anji said, the words dry in her throat.

The Bear let out a shrieking cackle, doubling over before snapping straight like a fired catapult. "Give up? What is there to give when you have nothing? You want to sue for change? Sue. You want to kill for peace? You'll kill for years, until your dying, pitiful last day, one hand wrapped round a rose and the other using the thorns to gouge the eyes of those *you* deem unfit to lead."

Something tugged hard at Anji's collar and she was dragged to her feet, the Ox panting at her back.

"We are but the mouths through which the One speaks, the air upon which Their winged truths ride." The Bear strode around the fire. "It is by Their design your path has met ours, Anji."

Anji heard the rasp of metal on leather and squirmed in the Ox's iron-hard grip, her vision sharp, a distant roaring in her ears. The blood in her veins pulsed like a drum, blotting out the crackling fire, the wind clipping through the ruined cathedral walls. The Bear held out a hand and the Ox let Anji go for an instant, slipping a gleaming dagger into those slender gloved fingers before holding Anji fast once more.

"You are not the One's warrior for justice in this world, child," said the Bear into Anji's ear. "You can fight your whole life, run toward the light you've convinced yourself *must* exist beyond the dark, but you'll find no answers in that void—only pain."

The Ox wrenched Anji's arm away from her side and pulled her to the lectern, the chipped marble shining in the sun's dying glow. The faded symbol of the candle wreathed in sunrays stood out among the white stone, black in shadow, like a forgotten verse of song. Anji felt the cold grip of flat rock beneath her exposed wrist and looked up to the Bear, her stomach dropping at the sight of the graven lines of the Bear's mask, stoic and still.

"Pain is all you will ever know, Anji. You *murdered* King Rolandrian, a man placed by the One's design. You spit on Their decree! You besmirch Their word, Their construction! For this your life on this plane is forfeit, but you may yet enter into the Realm Under by humbling your body. With ruination comes the dawn!"

"With ruination comes the dawn," echoed the Ox, her mask frigid as the stone Anji's hand rested on. The Bear raised her dagger.

"No," Anji breathed. "No, please—"

Anji balled her hand into a fist, but the Ox unfurled her fingers and pressed them hard to the stone. She separated her index and middle fingers and pressed at their tips. Anji squirmed and writhed, but the woman's body was like a brick wall, her arms a cage she couldn't escape.

"Don't! Please! I'm sorry! I didn't—"

She felt the dagger's edge kiss her skin.

"See us, oh *singularity*!" cried the Bear.

"Stop! Ox, don't let her—"

"For order defiled!"

Blood spurted across the white rock.

The blade clicked through Anji's bone.

At first Anji felt nothing, only the pumping fear in her bowels, the watery panic rushing, rushing, rushing. Then the pain came like a roaring storm as her vision tunneled on the length of reddened flesh lying in a thickening pool on the stone. She looked again at her own mangled hand and watched the knife slice into her middle finger where it met her palm. Another splatter of blood oozed and popped from the cut, and like an apple torn from a tree another part of her was wrenched away forever.

"For order restored," said the Bear, placing the second digit beside the first.

Anji screamed. She screeched and cried and bled and crumpled, kicking, in the Ox's arms.

Her cries echoed in the ruined church, and if a god or an entire pantheon was present in that holy place, it cared nothing for her.

22

Anji was six when her father first took her past Mudtown's border and into Linura proper. She'd begged him to bring her along on his many outings as far back as she could remember, and he'd always had an excuse for keeping her home. He couldn't carry her, she'd get lost, the meeting had to be kept secret—any and all reasons for her to stay put. But one day, while Anji was reading in the loft, she'd heard the familiar thuds of her father's large feet taking each rung of the ladder to her room.

"Come on, sprout," he'd said, and she'd bounded out the door still jumping into one of her shoes as her father locked up and ascended the steps from their basement into the alley above.

Her hand was swallowed in her father's grip as they'd navigated Linura's shouting, scrambling press, the gray stone arch of East Gate looming ahead. She'd waded toward it, her legs like jelly, breath caught in her chest at the noise and conglomerate bustle of it all. A voice called from high above, and before Anji could discern the source, something splashed at her feet, soaking the only dress she owned, coarse liquid coating her face and hair and shoes. Anji had stumbled back, one hand still gripped in her father's, and in the confusion felt an enormous weight pass over her toes, followed by the bellow of a gruff man sitting atop a cart led by a wide-eyed mule.

All at once everyone was shouting, her father included. But whether incensed at her or the driver or the mule or the entire mess, she didn't know. She only knew the breaking, pounding pulse in her toes. It felt as though shards of thick glass were being slowly pressed into the little bones, through to the marrow and out the other side. She screamed all the way home, wriggling and whimpering in her father's arms.

She thought she'd known pain then, as though it were the most she could feel.

She'd been wrong.

Anji lay in the cathedral's nave, wind howling through the cracked wall at her back. She curled in on herself, nursing the cauterized wound, the skin shriveled and warped and blackened. The burn stank of roasting meat. The pain came in endless, sickly waves. She'd cried out what felt like all the moisture in her body, and when she couldn't cry anymore she moaned and writhed on the cold stone.

At first she'd drifted in and out, the fire and its light dimming, the shapes on the ceiling sliding out of focus above, then the brief release of oblivion before the agony returned.

The Bear and the Ox held a hushed conversation until eventually the cathedral doors crashed open and the Goat's voice joined in. He'd issued a barking laugh when his steps came close to where Anji lay, then he left her alone.

The idea of escape had fled her mind entirely. She knew now the depth of her use, of her ability. She needed the Menagerie for the food and water they'd give her, if she could even bring herself to eat. Could she let herself die of starvation? Was she close already?

These thoughts tumbled through her, the pain a constant companion to the whirring blur of emotions and grief for her lost fingers, the fingers she'd taken for granted up until now. She lay on her back, felt something pinch her skin as she rolled to her side. Carefully, she untucked her shirt, took out the sliver of rock she'd found, and slipped it into her boot. She whimpered, embarrassed at her plan to somehow use a bit of broken stone to escape, at how foolish it all felt now, how small she really was. Then she drifted out of consciousness again, the black swirling to cover the heart-rending agony where her hand had been whole.

She woke to pain, of course. It wouldn't ever leave. It was hers now. She owned this pain more than she owned anything else in this world. Fresh tears blurred her vision, and she moved her arm to wipe them away, but stopped short as the bloodied, scarred lump of flesh came up to her cheek. She loosed another silent sob and rolled to her good side, searching for the dark.

Anji woke to loud, confused rustling. At first, she mistook it for the wind playing at the cathedral walls. But the noise toward the end of the aisle, at the nave where the fire had been snuffed out, wasn't the wind. Anji wiped at her nose with her uninjured hand, breath held and ears strained. Rasping breaths issued under the groaning of the wood and tile roof above. A rhythmic sort of chant, almost, though she couldn't discern any words being said. She sat up straighter, nursing her wound, and leaned away from the cold brick.

In the dim starlight seeping through the cathedral's cracked facade, she could make out two shapes. They writhed together, pale torsos moving in unison, and with every bucking, jerking motion, Anji heard another of those hushed intakes of air.

The Bear was perched on her hands and knees, her bare ass

to the Goat straddled behind her, the pale stretch of his back like the belly of a lizard. The Goat slammed into the Bear, silver scars shining, the muscles under his skin contracting with every shove forward. Their grunts and gasps echoed off the metal masks still tied tight, the only bits of clothing they hadn't shed.

Anji shifted, trying her best to keep silent, though she thought she could have made a decent amount of noise and not disturbed the two fucking at the altar. She instead watched with fascination, her jaw open, the hazy hope of escape just flickering back to life, when strong fingers grasped her shoulder.

✦23✦

The Hawk crouched at Anji's back, a finger raised to the gleaming mask where her mouth would be.

Anji's lip trembled, her mouth working to say . . . something, anything. A jumbled explosion of feeling swelled in her chest at the sight of the slight woman squatting in a pillar of moonlight. Anji tried to speak, but the Hawk held up a hand. Whatever condolence or condescension she may have had for Anji would have to wait, it seemed—she spun on the spot without a word, still crouched, and waved over one shoulder for Anji to follow.

She didn't make for the giant front doors. Instead, the Hawk led them to a shattered window in the arcade. They crept over broken boards, over the torn and musty carpet and onto the arcade's stone floor. The Hawk sank deeper into a crouch beneath the window, her fingers woven together in a step. Anji hopped onto the Hawk's hands and felt herself guided to the lintel. Cracked glass still marred the window's edge, but Anji thought there was just enough space to slip through without cutting herself. She grasped at the frame with both hands, wincing at the pain flaring from the wound and the slight jingle of her manacles.

With a clumsy final lurch, she hoisted herself onto the wide ledge.

From this vantage, she could clearly see the two at the altar. Their tangled breaths were louder now, one thrusting, the other letting out the occasional moan. Anji grimaced and studied them with a horrified fascination until the Hawk patted the stone below. Anji offered her hands, but the Hawk shook her head and pointed at the window. Frowning, Anji turned and peered through the opening. Minding the glass, she dropped to the rocky ground outside, her feet stinging with the impact. She looked around just as the Hawk landed behind her, already slinking into the darkness. Anji followed, thighs burning with the effort of staying crouched.

The moon cast a shallow light on the grass growing tall and thick along the long-forgotten path. Anji snuck along after the Hawk. A thousand questions burst into her head, not the least of which was how the Hawk had actually found her, but she kept her mouth shut. They could talk once they'd left this place behind.

The Hawk held up a fist as they came even with the cathedral's front corner.

A trio of horses, heads buried in the grass, stood at the cathedral entrance. Anji's stomach flipped. The blue bag was still dangling off the saddle of the Goat's horse. She made for it, but the Hawk yanked her back.

"Wait here."

Anji clenched her unmaimed hand into a fist, but stayed put as the Hawk parted the grass and padded toward the horses, then began untying the reins from two.

Something silver flashed through the air and stuck quivering in the earth at the Hawk's feet. A shadow emerged from the cathedral's opposite side.

"Leave it, Kit," came the Ox's voice from behind her mask.

Anji edged back behind the corner, hoping the stout woman hadn't seen her, that the doors wouldn't crash open, emitting the others. She listened for any sign that the two in the cathedral had heard, but so far there was no commotion, no additional voices. Anji couldn't even hear the sound of their panting any longer.

"Did you not hear me?" the Ox said, now stepping around the remaining horse. She slid another knife from her belt. "Kit, please. Just leave."

Kit?

"She's coming with me, Ox," said the Hawk. Anji inched forward, careful not to let her head come into view.

"Don't make me do this," the Ox said, voice hitching. Was she crying? The stalwart woman who had held Anji down and watched with a wooden face while her fingers had been cut off?

"You don't have to *do* anything," said the Hawk. She rolled the reigns in one hand, and began to back away.

"Kit, *stop*," hissed the Ox, her boots crunching on the gravel and broken glass as she closed in on the Hawk.

The Hawk kicked out once, and the Ox reeled back, clutching at her stomach and nearly tumbling over. The Ox whipped her knife at the Hawk, but in an instant, the Hawk's sword was out of its sheath. She batted the knife away, steel clanging and ringing out so loud Anji was sure the others would come clattering out of the cathedral at any moment. The Ox hissed and leapt across the short distance.

The next few seconds passed in a cacophony of grunts and thuds. The two women rolled in the dust, each in turn wrestling the other to the ground. Anji took an unsure step forward and felt a sharp bite at her ankle. Heart thundering, she whipped around, expecting to see the Goat jabbing a knife into her foot. But it was only the sliver of rock she'd hid in her boot. She bent and fished it out.

The fight around the corner barreled on. The Ox pivoted on her knees, hurled a punch into the Hawk's stomach, and pushed her writhing to the earth. She straddled the Hawk, shoulders heaving, her back a broad swath of black leathers, the skin of her neck exposed. Drawing a third knife, she whispered something in a shaking voice and raised the blade high.

Anji dashed forward and, just as that bovine mask turned toward her, plunged the sliver of rock into the Ox's exposed throat.

Rust red blood bubbled around Anji's fingers. She grunted and drove the rock deeper, then ripped it forward, teeth mashed together. She felt more than heard the Hawk scrabbling up, the anguished curse that issued from the woman's mouth. Anji sank to one knee as the Ox crashed to the ground, pushing the woman's limp form to her back and climbing onto her chest.

"It's done! Stop!"

Anji ignored the Hawk's shove to her shoulder, the pain of her lost fingers a distant thing. She gripped the shard so hard its edges cut into her skin.

She flipped the mask up.

The Ox's shock of blond hair framed an elegant, angular face. Her sharp cheekbones and prominent chin harbored dark brown eyes over an aquiline nose. Her mouth was thin and pretty but for a chunk missing from most of her top lip. Unlike the Hawk's, her face showed hardly any evidence of age save for neat laugh lines at her eyes and the corners of her mouth. Her skin shone ashen, lips and teeth coated with blood. Her hands twitched to her throat, trying to pull the rock free.

"No you don't," Anji growled, swatting the Ox's fingers away. The bloody stumps of her knuckles were now open wounds, smatters of red spotting onto the Ox's slack face, mixing in with the torrent of blood now spouting in an ever-weakening stream from the woman's ruined neck. The Ox gurgled, her eyes wide, the light and awareness in them fading fast.

"Stay with me," Anji said through gritted teeth, eyes blurred with tears. "Is your ruination coming? I don't see the dawn yet, you—"

Something crashed into her side and sent her rolling over the hard ground. A firm hand tugged her up by the elbow.

"On the horse," the Hawk hissed. She climbed onto her own and already had it wheeling around as Anji looked for a final time at the Ox's dying form.

Pain spiderwebbed through her jaw and she realized she'd bit a gouge in her own cheek. Her hands shook as she gathered the horse's reins. She would have liked the Goat and the Bear to turn up right then, reeling as she was with the rush of saving the Hawk. But if there was anything Anji could still do well in this world, it was running away. She spat and wiped warm blood from her lips and clambered into the saddle.

They rode in silence but for the thundering of their mounts' hooves. The cathedral atop the hill dwindled behind until it shone like a pebble left on the trail beneath the newborn, bloodred sun, and, finally, disappeared.

⊹24⊹

Anji's father gifted her a dagger on her thirteenth birthday.

Her mother had made a loaf of apricot cake and carved Anji's name and age into its glossy top. She'd filled the recesses with white icing, made with sugar and cream that hadn't come cheap. They'd wanted to surprise her.

Anji had barely had time to appreciate the cake as she pushed through the front door, her parents' faces shifting from excitement to distress as they saw the black bruise already beginning to blossom on her right cheek. They'd rushed forward and wrapped her in a hug, pelting her with a mix of frantic questions, outrage, and condolence. Her mother had yelped when she saw the ragged gash in Anji's forearm.

Tears in her eyes, her mother had applied a vinegary salve to Anji's stinging face, while her father cleaned and wrapped the wound on her arm. Then they'd gathered around the table for a small, subdued dinner. Anji had had to chew on the left side of her mouth, as the right side hurt so much. After dinner, Anji had helped clear the table and wash their few dishes, then they'd eaten Anji's cake in an awkward silence, her father muttering to himself, her mother darting worried glances at Anji, as though she would crumble into dust right in her chair. Only after Anji had reassured them that the mugging was over, that she was all right, that she would be more careful, had her mother finally gone to sleep, leaving Anji and her father alone at the table. They'd sat together without speaking for an interminable time, cinnamon-scented candles burning low.

"Do you want to talk about it?" her father had murmured, his eyes red with lack of sleep, brow knitted in a deep crease. He had to be dockside at dawn, but he'd stayed up with her, clasping her small hand in his large, callused one. Anjisaid no . She'd fought off the muggers—two ragged kids, little older than her—and that was enough. She hadn't even had anything for them to steal. She'd been shaken up, embarrassed, and her face hurt from the lucky punch one of the idiots had gotten in, but all in all she'd felt mostly okay. Angry, more than anything. The cut didn't even hurt anymore. It was her parents who had seemed the most upset by the whole affair.

Then her father had let out a heavy sigh, unclipped the blade from his belt, and ran a thumb across its edge.

"You shouldn't have to have it," he'd said, his voice hoarse. Then he'd cast around at their basement as though seeing it for the first time. "Your mother and I . . . we're working for something different. I wish so badly the world was just and kind, Anji. I wish people weren't so desperate. I wish . . ." He'd held back a sob.

Anji reached out and—

Manacles jingled, heavy on her wrists. She grasped at empty air. Someone coughed.

"Easy now."

The familiar scent of horse filled her nose, and she blinked and sat up straight, opening her eyes to pale sunlight, the plains spread around them like a rippling tablecloth. Ahead, enclosed by a wall of stone, lay a sprawl of rooftops interspersed with nearly a dozen gigantic windmills, their sails turning in lazy circles. Puffy clouds sped along above, tinged gold at their edges by the sun crawling toward the western horizon.

The Hawk rode at her side, mask raised over her head, face drawn, sea-green eyes glassy and distant.

"How long have we been riding?" Anji said, rubbing at her eyes.

"About . . . ten hours," said the Hawk, squinting at the sun.

Anji wiped sleep from her eyes, wincing at the lancing pain in her knuckles. The blistered wounds seeped a viscous, shiny fluid. She glanced at the town ahead. "That place have enough windmills?"

The Hawk said nothing.

"Water?"

The Hawk thrust a canteen at her, gaze still fixed on the road. Anji took it and drank deep, the tepid water dribbling down her chin. She chanced another question and asked where they were headed, and to her surprise the Hawk answered:

"Kiva," she said. "We're just passing through. I've an acquaintance there who owns an inn. We need to see to your wounds before infection sets in." She looked down the trail at their backs. "The others will follow. We may be half a day ahead of them. They'll be slower on one horse." Then she patted one of the Goat's saddlebags. "They don't have their scrying sheet either. That will buy us some time."

Anji was hardly listening. She looked down at her mangled hand, at the grisly gap between ring finger and thumb, and realized right then that she didn't care where they were going, as long as it wasn't back to the cathedral, back to the Menagerie.

Or what's left of it, she thought, allowing herself a satisfied smile. But something was still nagging at her.

"So," she said, "your name is Kit?"

The Hawk exhaled a long breath. "She shouldn't have used it. Not in front of you." She reached for the canteen. "Not that it matters now, I suppose."

Anji stoppered the skin and handed it back.

"You shouldn't have killed her," Kit said, her face hard, still not looking up.

Anji gaped. "I shouldn't have—" she sputtered. "I had to— another few seconds and she would have—"

"I was fine!" Kit yelled, startling a pair of black birds out of the foliage bordering the trail. They cawed and flapped away toward the distant mountains at Anji's back. Kit tugged on her horse's reins. She looked at Anji, her face drawn and haggard. "I had everything under control and you had to go and pull something cheap, something cowardly like that. There was no honor in what you did."

Anji scoffed. "You'd be some distance from your bounty with your guts spilling out on the rocks and them riding off with me if I hadn't done something. You should be thanking me!"

"Thanking you!" Kit rasped, her sarcastic laugh turning into a rattling cough. She cleared her throat, eyes piercing into Anji's. "Thank you for what, exactly? This whole farce of a trip has been a disaster from the moment I plucked your miserable hide from that tavern. I should have left you there to rot."

"I wish you had!" Anji said, heat rising in her cheeks. She'd saved the woman's life. She could have sat and watched the Ox cut into her, could have watched Kit's feeble attempts at defending herself and not done a thing. "You want to lecture me about honor?" She held up the ruin of her hand, manacles clanking. "Look at what they did to me! They cut my fucking fingers off! They killed my—" Tears seared at her eyes. "They tortured—"

And every terrifying, agonizing aspect of the previous week, every feeling she'd ever felt rose in a churning mass, like a kettle boiling over. The frantic escape through the north, the Hawk snatching her away, the fight with the Scorphice, the Goat's hand around her throat. The cathedral. The Bear.

Sharp metal clicking through bone.

Anji slammed her hands against the saddle, pain slicing through her wound. Then she screamed, her eyes shut tight. She let loose the knot that had been tightening inside her with each passing day, with every unfair hurt, every lonely second she'd spent running and fighting for her life.

"I can't do this anymore!" she screeched, cradling her mangled fingers. "I wish you *had* poisoned me. I wish you'd just fucking kill me! That's what you want, isn't it? Why don't you just do it, then?" Then her anger lifted its mask to reveal the sorrow beneath—the fear and confusion she'd borne and shoved down deep. Anji slumped against the horse's mane and choked out a sob, then another, until the torrent of tears came. Snot bubbled from her nose as she sat up, and she wiped it away.

"Please," she said, sniffling. "Please kill me. Just end it. I can't—I can't—" Her lungs were on fire, vision fogged over with tears. She slid off the horse, falling to her knees before the Hawk. The earth spun under her clutching fingers. A bead of blood dripped from her wound into the dirt. "Please, Kit, don't let them cut me again! Please!"

Then the Hawk slid from her own horse, her boots thudding into the ground.

"Get up, you moronic—"

Anji grabbed at the Hawk's boot, but the woman kicked her hand away with a snarl. The horse behind her nickered.

"You're so selfish," said Kit.

Anji's eyes went wide, and the anger came back with a fury so deep it drowned the fear. She pushed herself to her knees, still sniveling. "*I'm* selfish?" she spat. "You're about to trade *my* life, watch me get tortured, for some money! What could I possibly have done to—"

"Everything! Everything you've begged and cried about, killing Rolandrian, killing Ox—my damned horse is even dead because of you. Are you incapable of considering *anyone* but yourself?" Anji blinked up at her, mouth working.

"I didn't—"

"You think you *saved* me back there? You think you somehow saved Yem by murdering one old man? You've no notion of the damage you've caused! No inkling of the wider world around you. You think the miseries Yem's people endure are a snake with a head to be lopped off, and then like *maxia* everyone will be rich and fat and happy again? There are forces and systems in place you haven't even *attempted* to understand. You think you're the only child with dead parents? Look around you! The world is filled with starving orphans. You and I saw the same Silverton, did we not? We'll see the same in Kiva and Tideron and you'll see more in Linura before you die. The whole country is headed for ruin and you've practically sealed its fate because of your anger—your childish, ignorant bid to make a change when you know nothing of what that change could mean."

"I don't—"

"The Wardens, girl! They were vying for control while Rolandrian was still warm, making deals, clasping the country tighter in their grip than it already was—all under the guise of *order*. They'll set curfews. They'll start rounding up entire families. Public executions in Laurelside, in Mudtown, common turning on common. Many and more will suffer the same as you did: starving, freezing, without their parents. Was it worth it? Was it worth your petty fantasy?"

"You can't—"

"And now you want it all to end!" The Hawk barked a laugh.

"You were afraid of the consequences, so you ran, and now that those consequences are marching you back, you want to run again! Well, I won't save you—I'll not prevent your torture nor your execution. It will be the only decent thing you've done with your pathetic life."

Anji choked out another sob. "What difference does it make? If I'm going to die anyway, please just do it now! Haven't I gone through enough? Aren't you satisfied?"

The Hawk slapped her.

"This isn't a gods-damned story, you stupid girl! You think a little suffering makes you innocent? You think you've earned something? What good is your pain if you learn nothing from it?"

Anji held a hand to her stinging cheek, her lips trembling.

Kit sucked in a labored breath. "Get back on the horse."

"No," said Anji, wagging her head. "No, please, don't make me—"

The Hawk seized her arm and yanked Anji to her feet. "I said get up."

"No!" Anji screamed, batting at Kit's hands. She stumbled away, panting. "Why are you doing this? They said you'd left, that you weren't keeping the tenets. You're not working for the Wardens, for the Senate. What could you possibly need a million Rhoda—"

"That's not your—"

"You killed *royal* guards!" Anji said, pointing down the road. "You killed the Lynx! Your own friend! So tell me why you won't kill me right here. I deserve to know. I saved your life, you owe me—"

The Hawk snarled and leapt forward, and before Anji could dodge away the sky whirred past and her back slammed into the ground. She sputtered with the force of Kit's knee pressing into her chest.

"I owe you nothing!" the Hawk screamed in her face. "You hear me? Nothing!" Then she winced and began to cough, a crumbling, rattling choke Anji could feel through Kit's knee. The Hawk spit something black into the road, swatting Anji's flailing hand aside. Breathing hard, she reached up and grabbed at her horse's saddle, unwound a coil of rope, and tied it deftly to Anji's manacles. "Up. And not one more word, or I'll cut off another finger." She shoved off of Anji and tottered toward her horse.

Anji writhed in the dirt, her tears spent, gasping in cold air. Harness jingled as the Hawk climbed into her saddle, giving Anji hardly any time to haul herself up and into her own before the length of rope tightened, pulling her toward Kiva.

✦25✦

Black clouds hulked over Kiva as they approached the main gate. The thunderheads obscured the setting sun, casting the towering stone walls in a burnt glow. A pair of constables in bright yellow tunics stopped them, their eyes lingering on Anji's manacles. But one look at the Hawk's mask had allowed them passage without issue.

Kiva's famous windmills, so huge from a distance, were positively gigantic up close. Their sails revolved far above other buildings, canvas flapping, the huge frames groaning on giant axels built into bulky plaster structures. As they came to their first intersection, Anji and Kit passed close enough to one of the mills that they could hear the buzzing and clunking of machinery inside. The huge blades dipped between rooftops, nearly grazing the ground before ascending once more.

"You didn't even have to show your note," said Anji, now sparing a glance toward the open gate at their backs. She turned back to see Kit tipping some Rail onto the back of her hand. Kit lifted her mask just enough to snort the little pile, then stowed the thin green vial back in her leathers.

"Won't someone see—"

"It's fine," said Kit, clearing her throat. She adjusted the mask and tugged Anji's rope, leading them down a broad, crowded street as thunder crackled overhead. Lightning flared past Kiva's high wall, which surrounded the entire city.

"Let's be quick," said Kit, snapping her reins. Anji hardly had to urge her mount to follow.

Kiva's denizens gave her and Kit a wide berth, parting like water before a ship. Most hurried on without a second glance at the Hawk, but a few whispered and pointed as they passed. Their dress was simple, yet sturdy, their faces clean of any dirt or grime. Nobody was particularly fat, but neither were they as emaciated as the few people Anji had seen in Silverton. She wondered about the little boy with the doll, cold and frightened and missing a shoe. Where was he now? Anji's thoughts darkened with the weather, drifting from the boy to her friends. Kaia gushing about a pretty noble she'd seen. Libby showing Anji her hidden stash of pasties she'd kept under her cot. Anji blinked at Kiva's buildings as they rode. Libby had mentioned her dream of someday attending the university at this city's heart. Something involving medicine or herb lore. Libby had loved plants. She'd loved helping, when she could.

She'll never go to that school now.

Anji's horse followed the Hawk's through a cramped intersection and into a wide square surrounded by shops and three-story tenement houses. Below, the square's perimeter was lined with carts and wagons selling their wares, some packing up under threat of rain and the deepening dark. Regardless of the coming storm, however, the square teemed with people. Constables milled about amid the crowd, easy to spot in their yellow capes, but they simply watched. Some of their expressions were even bored. Despite the presence of constables, the air of anxiety Anji had felt in Silverton wasn't as thick here. It reminded her more of the natural, bustling-city energy she'd forgotten even existed in the six years she'd been trapped in Linura castle.

Anji considered her manacles, her mangy appearance. The thought of escape still tugged at her with every step toward Linura. The maxial tether around her ankle had been cut. She could chance the Hawk's exhaustion, her ability to hold on to the rope tied to Anji's manacles if she hopped off the horse and sprinted away. She could lose herself in the crowd . . . but what then? A filthy, maimed, and chained girl tearing through streets filled with constables and upstanding citizens about their business. The image didn't inspire much confidence that anyone would lend a helping hand. This wasn't Silverton, or some run-down bar in the far north. The people here seemed tolerant of the constables in their yellow finery, if not wholly content. And if indeed there were people, even here in Kiva, who were sympathetic to Anji and what she'd done, what could they do? Would they take her in? Give her a job? Would they lie for her when the Wardens came to their doors?

Of course not.

There were also her injuries to consider. She scanned the ugly stumps where her fingers had been the night before—they needed attention from this innkeeper friend of Kit's, or infection would surely set in. Anji scowled at the woman pulling her along.

Can't have me dying before we get to Linura.

A bell clanged somewhere distant, and the Hawk led them around the square's perimeter, sawing at her reins as a gang of squealing children sprinted across her horse's path. Anji watched the kids weave across the square until they joined a dense tangle of people gathered before an elaborately carved wooden box, its front an awninged window housing a trio of puppets bobbing back and forth, smacking at each other and shouting unintelligible lines. A constable stood to one side of the stage, a hand clapped around the hilt of her longsword, her face severe. And on the stage's other side, his eyes watching the crowd like a hungry dog, a Sun Warden in bright yellow robes.

"This way," said the Hawk, snapping Anji's gaze away from the puppets. The crowd's noise crawled after them through the maze of streets, finally receding as Kiva's wall came into view once more. The sun was sinking past the wall's crenellations now, casting long shadows on the cobbles underfoot, the cracked stones upturned and disorganized from what had once been a symmetrical design. Where the streets had been broad and clean before, they'd narrowed into trash-lined alleyways hemmed by grimy brick homes. Laundry flapped on lines strung between the shuttered windows above, and every square inch of unused wall had been plastered with posters, their moving images and words distorting the dimensions of the street, making the walls seem to shift as Anji continued on. Hardly anyone pushing past looked at Kit and Anji. The sour tang of unwashed bodies hung heavy, mixed with the stench of burning coal and oil. Aside from grungy apartments, most space was taken up by hulking buildings that belched greasy smoke from brick chimneys. A whistle squealed from above, and a large wooden door creaked open to Anji's right, emitting a group of adults and children wearing matching gray clothes, their faces smudged with dirt, their eyes downcast.

Anji could hardly believe that only a few streets away stood another crowd of people enjoying themselves, drunk and well-fed and laughing. She felt like she'd entered a wholly different city, one where children worked in factories alongside their parents, where any semblance of joy or comfort seemed stolen from the air. There were no puppet shows here.

You think you somehow saved Yem by murdering one old man?

Anji blinked her dry eyes. Heavy clouds crawled across the

sky. The smell of the sea to the east rode lightly on the breeze, kissing her nose, wafting through her blood-matted scalp. She looked down at her manacled hands. Blood had caked under her fingernails once more. She pushed down a wave of nausea.

"The inn with the red roof," said Kit, her voice so quiet Anji had to ask her to repeat herself. Kit pointed down the lane with a shaking hand to a lumbering brick-and-timber inn sitting in the shadow of Kiva's wall. Its dusty latticed windows were dark, the sagging shingled roof in desperate need of repair.

"Come on," said Kit, jerking the reins.

The inn stood three stories overhead, silent and grimed with mud and dirt where the walls had once been whitewashed. Kit fixed the horses' reins to a vacant hitching post, lifted the blue bag over one shoulder, then turned and unfastened the rope from Anji's manacles and tossed it to the ground. A ragged, rasping breath issued from behind the mask, and Anji realized she'd hardly heard a word out of the woman since they'd entered Kiva. Kit leaned slowly to one side, then righted herself with a shuddering step.

A shout echoed down the street from some unseen source, followed by the crack of breaking glass. Kit grabbed Anji's manacles in one gloved fist and pulled her toward the inn stairs. She swayed on her feet on the first step, shoulders rolling with a rumbling cough as she took the next.

"You're taking too much of that stuff, Kit—"

"I'm fine, girl, stop your chattering," said Kit, though her words slurred, like she'd drunk a barrel of wine. She took the last step, gave Anji's chain a final yank, and spewed a thin trickle of thick black fluid from beneath the mask onto her leathers.

"What the fuck!" Anji jumped aside as the Hawk rocked away, then slumped into Anji with so much momentum they both nearly tumbled down the steps. Anji held the woman in quivering arms, her hand flaring with pain. She sputtered and scanned the cluttered mass of run-down houses, sloping roofs of thatch and broken tile—some windows were either broken out or boarded up. The street was nearly empty now.

Anji grunted, "Wake up!"

Kit didn't stir—she could have been dead for all Anji knew. The blue bag dropped with a clatter from her limp hand. She thought she would drop Kit there on the ground, wounded hand screaming as she propped up her dead weight. The Hawk was small, to be sure, but so was Anji, and she was at the last of her strength now. Her knees quivered, and she almost dumped Kit's lifeless form to the wooden steps when the inn's door creaked open.

A man stood in the narrow gap between the door and the stone entryway, weak sunlight reflecting off his circular spectacles. His eyebrows lifted past the frames. He held a short crossbow in one hand, aimed at Anji as she struggled to hold Kit up.

"Kit? What are you—"

Anji shouldered past, shoving the man to the side. He might have a problem with her, but she'd rather deal with it inside than out in the street.

The light in the inn was near nonexistent, but Anji found the rough outline of a wooden high-backed chair and settled Kit into it, then collapsed to the floor. A tiny fire smoldered in a dusty black hearth in the main room's corner. Anji drew her knees to her chest and blinked, letting her eyes adjust to the dark.

A door crashed open behind the bar, seemingly of its own accord. Anji inched back against a table leg. She glanced up at the bespectacled man now striding across the room, the front door slamming shut at his back.

"Back in there, if you please," he said, motioning toward the bar, making a shooing motion with one hand. "Last time you left the stove you nearly burned the whole—"

"Who is that?"

A short, black-haired boy leaned around the paneled bar, green eyes wide and sparkling. He grinned at Anji, revealing an empty space where his two front teeth should be.

"Berip. Now." The man pointed back to the kitchen.

Berip threw Anji another gap-toothed grin and darted behind the bar, the door creaking open and slamming closed once more.

"Kids," the man said, running a hand over what remained of his hair. "Can't seem to keep him in one spot. You know how it is."

Anji didn't, but right then she also didn't care.

"On the steps," she said, her voice a croak. She scrabbled to her knees. "There's a bag, I need to—"

"I'll get it," the man said, raising the bow. "And get up off the floor for the Nine's sake." He pointed to another chair near the one Anji had dumped Kit into and was out the door before Anji had a chance to protest, though he kept it propped open as he crouched over the steps.

Anji rubbed at her arm and eased herself into the chair.

The room came into further relief as her eyes adjusted. Second-story windows let in weak shafts of pale, mote-filled light. The common room was cozy—a neat double row of tables and chairs, mismatched in height and grain but sturdy and clean. The fire popped under a brown brick mantel crowded with fat yellow candles and dusty wooden picture frames. A stout, wiry potted plant stood in the opposite corner, its leaves thin and yellowing, but alive. Frayed rugs ran the length of the empty walkway leading to a polished bar, with another door behind that must have led to the kitchen. An inn if she'd ever seen one, but this one was empty. That was a first.

The place smelled like dust and wood and stale beer, and she caught the acrid aroma of turmeric drifting out from the kitchen, along with the clatter of utensils and pots as Berip bustled about behind the door.

Her heart jumped as the man let himself back in, the blue bag in one hand, crossbow still perched in the other. He closed the door behind him with a solid click, then kneeled and surveyed Kit, his bow still trained on Anji.

He was old. Or, at least, older than Anji. She'd put him in his late forties or early fifties, but he'd obviously avoided an abundance of the drink he served. His round spectacles took up most of his face under a wide forehead grown wider by a receding line of gray and black hair. His thin lips were curled at the edges, like tiny hooks had been set in the lines of his sallow cheeks. He had no chin to speak of, but Anji thought he looked pleasant. Handsome even.

"That bag is mine," said Anji, pointing.

The man peered at Anji. "No, it isn't," he said, then stood and gestured at the ceiling and spoke before Anji could retort. "Let's get her upstairs, then," he said, not asking Anji what a girl in chains was doing in his inn or why she'd dumped an unconscious, vomit-covered bounty hunter into its common room. She opened her mouth but he held up a thin hand.

"Peace," he said, holding up the bag. "I've no quarrel with you, but this isn't mine to give. Let's get her in a bed and you can tell me what's going on. Over some food—and a drink, I think."

Despite herself, and the second crossbow held on her in as many days, Anji relaxed. She watched the man lift Kit easily over one shoulder, then motion for Anji to precede them up the narrow staircase onto the second floor and down a dim hallway where they stopped at the last room on the right.

"It's unlocked," said the man at her back. "Go in and sit on the bed to your right."

Her jaw tensed, Anji opened the door and sat on one of two thin mattresses piled high with down comforters on either side of a compact bedroom. Kit made a hitching sound in her throat as the man nestled her onto the opposite bed, but her eyes stayed closed. He slipped Kit's swords and knives out of their sheaths, the bow wavering, though still pointed at Anji. He opened a closet beside Kit's bed, then placed the swords, knives, and blue bag inside before locking the door with an iron key. Then he pointed toward the hallway.

Anji waited in the hall as he closed the door silently at his back, unsure of what to say.

"Sorry about that," he said, lowering the crossbow. He rubbed at the back of his neck. "Precautions, you know."

"I get it all the time," said Anji.

"You're wounded," he said, nodding to Anji's wrist.

"A bit," she said, her brain swimming.

He only let a steady breath through his nose, then without a word strode past and motioned for Anji to follow.

She was still in the hall as he descended the steps, wondering what the hell she was supposed to do now. The man—Kit's friend, allegedly—had just robbed and disarmed the Hawk and locked her things in a closet. Anji found she respected his cheek, even putting aside her confusion.

"She'll be fine," the man said from the stairwell, noting her hesitation. "I'm Jared, by the way. Let's get you something to eat."

⊰26⊱

"Berip," said Jared, ushering Anji through the kitchen door, "we have company."

The black-haired boy who'd appeared behind the bar earlier was now perched on a tall stool in front of an ancient-looking stove. A copper pot the size of his torso belched steam as he stirred with two hands, his face fixed in a concentrated frown. He cast a furtive glance at Anji, his eyes wide, then set back to work without a word as she stepped further into the narrow space.

Shelves ran the length of the walls, packed with glass jars containing various spices and ingredients, some Anji had seen and others she couldn't have guessed at. Cast-iron pans and dented tin pots hung from a rack bolted to the wooden ceiling over an island littered with cutting boards and wood-handled knives. In the room's corner sat a round brick oven, a hazy orange glow pulsing from within. Every inch of counter space was taken up by crates, racks of utensils, or dishes.

Jared clapped his hands together. "As you can see, we don't keep very organized."

"*You* don't," said Berip from his stool. He pointed at Jared,

207

green eyes now fixed on Anji. "He's messy—leaves his stuff all over the place. And his feet stink."

Anji blinked, still a bit frazzled. Less than a day ago she'd been held down and mutilated, and now here she stood, witness to good-natured, domestic bickering in this cozy little kitchen. The smell of turmeric wafted stronger in here, and she felt another wave of dizziness rack her head and her knees weaken with the mix of heat, fumes, and the throbbing pain in her hand.

"Over here," Jared said, touching her gently on the shoulder and leading her around the island counter to a burnished wooden table shoved against the only available space across from the little area where Berip worked. The boy stared wide-eyed at Anji but turned his back to her as he began stirring once more at a giant pot. "Berip, the salve and some vinegar, if you please."

Anji settled into a rickety rosewood chair and breathed through the pain as Jared sat at her side. He produced a folded heap of cloth that jangled as he unfurled it, revealing multiple instruments: a scalpel, razor-thin shears, a stack of cotton squares, a needle and spool of black thread, and a coarse wire brush balled into a tight knot.

"Are you sure you know how to—"

The door squealed open. Berip darted to the table's edge and set two fist-sized glass jars onto the burnished wood, his eyes darting to Anji before settling on Jared.

"We're almost out of this," said Berip, tapping the lid of one the jars.

"Thank you, Berip," Jared said, and began unscrewing the jar.

Berip grinned at Anji. "I burn myself a lot." Then without another word he scampered around the island and back onto his stool.

Anji watched him, smiling to herself despite her pain, which seemed to be getting worse the longer she stayed awake. Jared cleared his throat and Anji whirled around to face the assortment in front of her. One jar contained a thin layer of a yellow and greasy substance, and the other held what looked to Anji like water, but burned her nostrils when Jared pried off the lid.

"This is going to sting like hells," said Jared, dipping one of the squares into the clear liquid, "but if we don't do something now it's going to get infected. Whoever cauterized the wound didn't do a great job."

Anji's stomach turned, and she inched back in her chair. The smell of the vinegar hit her nose, tangy and sterile and sharp. She didn't want even a drop of that on her skin.

"I know," said Jared. "But you'll lose the whole hand and worse if we don't—"

"Just do it," Anji said.

Anji felt a shaking at her shoulder and opened her eyes. Jared sat at her side, folding his medical tools back into the cloth.

"You passed out," said Berip across the table, slurping on a metal spoon. He giggled and slammed his hand to the wood. "Like that."

Jared smiled as he folded the bundle back together. "Makes for an easy patient. How do you feel?"

Anji sat straighter in her chair. The agony that had made her lose consciousness was now only an echo where her fingers had been. The white bandages were speckled with dots of red, but the pain was nearly gone.

"How did you," she croaked. "How—"

"He *used* to be a surgeon," said Berip. He draped his scrawny arms over the scuffed wood, tufts of black hair dangling over the ridge of his brow, then pushed a ceramic bowl across the table and let a spoon clatter next to it. "Eat up. It's really good."

Anji tugged the bowl close and stared down into it with muggy eyes. Bits of meat and potatoes swimming in a thick gravy. Her stomach lurched, a mix of nausea and aching hunger, and she set into the bowl like a wolf, ignoring the weight of the manacles. The stew singed her tongue, but she spooned every morsel while the boy looked on, his own bowl neglected at his side.

"He worked in a big castle and everything," Berip said, leaning an elbow onto the table top.

"Berip." Jared rolled his eyes to the ceiling.

Anji glanced at Jared. "Must have been a good job."

"It really wasn't—"

"He doesn't like talking about it much," said Berip. "Says he likes this better." He gestured around the kitchen. "Says it's quiet." Then he made a stern face and lowered his voice. " 'Apart from tossing the drunks out every night.' "

Anji guffawed and swallowed the last bite of stew, letting the spoon clatter into the bowl.

"Hey, she has a gap tooth!" said Berip, baring his little teeth. "Just like me!"

"Berip, don't point things like that out, it isn't polite."

"It's alright," Anji said, facing Berip. She stuck her tongue into the gap in her teeth. "My dad had one too. I used to stick Celdia between them."

"Don't give him any ideas," said Jared.

Berip giggled. "I wouldn't do that—that's stupid."

"Berip, please." Jared ran a hand over his face.

Anji leaned over the table, every muscle in her body tense and sore. She felt like she'd been pushed down a rocky hill and fallen into a tub of thorns. She wondered how much time had passed, and whether the Hawk—Kit—had woken up yet. She glanced at Jared's bundle of surgical tools and imagined herself spiriting away the scissors and trying them on the blue bag upstairs. If she could find something sharp enough, something like shears with some leverage, she just might be able to cut into the bag and get her things and be away before Kit had a chance to wake up and realize what had happened.

The boy fidgeted in his chair, and for a moment Anji thought he was about to leave, but he stayed put, fingering his spoon, rocking it back and forth.

"Are you gonna kill us?"

"Berip," snapped Jared, "it isn't nice to—"

The pot on the stove sputtered, steam hissing up around the lid. The lid toppled over and yellow foam bubbled over the rim.

"Nine!" Berip shot up from his chair, eyes wide, and scurried around the clutter and up onto his stool again.

Jared rose from the table as Berip fussed and cursed over the soup.

"Berip, what did I—"

"It's fine! I like it like this!" Berip made a shooing motion with one hand while he stirred the pot, a gesture that made him look older than what Anji guessed couldn't be more than twelve years.

Jared sighed, then raised an eyebrow to Anji and motioned at the kitchen door and the common room beyond.

"I've got something out here I need a hand with—I mean." His jaw dropped and he slapped a palm to his forehead. "Nine, I'm sorry, I only meant—"

A muscle twitched in Anji's cheek. "Don't worry about it," she said, lifting herself gently from the chair. "I guess I'll have to get used to that. I don't know how much use I'll be, but I suppose I owe you." She didn't feel much like doing any physical labor, but the kitchen was stifling and filling with more smoke and steam the longer she sat there. She wanted some air.

"Excellent," Jared said, then he rounded on Berip. "Turn the heat down and keep stirring, Berip. Not everyone likes crust on their soup."

Berip waved them out, little teeth dug into his bottom lip as he stirred.

✦27✦

The common room was still empty, but the fire in the corner had been stacked to a merry roar. A poster identical to the ones she'd seen plastered on the buildings outside was tacked to the brick above the mantel, depicting a Dredger crawling toward the viewer with a red-eyed, snarling face. The caption underneath read the same as it had in the bar so many days past. Anji heard a clink behind her and whirled to see Jared shutting the door to the kitchen with one hand and offering two green vials of dark powder in the other.

The vials rolled to a stop in Jared's outstretched hand, and Anji looked up at him, confused. "I don't—"

"Not for you," he said, jerking his chin to the ceiling. "I saw the black phlegm she hacked up on the steps when I went out to get that bag of hers. She's thinner than I've ever seen her. I haven't checked under her clothes, but judging by her weight and the rattle in her throat, she's started to turn."

Anji thought of the Dredger Hectate had shown her, dragging its snout against the floor of its cage, its scaly gray hide scratched and seeping dark blood, the frustrated animal whimper as it snorted up dirt. A log cracked in the fire, bringing Anji's attention back to the common room and the man standing before her. She looked at the dusty rafters, at the poster above the fire, running her tongue along her teeth.

"I thought she had more time . . ." she said, the words trailing away.

"How often is she using?" said Jared.

"I don't know," Anji said. "I've only seen it a few times."

Jared nodded slowly, though her answer didn't seem to satisfy him. Anji couldn't fault his concern. The Hawk had puked up something vile on the steps outside, then passed out and hadn't yet woken up. If that Maxia, Alphoronse, was correct about his description of the drug's enhancing properties, it explained a lot about the woman's prowess despite her old age.

She's likely dosing herself as often as she can afford.

As though he were reading her mind, Jared adjusted his glasses, then took Anji's hand and set the vials clinking into her palm, closing her fingers around the glass.

"The change is visible on the torso first," he said, placing a hand to his chest. "Then the arms, hands . . . you'll see it in her neck soon, as it's the only bit of skin she's got showing. Since you're traveling, she needs to keep the mask on in public. Her eyes will turn bloodshot, then the irises will go red too. The teeth will lengthen. Her face will be the last to transform." He sighed and pointed at her hand. "This stuff is expensive. See that she parcels it out till you . . . till you get where you're going."

Anji gripped the vials tight in her hand, then looked up at Jared as she stowed them in her coat pocket. "How did you know?"

Jared shrugged. "I treated addicts for years. Not Dred—" He swallowed. "Not Rail addicts, specifically. But you don't need to be an expert to see her time is running out." He inclined his head at the vials in Anji's pocket. "That's to start weaning her off. If she doesn't quit soon . . ." He chewed at his lip.

"She mentioned something about quitting," said Anji, surprised at the defensive tone in her voice. "Once she got back to Linura . . ."

Jared clenched his jaw, his eyes cast toward the crackling fire and the creature depicted above it. Then he sighed and pointed to Anji's pocket. "Well, see she gets that. If she stops too quickly it could kill her."

"Why don't you give it to her?" Anji asked. "You think she'll take my advice?"

Jared laughed. "She's never once taken mine." He clasped his hands together and stepped around the bar. "Berip doesn't know I smoke," he said, plainly uninterested in speaking more about Rail. "But I'm headed out for a roll. Would you murder me if I offered you one?"

Anji groaned. "I'd murder you if you didn't."

They filed outside, letting the door close with a quiet thud at their backs. Jared leaned against the splintered wall of the inn and began rolling two cigars. Anji took the rolled-up wad of paper and cadroot he handed her, leaned forward into his lit match and inhaled the sweet tang of the plant. Nothing had tasted so good in weeks. She rolled it between her fingers as Jared lit his and waved the match out.

"You've got me in the same room as her," said Anji, gesturing with the cigar to the floor above.

"And?"

"Aren't you worried I'll kill her?"

"As if she'd let you."

Anji narrowed her eyes. "You know I killed Rolandrian, right? That's why the Hawk has me."

Jared ashed his smoke. "The Hawk," he said, rolling his eyes.

"Did you know her?" Anji waved a vague hand. "Before?"

"I did. Back when she only went by Kit."

"She'll always be the Hawk to me."

"You weren't always a killer," said Jared. "Neither was she." He scratched at his unshaven whiskers. "We go back pretty far, me and Kit. Both of us ran with one of the Spurs in Linura. Roped real deep into that shit. She got caught up as far as you can go, stealing, getting everyone from royalty to the urchins in Mudtown addicted to Snip, Faze, Sundown, you name it. It's a dangerous business, running drugs. Turf wars, internal disputes, power grabs. And that's without the Senate on your ass. Or the Sun Wardens now, I suppose." He cast a long glance at the filthy street, its sparse traffic beginning to thicken as the work day came to a close.

"Anyway," he went on with a heavy sigh, "I got out. They trade in services sometimes, the Spurs. I had a deft hand and they put me through school for surgery, but as the years passed they wanted fresh blood and sold me off to a duke in Tideron. Had it pretty cozy there for some time, but the sight of blood and bone grates on you after a while. Still.I got off easy."

He sucked at his cigar and went on. "Kit though. She stuck around, making her dead drops, paying tribute, torturing debtors. Then one day she's told she has to kill her father."

Anji stared, nearly crushing the cigar in her frigid fingers.

"He wasn't too high ranked, but he was influential. Revolutionary type. Wanted to change things up. So they made an example of him. The Peak—that's the leader—had her gag him with his own belt. Then she tied him to a chair and slit his throat in front of the whole Spur."

Silence settled like a curtain between them. A gust of sour wind wafted down the street, blowing a ragged bit of cloth across the cobbles. The cigar's taste no longer interested Anji.

"How could she do something like that?" she finally said, her voice cracking.

215

Jared exhaled a plume of smoke. "She was too involved," he said. "By the time they'd asked her to do it, she would have done anything. That's the trouble with the Spurs. No matter how terrible your Peak, no matter what they might ask you to do, they're your blanket against the cold. They're your source of security. I bet she didn't even see him as her father at the time, just another thing she was commanded to do. Another task assigned to one in a score of lowly Nails, on pain of having to sleep in the street, of being turned out by your friends. Living on the edge of everything like that for so long, you do what's best for you and no one else. I tell her every time she comes out this way, which isn't often, mind you, that we have plenty of space for her. I think something keeps her in Linura. Maybe it's the crowds. The noise."

Anji huffed out the last of her cigar and smashed it underfoot. It hissed as it went out. "Why are you telling me all of this?"

Jared ran a finger along his pursed lips.

"I just thought you should know who's doing it," he said.

"Doing what?"

He gave her a bemused look. "Killing you."

Anji didn't say anything, just followed his gaze around the dilapidated street. She drew her coat tighter against the wind.

"She's just another person," Jared continued, flicking out his cigar's tip. He scraped his shoe over the glowing cherry and stooped to pick Anji's butt off the stones and stowed it into his pocket.

"Yeah, and so am I," Anji said, hating how petulant she sounded. She crossed her arms. "And I don't much like the notion of my skin being peeled off."

He hummed an affirmative as he stood back up, and Anji realized as they stood close together under the inn's warped wooden eaves how tall he actually was. She took an unconscious step back.

"Why are you being so kind to me?"

Jared lifted a shoulder. "Kit wouldn't bring you here if she thought you were any real danger to me or to Berip. Like I said, you and I have no bad blood. I don't care what it is you did or didn't do. To be quite honest with you, my life would be the same whether you were guilty or not—whether you lived or died. I don't see the point being rude to someone like that."

If there was an insult in his words, Anji had a hard time finding it.

"Besides," Jared went on, "you're tiny, you're manacled, and one of your hands will be out of use for some time. I think I like my odds. And Kit's."

Anji opened her mouth, then closed it again.

"She isn't doing it out of hate or rage," he said, "though that might be the way it seems. She believes she has to do this, just as you believed you had to kill Rolandrian. We're all just doing what we think is right, till the bitter end."

"Do you give this little talk to everyone she brings out here?"

Jared laughed. "You're the first she's brought, actually," he said, motioning for her to follow him back into the house. "Maybe she sees something in you she wanted the rest of us to look at."

Jared led Anji upstairs and into the corner room where Kit lay sleeping, still but for the slight rise and fall of her chest. Anji slipped off her coat and set it on the back of the room's only chair before turning to Jared to thank him for the food and the room.

But he was already swinging the door closed on its oiled hinges, mouthing a silent "goodnight" over the single taper he carried. The door shut with a muted click, and Anji sank onto the bed opposite Kit.

Wind rattled the latticed window, the crowd filtering into the common room below a rising confusion of shouts and laughter. A lute began to play, then a fiddle followed by a chorus of drunken voices. She liked the noise. Absolute silence had always made it difficult for her to drift off. She slipped off her trousers, her mangled shirt, and crawled in among the scratchy linens, favoring her left hand, the pain only a mild throb now. The thin mattress eased her muscles like a feather bed after so long sleeping on the ground.

Her last thoughts were of Kit, of what she'd had to do to survive, the sacrifices she'd made, the horrors she must have seen. But she found it hard to feel bad for a person so focused on seeing her executed. Anji wouldn't march a person to their own torture for any sum of money, regardless of what they'd done. The Goat's mask appeared in her mind like a phantom, followed by the Bear's—firelight glinting as the old woman cut into her skin. Anji pictured her own father tied to a chair, eyes pleading, a knife poised in her hand. She shuddered at the thought, then rolled over and drifted off.

⊹ 28 ⊹

Anji flicked aside the rough-spun curtains, staring through warped glass at Kiva's scattered rooftops and empty streets shadowed pink under the new-day sun.

Sleep had come for a few fitful hours before the gnawing at her knuckles had her up and pacing the agony off, until finally she'd dragged the room's lone chair under the window to watch the sun rise. The inn lay still and quiet as its few stragglers had been herded out—but as morning crept into the street below she'd begun to hear the familiar rumblings of a house coming awake: pots clanking in the kitchen, doors creaking open and clicking closed, an armful of wood tumbling into the fireside grate.

Their room was sparsely furnished. Drafty, but dry. Anji wondered where all the warmth from the night before had gone. She picked at the chair's grainy armrest and glanced at the closet door, heart aching at the closeness of her only remaining possessions. Kit murmured something in her sleep, her chest rising and falling in rapid, irregular hitches.

Anji still feared the aged bounty hunter, still flinched at those calculating green eyes, the potential in those seasoned hands. Anji had been instructed in combat, yes, but her training had been simple sport compared to Kit's vast knowledge and experience. How many dozens of hearts had Kit stopped? How often had she felt the gush of warm, sticky blood run out of the hole she'd made in someone's skin and onto her own? Anji slouched in the chair, legs splayed, and wondered if she'd ever amount to anything like the woman curled in the bed in front of her. Whether, on the slight chance she escaped this mess, she'd amount to anything at all.

Anji dug into her coat and fished out the two vials of Rail.

I could sell it all, she thought, rolling the smooth glass back and forth in her palm. *This alone could get me enough Rhoda to fund a trip up north.* She squeezed the vials, the cork stoppers digging into her skin. She *could* slip out. There were no bars on the window. Strangling the Hawk in her sleep had lost its appeal, but she could still try to escape. All she needed lay in wait in this room: the Rail in her hand, and her coin and dagger. Both in the blue bag locked in the closet.

Anji bent over the chair's armrest and dug at the wood with her filthy nails. Along the grain at the edge she could make out a sliver the length of her middle finger, long and sharp and surprisingly stout. Tongue between her teeth, she peeled off the wooden shard, then rose from the chair and crossed the room to the closet and knelt down. She jammed the makeshift lockpick into the keyhole and set to work.

She had no idea what she was doing.

Prisoners had mounted daring escapes in the stories she'd read as a girl using this method, though they'd had metal tools and she had only a bit of wood. She tried to imagine the inside of the lock, where the little stick was, but she didn't know if she was any closer to getting the door unlocked than she was to ruining the mechanism altogether. She cursed, her hands sweating, and rattled the doorknob in frustration.

The slap of leather on wood reverberated through the room. Anji twisted as the Hawk murmured and shifted on the bed. The journal the woman had been keeping had fallen onto the floorboards. Anji dropped her makeshift lockpick and crept to the little book, hazarding a glance at Kit. Still asleep. Anji settled herself to the floor, legs crossed, and opened to a random page.

Kit's writing was so small and densely packed Anji could barely make any of it out in the low light. She hunched over, faced the pages toward the window, straining her eyes to see the minute words. She flipped through a few more pages to find more of the same tight scrawl covering every bit of paper.

A hand grabbed her wrist.

"What are you doing?"

Anji yelped and dropped the book. She wrenched away, but Kit's grip loosed in an instant. The woman shot up from the bed, swaying a little on her feet. . She blinked and took the room in. "Where—?" she said, rubbing at her eyes. Her knees buckled as she stepped toward the window and Anji sprang to her feet, one hand held out.

"Sit," Anji said, and to her surprise, Kit eased back onto the bed, running a hand through her gray hair. She hacked a weak succession of coughs, mucus crackling like a rockslide. Anji dragged the chair closer and sat down as Kit lifted the journal from where it lay upside down on the floor.

"You read my—" she said, her lip twitching. "This is private. You had no right to look through—"

"It fell on the ground while you were sleeping!"

Kit fanned the pages once, as though to check they were all still there, then with a glare at Anji, shoved the journal back into the folds of her leathers. She wiped at her mouth. Her body quaked from head to foot, like something inside her chest had set to vibrating. She patted the side of her neck. "Still intact. What's that, a whole day without you opening someone's throat?"

"Nearly two," Anji said. She took a step closer, studying the area of skin on Kit's neck where her leathers ended. Still clear, as far as she could tell.

"What are you looking at?" said Kit.

"Nothing," said Anji, holding out her hand. "Found these for you."

Kit looked the vials in Anji's palm, her eyes going wide. She reached out a shaking hand but Anji snatched hers away.

Confusion crossed Kit's face, but it quickly shifted to anger. "Give me those."

"No," Anji said, lifting her chin. "Not unless you give my things back."

"And arm you in the process? I think not. Hand them over."

"You'll die if you stop taking it."

"Not before I kill you."

"Just the dagger?"

"Girl."

"The coin?"

Kit sprang from the bed with a snarl—

"Okay, okay!" Anji said, tottering back. "The manacles then."

The Hawk paused, already rocking a little on her feet.

"I could have killed you in your sleep," said Anji, "but I didn't. It's the least you could do."

Kit snorted. "The least I could . . ." she said to herself. She glared at Anji. "I would have woken up. There's no way—"

"You were dead to the world," Anji said, and after a long silence, "Please."

Kit's eyes rolled between Anji and her chains.

"Fine."

Anji had barely held out her hand before Kit snatched the vials and popped one of the corks with a practiced fingernail.

She sank back onto the bed and tipped black powder onto one quivering fingertip. She snorted, capping the vial as she tilted her head back. Some of the powder sprinkled to the floor, but Kit didn't seem to notice, and Anji didn't mention it. Instead she pointed to the closet door.

"The blue bag is in there, along with your swords. Still can't get the damned thing open. Once I do though—"

"Your father's dagger straight through the heart," Kit said, patting her chest. "I'm terrified." She blinked hard, the skin at the corners of her eyes bunching. "Where are we? The coast?"

"Kiva."

Kit stiffened, her mouth a thin line. "I told you we were riding *through* Kiva. Not stopping for the night. I specifically said—"

"Well, you didn't give me much choice, did you?" Anji said. "You passed out in the middle of the damned street. What was I supposed to do, leave you lying there for your old friends to find? They would have *actually* slit your throat, and I wouldn't have been any closer to getting my things back." She turned away. "Though I would have been rid of you at least."

"So that's it then?" Kit said. "You have to get the bag open, so you save my life, bring me in here and get us a room, and somehow buy me—"

She stopped, her eyes narrowed. She looked around the dingy room as though she'd never been inside an inn in her life. Anji twitched away from the finger Kit leveled at her.

"How did you pay for this?" She dug out the other vial and joined it with the first. "For these?"

"I didn't have to—"

"Wait." Kit reached for her belt where her pouch usually hung. "You stole my money?" She threw a spitting glare at Anji and stormed across the room to the bundle of clothes Anji had set atop the dresser at the window's edge.

"If you'd just let me—"

"Shut the hell up."

Kit rummaged through her things until she found her pouch and lifted it, Celdia clinking together inside. She wrenched it open, fished around with a finger, and glanced back at Anji.

"Well," Kit said, strapping the bag back to her belt, "you don't have a Celdia to spare yourself—".

"You made sure of that."

"How did you pay for the room?"

"Am I interrupting?"

They both whirled. Jared stood in the now open doorway, one spindly hand on the knob.

The room rang with silence. Kit opened her mouth, then closed it again, staring at Jared with wide eyes. Anji tried and failed to hide a grin and nearly broke the silence when Jared cleared his throat.

"Sorry about the linens," he said, straightening. He scratched at the corner of his mouth. "This room hadn't been used in a while and I—"

Then Kit did something Anji had neither heard nor ever expected to hear out of her. She laughed. Not a scoff or a snort. It was a small titter that grew into a rasping, relieved cascade. She sniffed and bounded across the tiny space, bare feet slapping on the boards, and into Jared's now outstretched arms.

Anji felt her cheeks flush and looked around the room while Kit said something unintelligible into Jared's shoulder. He held Kit at arm's length, wiping away a tear and coughing a choked laugh, his hands on Kit's bony shoulders.

"Food," he said, "and tea." He looked her up and down. "Maybe something a bit stronger."

Kit actually giggled, then let herself out of Jared's grasp and bent to the mattress to gather her things. She was nearly back to the door where Jared stood waiting when she caught Anji's eye.

The room rang with a terse silence, and Anji caught a frown twisting at Jared's mouth, but Kit spoke before either of them could.

"Up," said Kit, her face stony once more. She ran shaking fingers through her gray tangles and rolled her eyes to Jared. "I hope she hasn't given you any trouble. She isn't exactly—"

Jared held up a hand. "None at all," he said. "Let's eat."

⊹29⊹

Berip skirted around the table, hardly making eye contact with Kit. Anji sagged in her chair and relished her wrists' newfound freedom, the absence of the hunger that had taken root in her stomach over the last few days. The kitchen gurgled and creaked around her, steam wafting from the ever-churning stew on the stove. The little boy flashed his giant green eyes once at the woman sitting at Jared's side, then scooped up a dirty dish from the middle of the table and brought it to the wash basin.

"Quite the cook," said Kit, shoving her half-eaten bowl toward the table's center.

"He's not useful for much else around here," Jared said, not unkindly. He cast a look across the space at Berip who was now pushing a broom with mixed success across the floor on the island's opposite side. The scratching bits of straw filled the silence for a moment before Kit leaned forward across the table and grabbed Jared's veiny hand with her liver-spotted one.

"I meant to come back," she said, as though Anji wasn't in the room. "There weren't enough of us yet, and I didn't know—"

Jared waved away her comment, but didn't remove his other

hand from hers. "There's no need, Kit. I'm doing alright for myself here."

"We have the numbers now," said Kit, her voice even. Her slim frame was perched halfway over the table. "This job will more than cover bribes and supplies. There's a garrison stationed on the Everrun's western shore—out of sight, with more coming in every day. We could still do this. It's already happening."

These words brought a flurry of questions to Anji's mind, but she knew Kit wouldn't answer them. She took another spoonful of the stew and let a strip of meat disintegrate on her tongue, savoring the salty tang and toughness of something warm and spiced. Jared slipped his hand out of Kit's and settled his narrow chin into his palm.

"Politics. Scheming. No, Kit. I appreciate what you're doing and what you've got planned. Really, I do. But I'm out. Hells, you might have saved me another decade or two of running for my life. I can't stomach the garden-walk plotting or the back-door, smoke filled room–type things anymore." He winked at Anji and padded at his coat pockets. "Speaking of, I think I'll get some air."

His chair creaked as he eased up and sidled out of the smoky kitchen. Anji grinned at Kit.

"So," she said, raising a brow, "you two—"

"Not another word," Kit said, dipping back into her stew. Her face reverted to the hard planes and lines Anji had been so used to seeing over the last few weeks, as though the woman hadn't just spent the morning with an old friend. Anji raised both her hands and her eyebrows before joining Kit in silently lapping up the rest of their meal.

"He's been smoking a lot more lately," came a voice from near the stove. Anji looked around in time to see Berip's scrubby face emerge from behind the counter.

"A surgeon should know better," Kit said, running a finger

along the inside of her bowl. She sucked the last morsel of stew and leaned over the table's burnished surface, arms crossed.

Anji thought that was rich, coming from someone constantly dosing herself with Rail, but she remained silent. She pushed her bowl aside with a clatter and leaned back in her chair, relishing what might be her last shred of comfort. The warmth of this dingy kitchen reminded her of the intimate laundresses' quarters under Linura Castle. She thought if she closed her eyes the simmering pot and rickety plumbing of the inn might make her feel like she was home again.

"Surgeons smoke more than anyone," said Berip, sliding Jared's chair out with a loud scrape. He hopped up and set into his stew. Anji watched a dribble leak onto his chin and twitched to wipe it away, but Berip ran his forearm along his mouth. "He doesn't want to do it around me, but I don't mind. Whenever I smell it outside, on other people, it reminds me of him."

Anji watched him eat, those shocking green eyes not focused on anything and staring intently at everything all at once. She couldn't believe she'd ever been that small. He was so skinny, a runt if she ever saw one, but cute as hell. She wished she could bring him along with her and Kit, but then her stomach sank at the thought of what waited at the end of whatever road this was. At least after she died there would still be one child in a safe, cozy place like this.

He doesn't know how good he has it.

"Just don't start up yourself," Anji said. "It'll make you stink."

Berip wrinkled his nose and took another spoonful of stew. "Jared says I can't race if I don't maintain lung capacity." He pronounced this last word as though he'd just learned it, slowly, with all of his mouth. "I'm gonna be the fastest there ever was."

"You should see the races in Linura," said Kit. "The champions would overtake anyone from Kiva in a single lap. Some of the best runners I've ever seen. A fair few of them are graduated to messengers in the king's army."

"Not faster than me," Berip said, and Anji nearly cackled at the boy's unshakable confidence. "Just wait, I'll come to Linura and beat all those cows." He grinned and slurped another mouthful, legs kicking out from under the table.

"I'm sure you will," said Kit, rising from her chair. She stretched her arms out and shot Anji a look. "We need to be off."

The door to the kitchen cracked open and Jared appeared again, the waft of fresh cadroot sifting into the room to join the scent of cloves and garlic. Anji found she liked the smell as much as Berip did.

"Storm's coming in," said Jared, brushing raindrops off his coat. He crossed to the stove and blew out the flames at a low simmer under the pot. "Make sure this is packed and sealed, Berip," he said, clearing the counter of ingredients. Berip raised his bowl, drinking the last of the stew's dregs.

Jared looked around at Kit. "Leaving already?"

"We've taken enough of your hospitality," said Kit, not quite meeting Jared's eye. Anji stood from her chair.

"Thanks very much for the food, Berip," she said. The boy's jaw hung open.

"You're leaving? You just got here!"

"Yes, but we have to get to Linura," said Kit. She locked eyes with Jared, but he just slid the iron closet door key across to her and busied himself at the island counter.

"Kit's very busy with work, Berip," he said, then looked around with mock severity. "We can detail the kitchen today."

Berip groaned into his bowl. "We did that last week! How much cleaner could this place possibly get?"

With a wink, Jared jerked his head toward the common room, and Anji and Kit slipped through the door and made for the stairs, the sounds of a lively argument following them up.

⊹ 30 ⊹

"He's cute," Anji said, struggling with her bootlaces. "You could send me off to Conifor and stay here. No one would know."

"Quiet," said Kit from the room's opposite side. She'd returned her swords and knives to their sheaths and now sat on her mattress strapping her boots on. That finished, she gathered up her mask and clipped it to her belt, the blue bag's handle clutched in her other hand. Jared had left a canvas bag bulging with food and changes of clothes for them on Kit's bed, which she grabbed and pushed into Anji's arms. "Looks like we're packed. Are you ready?"

"Hang on," Anji said, scanning the room. "Oh yeah, you have everything I own."

"That wasn't funny the first time you said it."

"Not much of a joke if it's true."

Kit inhaled deeply and said, "You've still got your clothes and boots. I could ride you through town naked."

Anji raised her eyebrows. "You into that?"

A voice called from outside. Another answered. A cart rattled past on the stones, horse whickering.

"What were you two talking about?" Anji said, standing from the bed. "At the table. You mentioned something to Jared about having numbers . . ."

"If it concerned you I would tell you about it," snapped the Hawk.

"Fine, fine," Anji said with a mock sigh. "But I'm not convinced you—"

A wooden crash echoed downstairs.

"What was that?" Anji said, blinking around at the room.

"Be silent," whispered Kit, slipping her mask on. She moved across the room to the door, pressing an ear to the wood.

Another crash sounded. Harsh voices arguing.

"Berip and Jared are down—"

"I said *quiet*," Kit hissed, backing away from the door. "It's her. We have to leave."

Anji's heart hammered against her ribs. Her lower lip trembled. *Knife flashing, clicking through bone.* The pain flooding after, followed by that scouring darkness. She flexed her uninjured hand, now slick with sweat.

"What do we do? Nine, how can we fight both of them? I don't even have two working hands—"

"Stop," Kit spat. She pointed to Anji's other boot, still unlaced. "Tie that, listen to what I say, and keep your mouth shut or we all die."

The tone in Kit's voice gave Anji pause; she'd never heard the woman this . . . afraid? She chanced a look outside. "Maybe we could signal for help?" She turned to ask again when Kit didn't say anything but found the woman facing her, a knife in one hand. Anji's heart leapt into her throat and she took a step back.

Anji glanced at the window—thought about jumping out, about her chances grappling with Kit here on the floorboards. Kit crossed to her bed and sliced a long strip of cloth from the sheets.

She ripped the strip away and sheathed the knife, handing the cloth to Anji.

"Tie this around your nose and mouth," she said.

Anji hesitated, frowning, but took the cloth. Kit swung the bag around and crossed to the dresser.

"What the hell is going on?" Anji said, but she tied the cloth to her face regardless. Her voice was muffled under the moldy fabric as she said, "Are we robbing the place or something?"

"Shut up and listen," Kit said. She opened the bag and Anji felt a wave of embarrassed frustration wash over her as she tried and failed again to see how Kit opened it. The Hawk fished out a vial.

"Oh, we're just going to get high, is that the plan?"

"I said shut *up*," Kit hissed, jerking the bag closed once more. Anji snapped her mouth closed, studying the container. It looked much different from the vials of Rail Kit had been sniffing at. This one was bulbous and squat, made of a thick, clear glass much sturdier than the leaf-green vial of Rail. A sphere filled with amber powder, perfect save for the cork smothered with hard yellow wax.

Another crash issued from the common room below, followed by a tangle of barked commands and high-pitched yelping. Anji rushed forward but was stopped by Kit's outstretched hand. The Hawk's mask shifted in the dim light of the coming storm outside, traced in latticed shadows.

"Kit!"

They both twisted toward the room's door.

"That was Berip," said Anji. "We have to get down there—"

"We will, but you need to listen," Kit said, running a slender thumb against the sphere. "The cloth will hold most of it back, but try not to breathe until you're—"

"I don't understand why you won't—"

"Will you for once in your miserable life stop *fucking* talking," Kit said, holding a hand up, her voice so quiet a slight breeze would have drowned it out. Anji snapped her mouth closed. She glanced at the open door once more, and they both heard a sound like a hammer slapping meat followed by a grunt of pain and a tangled clatter of wood. Kit turned back to Anji. "If there was ever a time you would be silent and do as I say, let it be now, both for our sakes and theirs."

Then Kit squeezed Anji's uninjured hand, and she felt a rush of—was it comfort? Fear? Anji buried her questions, heart thundering against her ribs. Kit slipped the blue bag off one thin shoulder and piled it along with their other things unceremoniously into Anji's arms.

"When I throw this," Kit said, hefting the vial, "make for the front door. It will be difficult to see—you'll have to feel for it. You get outside, and ready the horses." She tapped at Anji's cheek, at the strip of rough cloth. "And be sure this doesn't slip. Got it?"

Anji blinked, still staring at the vial. The cumbersome bag didn't make for much of a weapon. She wanted to fight too. It felt odd, but she found herself picturing a battle in the dim common room, Kit at her side, the two of them fighting their way through countless brutes, though she knew there were only two.

"Girl," Kit said, snapping Anji back to the present. Her voice carried a pleading tone along with its usual stony force. The whites of her eyes shone bright in the shadowy room. A gust of wind shrieked through the drafty planks, sending the inn sign's iron hinges screeching. Anji swallowed and nodded.

The hall was darker than their room. Anji crept behind Kit to the stairwell, hurrying but trying to stay silent at the same time. As they gained the staircase, she spotted shadows flitting across the knee wall and scarred railing. The sounds below ceased as Kit straightened. She let her shoulders rise and fall with a steady breath, vial at her side. Anji was about to ask what Kit thought she was doing when Kit began walking down the stairs, head high, back straight. The steps groaned underfoot, ancient and splintered.

Anji followed down, digging for a shred of the same composure Kit held. *Get to the door. Get to the horse. The door, the horse.*

"Hawk!"

The common room's mismatched tables had been flipped over, their chairs knocked to the ground. The hearth still held a meager clump of orange coals, but if any heat emanated, Anji couldn't feel it. The sun's obscured glow filtered through the latticed windows, throwing diamond lines into the pool of soft light Kit walked into. Ahead of Kit, facing the stairs, were the Goat and the Bear.

✦ 31 ✦

Jared sat slumped over in a chair near the bar, his chest heaving. A streak of dark blood ran from his brow, dripping onto the flagstones beside his shattered spectacles. His fists were clenched, every muscle straining against the chair's arms, but no visible bonds held his wrists or ankles. The Goat stepped to Jared's side, a glowing rock curled in one finger. That hideous horned mask twitched toward Anji as she followed Kit down the steps, then shifted to Kit herself and watched her clear the final step and creep into the common room, the spherical vial held high in one hand. Jared let out a sob. One eye was closed in a nasty purple bruise. The other swiveled to Berip, struggling despite the vise grip the Bear had on his upper arms. Kit took a step forward, and the Bear slipped a slender dagger from her belt.

"That's far enough!" she said, moving the knife's edge to Berip's skinny neck. "You try anything and by the One's radiance I will open the boy's throat right here."

"Kit," breathed Jared, his voice weak. "Don't let them—"

"Keep him silent!"

The Goat sank a gloved fist into Jared's cheek, spraying a fount of blood in a wide arc. Jared moaned again, but said no more. The Bear rounded on Kit, her breath coming in sharp spurts behind her mask. Her neck muscles were strained, the sliver of her jaw tight and blooming red.

"Goat, I will interrogate the Hawk. For every hesitation, for every answer I mislike, you rip out one of the bartender's impious teeth."

"My pleasure, boss," said the Goat. The Bear's stoic white mask contrasted with the shaking rage of the voice beneath it.

"You will answer my questions, Hawk. Then you will give up your charge. You are no longer beholden to Menagerie tenets."

Kit said nothing, and enough time passed that Anji wondered if the woman had heard the Bear. She was about to speak herself when Kit's voice rang out from behind the mask.

"The girl is my charge by right of conquest and acquisition."

"Now she remembers the tenets," said the Goat. Let's get on with it, Bear. I didn't come here for a lecture."

"You didn't come here to die either," said Kit, her eyes not leaving the Bear. She hefted the vial above her head. "But you'll choke on your own blood in thirty seconds if you don't release that boy. Decide."

"Dabbling in maxia now, Hawk?" said the Goat, jerking his head at the vial. "How much will that piece set you back?"

The Hawk said nothing.

Anji felt the tension in the room like a harp string tightened to breaking. Jared's breath whistled through his lungs, and she wondered distantly if one had collapsed. Berip was still struggling, though the fight seemed to be leaving him. The common room swelled with silence. The tiny mound of coals cracked in the hearth. Anji flexed her feet, her uninjured hand tight against the railing. Her legs shook.

"Berip," said Jared, his voice wavering, "it'll be alright. Just do as they say." Anji's heart sank. He and Berip weren't wearing masks. She met Jared's eye as it swiveled from her to Kit.

"Bear," Kit croaked, "please. We don't have to—"

"We don't *have* to!" shrieked the Bear, wrestling the struggling Berip tighter in her arms. Anji's heart skipped in her chest. A red line had appeared at the boy's neck as he struggled. The Bear went on. "Of course we don't have to, Hawk! I command you to lay your arms down this moment! This was not part of Their decree!"

"There is no decree, Bear!" said Kit. "This isn't right! You can't—"

"Do *not* tell me what I may do!" the Bear screamed. "Why are you doing this? Why have you abandoned us? For her?" She jerked her head at Anji. "For these traitors and idlers? Have I taught you nothing? Have I *given* you nothing?"

Kit stood still, the orb full of orange powder still raised. The mask betrayed nothing.

"Waste of time, Bear," said the Goat. "Look at her hair. It's falling out as we speak. She'll be bald before we're through here." He raised his voice over another groan from Jared. "Had enough of that Rail, bitch? Looks to me like it's going to do you in soon."

Silence cut through the room apart from the crackling fire and Berip's continued struggles. The Bear rounded on Kit, her mask angled in a question. "Is this true, Hawk?"

Kit let a heartbeat of silence pass, then said, "Let us pass, Bear."

The Bear snarled and shouted, "A tooth, Goat!"

The Goat chuckled and said a string of tangled words, and before Jared could finish the pleading look he gave Kit, he screamed as a gout of blood welled from his mouth and a pearl-white tooth flew into the air and landed in the Goat's waiting palm. Berip yelled for Anji, for Kit, but Anji held her ground, reluctant to cause the boy's throat any more damage.

"Bear!" said Kit. "Stop this!"

"Answer my question, or on the One's own grace I will have Goat rip his heart out!"

Kit stiffened, and though it was the worst possible timing, hacked a cough so deep it rattled her mask and doubled the woman over. Everyone watched for an interminable time as Kit coughed and sputtered, then finally the Hawk straightened and looked at the Bear, gasping a little around the next words she spoke.

"I have it under control. I'm going to stop once I'm back to Linura—"

The Bear let out a strangled yell, so full of frustration and betrayal and anger Anji almost felt sorry for her. "Poison!" she screamed, her hands shaking. "You would defile yourself! You would dishonor your blood, when you were given *everything*! Is this why you left? Why you decided to shepherd this slut yourself?" She pointed at Anji with the knife, but then slammed it right back against Berip's throat and bellowed, "You made a blood oath to us, Hawk!" Anji could hear that behind the mask the Bear was crying now. "To me. To Ox and Lynx, who lie dead now by *your hands*! Do you deny it? Thirty years! Thirty years we've been friends. I loved you, Kit! You would be sniveling in some Spur's den if not for me, meting out Phase and Snip and all the other vile things the vermin smoke. And you chose to throw it all away? Why, Kit? Why did you do it? Why are you doing this?"

To Anji's surprise, Kit lowered the orb. She sniffed, and Anji realized she was crying too. "Just let the boy go, Bear. Let them both go, and I'll explain. I'll tell you everything you want. I didn't think you would listen to me, but I know if I just—"

"No!" the Bear screamed and gripped Berip even tighter, and now Berip wasn't struggling anymore, only staring at Anji and Kit, his fighting energy all but spent, his eyes pleading, understanding beyond what any child should endure etched in every plane of his face. "Shut your traitor mouth! You've gone too far! We will take the girl and leave your pathetic blasphemer corpse to rot. I'm done with you."

"Bear, don't, please—"

Time slowed. Anji watched as though from a great distance, as if a Maxia had somehow altered the flow of events. Jared sucking in a shuddering breath. The Goat twisting to face them, Kit raising the vial overhead.

The Bear dragging the blade across Berip's throat.

The world sped up as Berip's green eyes widened. He slapped a hand to his neck, but bubbles of dark blood were already welling from between his slender fingers. His mouth worked for air, and he locked pleading eyes with Anji before falling to the floor in a gathering pool of red already soaking into the planks.

Jared let out a wail so jagged Anji could actually feel the fibers of her heart contract. She gaped at the scene, and nearly dropped the bag down the stairs in her mad dash to get to Berip, to help, to shove all the blood back into his throat.

The Goat yelled a jumble of unintelligible words and smashed one of his glowing purple vials against his chest. Kit slammed her vial to the floor in a fluid motion with one hand as she raised her dagger in the other. The glass crashed, and with a complex word of instruction, everything went white. Anji had been expecting an explosion, but the only issuing sound was that of the vial breaking against wood, followed by a confusion of scuffling feet and shouts of alarm, followed by coughs and gasps. The shock of white seared into Anji's eyes for a heartbeat, then mercifully began to dissipate.

Disregarding the blur of motion below, Anji leapt down the stairs onto the common room floor as a cloud of acrid orange smoke began to fill the room. Her breath rasped under the mask as she darted through the confused tangle of blades and limbs. Jared lay on the ground on his side, his legs curled, holding the bloody form of Berip in his arms. He loosed a shuddering cry and

239

began to cough and retch. A weight plummeted into Anji's throat, and for a heartbeat she thought to scoop him up, wanted to drop down to help the lifeless body of the little boy she'd shared a table with minutes before, but her mangled hand was barely holding on to their bags, and she had to get outside to the horse.

I can't fuck this up. This one thing.

Anji twisted away from Jared as he hurled up another cough and began to convulse. She crossed through the tangle of tables and chairs, her thighs ramming against hard wood, knocking a stool clattering to the floor. The door was still ajar from where the Bear and the Goat had broken through, and she made for it. A hand caught her boot for a moment before she kicked it away and bolted out of the inn.

Oily black clouds swirled overhead. The street had begun to fill with Kiva's early morning crowd. The horses stood in a line where Kit had left them, huddled against the cold with another, tied to the single post. The Goat's gray rolled an eye at her as she approached and sidestepped. Anji knotted the bag to the saddle. She bunched the other things into their places, and loosed the lead line.

Her throat convulsed, and for a stomach-churning moment she felt her lungs hitch. She gasped, vision tunneling, felt a sliver of air through her nostrils. Her breath wouldn't come. She ripped the makeshift mask from her face and with a shaking hand grasped at the horse's saddle, straightening her back and gulping clean air. Sharp pain sliced through her chest, and she didn't know if it was the frigid air or the substance Kit had thrown or both. Had she inhaled it—whatever it was? Had the mask worked? She felt her heart racing more than it had inside, and what little light the storm overhead allowed began to dim. She couldn't feel her hands. She looked down at her maimed fingers, wiggled the remaining digits, and felt the world tilt.

Crashing and bellowing issued from the tavern, the scrape and clang of metal. Anji let go of the saddle and dropped to one knee. She gripped a tuft of weeds poking through the chipped cobble-stone and focused on it, as though holding on to the earth would right the spinning, fading sensation enveloping her every sense. She couldn't process anything but the immeasurable darkness creeping on the edges of her vision. Another cut of pain racked her chest, and she felt tears of fear and frustration and confusion bubble up at her eyes. The tears stung in the cold, and she wiped them away with her mangled hand.

It began to rain.

As the eddies of vague darkness closed in, the inn door burst open and Kit appeared, leathers flecked with dark blood. Anji watched the woman kick the door shut and spring down the steps into the street, favoring her left leg, but losing no speed as she came level with Anji and the horses.

Anji felt a tug on her upper arm, and the world spun once more. She waved Kit off.

"I can't—"

"Get on the damned horse or you die!"

A splintering, squeaking noise issued from the inn's facade and the door exploded out in a shower of stone and wood. The Goat thundered into the light, his monstrous horns nearly at a height with the second-story windows. He loosed a roar so loud it vibrated in Anji's chest, his eyes shut tight, claws swiping at empty air. Screams issued all around the street, townsfolk sprinting for cover. Doors and shutters slammed shut as the Goat stomped toward Anji and Kit, footsteps shaking the ground at their feet. He stumbled to one knee, still huffing and bellowing, black blood seeping from his eyes. As he fell, he gurgled and coughed and belched a gout of amber-coated bile onto the stones.

The Goat rolled onto his side, his limbs convulsing, kicking up broken cobbles and sprays of dirt. A final shuddering breath escaped his open maw and he lay still. His bulbous mask shimmered like an obsidian scab atop his broad, fur-lined head.

Anji felt a writhing in her throat and coughed up a dribble of vomit or blood. It was cold on her chin. Then she felt herself lifted from the ground.

"Up you get."

She cast about, confused—she was in the saddle. She looked down at Kit, who was now slapping at Anji's legs. Wood clattered inside the inn, followed by a strangled yell.

"The other one. Up. There."

The Bear crawled on hands and knees through the ruin of the inn's facade, her mask reflecting the dim light. It was smeared with blood and shattered on one side, revealing a single brown eye underneath, rolling in its wrinkled socket. It settled on Anji for half a second before the woman collapsed.

Anji swayed on the horse's back, but before she could fall Kit was behind her, reigns in hand, and the world lurched along with Anji's stomach.

She vomited all down her shirt.

The horse thundered down the lane, hooves clapping against stone. The saddle was too small for them both, the swells digging deep into her thighs. Anji tried shifting on it, gripped tight to the horn with her uninjured hand. She took a heaving, sobbing breath as though it were her last in the world. The dilapidated buildings raced past at an angle.

Air rushed past her ears and she slammed into the frozen dirt, searing pain shooting up her ankle and into the meat of her calf. Anji twisted in the mud, a moan bubbling out. She searched for the horse. Kit halted and dismounted, sprinting back to where Anji lay.

"Get up!" she barked, gesturing at the horse. "Get up *now*!"

Anji tried speaking through the pain, tried to voice the awful

242

clutching panic pulsing through her, but the agony was setting in now. All she could do was cry out and struggle to stand.

Kit growled and Anji felt strong arms around her torso. The ground drifted away from her aching face, drops of blood and spit and vomit spattering into the gray dust. She retched again. The world righted itself and she hopped along at Kit's side on one foot, one arm around the woman's tiny shoulder. She had no idea how she got back onto the horse. It must have been Kit's doing, but soon they were on their way again, bouncing along in the saddle, Anji's ankle throbbing, her breath shallow and uneven. Rain spattered against her cheeks, into her eyes. Lightning cracked somewhere up ahead, illuminating the world in a beautiful flash. Anji shivered in the Hawk's thin arms. Maybe Kit would just let her see the coin, the dagger. They were Anji's after all. They were hers. *Hers*.

A scattering of grubby townsfolk appeared at their doors as they sped out of town, but none stepped past the thresholds. Either they had no idea what had just happened, or they did and didn't want to get involved. Smart of them. Death followed wherever Anji went, wherever this woman took her. She was Death on horseback, shattered ankle and all. The Hawk had come after her and still she breathed, still she rode out from a massacre with only a bloody nose and a broken foot and a destroyed hand to show for it.

"Hang on," Kit said as they left Kiva behind, as the far horizon lightened, clouds roiling overhead. Anji held tight to the horse's mane, tears freezing on her cheeks, a shimmering dark veil sliding over the world.

"Hang on, Anji."

✦ 32 ✦

Bashing waves woke Anji from a fitful sleep. Rainclouds had followed them as they fled from Kiva—from a dead Berip and a dying Jared and whatever was left of the Menagerie. Anji had passed out multiple times, rain drumming on her face, shivering, and dreaming of Berip's tiny form lying in a spreading pool of blood. She saw his wide, accusing green eyes begging her to help, his throat a red bloom.

While Anji fought for sleep, Kit had hastened them toward the coast, muttering to herself and hacking her now ever-present cough. At last, as the storm at their backs gave up the chase, Anji had sunken into a longer darkness. When she finally regained consciousness she'd found herself at the edge of the world, covered in her own sick, a pounding in her temples and the clawing, knife-edge pain digging at her ankle with every motion of their mount.

Now Kit slowed the horse to a walk. Thunderheads grumbled above, iron gray with rain and dirty brown where the sun fought to shine as it set. The thin trail they'd found wound along a ridge overlooking the churning gray surf. Anji looked out across that wrinkling expanse, tears frozen on her wind-scarred cheeks.

Gods, I hate the fucking ocean.

The Kalafran consumed the eastern horizon, too big, too loud, and ever-crashing against the rocky shore below. Her father had romanticized the sea. He'd once told her the ocean meant freedom, but for Anji it was just a giant, mindless mouth that could swallow her whole. No matter how much she fought, the sea would always win. A bay she could handle. A lagoon or a lake or an inlet, all of no consequence. Those were closed, controlled things—harnessed by people. Girls didn't drown in ponds or streams. A lake wouldn't drag you screaming into its jaws. But this untamable vastness had always terrified her, much to her father's disbelief. A fisherman's daughter should share his love for the sea. She averted her eyes as they followed the sedge-lined path, the tundra a distant, frosted memory at her back. This ocean in particular only meant one thing: the end of her journey.

Don't forget the torture, she thought, *can't forget the torture. Oh and the execution, that'll be fun. It'll be its own kind of torture in itself. The crowds, more insane Wardens shouting in their yellow robes. Looking down at me like they aren't happy I did it, like they wouldn't have done it themselves if they'd only—*

"There," Kit said, shaking Anji out of her thoughts. "Just a bit farther."

Anji blinked and followed Kit's outstretched hand to a bulbous stone tower perched on a narrow hill facing the sea. Anji could just make out the shape: a pillar of wind-blasted rock, topped with a domed iron roof. A lighthouse, but judging by its precarious tilt and the gaping hole in its side, Anji thought it a wonder it was still standing.

"It's a ruin," Anji said. "We're not going in there."

Kit flicked the reins, guiding the horse over a slight rise.

A white flash splintered between the distant clouds, thunder drowning out Anji's exasperated sigh.

The trail spun down until they met the base of the rocky hill. Boulders lay stacked in haphazard piles up and down the slope, any hint of a road or path long obscured by weeds and brush. Scraggly trees leaned in unison with the salt-heavy wind. Kit dismounted, her mask jostling at her belt, swords on her other side clanking as she settled to the ground. She coughed more black spittle into her hand and wiped it on her thigh. The woman's leathers didn't seem as tight as they'd been days past. The material was wrinkled and sagging around her hips, at the joints of her shoulders and elbows. The Goat had been right, her hair *was* falling out. It had been thin when they'd first met, but now there were whole patches of bare scalp near the back of her skull.

How much time does she have left? Days? Hours? The maxia Kit had been using since the start of their journey likely wasn't helping matters either. Anji tore her gaze from Kit to the hill and the relic at its crown. She ran her tongue along her bottom lip, but stopped and wiped at it. Too cold for that.

"Off," said Kit, patting at the horse's flank. "Let her rest."

"You might take that advice yourself."

"What's that supposed to mean?"

Anji scoffed and looked back at Kit. "You look ready to transform right here. You're losing weight, your eyes are getting red."

Kit glared up at her. "I'm fine. Get off."

"What happened to the Bear?" said Anji.

"I don't know," said Kit. She sniffed and wiped at her nose and motioned for Anji to dismount. Anji stayed in the saddle.

"You *don't know*? What about Jared? Is the Goat even dead?" Her lip trembled. "Oh gods, she killed Berip, Kit, she just—"

"Stop that," said Kit. "We can't do this here. Please, we can't—" She doubled over, coughing, one hand to her knee. The Hawk groaned and spat and stood straight again, her eyes puffed, the whites veined with red. "We need to get out of the cold."

Anji slid out of the saddle. She thought she heard Kit mutter a thank-you, but the wind was starting to pick up.

They trekked up the slope in silence apart from their panting. Anji didn't mind. She'd wanted answers, something Kit might have been holding back till now, something that might justify the death of a little boy. But what she wanted wouldn't make a difference. She didn't feel much like talking anymore. Didn't feel much like anything. What was the point of going on? Even if she were somehow able to get the bag open, to get Kit to tell her how—if she could, what then? If she killed Kit and took back her things, there would only be this: a barren expanse of moss and rock and dirt at her back, and the ocean ahead. Hills tumbling on and on until they grew to mountains unpassable. She could run, but the hiding would never stop. Death would follow her forever.

If not for me, Berip would still be alive. Kaia. Libby.

Was that Kit's reason for wanting to spirit her through Kiva so quickly? Did she know Anji's mere presence would mean death for the people the Hawk loved? Anji felt unclean, like poison, a spreading sickness to be burned away. No good could come of her going on. No good had come from anything she'd thought she'd accomplished.

She'd done nothing. Whatever remained of her life was forfeit however she looked at it.

"I'll take her," Kit said, and she was there. She waved a hand up the hill. "Go on, it'll be hard enough with your foot like that."

Anji scowled. "Like what?"

Kit's nostrils flared, but she only coiled the reins in one gloved hand and threw the two bags over her shoulder. "You're limping. We need to get you off that ankle."

Anji stared at Kit as though seeing her for the first time. Whoever the Hawk—Kit—had been, she was no longer under Senate or Warden control. Whether outcast or gone of her own volition, she was a wholly different woman from the Hawk Anji had sung about in her youth. One who'd killed royal guards on the road to Silverton, who'd shown such disdain for Hectate and Alphoronse and an absolute resolve not to let Anji fall into the Menagerie's hands, even if it meant killing people she'd known for decades. The Bear, who had seemed so stoic at Sheertop's altar, had been beside herself with anger at Kit, at the betrayal she had endured at the hands of an old friend, all to spirit Anji away for a bounty Kit likely wouldn't even have the chance to spend.

There has to be a reason.

"Kit," Anji said, "why are you—"

"Not here," said Kit, shaking her head. Then she clicked her tongue at the horse and heaved herself forward. Anji limped up the hill after, drops of rain just beginning to fall.

⊰ 33 ⊱

The lighthouse looked ready to collapse at any moment, but Anji hauled herself inside anyway. She felt along the inside wall of the darkened, circular room and let herself slide to the floor, legs crossed. Her shirt hung heavy with sweat, freezing where it touched her skin. The wind was kinder in here, at least.

Kit rustled through the empty doorway, blotting out storm-gray light. She dropped the bags to the floor and lowered herself across from Anji, onto the first steps circling to the tower's top, where giant fires had been stoked so long ago. With a ragged sigh, she bent forward, hands reaching for her toes.

"What is that," Anji said, her voice scratchy and dry. She pointed at Kit, rolling a finger in the air. "That thing you're doing?"

"Stretching," Kit said, bending one wrist, then the other. Her arms were so thin, shaking from shoulder to forearm to fingers. Kit's whole body quaked with the effort, whatever it was, but she continued. Eyes closed, she let an uneasy breath out through her nose once, twice. The third sounded smoother.

"What does it do?"

"It relaxes me," Kit said.

"Doesn't look relaxing."

Kit opened her eyes and dragged the brown sack toward her. After digging around, she threw Anji a dried piece of meat and a hunk of brown bread, and set to her own with quick, greedy chomps.

The bread was dry, but full of flavor. Honey and nutmeg, hints of cinnamon. Had Berip baked this bread the day he died? Anji curled in on herself, favoring the ankle, wrapping her body around the bread. She pictured the cozy kitchen where it had been baked and felt a tear well up, blinked it away, and started on the meat. Tough. Tasteless. She ate it in two bites.

They sat still, the wind dropping with the temperature. Kit inched back against the weathered stone opposite Anji. She let her hands drop together in her lap, legs crossed, and breathed those long, crackling breaths, like a bellows clogged with wet clay.

"Why do you do that before you fight?" Anji asked.

"What?"

"That thing, that pose."

Kit blinked. "I have many poses. Which are you referring to?"

Anji rolled her eyes and laid her arms on the ground. "You know, before you start fighting, you go all limp."

"It's a basic technique. Your aunt never taught you?"

Anji shook her head.

"I still the body, and the mind follows. The still mind may do anything. I can tear through anyone, I can win mismatched fights. With a mind unclouded, pain is nothing, fear is no one."

The words sounded like a mantra more than an explanation.

"Could you show me how you—" The question fell out of Anji's mouth before she had time to stuff it back in.

"I don't see the use in—"

"Please," Anji said, "for what's to come. If what you say is true, if it can help with the pain . . . let me face it with—with a still mind."

Both of them jumped at the distant crack of thunder outside. Kit turned back to Anji.

"Do you feel the tips of your fingers?" she said, sitting straighter. Her face was sheened with sweat. Anji wondered if it was a good idea after all to be asking for this. Maybe the woman needed sleep. Maybe they both did, and these kinds of exercises would prove less than useless for what lay ahead. No amount of whatever it was Kit did before a fight could help with actual *torture*, could it?

"You're not even trying," Kit said, slumping and sliding back against the wall.

"No!" Anji said. "I'm sorry, I wasn't—it doesn't matter. I was just thinking—"

"Yes," Kit said slowly, head bobbing slowly up and down. "That's your first problem."

Anji frowned. "What, thinking?"

"Too much of it," Kit said. "I asked if you could feel your fingertips, and you went off somewhere else." She patted at the ground. "Stay here."

Anji sat straight, trying her best to mimic Kit's posture.

"Your fingertips—feel them buzzing?" Kit said. "And it helps to close your eyes."

Of course, Anji thought, but she closed them.

"Notice what you feel," she said. "Your fingers, your limbs, air in and out of your lungs. All happening without you. Sounds and smells and even the taste in your mouth. You're aware of these things, but you assign them no emotion. No feeling. You watch those thoughts float past like clouds. They simply are—as you are."

Anji frowned. *Okay. Focus. Or don't focus?* Which was it? Anji inched forward, the sharp edges of the weathered rock digging into her thighs.

How long would she have to do this?

Berip and Jared died because of me.

She had to stop thinking.

I'm not ready to die!

Images flew past like birds on the wing. A broken door. Her parents' lifeless eyes. Linura's Order cathedral, stained glass twinkling in the sun. Warm blood pumping over her hand. A Dredger in a cage. Sheertop. The Bear's mask.

Blade clicking through bone.

What had Kit said earlier?

Pages stuffed into their mouths.

"You're still thinking too much."

"I'm sorry, I can't just—"

"I told you to clear your mind."

"A little difficult with you barking orders, don't you think?"

Anji waited for a reply but none came. She tried to identify the sounds around her. Wind buffeting against the lighthouse. Brush cracking on the breeze. The horse's hoofs knocking against the mossy rocks outside. She tasted the brackish water and dry meat still resonant in her mouth. Her fingertips grew heavy, then her arms. The tension in her neck eased, and the pain in her ankle became distant, though still present.

"You are not your body," said Kit. "Not the wind outside or my voice or your thoughts."

Anji kept her eyes closed, and as though she were watching a school of fish gather and flow, a murmuration of birds flapping between chaos and order, the myriad thoughts bustling for purchase in her mind began to drift from a center where she was and was not. She wasn't sure if she was actually doing it—but she had the stray thought that doing it didn't matter. None of this did. Nothing.

She opened her eyes.

Kit sat across from her, knees folded in, her eyes bright.

"I couldn't hold on to—whatever I was—" Anji broke eye contact. She didn't want to see her failure in Kit's eyes.

"You wouldn't have even if we'd sat here a week," Kit said, waving a hand, though the look of annoyance Anji had anticipated was absent. "That practice is not meant to be done right the first time, or the fiftieth. It takes years of patience, of dedication, and you have quite a bit on your mind." She tucked a lock of hair behind one ear and cleared her throat. "You did well though. I could tell you were trying, at least. A mistake most make, but difficult to avoid."

Anji didn't know what to say. How could trying be a mistake?

"What's the use in knowing all this?" Anji finally said after a moment of awkward silence.

"I already told you—"

"You told me it helped," Anji said, "but I don't really understand how."

Kit shifted on the rock and unsheathed her dagger, flipping it in her bony fingers. Her eyes were dull with exhaustion, and Anji nearly said they should just forget it and go to bed before she began.

"Your opponent is rarely in such a state," Kit said, eyes still fixed on the dagger. "It's best to have every advantage. These methods, basic as they are, are not widely mastered. I have only met two other people with my aptitude."

Anji didn't want to guess who, but she had a feeling. It didn't feel like an advantage. If anything, she felt more tired.

"We should sleep," Kit said, scratching at her wrist.

"I don't think I'll be able to." She still had questions, but she didn't think the Hawk would answer if she just came right out with them. Anji scraped a hand along the floor, feeling the centuries of rot and long-gone memory seeping through the chipped rock, the mortar holding it all together.

"Nothing like this back home," she said, more to herself than to Kit.

"What do you mean?" Kit said. "Rock all over the place in the city."

"Not this rock," said Anji, still feeling the stone. "Not in Mudtown. All the buildings in Mudtown are built of wood or stone quarried from Dorodad. My dad told me they don't pay Dorodi miners as much as they would have to in Yem. He complained that Linura had forgotten its roots, the hard work of all the ones who'd come before. Old Linura was built by the Order from coastal stone. It's all but buried now. We'd go on walks and Dad would point out how you could tell it was all new, all stained with foreign, oppressed blood. Like the city was trying to erase its own past. He was attracted to ancient things. My mother said she had to keep an eye on him or he'd run off with an old woman and leave her alone to take care of me."

"You miss them," Kit said.

Anji nodded. "Most kids don't like their parents." She picked up a pebble and rolled it between her fingers. "The few years Mudtown's schools were open, I heard others complaining about their lives at home. Even poor kids can be entitled sometimes. They don't even know what they've avoided; what it's like having them and losing them."

Anji didn't know if Kit was listening, but she continued. The last week had been the epitome of confused thoughts, black whirls of ideas and worries and memories and now, revelation. She felt an elemental need to lay them out to another person, to bare her humanity and ask someone, anyone to share the load of all these past years. She'd always imagined herself confiding in Kaia and Libby, eventually, but the walls she'd put up between her past and present had remained firm. How ironic that the person marching her toward death would be the person who brought the walls down.

"Every day I wake up afraid I'll forget their faces. But they never fade. Everything is clear as the day I lost them. Their voices, their hands, how they walked." She pulled her coat tight. "The way they smelled. Toward the end, they were arguing more, but they always made up. I got kicked out of the house a few times so they could be alone.

"People aren't happy together just . . . ," she waved a hand, "because they're together. There has to be more there, and there really was. It was love. They made each other laugh every day. I remember I'd come home once, sweet on one of the kids from school because of a stupid joke they'd told, and my mother told me: 'Anji, dear, I'm so sorry to tell you this, but you're screwed. If they make you laugh, you're already chasing.' " Anji cast her eyes to the ground. "You would have liked her."

"I'm sure."

"I still dream about her," Anji said. She wiped at one eye, feeling stupid for crying in front of Kit and emboldened all at once. "Dad too, of course, but not as much. Mom and I didn't even talk as often, but we had a different understanding. We didn't need words." Anji stared across the open space at the brick and chipped mortar of the lighthouse stairs, spiraling up and up. "I dream of her at home sometimes, sitting at the table, looking through the tiny window facing the street, watching people's feet swing past. Or I'm at school and she's come to surprise me. In others it's the street right outside our house, and I'm running home with my bag flapping behind me and I'm jumping into her arms. And then I'm yelling and smacking at her arm because she wasn't supposed to just . . . come back like that. Not after she was gone for so long without saying goodbye." Anji ran a hand over her shaved scalp. "And then I wake up, and she's gone again."

Thunder crackled, a flash of light following after.

"When I killed him—Rolandrian. It wasn't planned or anything.

I was just in the right place at the right time. I wasn't even supposed to be in that part of the castle that night. I was taking over a shift for a laundress with a fever. I'd never even been in those chambers before.

"He didn't even notice when I came in. The guards outside, they didn't hear anything. Didn't ask what I was doing there. I was just a servant to them, another girl from below the castle. That's the trouble with servants."

"What's that?"

"We're invisible," Anji said. "There's always lowborn work in high places. 'The grease to the gears,' Matron said to me once. The grease made everything so quiet I wasn't noticed.

"He didn't notice when I grabbed the letter opener, either. He was just—staring out the window. I grabbed the blade off his desk, walked into the room, and I shoved it into his neck. And he just died."

She'd thought her parents, in whatever eternity they were in—if indeed there was one—would have reveled in that moment and felt a beaming affection for the girl she'd grown into. But that moment had never come. It was only fleeting excitement and tremendous anticipation followed by more fear than she'd ever known.

Anji brought her knees to her chest. "My mother was a Maxia." There. The words were said. She glanced at the Hawk, their eyes meeting for a heartbeat before she swallowed and went on, "She worked for *The Tide*. It was an underground newspaper, named after a rebel group my parents helped form. I don't know if you've heard of it . . ."

"I have," said Kit.

"That scrying sheet," Anji said, pointing outside to where the Goat's horse grazed. "She was trying to figure out how the charm worked. My coin . . . one of two. It was her first experiment, her first attempt to understand how maxia could be used to communicate messages. She charmed her coin to match her own heartbeat—called it a "recording." The closer she was to me, the stronger the pulse in my coin. She carried the other with her always, but I never found it on her body . . . that day. I imagine it was destroyed along with all her other work, but I can still feel mine pulsing. Her dying breath must have kept the charm working forever. I slept with it every night, right up until you took it."

Anji paused, unsure what she hoped the Hawk would say, but she said nothing.

I've already said everything else, Anji thought, and with a heavy sigh, she went on.

"It had just rained. I'd been building mud castles in the street. So stupid." She sniffed, one of her nostrils clogged from crying. "I came home and the door, our only door, was busted in."

Kit stiffened. "You don't have to—"

"It's alright," said Anji. "I found my mother lying near the table, on her back. Dad was on the stairs to my loft. There was so much blood. I didn't know bodies could hold so much of it, or lose so much. It was like someone had come in while I was gone and painted the floor red. They were both stabbed to death and," she pressed a hand to her forehead, "pages of *The Tide* had been stuffed into their mouths.

"Someone must have found out what they'd been up to, who they were working with. An informant in the rebellion. One of the Wardens, maybe. I never found out. Anything not Senate-approved, newspapers, plays, songs—forbidden, of course, but an unregistered Maxia . . . tinkering with Senate secrets . . .

"My parents believed in a better life for us, for people like us. They were so smart, Kit. They could have done anything—could have made more money and gotten us out of that basement, but they believed in something, and Rolandrian had them murdered for it. *I* would have been murdered for it if I'd been there.

"I wanted him to feel the pain I felt, the loss I endured for six years. I wanted him to feel alone and terrified and helpless, because of what he did to my parents. To me."

A thick silence stood between them, the horse nickered outside.

"I'm so sorry, Anji."

Anji leaned her head against the cool stone. "Like you said, it didn't do anything. Mostly I felt the same amount of awful and alone. The only thing that changed was I'd murdered someone, and that someone being gone won't put food on anyone's table. It won't raise wages for a single factory worker. Laundresses will still be treated like prisoners. It didn't save my parents. It won't bring them back. My only friends in the world were tortured and killed. All because of me.

"Some part of me thought I would change things, that I would lead the revolution my parents dreamed about. The uprising they must have argued over and planned and spread. But that was only a shallow justification. I wanted to feel better, so I took the simplest path. I think if I really wanted to help, I would have searched for another way. A better way." She buried her face in her hands. "And now it's too late."

"There is one," said Kit, her voice cracking. "Another way."

Anji listened then. Not out of deference, but because behind this woman's bile was someone who'd been where Anji had: cold and alone and afraid. Orphaned, blood-stained, and without direction.

"If you want real change, the kind that lasts, you have to accept that you're a small part of the larger whole. That out of many"—she held her fingers splayed and bunched them into a fist—"one force may yet overcome. We *are* the many, Anji. The lowborn, the common. The laborers and farmers and fishermen.

258

One act like the one you committed will not dismantle years of oppression and greed. One murder, regardless of its rank, will not grant the many their due.

"You thought Rolandrian had ultimate authority. It's a simple story told to people like us. He was a distraction. A figurehead. A conduit for the common folk to focus their hatred." She locked eyes with Anji. "He likely had no idea who your parents were."

This last sent a surge of indignation through Anji. How could he not have known?

"Those few who advised the king," Kit went on, "the Senate, the Governors, the Sun Wardens, their subordinates, their lords and ladies—they are the real, unseen force, and they fear the many. You look around and you see poverty and strife, hunger and insecurity, and I warrant your feelings on all those things are valid—I share them with you. You and your parents lived through it all, like so many others. But you cannot topple a pyramid by cracking its crown. You must dismantle it, brick by brick, until its weight is lifted free and you can begin again. And for that, you need numbers. You need organization. You need an army." Her eyes flicked over Anji. "And an army needs . . . investment."

Anji inched forward. "A million Rhoda," she said, "that's why you need me alive. You want to fund the Tide."

"I want to contribute. I'm one small part of an organized whole. The tide against the levees being built. The Wardens have taken their time, playing their games behind the Senate's back, but they've grown bolder these past months, and bolder still now Rolandrian is in the ground without an heir. But they are not invincible. They can be deposed. But not by reckless murder or blind hate or ignorance. It will take a collective. It will take time and planning. One shared vision distributed among the masses. Anything else, any fractured action like the one you took only feeds the monster that stomps on the necks of good people like your parents."

They sat in silence for a heartbeat before Anji said, her voice hoarse, "You don't have to do any of this. I agree with everything you're saying. Let me help. Take me with you to where the rebels are camped and I can—"

"You're not listening."

"I'm not—" Anji stuttered, then tried a new tack. "How do you know they'll even pay you? The Wardens? How can you trust anything they say?"

"They'll pay. If there's one thing the Wardens and the remnants of the Senate are known for, it's paying their debts in a very public way. This is all a show, Anji. They intend to make an example of you, of the futility of your crimes. You will become the ultimate caution against revolt. They'll take you to Laurelside, right to the center of Mudtown, and execute you to prove their hold over Yem. They'll prop me up, the loyal bounty hunter who ensured Rolandrian's killer was brought to justice. And then I'll use their own money to topple their regime."

Anji bit at her lip, her mind working. There had to be a hole somewhere in this plan for her to squeeze through. She just had to find it.

"What about the Bear? Won't she tell the Wardens that you left? That you killed the others?"

Kit shrugged. "There's no shortage of bounty hunters in the world. We were simply the most well-known, but past our prime. The Wardens won't care if a few old killers for hire are dead. Besides, our tenets hold for each other as well as anyone else trying to take a charge. They'll see it as infighting, nothing more, so long as you're delivered."

"But the Bear—"

"Is now the Menagerie's last remaining member, and she'll not stop until she has you. She's likely following our tail right now. We have her scrying sheet, so she'll not be able to contact the

Wardens from the road. Even if she did, the embarrassment of losing you when you were in her grasp, of losing her fellows . . . of losing me." Kit scoffed. "She could never endure the shame. No, she'll die before giving you up, especially to me."

The thought of seeing that pearl-white mask again sent a chill down Anji's spine. She sat straighter against the rock. "And you'll be the one to kill her?"

Silence pressed between them. Kit sniffed, and though she'd gone through her stretches a few moments before, her body seemed to tense like a bow string before she looked at her gloved hands. "I will."

A thought occurred to Anji then, her last desperate grasp at freedom.

"*I'll* tell the Wardens then," she said, hardly believing the words as she said them, but she went on despite the grave look on the Hawk's face. "Before they torture me. I'll tell them you're aiding the Tide, unless you let me go. Right now."

To Anji's surprise, Kit laughed, that bell-like burst she'd heard for the first time in Jared's inn.

"You killed for your parents' vision, Anji. Running was cowardly. The act was ill-advised and ill-informed, but not without reason. Not without passion. You believed in that vision then, and you believe in it now. You and I both know you won't breathe a word. Besides, look at me. We both know that by the time we've turned you in, I won't be in a state to reap any consequences for you telling anyone. I'll just be another Dredger living in the slums, likely hunted down and slaughtered without anyone knowing who I was."

"But you're leading *me* to slaughter!" Anji's words rang off the empty tower walls. "You *know* about my parents. We're on the same side!"

Kit sighed, her shoulders dropping. "I have to do it, Anji. I find this all . . . distasteful, yes, but you signed your death warrant the moment you put that blade to Rolandrian's throat. We have similar goals, perhaps, but you're forgetting your role in all this. The role you put yourself into. If you're willing to kill for a cause, you should be ready to die for one too."

Anji stared across the darkened space, lips pressed hard together. A thousand retorts flitted through her head, but they all led to the same place.

Kit opened her mouth to say more, but lapsed into a fit of coughs again, bent double with the force. She spat onto the stone, fished out a vial of Rail, and tipped its remaining contents onto the flat of her hand, then snorted up the sizable mound of powder. Nostrils flaring, she tilted her head back, sniffing hard, and wiped at her eyes.

"Don't you need to sleep?" said Anji.

"After everything I've told you?" said Kit, letting the vial clatter to the floor. She leveled a look at Anji. "I don't think so."

"You didn't have to tell me anything," said Anji, avoiding the instinct to deny the Hawk's unspoken accusation.

Kit shrugged. "No," was all she said.

Anji searched for something else to say, some final argument that would get her out of this corner. But nothing came. She pulled her coat tight and sank to her side, favoring her injured hand. Jared had treated the wounds better than she could have expected, but the effects of the salve had begun wearing off. The pain had come back. She turned her back to the Hawk and closed her eyes, her thoughts swirling like the rain outside.

⊶34⊷

Morning saw the storm blown out, leaving sunlight and birdsong in its wake. Anji had said little and Kit even less as they packed their scant supplies and set off, waves crashing on the beach far below. The lighthouse was a distant shape at their backs when Anji finally relinquished the saddle and motioned for Kit to mount. Her ankle still smarted when she put too much weight on it, but she could take only so much pleasure watching her captor stumble in a sleepless haze as their sedge-lined path shifted to a broader road. She'd expected an argument, but Kit simply stood on twitching legs while Anji dismounted, then climbed on without a word before they moved on, plodding toward the columns of chimney smoke that marked the borderlands of Tideron.

The coast road ran empty but for a few carts drawn by haggard draft animals. Their riders tipped their hats as they creaked past, one dray weighed down by an entire family dressed in filthy rags. As Tideron's outskirts began to materialize, Anji spotted a spindly wagon covered in a patched tarp angled into a ditch, its front wheel in a splintered heap among the dirt. A grubby woman and her brood loitered at the roadside in rough, greasy homespun, begging any passerby to help.

Kit flipped a Celdia toward them, but clicked her tongue at the horse. They pressed on.

"You're quiet today," said Kit, stuffing a piece of dried meat into her mouth.

Anji glanced back at the woman and her children, her mouth dry. She said nothing.

The Hawk spat into the grass.

They walked in silence, level with the coast for a quarter hour before coming to the base of a large hill. Anji untied the canteen from the saddle, frowning at the hollow splash slapping against the bottom. She took a drink and watched a scattered cloud formation collecting in the eastern sky, stirred by a robust strand of wind that fluttered her coat. A screech rent the air, followed by the stark black shapes of two large birds riding the buffeting currents. The birds circled and weaved, dancing together over the sprawling gray sea. Anji took a long, deep breath of salty air as the pair flew off, dark specks against the deep blue.

"Water's nearly gone," she said. She took another sip and corked the canteen. "Kit, did you—"

Kit was slumped over in the saddle, her shoulders caved over the swells, chest shuddering in and out. A small dribble of black saliva leaked from the corner of her mouth. Her eyelids fluttered closed. At the neckline where her leathers ended, Anji could see tendrils of gray running like filthy veins under her skin.

Anji's stomach went cold.

You'll see it in her neck soon.

"Hey! Kit!" Anji shoved the woman's shoulder to no avail, gathered the horse's reins, and tugged it up the rise. As they crested, Anji's ankle a dull, endless throb, Yem's largest coastal city came into view.

Tideron sat like a god's wagon wheel sawed in half and laid along the rocky coast. Its thick stone wall hemmed in clusters of white and gray buildings wedged between broad avenues that ran like spokes toward the hub of masts and sails standing at its eastern end. A solitary finger of black rock curled out from the city's southern edge, its tip dominated by a white-brick lighthouse twice the size of the ruin they'd sheltered in the night before. Seabound ships in full sail crept over the waves, bound for Kardisa, for Blackwater Gulf, for Linura.

Anji turned to try to wake Kit again, but the Hawk was now blinking at her from her perch on the saddle.

"We're here," said Anji, tossing the reins toward Kit. She pointed down the slope. "Harbor's right there. We don't even have to go through the gates. There's a separate entrance from the headland."

Kit levered herself higher in the saddle, massaging her throat. She met Anji's gaze. "What is it?"

"Your neck," Anji said, pointing at the gray lines peeking above the leather. She didn't know what else to say. *Right, didn't know if you noticed, Kit, but you're slowly turning into that monster on every poster between Linura and Conifor.*

Kit pulled her collar over the markings without acknowledgment and cleared her throat.

"We're not going to the harbor. Not yet."

Anji rolled her eyes. "Look, I'm not stupid. You need to find a ship home just as much as I—"

"Enough!" said Kit, raising a hand. "Enough. I have to go in. I need . . ." She scratched at her thigh, twisting her neck until it popped.

"What?" said Anji. "What do you—oh."

Kit slipped twitching fingers into her leathers for her last vial of Rail. She thumbed the cork off, turned the entire tube up and stuffed it into her nostril, leaning her head back. Sniffing hard, she tapped at the emerald-green glass, ensuring every morsel dropped out. With a final snort, Kit tossed the vial into the dirt, wiping at her watering eyes.

Arms crossed, Anji watched Kit gulp down the last of their water. Contrary to Jared's advice, the Hawk had been inhaling more and more of the Rail. What vile changes were happening under all that leather? How much longer before the signs of turning showed in her face? Would she fully transform into a mindless, sniveling Dredger while they were at sea? Surely any competent captain would toss her over the ship's side if they found out what they'd brought aboard. The thought brought a faint glimmer of hope, but something nagged at Anji as Kit shuddered in the saddle and nudged the horse down the trail.

"Jared said you were supposed to start weaning off."

Kit cast Anji a sidelong look as they walked, her eyes dull red. "Wouldn't do much good now. Besides, a sea voyage, stuck with you and your mouth? I'll not endure that without a fix." She gestured at Tideron's approaching wall with the empty canteen. "We'll go in, get more Rail, then find a ship for Linura."

"How do you know we'll even find any Rail in there?" Anji asked, stumbling through the sand. Her ankle was beginning to throb again.

"There's a building marked."

"I didn't see anything," Anji said.

"You don't know what to look for."

⇥35⇤

They gained flat ground once more and joined the milling trail of wagons and gruff townsfolk snaking toward Tideron's main gate, an archway two stories tall, its bronze doors thrown open against the towering wall. The stone stood cracked and bleeding decades of lichen and moss. A wooden coat of arms topped the gate's archway, depicting a black squid over checkered purple-and-white squares. Four constables in yellow tunics stood in the arch's shadow. From this distance Anji could just make out the scruff of their beards and the practiced way they gripped the swords in their golden sheaths. The constables stopped each group as it reached the gate, barking commands and sifting through carts.

As they moved with the throng, Anji wondered if they'd be better off tying the horse up somewhere and continuing on without it. Few others in the crowd had proper horses, and theirs was bigger and better fed than most.

Ahead, a cart and driver trundled through the gate and one of the guards waved the next wagon forward. The crowd inched along. Anji felt a shiver as they walked into the shadow cast by the salt-stained walls.

Something gurgled from behind Kit's mask and a trail of gray vomit dripped down into the saddle between her legs. Kit swayed and gripped at the swells. Anji reached instinctively for Kit's leg, but stayed her hand and stepped aside as Kit shuddered and spat a glob of something yellow to the coarse sand underfoot.

"You've got a trial set day after next," Kit said, wiping at her mouth. "Thievery. From a spice merchant in Kiva. I was in the area on another job. Got it?"

Anji groaned. "Couldn't I be in trouble for something more exciting?"

"You already are, and you're about to be executed for it. Don't you want to even pretend that's not the case?" She began to say more, but a croaky voice cut the air ahead.

"Oh, but this is ridiculous!"

Anji and Kit spun toward the wagon ahead and the old man standing near its front wheel. The man threw his hat into the dirt and stamped on it, waving a crooked finger in a burly constable's face.

"You mean to tell me I have to *pay* to enter a city I've lived in for forty years? Bah!" He waved a hand, turned to the wagon, and began climbing back into the driver's box. "I've been coming and going through this gate since you were sucking on your mama's teat, *boy,* and I don't need you or anyone else—"

The guard grabbed the man by the collar and pulled him back into the dirt. The old man stumbled and yelped and landed in a tangle of limbs. "You bastards!" he shouted, and as one of the guards bent to bind his hands the old man pulled a knife from his belt and scrabbled to his knees. "Warden pigs, the lot of you!" Another constable stepped forward and without a word drove his sword neatly into the commoner's chest and out through his back. The old man gasped and clapped his hands to the guard's wrist, but after a moment went still as the soldier slid him off his sword with a booted foot.

The guard spat into the dust, ignoring the halfhearted cries from some of the crowd. He wiped his sword on the old man's shirt, then dug into a pocket and produced a yellow sheet of paper, which he held high overhead as he shouted over the gathered crowd.

"Listen up, you lot!" he said, his voice competing with the roaring sea. "This here is a decree from Illuminator Escadora! His words give us the power to charge a fee to any seeking entrance to Tideron and its custom, be you citizens or foreigners." He nudged the lifeless old man with his boot. "I want no trouble, you hear?" He gestured at the other constables standing in a line at his back. "We're here to collect proper tolls and see no trouble is started. Anyone have a problem with that?"

The crowd went on murmuring, but none came forward. The guard barked a command for the others to take the old man's body away before resuming his spot under the archway and out of the sun. The cart was pushed aside, likely to be ransacked at a later hour, and Anji and Kit were ushered forward.

They stayed silent as they came level with the gate. Anji tried her best to look deferent and ashamed of herself, avoiding the eyes of the thickset, well-armed men now crowding around the horse. She raised her eyes a fraction and looked through the archway at Tideron's gate-side plaza.

The sun-scorched roofs shone so bright she had to squint. Every surface seemed coated in fresh white paint. Brick and plaster houses crowded together like the spines of books stacked neatly on their shelves. A pair of well-dressed children darted across the square, skirting a pale statue at its center depicting an elegantly carved squid, its tentacles wrapped around a towering marble obelisk. The square was half-filled with townsfolk trudging to and fro, some carrying bulging satchels, others hand in hand as they passed by clean-swept alleyways. Another child, full-cheeked

269

and jabbering, broke off from her parents to set off a congress of seagulls toward the forest of masts standing sentinel in the hazy distance.

". . . this one here."

Anji blinked and returned her attention to the voices close by, remembering to keep her head bowed as one of the constables came close. His greaves were polished mirror bright, neither dented nor scratched.

"Prisoner I'm seeing to," came Kit's voice, steady and solid yet tinny as it always was behind the mask.

"Yeah?" said the guard. "What'd he do?"

"I am forbidden from speaking my charges' crimes," Kit said. Anji looked up just as the guard's hand flapped back to his side, near a burnished leather sword hilt. *Was he about to touch me?*

The guard motioned to Anji's hand. "What happened to his fingers?"

"I cut one off for every annoying question he asked me," came Kit's reply. Anji held her breath to stop a laugh. "And the next time he delays me it'll be the whole hand." Kit held out the same letter she'd given Hectate, pressed between two fingers. The guard took it with a frown and scanned the words.

An interminable silence stretched, filled only by the murmuring crowd ahead in the square and the squalid fold behind. The guard gave a curt nod and waved them through without a word. Anji caught a glimpse of him joining his comrades at the arch's side to let them pass, his face impassive if a little shaken.

"You scared the shit out of him," Anji said.

"Hush," said Kit, but whatever bark she'd had for the guard was absent now.

⊹ 36 ⊹

The Hawk hitched the horse at a vacant post, tying the blue satchel to her belt and leaving the rest. She led them on foot through Tideron's midday crowd and out of the plaza, one hand clamped to Anji's bicep. They weaved through a maze of shrub-lined streets, the white cobbles underfoot gleaming like snow in the sun. Stone façades of houses and shops lined the thoroughfares, their windows intact, lintels filled with potted flowers, shutters painted in even coats of varying colors. Eventually they came upon a broad street lined with market stalls, packed shoulder to shoulder with townsfolk clamoring for stacks of fruit, cheese, and linen billowing on the breeze. A white-and-gold wagon trundled past bearing a Sun Warden in hushed conversation with a white-jacketed woman with gleaming purple eyes. They were pulled by one of the enormous black birds that had driven Hectate's own cart, its squawk jostling the crowd just enough to haul the cart through. Kit pulled Anji through the press, clicking her tongue at one stall in particular, manned by a woman wearing at least two dozen rings who claimed she knew what day Anji would die. Every person gave the Hawk and her charge a wide berth, averting their eyes but staring all the same when they thought the woman's gaze had moved on. A girl with frizzy red hair pointed and mouthed "hawk" to her mother, who shushed her and dipped her head as they passed.

"This way," said Kit, leading them out of the cluster of stalls and into another square, this one smaller than the one at the main gate. A bell tolled from some unseen structure, followed by raised voices at their backs. People pushed forward on all sides now, some of their faces excited and murmuring, but others mostly nervous or confused, their voices low, heads bent as they scuttled into the massing crowd.

"What's going on?" said Anji.

"Keep your mouth shut and your head down," said Kit. She grabbed Anji's wrist and attempted to wade them through the oncoming throng, but the crowd was too thick now, and they were taken up into the stream. Anji twisted with the mass of writhing and whispering bodies, toward the focus of everyone's attention. She stood up on her toes.

A structure of brilliant white stone dominated the square's opposite end. It harbored one enormous door at its center, black oak bolted with black iron. Unlike the Order cathedrals, the structure had no nave, no buttresses, no spanning arcades. The windowless facade towered over Tideron's rooftops, a symmetrical elongated pyramid shielded by a layer of scaffolding. Bent-backed workers lumbered up the ramps and ladders with wheelbarrows and sacks, hunched under the weight of brick hods. Hammers, chisels, and the calls of other workers competed with the murmuring press now focused on what stood in the space shadowed by the tower.

A wooden platform, raised to chest height.

One long beam ran the length of the platform over the heads of five figures assembled in a line facing the crowd, hands tied behind their backs. Five thick ropes hung from the beam. A giant in a red hooded robe, face a mask of pure black, stepped between each of the figures in turn, tugging the nooses tight around each of their necks. One of the condemned, a man with salt-and-pepper hair and a hooked nose, slumped to his knees, his eyes full of tears.

"This isn't right!" he cried. "We've done nothing! This is murder!" But nobody in the crowd rushed forward onto the platform to free him. The woman beside him stared silently at the crowd, her eyes wide, as though she'd just realized where she was. She might have been a few years older than Anji.

The crowd murmured on as the man wept, as the woman at his side picked at her noose. The others were a pair of men with barely enough scruff between them to make a full beard and an old woman shivering with cold and fright. Her pale legs were webbed with varicose veins.

Another figure wearing a bright yellow robe took the stage.

His dress was so garish it made the square and surrounding buildings look grubby by comparison. The figure glided across the planks on slippered feet to the platform's front edge and lifted his hood. An old man, balding, with streaks of gray hair riding above his long ears. His pallid skin hung like melted wax, wrinkled and fixed in a deep frown. The eyes sucking in the gathered citizens were gray and hard as steel. He looked over the crowd, sparing not a glance for the condemned at his back. In his stubby fingers he clutched a leather-bound book with a circle embossed in gold on its cover. He held a hand up, and the crowd quieted, though some of them still whispered to each other. The man kept his hand raised until silence overtook the square.

"Citizens of Tideron!" the man said, ignoring the whimpering at his back. "I am Illuminator Escadora, of the Conclave Wardens

Sun. I apologize for the disruption of your daily tasks," he said, simpering. He gazed across the crowd, and shook his head. "A market day. Such a blessing, especially on a day granted so blue a sky by the One On High. But disruption can so often bring forth the milk of tomorrow's virtue, if you've the courage to drink."

Though he spoke softly, his voice rang clear as a bell. The crowd was enraptured. He went on.

"Behind me you see the worst of you! The scum that walks your streets, those who would spit upon the good work you good people do! Fornicators! Reformers! Thieves! Traitors to the *Crown*! Would you have your homes, your streets, clogged with such sin? Would you have your children witness such degeneracy? Are we not entitled to cleanliness and class? Shall we purge this mortal realm of the filth and muck which has descended upon—"

"Gods! We've done nothing wrong!" said the man on his knees, his voice a shriek so high-pitched Anji had to wince. He sobbed, his fingers clenched into fists, and stared out at the crowd. "Why are you letting them do this?"

The man in the yellow robes flicked his fingers at the giant in red, who smashed his fist into the crying man's mouth. Teeth clattered over the planks in a spray of blood. The giant whipped a strip of cloth out from inside his robes and tied it around the man's mouth. Anji felt Kit stiffen at her side.

"There are no *gods* here," said Escadora, turning back to the crowd. "Only the One, in whose benevolence you may choose to bask. Think me not an executioner," said the yellow-robed man, pressing a spindly hand to his chest, "not a judge—no. I am a messenger, instructed by the One to shed this good city of its villainy, its idleness, as is Their design with all things. I am but one of you! One of you indignant citizens who has chosen to heed the One's word and *abolish* and *abort* those who defile Their cosmic decree. For what are we without the rules set down in this good

274

book?" He slapped at the leather and shook it over his head. "We are no better than the bugs you squash underfoot without order, without law! And these," he gestured at the five figures behind him, "these sinners spit upon order. They make the streets you walk unsafe with their sin, their disgusting vice and vapidity and *vagrancy*. Laziness! Ingratitude! Shall we purge them from these streets?"

A few calls of agreement came from the crowd.

"Shall we make safe the city once more?"

The calls came a bit stronger.

"Shall we live not in black fear, but in the white light of grace bestowed *only* by the One On High?"

Claps and cheers now, though Anji noticed a few people at the back were making their way out of the square. She turned back to the platform.

"With ruination comes the dawn!"

The crowd chanted this back.

"With ruination comes the dawn!"

The crowd screamed this back.

"Squash these bugs!"

The red-robed giant grabbed the man on his knees by the hair and stood him up. The man squirmed and cried out through his gag. The others stood still, their ropes like dead snakes looped around their necks.

"Kill them!" someone screamed in the crowd.

"This isn't right," said someone at Anji's back, but she didn't see who it was.

Escadora clasped his hands together, his face a swirl of sorrow and pride and pleasure. He blinked at the crowd and bowed his head, then stepped aside and, at a wave of his hand, the five on the platform dropped through gaps in the stage.

Five cracks, like knuckles popping.

The sound resounded off the walls. Gasps issued from the crowd; some were shocked to silence—others, who must have been to one of these executions before, cheered and rushed toward the man in the yellow robes, who was now taking paper pamphlets from a wooden box and distributing them to outstretched hands.

"Come on," said the Hawk, grabbing Anji's arm.

⊰ 37 ⊱

Kit ushered them into an alley and slumped against the wall, chest heaving. She gripped the blue satchel's strap strung over her chest like the rigging of a ship in storm.

"He sounded like the Bear," said Anji, her back to the opposite wall. "How could they—what was—" She rubbed at her eyes. "That wasn't a trial—it wasn't anything! It was just—just—"

"Murder," said Kit, sliding to squat against the brick. "No need for a trial when *the One On High* has already decreed who is damned and who isn't." She ripped her mask off, tearing a chunk of gray hair away with it. Her lips were bulbous and pale, the tips of her elongated teeth just showing behind them.

"That doesn't make any sense," said Anji, averting her eyes. "Everything I've heard from them is just a jumble of meaningless words. That man—Escadora—he said people had to choose . . ."

"It's not supposed to make sense," said Kit. She wiped a run of black snot from her lip. "It's supposed to make you feel what they want you to feel. You want people under your control? Divide them. Fill them with fear. Then point that fear at something to hate and they'll do whatever you say."

A man pushing a wooden cart ambled past the alley mouth, and Kit motioned for Anji to move farther into the dim corridor. The tiled rooftops above framed a sliver of darkening sky, its light reflected dully off the scattered puddles of water underfoot. Iron pipes crossed the gap at haphazard intervals, dripping and hissing thin streams of steam. They passed a vacant alcove littered with piled, rotted wood and a tangle of metal that looked like it had once been a baby's carriage. Kit tottered to a stop and slammed against the wall once more. She let out a sharp gasp and finally sat on the muddy ground.

"Come on," said Anji. "Can't be much farther, right?"

Kit held a gloved palm up. She retched and planted one hand on the cobbles. Anji took a tentative step forward, then rushed ahead as Kit sagged to her side.

"What do I—"

"Just—" Kit coughed into her fist. Anji grasped Kit's bony shoulders and hauled her sitting straight.

"This place is filthy," she murmured. "Let's get you on your feet."

"I need a moment," Kit said. "Just a moment, Anji, please."

Anji cast around the alley, not sure what she was looking for. Her eyes locked on the blue bag still slung across the Hawk's chest.

"Anything in there that can help?" she said, pointing at the bag.

"Nothing," said Kit. "I need a fix. I need—" Her chest heaved in tiny, hitched gasps.

Anji frowned. "Are we close?" She snapped her fingers in Kit's face. "Kit, are we close?"

Kit pointed a finger to the alley mouth. Anji released Kit and, still at a crouch, moved to the corner and looked across the way.

"What am I looking at, exactly?"

"It's a bathhouse," Kit said, rising first to her knees, then shakily to her feet.

"Are you sure you're okay to—"

"I'm fine," said Kit, coming level with Anji. They both stared across the street, their backs to the alley. "Let's get a move—"

Something mewled behind them, like a large cat. Anji spun and nearly tumbled back.

The Dredger shambled toward them, its eyes sunken and gone to a red so deep Anji wondered how it could see. Its too-long arms hung like anchors from narrow shoulders, the gray, scaly skin drawn tight over its clavicles and clenching neck muscles. Another mewling sound issued from its mass of tangled, protruding teeth. It dragged one of its clawed feet, trailing a line of black blood.

"Don't startle him," said Kit at Anji's side, any hint of exhaustion now gone from her voice. She slipped the blue satchel around, opened it with one hand, and pulled out two empty Rail vials.

"What are you—"

Kit held up her other hand, eyes still fixed on the Dredger as it whimpered and stuttered toward them. The creature flexed its taloned fingers, its stomach bulging in and out like a bellows.

"Peessss," it gurgled, holding out a trembling hand. Its nails were caked in more blood, and Anji noticed razor-thin scratches all along its thighs, dribbling over the patchy fur where the scales ended.

"It's okay," said Kit. She sniffed, and Anji's brow furrowed. The Hawk was crying. She uncorked the vials.

The Dredger barked another cry and hurtled forward, its bloodred eyes blinking.

Kit tossed the vials over the Dredger's head. It hissed and whirled and dove onto the vials as they shattered against the alley floor. Horrid snorting and gasping issued from where the creature lay, inhaling bits of glass and dirt and grimy water.

Kit straightened and wiped at her nose. She pulled the bag open and stuffed her mask inside, then led them out of the alley while the Dredger snuffed at the broken glass behind them.

⊹38⊹

"Why aren't you wearing your mask? Won't they—"

"Spurs don't sell to Senate affiliations," said Kit, hustling them along. The gray tendrils in her neck had smoothed to a patina of fine fur and hard ridges. Anji opened her mouth to point it out, but Kit tugged her along, shaking her head. "Don't ask questions. You're a new recruit. My subordinate. Got it?"

Anji had a retort ready, but she stopped short as they entered the bathhouse's shadow. The building was painted a garish red, its shutters closed on all of its four levels. Anji marveled at the woman now taking the crumbling front steps. Kit had truly gone mad with withdrawal if she thought anyone would be inside. But despite its run-down facade, the bathhouse still dominated the entire block like a bruised tongue among the whitewashed structures littered like broken teeth along the street. Harbor bells clanged in the distance. A door down the street slammed shut, and farther off Anji heard the clatter of a cart and horse before both came into view, crossing the intersection then moving out of sight. As they climbed the steps, Anji spotted a chimney topping the square roof, and now that she'd come closer she could see a thick column of steam billowing in a lazy plume from its spout. The wind carried the vapor away as soon as it crested over the metal pipe's top. Anji rubbed at the back of her neck.

Alright, it's open at least, she thought, looking around, *open in the scrubbiest, scummiest part of town, but still—*

The wooden double doors ahead clicked open and a short, balding man in a tiny vest sauntered out, followed by the sounds of muted, murmuring voices and a stringed instrument Anji couldn't quite place. The brawny doorman barely topped Anji's shoulder, but the stare he offered as she crested the final step sent a chill up her spine. His eyes scanned Kit up and down, assessing her lank figure, the black scale and tufts of fur beginning to creep up her neck.

"Misses," said the doorman with a tight bow. "I regret to say we are prioritizing reservations at present. If you like, I can recommend any number of other accommodations for—"

"How much?" said Kit, untying her purse.

The doorman wrinkled his nose. "Madam, as I said before, we are prioritizing—"

"I'm here on Spur business, you stupid little man," said Kit, her voice hard. "Call the Peak down if you've an issue with a sale. I don't have time to jaw with you."

The man leveled a look at Kit's neck—at her reddening eyes, the black crust around her nostrils. He obviously agreed Kit didn't have much time at all. He straightened his vest and held out a fleshy hand. "For you both, twenty."

Anji gaped as she watched the Hawk produce a wad of paper bills, fan through them, then clasp the bag shut in one neat motion.

"*Twenty* Rhoda?" Anji said, eyes wide. She gestured at the street, the doorman's censorious glare, the bathhouse in general. "There's no way it's that much." She made to grab the bills but Kit snatched her hand, twisting until pain bolted through Anji's fingers.

281

The doorman offered a humoring smile, his hand still out-stretched. Kit slapped the bills into his palm before releasing Anji.

"Our thanks," Kit said as the doorman stepped aside to let them through. She motioned for Anji to follow and said, so quiet Anji could only just hear, "If one were in need of a powder room, preferably a green-glass mirror . . ."

The man turned back to the street, his hands clasped. "Top floor, door o' blue."

Kit dipped her head and ushered Anji into the bathhouse, a hand pressed to her back.

Anji heard the door close behind her and let her eyes adjust to the musty dark as a host of heady aromas assaulted her nose. Eucalyptus, sage, chamomile, and foreign herbs Anji couldn't place. The mixture of smells summoned vivid images of her family's basement apartment and the chandler working above. She pulled her coat tighter despite the clawing, humid air filling the room.

Bodies in cream-colored towels and robes (some of them draped in a way that was all too revealing) lounged in groups and intimate pairs in a scattering of plush chairs and couches. Knee-high glass tables footed the furniture, supporting smoking smudge bowls, ashtrays, water pipes, and platters of food. Anji's mouth watered as she watched a squat old man testing the limits of a tiny white towel stuff a stack of bread and cheese into his mouth.

The ceiling towered high above, railways and walkways lining the square room. At the center of the space, sunk down with cushy benches lined in a circle, lay a fire pit crackling and shifting color with every passing second.

"Come on," Kit said, still pushing at Anji's back. "Top floor. The smell is making me sick." Anji followed close behind, wiping at the sweat already forming on her brow.

The halls on either side of the large main space branched off into smaller capillaries, all leading to what Anji assumed were private parlors. Sighs of pleasure and instructive, professional voices issued from behind screen doors. Kit led Anji up a flight of stairs, both of them huffing and puffing by the time they reached the top floor. Anji's ankle protested with each step, the pain sharper than it had been that morning. Had she really woken up in a crumbling lighthouse down the beach only hours before? She hunched over after taking the final stair, gasping with hands on her knees.

"Quite the pair we make," Kit breathed beside her. "A lame regicide and a decrepit drug addict—bested by stairs."

"Handled that Scorphice just fine," Anji said, waving the comment away. She looked around. "You're sure we're on the last floor? Any attics I should know about?"

"We're nearly there," said Kit, watching a flabby, silver-haired man saunter past, naked save for a small towel slung around his ample waist and an assortment of gold chains thick as Anji's fingers. He trailed an attendant waving a censer billowing clouds of thick green smoke.

"How can anyone afford all this?" Anji said as the man turned a far corner.

Kit opened her mouth to speak when two figures emerged from the door across the hall, their eyes glassy, tranquility writ on their faces. One of the figures, a lithe man no older than Anji, wore a purple robe hanging loose over his chiseled stomach. He sniffed and tittered as a bare-chested man in pale yellow trousers ambled out behind him.

Anji recognized the old man's face.

"That's Esca—"

Kit cuffed Anji's ear with the palm of one gloved hand.

The door clapped shut behind the couple, the bang of its closing reverberating off the wooden floor and walls. The pair wandered off arm in arm as Kit straightened and motioned for Anji to do the same.

"Don't act so shocked," said the Hawk. "You'll give us away if you look like you've never been to a place like this." She pointed to the door Escadora and his escort had just vacated. "Not a word while we're in there. I'm not used to buying like this."

Anji narrowed her eyes. "Like what? Aren't all deals the same?"

"I don't know which Spur operates in this neighborhood."

"You mean you don't know how—"

A scream issued from behind the door, sharp and breathless. Anji winced and stepped back.

"You can't wait out here," Kit said, one hand on her knife. Her face was drawn, sweating. Anji wondered for what felt like the hundredth time in the last few days whether she could take the woman right there on this landing. The Hawk seemed to be dying right before her eyes. But deep down, Anji knew better. She'd been bested on the tundra, with and without a sword, and she didn't much like her odds no matter what Kit looked like now. Even in her worst state, even this close to succumbing to her addiction, Kit was a hardened warrior, and she would do whatever she could to keep herself alive until Anji was locked up on a ship bound for Linura. No, she'd go along with this, if only to avoid a beating and, most of all, for her possessions. She glanced once more at the bag around Kit's shoulder.

Another screech sounded behind the door, followed by harsh, raised voices.

Kit knocked in a strange pattern. One knock, then three in quick succession, then a final deliberate boom that shook the door on its hinges. She pulled up the collar of her leathers, covering what she could of the graying skin. Anji thought it was a waste of time, considering the crusted black snot around her nose. The shrieking and arguing on the other side faltered before the door was pulled in a few inches, revealing a red-rimmed eyeball in a hairy, greasy face.

"Out," said the face, closing the door.

"Not one step back," Kit said.

The door stopped, then the eye disappeared for an instant, looking back into the room. Anji caught a shock of oil-black hair to accompany the face before the eye shot back into the crack. "Fiacco then?"

"Fiacco," said Kit. To Anji it sounded as if she were about to collapse from sheer exhaustion right there in front of the open door. What would Anji do if that happened?

The eye swiveled to where Anji stood. "She in too?"

Kit grunted, "New blood," and made a complicated hand signal to Anji that made no sense at all, but Anji played along and made one back to her. The man in the doorway seemed appeased. He opened the door just enough for the two of them to squeeze through.

+ 39 +

The stench of blood and piss and sweat racked Anji's nose as the door closed at her back. Frayed curtains hung over a shuttered window, letting pillars of dusty light through to a sort of sitting room. Two stiff couches flanked a squat table perched on a moldy rug. A bald, shirtless man sat like a boulder on the right-hand couch, beady eyes focused on Kit and Anji from the moment they walked in. Anji spared him a glance, but her eyes were drawn to the scrawny middle-aged man in soiled clothes strapped to a chair in front of the window, chest heaving, skin sliced in a dozen places. Anji looked down to the floor, feigning a silent deference to Kit and thankful she'd been instructed not to make a sound. She thought if she tried she would throw up.

"What's all this?"

A raven-haired woman in a patched blue smoking jacket appeared from behind the whimpering man. Anji figured her of an age with Kit, if not a little younger. A slender sheathed sword bounced against her leg as she stepped around the bloody mess on the floorboards. She wiped at her nose with the back of one gloved hand. "I'm a bit busy right now—"

"Fiacco," the man with the greasy hair murmured. "Rail." He grinned, teeth milky white.

"Ah," the woman said, "thank you, Devas."

She stripped off her leather gloves and slipped around the tortured man, dropping a long, blood-spattered knife clattering to the table, then crossed the room to the vacant couch. Anji watched as she reached into the space between the couch and moldy carpet, sliding a sturdy leather case out from beneath the frame. She rose and tossed her blood-stained gloves onto the table beside the knife. "You're far out of your jurisdiction, Miss . . ."

"Kit," said Kit, eyes glued to the leather case. "I—we're headed back to Linura," she said, her voice firm for all it had quavered out in the hall.

The woman gave them an amused frown. "Long trip." She cracked the case open and wagged a knowing finger at Kit. "It just *tickles* me when city Spurs employ users," she said, taking out two green-glass vials. Anji felt Kit straighten at her side, but nobody else in the room seemed to notice. "I always tell my crew," she said, gesturing at the hulking man on the couch, "how are you supposed to *move* the stuff if you've never tried it? What do you tell a slop looking for something they've never had? 'It'll make you feel . . . things'?" She giggled and looked Kit up and down. "Though you're looking fairly far along."

"I've started weaning off."

The woman's grin widened. "Of course," she said in a singsong voice, and pointed to the man in the chair. "If only my friend here had a similar taste for restraint." She raised her voice. "Hear that, Bras? *Small doses! Dilution!* Or we have to cut the shit right off you!" She swiveled back to Kit and Anji, still standing in front of the door. "That's . . . one hundred Rhoda, if you please."

Anji started, but Kit flashed her a look, then reached into her purse and set two neat stacks of bills at the table's edge. She inched farther forward and accepted the two vials, which she stowed in the folds of her leathers.

"Appreciated much," said Kit, bobbing her head. She tied the purse and motioned for Anji to precede her through the door. The door Devas still guarded.

The woman clicked the case shut and sat back on the couch, one leg folded over the other. "Don't rush off now, Kit," she said, a hand to her chest. "Compared to Linura, we're positively rural, but not without our manners." She snapped her finger at Devas, who immediately dipped his head, abandoned his post, and pushed through another door across the room.

"Clean this up, will you?" The woman flicked a hand toward Bras, his shoulders shaking in silent sobs. Bras looked up as the bald giant lumbered to his feet and began unstrapping him.

"Help me! I didn't—"

The guard dealt Bras an open-palmed smack that took up most of the poor man's face. A fresh spray of blood spackled the floorboards. Kit watched in silence as Bras was hauled out of the chair, gurgling and spitting and shouting, too weak to struggle against the huge man's grip as they left out the room's main door.

Anji felt her gorge rise again.

Kit motioned for Anji to sit as though nothing untoward had just happened. Anji settled onto the cushion and watched Kit dose herself.

"Wonderful, isn't it?" the woman said, chuckling, her laughter cracking like glass. "Our first batch since Rolandrian got pricked. Linura is in such an uproar—we've been able to move much easier. Of course you'll know all about that." The woman ran a hand through her hair and sat forward on the couch as Devas came through the door once more with a tray balanced on one hand. He stepped through the tangle of legs and furniture and set the tray on the table. A green unmarked bottle sat atop the tray along with three bulbous wineglasses. The woman waved Devas away and he returned to his place at the door.

"My name is Jorgina, by the way," the woman said, pouring the wine into the glasses. "But for you, Gina will do." She eyed the level in her glass, poured an extra bit, and set the bottle down.

"A pleasure," Kit said, taking a sip from her glass and prompting Anji to do the same. The wine was delicious. Anji couldn't remember the last time she'd tasted something like it.

"To the host," said Kit, raising her glass, "and to the death."

Anji spit her wine out. She looked from Kit to the woman on the couch. Gina ignored her, one leg folded over the other, the wineglass—nearly empty now—balanced in one hand on her knee. Her voice was solid and firm when she spoke, however. "Are you ready?"

"Another moment, if you please," Kit said, taking a steady breath. She drained her glass and set it down. "What news from Linura?"

What news from—what the fuck is going on?

Anji inched back in her seat, clutching the wineglass like it was her last anchor to sanity.

Gina swirled her wine. "Oh it's 'sanctity' this and 'appointments' that," she said, waving a hand. "Some rebel force has been gaining traction, but I hardly think they'll kick up any dust. The Sun Wardens have their constables out in force, bashing doors in, putting on public displays. Barbaric bunch, if you ask me. Senate is all aflutter, voting on whom to put in Rolandrian's place—him being without an heir and all—someone to rally behind. The Wardens claim the successor will be chosen in due course by their god. Your standard transfer of power. Don't ask me for specifics. I don't get out to Linura much these days." She leaned forward. Anji felt Kit inch back.

"I *have* heard it said that since the king was killed, they're having issues in some of the factories. Strange, isn't it?" And Anji really believed the woman was confused. "You'd think order a balm to chaos. That the foundations, cracked as they were, were enough to hold everyone up. But they obviously weren't. There have been attempts to climb the revolutionary ladder for years, decades even." She tapped her lip. "But it seems they—this rebel group, I mean—the Tide, may yet gain a foothold. Who's to say?" Gina sat back in her seat. "It's all rather droll to me."

Anji locked eyes with Gina. "Revolution bores you?"

"Quiet," snapped Kit.

Gina barked a laugh. "*Futility* bores me, child. Who gets to eat what? Who dies when? Who shits where? Do all you like. Set fires in all the places you deem necessary. It's all the same in the end. Some people have things, others don't. No amount of protest will make it any different. The revolution ends, and people are still starving somewhere."

"Easy words for someone with food."

Gina tapped a finger against the glass. "I like this one, Kit," she said, eyes fixed on Anji. "But then again, I've always had a weakness for weakness."

In response, Kit dosed herself again. She sniffed and held her head back, letting the powder do its work.

"A piece of advice for you," Gina continued, her misty eyes meeting Anji's, "whatever your name is. The world won't make space for you or your ideals." She weighed her hands. "There's the reality you wish for, and the one which exists. Try to remember which will keep you alive."

Kit set a hand on Anji's knee, steady now. Firm.

Gina tittered another laugh, drained the last of her wine, and set the glass on the table. "It's no matter to me. People will be looking for a fix till the world ends."

A retort was ready on Anji's lips, but Kit squeezed her knee and inched forward.

"Day is fading," she said, "and I must be on my way. Much as it pains me."

The two women shot to their feet, swords drawn. Anji felt herself shoved aside as Gina's sword came flashing down into the cushion where Kit had been sitting a heartbeat before. Kit rolled over the back of the couch while Anji slammed herself to the floor. Metal clanged, deafening in the small space, as Kit and Gina swirled among the various pieces of furniture, grunting and slashing with their short swords. Gina's movements were fluid, like a dancer's, but she was impeded by the number of things in her way. Kit moved like a boulder rolling down a hill, not caring for the couches and chairs she had to avoid, knocking over a shelf that came clattering to the floor. Anji got to her feet, reaching for a dagger that wasn't there. She felt a speeding rush of panic as Gina struck Kit a glancing blow that sliced into the Hawk's shoulder. Kit ignored the wound and pressed another attack.

Gina grunted and kicked the table on its side, trying to get inside Kit's considerable reach. She edged forward, sword raised, but hopped back with a cry, holding a hand to her stomach.

"Yield and we can leave," said Kit, her chest heaving. "I've no wish to kill you."

"Stop with the formalities," Gina said before lunging at Kit.

As Anji got to her knees, she felt a sharp, biting pain. Gina's discarded dagger, still covered in Bras's blood, the blade's edge digging into her skin. She snatched it from the floor just as Gina cried out and backed away once more, her steps clumsy and lopsided now. She swiped at Kit, who pushed ahead with her sword raised for a final blow.

Devas pounced across the room toward Kit, a dagger of his own raised high. He stumbled on an overturned couch cushion but barreled ahead, his girth propelling him toward the Hawk.

"Kit, look out!"

But Anji was already bounding toward Devas, the dagger held firm in her hand. She stepped onto the splintered couch and leapt onto Devas's back just as he began bringing his dagger down toward Kit.

Anji slammed her knife into Devas's chest—once, twice—feeling the blade separate tendon and muscle. A jet of hot blood sprayed out from the wounds, coating Anji's fingers. Devas crashed to the floor under her, gurgling and twitching. He made a feeble attempt to wrench Anji off, but she was already clambering away from him, watching with wide-eyed horror as he choked his last breath.

The fight on the room's other side was slowing down. Anji scrambled to her feet, flexing her fingers as she watched Kit advance, eyes bright, her body tensed. Gina fell back, knocking a side table clattering to the floor. A moment of tense silence rang through the room before the two women launched at each other once more in a flurry of sword strikes and grunts. Kit yelled and pressed forward, feinting to her left side, then drove up in a stab just as Gina raised her blade.

A sickening punching sound rent the air. Gina gasped, still swiping her sword—but even Anji could tell all the woman's strength had been sapped. The blade tumbled from her hand onto the carpet below with a defeated thud.

Kit took a step back and wrenched her sword free from Gina's sternum. She caught Gina with one arm around her shoulders and cradled her to the floor, letting the blade rest on the planks at her side. Anji stepped forward, still fighting for a breath.

Kit lay Gina down on the carpet, smoothing her hair out. Blood was already pooling into the moldy fabric. She made cooing, shushing noises and stroked Gina's cheek. "You were honorable to the last," she said, her voice low, reverent.

Gina's chest heaved, blood bubbling from the wound at its

center. She closed her eyes tight and opened them once more, their whites rimmed with red.

"Peace," said Kit, and the woman rattled her last breath, limp in the Hawk's arms.

Anji snatched the bottle of wine, still intact, from the floor and took a greedy swig. She wiped at her mouth and looked around the decimated room.

"What in the fucking million hells was that all about?"

Kit said nothing, just folded Gina's eyes shut and stood, brushing off the dust and blood from her thighs. Devas had stopped his death twitches on the room's other side, blood ringing his still form. Kit spared him a glance, then locked eyes with Anji.

A wave of pure terror flooded through Anji as Kit rushed forward, arms raised. She held the bottle ready like a hammer and stammered as Kit's boots thundered across to her.

But Kit only wrapped Anji in a tight hug.

Anji was so surprised she dropped the bottle.

Kit leaned back, her hands still on Anji's arms. She smiled then, and Anji realized she'd never seen the woman grin like this. She could see nearly every one of her straight white teeth. She had a single dimple on her left cheek. Kit's wrinkles bunched at her eyes, and though Anji looked for a word, she couldn't find one as they stood together among the wreckage.

There was no disturbance or sound of rushing steps in the hall outside. Anji wondered whether anyone would have intervened if they had heard anything.

"Grab everything you can," said Kit. "There will be money— lots of it. We have a few minutes, but I'm not sure when the other will return."

"What are you—"

Kit released Anji and began rooting around the room. She grabbed up the leather case and checked the locks before stepping over Devas's limp form and swinging open the doors to a broken cabinet. Anji watched her pull another case out from the cabinet's depths, crack it open, and swing it around to Anji. It took her a moment to process just how much it held.

Half a million Rhoda, at least.

"If you're planning on telling me what just happened," Anji said, her mouth dry, "I'd really love to—"

"Not here," Kit said. She slung the blue bag over one shoulder. "Wipe what blood you can from your hands," said Kit, slamming the case closed. "Time to find a ship."

–+ 40 +–

"I didn't know when we arrived which Spur we'd be dealing with. I had to take the chance it was my own, or an ally to my own, but it was not."

They'd rushed out of the bathhouse and down a maze of alleyways, Kit stumbling with exhaustion, Anji breathless with fear at her side. The few people they'd passed walked by without a word to either of them, though a fair number spared a curious glance for the Hawk and her charge as they hobbled past.

"So Gina tried to kill you?" Anji said.

"It's an old rivalry. There are a dozen Spurs around Makona, and not all of them friendly. If we ever meet, we're to offer unpoisoned food or drink and exchange certain—pleasantries, before fighting."

Anji's arm ached with the weight of the leather case banging against her leg. More money than she'd ever seen in one place, right there in her hand.

"You knew the whole time you'd have to fight," Anji said, trying and failing to keep the mix of awe and disgust out of her voice.

"I didn't *know* until we sat down," said Kit. "This way." She directed them down a short set of stairs and onto the docks proper, then paused at a bench facing the waves and sank into it with a heavy breath.

Anji sat beside her, her ankle and knuckles flaring like burning coals. The docks bustled with a heart-wrenchingly familiar routine. Sailors and dockworkers calling out to each other in their jargon, the creak of old, sea-tested wood, waves slurping against hulls and barnacle-crusted pilings; even the briny reek of fresh fish brought memories from her childhood. An iron crane squealed on its bearings as it swung roped crates over the heads of a crew unloading a double-masted ship. The sodden workers had formed a line from deck to dock, hauling barrels and canvas-wrapped bundles onto a wide cart. One of the ship's crew stopped to stare at them, but he was cuffed on the ear by another worker and averted his gaze.

As though it were a cue, Kit ripped her mask off. A pair of bearded sailors rolling a hand cart shot Kit a narrow-eyed glance as they passed, but they continued on without a word.

"What are you doing?" Anji said. "They'll see your—"

But Anji stopped, her breath caught in her chest. The graying skin and tufts of rough fur that had begun creeping up Kit's neck that morning had grown over her jawline now. Her lips pushed outward, like she'd lined her mouth with wool. Her eyes blazed where their whites had been, and the green of her irises was saturated with red. Anji had noticed the Hawk's already thin hair growing patchy, but with the mask removed it was clear how much she'd really lost. She'd be bald before long.

"Kit . . ."

Staring at the mask in her shaking hands, Kit said, "Peace. I want a minute of free air."

Anji sat back on the bench, trying not to stare at Kit's disfigured face. A bell clanged from a distant mast, and Kit shifted away.

"If the One's hell existed," she said, more to herself than to Anji, "there's a special place there for whoever made Rail."

"I don't understand why anyone would sell it in the first place," said Anji.

Kit coughed and cleared her throat, throwing Anji a haughty glance. "Same reason anyone does anything terrible—money."

Anji picked at a fingernail, studying the Hawk's mask in Kit's lap. She'd never been much for conversation, for reading how people felt—but something told her Kit felt that same urge Anji had felt in the lighthouse. That yearning to bare yourself as the short time you had left ticked past.

She inched forward.

"Jared mentioned you were involved with a Spur . . . ," Anji said, "with him . . . when you were younger." If Kit was annoyed at Jared's admission, she didn't show it. She only stared out toward the churning waves, the sky lightening to gold.

"It's a long story," she said, her voice soft. "Long and sad."

Anji forced a weak smile. She hated the thought of prodding Kit in what might be the woman's final hours. But apart from a selfish desire to know more about the Hawk, a desire that might never fully fade, she wanted to afford the woman the opportunity, the dignity, of her attention.

I might be the last person she speaks to.

"Take a second to rest," she said. Then she gave Kit's shoulder a light punch. "Anyone interrupts you and I'll fight them off."

Another shout came from one of the crewmen on deck, and the others responded in kind. Kit settled back against the bench, her mouth a thin line. Anji's smile faltered. Then Kit spoke.

"I ran with Spur Fiacco before I could walk," she said. "I've watched my best friends die, people I considered family, at each other's throats." She scratched at her hand and went on, "I've seen a man's entrails torn out while living. Faze fiends hallucinating in sewers. The worst a person could endure, and then some.

"The Peaks—heads of the Spurs—teach you not to care. 'They want what they want. They bring it on themselves.' That's what I was told, and I believed every word. I believed it when I made my drops, knowing the hands they would fill—the lungs. I believed it when I skewered a Faze addict for a being a Celdia short on what she owed. I melted a man's hand off for buying in different territory, and I sold him a ream of Snip as he screamed. I killed and maimed and tortured so many. I got promoted. Given more command, more responsibility. More respect.

"In all those years, I never asked why. Why buy something you know will ruin you? Why give up your job, your family, everything? Why do they feel such a *need* to escape? What is it they're escaping from?"

Her shoulders rocked with each breath—Anji could hear air rattling through Kit's spent lungs, but she stayed silent as Kit continued.

"I did everything they asked of me," she said. *"Everything."*

Anji held her breath, unsure of what to say. She imagined the Hawk cutting her own father's throat, the way the knife had felt digging into skin. An urge rose in her to comfort Kit, to say she knew everything and none of it was her fault. She was about to speak when Kit went on.

"Years passed, and when calls for change began from inside the Spur, I silenced them. I was devoted. I would have done more, had I been asked." She gazed out at the distant surf.

"Then they just . . . sent me away. They had me trained like a dog, then when the Bear came calling, with her grandfather's connections to the Senate, my Peak couldn't resist. He offered my skill, my loyalty and devotion, to the Menagerie just as it was being formed. He wanted a spy in the Senate, someone to guide their efforts away from the Spur's trade. I never wanted to go, but something happened that I didn't expect: I made friends. I traveled the world with them. I loved them.

"But I didn't close all contact with my former life, or my old friends. I was still close with Jared, though he'd been sold off to a duke to be his household surgeon. We exchanged letters, and over the years Jared became more sympathetic to a growing reform movement: the Tide. Whispers became rumors, rumors led to my own thoughts on what I'd seen—what I'd done. Then the Bear started attending masses for the One Path, started preaching to us. It took far too many jobs with cruelty at their heart before I began to realize how we had changed, how the Bear had changed. We'd become no better than mercenaries; thugs for the Senate, and eventually for the Sun Wardens themselves. We silenced dissent, strangled calls for change. I had become the tool I was always intended to be, but I kept on. Bear had always been our leader, and I'd been bred to be led.

"Then, one day, I ran into a man I'd known in the Spur. It was like light had been let back into the world. We began seeing more of each other, and before long I fell back in with my contacts," she said, "others from those days, who had also left the life behind. Most of them had begun working in factories or mills, and there their sympathy to the Tide had grown. They convinced me to accompany them to their secret meetings, and I learned more. I listened more. They gave me banned books they'd hoarded as the Wardens began to squeeze the city of all dissent. Books about change. About how we could effect it if we only had the means, the organization, the numbers." She glanced at Anji. "The funds."

"Did you tell them?" said Anji, "who you really were?"

Kit nodded, knuckling black drip from her nose.

"I told them everything. About the Menagerie, every horrid thing I'd done. But still, I couldn't just . . . leave. The Menagerie, I mean. Bear had grown more paranoid and—well, you've seen her yourself. I was afraid of her. Of what she would do if she found me out.

"Living two lives, two identities—it takes its own toll. I managed for a few years, attending Tide meetings one day and off hunting with the Menagerie the next. But I became less reliable, less interested in taking jobs. I had money enough for the rest of my life, and the work made me sick. We'd known each other for so long—they thought I was merely feeling my age. I began to spy on them for the Tide. I helped the revolution gain more knowledge we could use against the Wardens. I wish it hadn't felt like a betrayal, but it did. I knew what my old friends had become, but I grieved for the friends they had been.

"So, about a year ago, I began using Rail. The smallest doses at first." She coughed a laugh, fingering a vial in her pocket. "I was already a monster in mind, so why not a monster in body? Nightmares plagued my attempts to sleep, so I stayed awake, euphoric and numb, so lonely and filled with secrets I could hardly function. I felt I'd lost and found myself all at once, but in pieces I couldn't fit together."

Kit swallowed, wiped a tear from one bloodshot eye.

"Kit—" Anji started, but the Hawk held up a hand.

"Listen to me," said Kit, her voice hoarse. She dug a Rail vial out of her leathers and took another dose, then nudged the leather case with one booted foot. "You'll take half the Rhoda in there, get on a ship, and make for a northern town—wherever suits you. Find a man, a woman." She flailed a hand. "Get a cat. Whatever you like. Just stay out of Linura for the rest of your life. Else I'll have to find you all over again."

With every word, a lightness filled Anji from her toes to her maimed hand; her throat swelled with an air she never knew tasted so sweet. "I don't—" she sputtered, her eyes stinging. "Why?"

Kit's jaw clenched, the blackening skin around her neck going taut. She flexed her hand and sat straighter on the bench. "I'll not spend my last days as a mercenary—even if the cause is just. Besides, that's twice you've saved my life now," said Kit. "Fair is fair."

"What about my bounty?" said Anji, hardly believing she was arguing the point. "Don't you need me so you can get paid?"

Kit shook her head and pointed to the leather case. "There's half a million Rhoda in there, at least. It's not as much as I'd signed up for, but I'll eat the loss to spare your life. Revolutions are underfunded by nature, even the successful ones."

They sat together in silence. A crippled, directionless woman and her dying captor. Anji searched for something to say, her mouth working.

"Stop licking your lips," said Kit. She clapped Anji on the knee and slipped her mask back on, then rose from the bench. "Let's find you a ship." Anji sprang up to support her before she fell.

✦ 41 ✦

They walked along the pier, the many berths on their left branching out like claws into the placid bay. On their right stood the grime-crusted walls of houses and shops worn by years of storm and sea. The weight of Kit's slight, quivering body wasn't much burden for Anji to bear, but the combination of a day without food, a night with little sleep, and the endless jabbing pain in her hand and ankle was enough to keep them at a slow pace as they crawled up the quay. The workers on the opposite side continued on with their unloading, but one of them, a bearded mountain of a man in suspenders, corncob pipe sticking from the corner of his mouth, called a halt to their work as Anji and Kit made their way closer.

"Stand me up," Kit said, letting go of Anji's arm. "I'll do the talking."

The ship's crew began to disperse as the bearded man ambled toward them. He tapped a finger to his brow.

"Afternoon," he said, not quite meeting her eyes.

Kit inclined her head. "Harbormaster?"

"Captain." He took his pipe from between his teeth and

motioned with it to the ship at his back. "Harbormaster's got an office back the way you came."

"We're looking for a ship," said Kit.

"Something small," said Anji.

"Anji, please."

"Sorry."

Anji couldn't help but beam at the rows of ships—even the ocean looked inviting. She was *free*. She was leaving this entire mess behind. A lightness she hadn't felt in weeks dared to spread through her chest, and she allowed the feeling to permeate for an instant. She smiled despite the man's gruff expression, despite the woman at her side dying on her feet.

"Got a sloop tied up down the dock," the man said, hooking a thumb behind one shoulder. "Shouldn't be much hassle for the two of you, though I'd suggest hiring on a hand or two extra." He glanced down the length of Kit's emaciated form.

"A sloop will be fine, sir," said Kit.

Without another word he turned and led them down the quay, past empty bilge holds, barnacle-studded piers shining in the late afternoon sun. The surf foamed at Anji's left side, bubbling around the ships tied to their moorings. Kit, limping along at Anji's side, began rummaging in the blue bag. Anji watched as they came to a stop at a narrow-hulled, single-masted boat bobbing along in the rising tide at the far end of the pier, nearest the cliffside overlooking the docks.

"Here we are," said the captain, turning to face Anji and Kit. He scratched at his beard. "Few traders from Kardisa sold it to me. What with the Rain Plague and all, they won't be back for some time. Like I said, not much in the way of a ship, but it'll get you up to the next town north if you know how to tack." He looked over his bulbous nose at Kit, who had now thrown the bag to the ground to continue rummaging through.

"We'll manage just fine," she said, the voice behind the mask weak and wavering. She held out a wad of Rhoda without looking up. "For your trouble, and for the sloop."

The captain frowned. "I never said how much—"

Kit thrust the fold of notes forward. "Is this sufficient?"

Anji felt a tension in her shoulders, a pang of worry at the captain's stricken face. They'd already dealt with enough today. If this turned into a fight, she wasn't sure how well she'd be able to defend Kit against a man this size.

But the captain only pocketed the bills. "More than she's worth," he said, glancing toward the setting sun. "Wind's blowing a strong south, but it'll die down with the day. I'd advise against sailing in the dead of night if it's just you two, but that's your . . ." he trailed off, looking over Kit's shoulder. His eyes had shifted past the Hawk, past the teeming wharf and equipment, to the steps leading toward the dock.

What little skin showed around his beard had gone white.

Anji followed the man's gaze and sucked in a breath of salty air. The fleshy spots where her fingers had been twinged.

Metal clicking through bone.

✛42✛

"Hawk!"

Heads turned along the quay as the Bear descended the steps. She pulled her longsword from its sheath.

"Hawk!"

The assorted dockworkers parted for that white mask, the single brown eye glaring through the destroyed mesh of its left eye socket.

"Get in the boat, Anji," said Kit.

"*Hawk!*"

Anji pushed down a lurching wave of nausea as the woman strode down the quay, her long legs eating up the planks. The Bear's bootheels clapped against the wooden boards with every step until she stopped ten paces away.

A seagull cried above their heads, circling over the creaking ships. The Bear's shoulders rocked with each of her gasping breaths. She leveled her blade at Kit, its tip trembling.

The ship's captain took a tentative step forward. "If you don't mind," he said in a quavering voice, "I've just sold this here sloop, and I mean to draw up a purchase document if you'd—"

"Off with you, old man," the Bear said, her mask not twitching an inch. "Your business is finished."

The captain licked his lips, and with a glance back at Anji and Kit, slumped off down the dock, calling for his crew to get off their asses and back to work. Anji wished for a fleeting moment she were part of the crew, her only concern the pain in her back and her next meal. But a peal of raw anger was coursing through her, a thirst no menial work would quench.

"Give me a sword," she said, and without a word, the Hawk unsheathed both her longsword and her short, handing the latter to Anji. Anji let the sturdy blade cut once through the air and stood her ground at Kit's side.

"You will not win, Hawk," said the Bear. "Even with your hapless cripple." She shifted to the balls of her feet and pointed toward the dock's exit. "Take what little respect I still hold for you, make your way out of town, and hole up with your drugs. Spend your few remaining days in what comfort you can. I'll say it for the final time: give me the girl or die by my hand." She pointed to Anji. "She is a traitor to order. She would drag the One's Decree through the muck." Her voice rose in pitch. "I'll see her strung up in Laurelside Square for all of Linura to see. Her blasphemer guts will festoon the Pearl District—the Sun Wardens will make such an example of her as to cast all would-be dissenters in the glorious light of truth. The One Path will reign supreme, and I will be its spear! All has been preordained. This is the One's will! We will have peace. We will have law and decency once more in our streets. I will usher in a new reign of prosperity and wipe the degenerates from—"

"She really goes on, doesn't she?" Anji said.

Kit spat to the planks, the glob of inky mucus laced with blood. "She's only gotten worse." She placed a hand on Anji's shoulder. "Remember what I showed you at the lighthouse," she said. "Focus."

Anji had barely taken a breath in before the Bear lunged forward with a yell. The woman covered the space between herself and Kit in two strides, clashed, rebounded, and was already twisting for a second attack by the time Anji had found her feet.

The woman was a flurry of steel and leather, jarring left and right so fast Anji could only hold her sword out in shaking hands as the Bear danced between her and Kit. Kit slumped forward, lashing out with her sword, her legs shaking with each step. The Bear's steel scratched against Kit's outstretched blade and slid down with a squeal. Anji lunged forward at what she thought was an opening, but met only empty air as the Bear vaulted back, swinging in a wide arc that barely missed Anji's chest.

A crowd had formed, the dockworkers' tasks forgotten. A trio of constables in yellow tunics sifted through the press, but they only stopped at the crowd's edge to watch.

Anji lunged just as the Bear sliced her sword in a wide arc. The blade came down, scraping against Anji's arm, cutting through the leather of her coat and into skin. A flash of searing heat lanced through her arm and she scrambled back, raising her sword in one hand as another blow shot toward her stomach. Kit leapt toward the Bear with a strangled cry, sword raised, but the woman twirled like a streamer caught in an upward draft and evaded Kit's shambling cut.

Kit jumped back, her shoulders heaving, her weight to one side. Anji could hear the rasping, clogged throat whining in tune with the breeze above. The masts creaked in a fresh groan of wind.

"Why are you *protecting* her, Hawk?" said the Bear, ignoring the jeers of the gathered crowd. "One last good turn before the void takes you? You think it will save you? You think the One harbors turncoats and fools? That They forgive those who betray their friends?" Anji felt a flutter of hope watching the woman's shoulders heave.

She's winded too, Anji thought. *If I can just get around her while she's distracted with Kit.*

Kit rolled a thin shoulder and spun her sword once.

The town guards had gained a bit more courage and were now making their way toward the pair, weapons still scabbarded at their waists. Anji didn't know what they would do once they got to the fight, but she had a feeling it would be over before they could decide for themselves. She tensed her legs and watched as the Bear bore down once more on Kit, hacking and spinning, their swords clanging together. She tried her best to find an opening, but the two women moved like swirls of current in a raging river.

Kit advanced, feinted left, then shifted right and stabbed empty air as the Bear maneuvered around, her side exposed. Anji bounded forward, but the Bear pivoted and shot a booted foot straight into her stomach. All her breath whooshed from her lungs and Anji collapsed gasping to the ground. She scrambled on the planks as the Bear and the Hawk danced in a tangled embrace, got to her knees as the Hawk's back came into view.

The tip of the Bear's gleaming steel burst through Kit's leathers, dripping dark blood onto the dock. The world stopped; the guards halted in place and watched Kit drop her sword clattering to the ground. The Bear leaned close enough for their masks to touch.

"You'll die a Dredger, you heretic whore," she said, "I can smell it on you! You think I wanted this? I gave you love! I gave you *life*! I—"

The Hawk pulled one of her knives from her belt and rammed it to the hilt into the Bear's exposed throat.

The gathered crowd let out a collective gasp as Kit pushed the Bear away, the sword grinding back out of her stomach. The Bear crumpled to the ground, Kit's knife still lodged in the space between mask and leathers. Anji got to her feet and stumbled forward as Kit cried out, slumping to the planks. A wine-dark pool of red was already forming, seeping into the black cracks between boards.

The Bear choked and convulsed and rolled to her back, strings of blood flowing past the mask and onto the dock. Her legs kicked and scraped against the wood. She gurgled something and reached a trembling hand to her blood-drenched sword, but Anji kicked it away.

Days past, Anji might have stood over the Bear and relished the woman's dying breaths. She would have ripped the mask off and exposed that evil face for all Tideron to see. She would have shoved her blistering wound between blood-coated lips. She would have mocked her god, her vision, and her faith, and laughed while her life leaked out.

But Anji knew now. Knew it would do no good. Her taunts wouldn't grow her fingers back. Her satisfaction would turn to ash.

So she turned away, and left the Bear to die alone.

⚜ 43 ⚜

Anji hobbled to Kit, still lying on her back paces away. The pool of blood had grown to engulf her still form.

"Somebody get a doctor! A surgeon!"

"Anji—"

Nobody in the crowd said a word.

"She needs help!" Anji screamed.

"Anji," Kit said again, her voice weak. "We—" She coughed up a dribble of blood. Anji wiped it away. "The boat."

"Okay." Anji grabbed Kit's arm and hauled her up, relief flooding through her at her groan of protest. "Okay, the boat. I've got you," Anji said, her voice sounding a million worlds away. "Let's get you out of here. I'll take care of—"

"Stop!"

A constable had come forward, one hand on the hilt of his sword. Anji disregarded him as she scrabbled with Kit's dead weight.

"My fault . . . ," murmured Kit, "all my fault. Anji, my—"

"Shush," Anji said, teeth bared. "It's alright now. Don't talk."

The guard cleared his throat. Anji heard the rasp of steel on leather.

"In the name of King Rol—"

"He's dead, remember?" Anji said, wincing at Kit's slumped weight and the searing pain in her arm. "This was Menagerie business."

The guard said nothing, glancing at the Bear's lifeless form, at her mask, at the Hawk's. Anji turned her attention to the sloop ahead, the two bags sitting undisturbed on the dock's edge. As they approached, Anji heard the guard rounding the populace up and telling them to be on their way. She hauled Kit off the pier and into the sloop, laying her down in a bloody, coughing heap on one of the benches. Kit clattered against a pair of oars as Anji bent and tossed the bags in before climbing aboard.

The sun was setting as they left the dock, left the Bear lying still on the planks, and sailed away from Tideron.

✛44✛

The sloop's deck was plastered in blood. Anji could smell the metallic stench even over the salted air. The Hawk sat hunched on a plank bench, gloved hands pressed to her stomach. Dark pools gathered in the pockets where her leathers met and stained the tangled netting at her feet. The last whisps of her matted gray hair spun on the breeze as she gazed out across the roiling surf. She tore her mask off and set in on the bench.

Kit's face was drenched in sweat despite the chill; the muscles of her jaw flexed. The fur and scales creeping up her neck had spread to her cheeks, her nose, her temples, the texture of gray tree bark. Her teeth were a crowded mess of fangs stained with blood, sharp and lengthened past her lips. Her eyes glowed like bloody coals, gazing out across the waves as the sail ballooned out above.

"My fault. My fault, my fault . . ."

Anji followed Kit's gaze over the churning sea, then she bent to face her.

"What's your fault?" Anji said, huffing a little laugh. She slapped a hand to Kit's knee. "That's all of them, Kit. The Menagerie is—"

"Anji," said Kit, her swollen red eyes swimming with tears. "My—" Kit coughed, black spittle running onto her chin. She fumbled for the pocket of her leathers, one hand still clutched at her gut, and flipped out a vial of Rail. It tumbled out of her twitching fingers and clattered to the planks.

Anji snatched it up. She tilted some powder out onto her finger and lifted it to Kit's nose. Her cracked nostril flared around Anji's fingertip.

Waves slammed against the sloop's side, sending spray in freezing plumes. The land behind them grew smaller with each passing minute, Tideron's lights flickering as the sun finally sank past the horizon. Anji began tearing off a piece of her shirt.

"What are you doing?"

"I'm seeing to this," said Anji, gesturing at the mess of Kit's stomach. "We have to stop the bleeding. You've lost too much—"

"Leave it," said Kit. She hunched away from Anji and farther in on herself.

"I can't just let you bleed out—"

"Leave me be." A shudder passed through Kit's narrow shoulders. She shifted on the bench and the Hawk mask clattered to the planks. Kit ignored it, staring out across the waves. "It's over, Anji. Over for me."

Anji hunkered down in front of Kit, her uninjured hand gripped tight to the woman's bony knee.

"What are you talking about?" she said, her voice a croak. "You're the Hawk, you've been through worse than this." She glanced at the empty vial floating in the pool of blood and salt water at their feet. "You're going home. We're going to get you help. You still have—"

"The bag," Kit said. "Bring it here."

Anji frowned but lifted the blue bag and set it clinking in Kit's lap. The Hawk slipped one of her gloves off, revealing a hand

313

sprouting fur and hard ridges, taloned black nails at the tips of her fingers.

Kit handed her the glove.

"Put it on," said Kit, motioning to the bag.

Anji did so, the glove still warm from Kit's hand. She reached out to the bag and touched the silky cloth. It sprang open from a hidden seam.

Anji laughed despite herself. "The *gloves*," she said, wiping away a tear. "You never took them off."

"Mmm," said Kit, her head hanging.

Anji upended the bag. Inside were a change of Kit's clothes, assorted bits of food and wrappings, a battered pair of shackles, a collection of empty vials, and Anji's dagger in its leather sheath. She slipped the blade free, her fingers tight around the familiar handle, then spotted a gleam of dull metal soaking in Kit's blood.

Two coins. One Anji's, the other its twin.

"What—I don't—Kit, what is this?"

"I took it, Anji," said Kit, her chest heaving. "Me."

Anji picked up the coins, both pulsing with maxia.

"You took . . ." Anji squeezed the coins, the edges digging into her skin.

"All my fault," Kit said, fresh tears spilling down her cheeks. She spat a thick glob of blood and mucus and sank lower on the bench. "I killed them. Stuffed the pages into their mouths. I took your coin before the Goat could guess what it was. Found you on the streets. Paid to have you taken to the castle."

Anji stared, a buzzing filled her ears. Her vision tunneled, her hands shook.

"I thought you'd be safe," said Kit, "and you were, for six years. Even when the castle bells began to ring, I knew you would be okay. Then, when I heard your description—when I heard about what you'd done—I cursed myself for putting you there. I cursed gods I don't even believe in and thanked them when I found out you'd escaped.

"Then," and now Kit's voice was a croak, "I heard about your bounty. A million Rhoda. All that money . . . for the Tide. I told myself I had no choice. I had to track you down, to finish the horrible job we'd started with your parents all those years ago." Kit whimpered and reached out a trembling hand. "I'm so sorry, Anji."

"That's how you found me," Anji said, eyes wide. "On the streets . . . in that tavern . . . Sheertop." She flexed her mangled hand, the phantom pain still present, still an aching loss she'd bear forever.

"Anji, I didn't—"

Anji stumbled to the edge of the boat, to the rail, to the endless sea bearing down on their little craft, felt her gorge rise and pushed it down. If not for the Hawk, for the Menagerie, she would never have set foot in the castle, would never have killed Rolandrian. She'd still have her fingers. She'd still have her parents.

"Anji," Kit said, her head lolling on her neck. "Anji, I'm so . . . I'm—"

"You," Anji sputtered, "you! You—"

Anji screamed. She tore at her scalp, her remaining fingers digging filthy streaks down her cheeks.

"Please, Anji," said Kit, her voice a whisper. "It hurts. I can't—"

Anji rushed forward, ignoring the pain, the obstinate agony in her half-healed hand she'd never escape as long as she lived. She took up her father's dagger in one shaking fist and slammed it into Kit's heart.

The sea seemed to freeze, the sloop's tattered sail drooped above, caught in a pocket of empty air. Anji locked eyes with the Hawk, pushing her weight into the dagger's hilt, tears and snot and spittle dripping onto those leathers, mixing with Kit's blood.

Kit convulsed under her. Warm blood gushed along the

dagger's blade. It ran down to join the pool. Anji choked a sob and felt something release in her throat, in the depths of her chest, like a knot untying and laying limp around her heart. She lowered herself to lay beside Kit and draped an arm over the Hawk, monster of the Menagerie. Would-be hero of a revolution.

Kit twitched, and Anji met her eyes again. In those glassy red wells, she could see a lifetime of murder and sorrow and regret. Years of remorse, of the needle-sharp knowledge of what she'd done, stared at Anji through those heavy lids. Kit's lips parted, as though to say a final word. She lifted her taloned hand to touch Anji's cheek, then the hand went slack. Her eyes reflected the milky gust of emerging stars overhead.

⊹ 45 ⊹

Anji lay alongside Kit on the deck, her body shivering and twitching. Strands of Kit's gray hair twirled in the breeze, tangled in sodden knots, slapping at her cheeks. The wind picked up in a gust, as though Kit's last breath had shot around the world and returned to speed Anji along the careless sea. She held Kit's body tight against the pain and the betrayal, the loss and the weariness and the resounding, immovable loneliness that seemed determined to follow her to the earth's end.

She cried in a puddle of ice-cold blood beside her dead friend.

Anji looked to the deck where the Hawk mask lay, gleaming under moonlight obscured by coming clouds. The boat trudged across the waves, rigging and mast groaning with the wind. Rain began pattering on the pitted wood. She shifted to her knees and picked up the mask.

It was cold in her mangled hand, its edges chipped and scratched. Anji wondered how many sword tips had glanced off the battered face, how much of Kit's sweat had soaked into the leather band lining its inside lip. She realized she was still holding the two coins tight in one hand and stuffed them snug in her coat pocket. They vibrated together against her breast, and she felt the corners of her mouth twitch ever so slightly up.

The wind blasted south against the ship's tack, buffeting the heaving sail, throwing waves against the groaning wood that had become Kit's final stand, her confession ground. Anji stared down at the woman who had shepherded her away from the salvation she now faced, the Hawk who'd taken her captive and set her free in so many ways with her final breath.

Anji sat against the stern, the tiller wobbling against the tugging waves underfoot. She took in a lungful of icy, salted air, then another, and another until she at last released a steady breath. Every muscle in her body throbbed, every bone felt ground to dust. A rumble shook through her stomach, and she loosed a tiny laugh at the thought that she could possibly be hungry now, but there it was.

People get hungry, kings and killers die, and the wind turns its course.

She grasped the tiller and turned with it.

✦ 46 ✦

Anji hauled herself out of the sloop and onto the dock, cradling Kit's emaciated body in her arms.

"Two Celdia for the dock," called the attendant, blinking in the sun. She shaded her eyes against the glare and shoved a thin cigar into the corner of her mouth. "You'll want to speak with the port master about—Nine Gods!" she yelled, the cigar tumbling from her lips. "You can't just bring one of those things onto the dock! What are you—"

"Stop your prattling, girl," Anji said, her voice ringing behind the mask. The sound reverberated up the metal and through her skull. She was shocked at how much it had enhanced her vision and hearing the moment she slipped it on. The damned things really were maxial. And heavy. And itchy.

A bell clanged somewhere distant. Gulls cried overhead. The docks had teemed with their usual activity at her approach, but a crowd had already begun to gather around the Hawk and her dead charge. High above the crowd sat a young girl on her mother's shoulders, her hands tangled in the woman's dark hair. The girl's eyes were wide as saucers, staring at Anji as though she'd walked right out of a story. Anji turned away as the dock attendant crept forward, adjusting her tricorn hat, and studied Kit's body and face.

"Is that—"

Anji lowered herself down, the Hawk's leathers bunching around her knees, her elbows. She laid Kit on the planks, then dug into her purse and held out a full Rhoda to the attendant. "Find whoever set the bounty on Rolandrian's killer. Tell them she has been apprehended by the Hawk. Go!" The attendant chanced a wide-eyed look at the body and scampered off the dock and out of sight.

⊹ 47 ⊹

Two constables hauled Kit's body on a stretcher through Linura's streets, preceded by a Sun Warden who shouted at the crowds gathered on sidewalks.

"See the fruits of idleness and ingratitude! An addict! A Dredger! This *monster* killed your beloved king! Rolandrian of House Demuratia lies cold in his crypt by the hands of this vagabond!"

Anji marched at their backs, her heart fluttering with anxiety and a spreading, sickening dread at the sight of so many people. Constables lined the sides of the street, holding back the churning, chattering crowd. Streamers and other garbage fell from windows, from people crammed onto rooftops to get a view of the Hawk and her charge. Linurans from every neighborhood had come to see the king killer. Some whispered and pointed as Anji passed; some cried; some called out angry taunts.

After an interminable time, Anji was led into a giant, spherical building in Laurelside, newly built, shining under the blue sky. Kit's body was hauled through the open door, and Anji followed in after. The Warden led Anji up a wide flight of carpeted steps, along a short hall hung with gilt-framed paintings, and stopped at a pair of double doors gilded with the symbol of the One Path.

The Warden knocked once and opened the door as a gruff command to enter issued from inside.

A fleshy man in a yellow robe sat at a polished wood desk on the room's far side. He sported a crop of salt-and-pepper hair slicked back with a shiny oil Anji could smell before the door had even opened. Rosemary to cover the scent of sweat. He thumbed through a few papers as the group filed in and took a sip from a silver flask before leaning back in his chair to survey them. A pair of latticed windows were opened to the city streets below, ushering in the distant sounds of a still-screaming crowd.

The Warden gestured for Kit to be deposited on the carpeted floor before the desk, and with a slight bow to the man on its other side, he and his handlers left the room.

The other Warden's mouth bent down in a frown, his thick brow furrowed. He offered Anji a cursory glance and rose to get a closer look at Kit.

"You're sure this is her?" he said, his nose wrinkling. He produced a gold handkerchief from his robes and pressed it against his nose. Anji felt an urge to slap him, but she remained stoic and still. He'd obviously worked with the Menagerie before.

Anji inclined her head. "Positive. She wasn't near this close to turning when I found her. Fit the poster's picture. Admitted to everything." She sniffed for good measure. "Vermin was proud of what she'd done." She finished her monologue with what she hoped was a silent exhale of steady breath. Her chest felt like it would explode with her heart thundering against her ribs.

The Warden clicked his tongue. Ambled back around the desk and sank once more into his chair, his eyes still fixed on Kit's body.

"How did you find her?"

Anji pictured the Goat sitting opposite her, his shoulders shaking with mirth. She spared a thought for her friends, who'd met their ends by his hand.

"Two laundresses informed us of her desire to flee to Conifor should she ever escape the castle."

The Warden leaned over his desk, then flipped open a slender silver box and fished out a thin cigar, which he lit. "Likely they helped her with the assassination," he said, blowing out a plume of white smoke. He huffed a laugh. "Damned servants."

"Their names were Kaia and Libby," said Anji, clenching a fist.

If the Warden heard insubordination in Anji's tone, he didn't show it. He waved this last comment away like a fly pestering him and settled into his high-backed chair.

"Bounty was one million alive," he said, sucking on the cigar. "Half for a corpse. Why did you kill her?"

Anji's shoulders tightened. "She did it herself," she said, gesturing at the body. "While I slept. Didn't want to live like this, I imagine."

"Hmm. She wouldn't have lived long." His lips drew into a thin line as he surveyed Anji. "Still, sloppy work, Hawk."

Kit wouldn't say anything she didn't need to. And she'd already let her temper flare. She stood still and waited.

The Warden stubbed out his cigar into a crystal ashtray, then reached across his desk for a slip of paper.

"Bring this to Bilingues and Colk," he said, scribbling with a stubby pen. He scratched out a signature and stamped a tiny sigil onto the page's corner, then folded it once and held it out to her between two pudgy fingers.

Anji stepped gingerly around Kit, taking in her features for the last time, the twisted face that Anji had first seen unmarred save by age, all those miles past across a campfire. The face of the woman who had damned then saved her. She snatched the note from the Warden's hand. He stood from the desk, hands behind his back, and paced to the window.

"As to your next assignment," he said, "round up your fellows and report to Illuminess Starkwald. We've heard rumors of an insurrectionist camp in place at the Everrun's western bend, growing in force." He mashed a fist into one hand. "We'll crush them. We will ensure our order."

The Warden stared out across the city, running a hand through his hair as Anji inclined her head and turned for the door. She said a silent goodbye to Kit, and slipped out of the building like a ghost.

⤙ EPILOGUE ⤚

The Tide's camp was an orderly row of patched tents, cookfires, and racks of weapons. Men and women in homespun paced around the lanes, hauling water and wheeling bundles of cloth and food. Anji trudged up the main thoroughfare against a press of figures in mismatched armor, officers calling out orders to fall in. The clang of a blacksmith hammer rang out above the concert of yells and commands. She even heard a patch of laughter among the din.

She made her way to a tall, white canvas pavilion at the camp's far end. The rising sun was a warm pink against the line of trees standing like sentinels at its back. The mask felt lighter today. One pothole tripped her up as she came to the pavilion's front entrance, but if the guards manning either side noticed, they said nothing.

Anji flexed her left hand around her dagger's hilt, the remaining fingers dry and stiff in the early morning chill. She looked one of the guards up and down, her father's coat flapping behind her, the coins in her pocket tingling with their loving song.

"Who's in charge here?"

ACKNOWLEDGMENTS

This book would not exist without the following people. It is to you I owe everything.

To my agent, Seth Fishman: you pulled me out of a livestream, and look what we've built together. Thank you for believing in a random nerd on the internet. You're my goddamned anchor.

To my editor, Stephanie Stein: thank you for seeing what this book could be, for giving me a chance, and for never holding back. You challenged me to dig deeper, to pull out everything I had to make this what it is. Your honesty, attention to detail, and passion for stories carried Anji farther than I ever thought she could go.

To my brother Vaughn: I don't think a day has passed where we haven't talked. You read this in its early stages and told me you liked it. That's all the motivation I'll ever need. You always had better taste than me.

To my dad: I called you a few years ago to tell you I quit my job to write books, and you didn't bat an eye (even though that plan ended up being a little shakier than we thought). What a blessing it is to feel your father's pride and reassurance.

To my sister, Sarah, my other brother, David, and my nephew, Jameson: even from across the country, I can feel your love and joy. You're three of the most beautiful people I have the pleasure of knowing.

To the rest of my family: your unwavering support means the world to me. The news I broke about being a writer was met with enthusiasm, encouragement, and love. I'm so lucky to have all of you.

To Cody King: you made the best damn map I could have asked for. Let's hang soon.

To Oliver Barrett: I never thought I'd have a cover so good. Thank you for patiently reading the many notes you had to sift through.

To Danny Hertz: thank you for your excitement, your kind words, and your hard work. You helped me more than you know.

I'm going to rattle off some more names here. This is a lonely job, but these people made it far less so and, even if we haven't seen much of each other, helped get me to where I am. My infinite gratitude to: Dan Pantenburg, Chad Klein, Matt Hester, Kyle Cregan, Kymm Meyers, Christian Zomer, Christian Snow, Ross Burford, Lindsey Uhl, Joy Payne, Dominik Schmidt, Dylan Rudlof, Jesse Suihkonen, Devin Brown, Kai Nehas, Max McClusky, Steve Jardin, Tim Howe, and Zach Rowland. Friends forever.

Even as a debut author, I've built up quite the network of support. I would be remiss if I didn't thank all the wonderful writers I've met online who have cheered me on in more ways than I can count. Thank you: Daniel Greene, M. J. Kuhn, H. M. Long, Nicholas Eames, Adam Cesare, Jason Pargin, Travis Baldree, Amber Nicole, Ben Alderson, Kaven Hirning, Adrian Gibson, Andy Peloquin, Alexander Darwin, Michael Michel, and Will Wight. Authors don't have competition—we just have talented friends who inspire us.

I am under no delusion that I would be here without the enormous number of people online who have been around every step of the way.

To the millions of readers who have engaged with the content I've made over the years: you did this. Thank you from the bottom of my heart.

To A Chat Of Books And Besties (Zoranne, Jaysen, Eryn, Kevin, Jenna, Deirdre, Johnee, Tre, and Laura): thank you for putting up with my voice messages. You're the best online friends I could ask for. Our eventual meetup will be the stuff of legends.

To my fellow content creators: Maggie Siciliano, Petrik Leo, Alex Andros, Nina Haines, Nick Parry, Austin and Richard from 2 To Ramble, and a few dozen more I'm probably not mentioning: thank you for the work you do.

To everyone in the BRK Discord (and of course, my mods and dear friends, Kyle, Marissa, Lindsay, and Ryan): you're the best reading community in the world. We all know it. Thank you for being there for me, and for championing my every effort.

To all the BRK Patrons: you saved me from living on the street. I'm not kidding.

Overwhelming gratitude to the team at Tor, who've had my back from the moment I signed on: Sanaa Ali-Virani, Libby Collins, Samantha Friedlander, Shreya Gupta, Christine Foltzer, Donna Noetzel, Jessica Katz, Steven Bucsok, Rafal Gibek, Stephanie Sirabian, Megan Barnard, Claire Eddy, Will Hinton, and Devi Pillai. You are an amazing group of passionate people. I am honored beyond words to add my work to such an incredible roster.

Whew.

And finally, to you. Yes, you, the one reading this. You picked this book up and read the words I wrote when there are a million other stories to read, shows to watch, and games to play. Thank you for your time, precious as it is.

One last thing. I listen to music while I write, so I would also like to express my sincerest appreciation to the following albums and the artists who made them:

Age of Winters by The Sword

Sunbather by Deafheaven

End by Explosions in the Sky

Take Care, Take Care, Take Care by Explosions in the Sky

Volume 1 by Magic Sword

Loveless by My Bloody Valentine

Young Mountain by This Will Destroy You

Commit This to Memory by Motion City Soundtrack

D by White Denim

Dopesmoker by Sleep

Go Tell Fire to the Mountain by WU LYF

Inhuman Rampage by DragonForce

De-Loused in the Comatorium by The Mars Volta

Ambient 1: Music for Airports by Brian Eno

ABOUT THE AUTHOR

EVAN LEIKAM grew up among the forests of Central Oregon, reading fantasy and science fiction from a young age. While touring the United States and Europe with an independent rock band, he began tinkering with his own stories to pass time in vans and music venues. Apart from writing, he enjoys cooking, producing music, riding his bike, and FromSoftware games. He is the host of the *Book Reviews Kill* podcast, and his social media pages have turned thousands on to new books. He currently lives in Portland, Oregon.

For more fantastic fiction, author events,
exclusive excerpts, competitions, limited editions and more

VISIT OUR WEBSITE
titanbooks.com

LIKE US ON FACEBOOK
facebook.com/titanbooks

FOLLOW US ON TWITTER AND INSTAGRAM
@TitanBooks

EMAIL US
readerfeedback@titanemail.com